Second Journal of the Ancient Ones

LEGACY
of the
ELDER GODS

M. DON SCHORN

OZARK
MOUNTAIN
PUBLISHING

For permission, or serialization, condensation, adaptions, or for catalog of other publications, write to: Ozark Mountain Publishing, Inc., PO Box 754, Huntsville, AR 72740, Attn: Permissions Department.

Library of Congress Cataloging-in-Publication Data
Schorn, M. Don - 1947 -
"Legacy of the Elder Gods" by M. Don Schorn
The second book of a series based on the elder gods theory of a revised account of human history.
1. Ancient History 2. Archeology 3. Lost Civilizations
4. Extraterrestrials
I. Schorn, M. Don 1947 -   II. Title
Library of Congress Catalog Number: 2008940344
ISBN: 978-1-886940-58-1
Cover Art and Layout by www.enki3d.com
Bok Design: Julia Degan
Book Set in: Times New Roman

Published by

OZARK
MOUNTAIN
PUBLISHING

PO Box 754
Huntsville, AR 72740

www.ozarkmt.com
Printed in the United States of America

Other Books by M. Don Schorn:

First Journal of the Ancient Ones

Elder Gods of Antiquity

Third Journal of the Ancient Ones

Gardens of the Elder Gods

A Spiritual Belief, A Way of Life, And Much More

Reincarnation...
Stepping Stones of Life

A Novel of Modern Exploration, Discovery, & Ancient
Revelations, Set in the Near Future

Emerging Dawn

Table of Contents

Chapter 1

Origins of the Universe

Science has determined that the universe formed roughly 13.5 billion years ago, although certain disputed cosmic structures are thought to be as old as 15 billion years. These facts were derived from a research endeavor called Project Boomerang, an international effort that included Andrew Lange of the California Institute of Technology.[1] This study was organized to detect the earliest formations within our universe that resulted from the Big Bang event. That project deployed an aerial balloon over Antarctica in late 1998, which was equipped with a telescope to photograph cosmic microwave background radiation to collect its main data. Additional measurements were also made from ground-based sites located high in the mountains. The ensuing data exposed slight ripples or irregularities in the faint glow of what is thought to be the earliest remnants from the Big Bang genesis, which further implied detection of those 'older' anomalous formations. Those enigmatic primordial cosmic structures are thought to actually predate the oldest particle remnants that formed the earliest stars and galaxies connected with the Big Bang event, thereby eluding any plausible explanation for their existence, while also generating abundant debate.[2]

Further collaboration of these findings included data from the Microwave Anisotropy Probe (aka MAP or WMAP observatory) launched in June 2001, which studied the oldest light in the universe, dating to mere moments after creation.[3] From an orbit one million miles from Earth, its two-year mission collected data to confirm and date the Big Bang event. It measured the slight temperature variations within the cosmic microwave remnants of those once ultraviolet rays emitted by the Big Bang genesis. Our constantly expanding universe has stretched those original ultraviolet light waves into microwaves, after their more than 13 billion years of travel since the Big Bang occurrence. Ongoing collection and dissemination of the latest cosmological data has allowed further refinement of the universe's age, which is now concluded as having originated about 13.7 billion years ago.

Currently collected information has revealed the underlying cosmic geometry associated with the earliest formations within our universe. Such delicate measurements have recorded ripple patterns that match the scenario of a 'flat' universe in which parallel lines never cross. Author Murry Hope reported on a much earlier but similar definitive work performed by Professor Richard Ellis and his colleagues at Durham University. That team developed an astronomical fiber-optic scanner for use with cosmic probes that produced a three-dimensional representation of galaxies comprising our universe.[4] The data derived using that technology indicated that galaxies were usually formed in clusters that occurred at regular intervals of about 400 million light years, which were evenly distributed along a narrow cone of the universe.[5] Such cosmic geometry essentially produced a universe resembling a gigantic honeycomb of regular repeating cells, separated by vast voids or regions of nothingness.

Additional conclusions derived from Project Boomerang further confirmed the continuing expansion of our universe, one determined to be at an accelerated rate from its original expansion speed during its earlier pace of inflation. This increased expansion rate is believed to be caused by the influence of a strange form of energy that fills empty space. This exotic force apparently acts against gravity, a conclusion that was also derived from observational data taken from Project Boomerang, which supported the existence of such an unknown energy commodity.[6]

Furthermore, the amount of matter found by astronomers can not account for the 'flat' configuration of our universe. According to Dr. Scott Dodelson, a cosmologist at the University of Chicago, some unknown form of energy is contributing to the total density known to be contained in the universe.[7] This unknown energy, a repulsive force or anti-gravity commodity, is believed to be contained in the voids of apparently empty space. This mysterious energy form is sometimes referred to as a cosmological constant, and is commonly called 'dark energy.'[8]

Such an energy commodity should not be confused with dark matter, the mysterious dense particles that are believed to weigh at least 50 times as much as a proton. These heavy particles are believed capable of passing through other matter without a trace, because of their extremely weak ability to interact with other particles. The particles thought to make up such dark matter are variously called neutralinos, gravitinos, or WIMPs (a Weakly Interactive, Massive Particle).[9] This dark matter is thought to comprise roughly 85% of all physical matter in the universe,[10] with bright matter comprising the balance, although these two types of matter are entirely different. The existence of dark matter had only been theorized through its gravitational effect on ordinary or bright matter, but was finally directly detected using the Hubble Space Telescope in late 2004.[11]

All observed matter in the universe, including humans, is composed only of bright or ordinary matter, even though the bulk (85%) of physical matter in our universe consists of the entirely different and unseen mass of dark matter. Yet both forms of physical matter when combined still make up only about 27% of the entire universe, with the vast remaining balance consisting of the previously mentioned exotic 'dark energy' commodity. Thus, the universe consists of about four percent bright (ordinary) matter, 23% dark matter, and 73% dark energy.

An alternate theory attempting to explain such anomalous undetected matter requires the introduction of 'extra' dimensions beyond our perceived three-dimensional world. Such a concept is sometimes referred to as the Hyperdimensional Physics Model. One theory, proposed by researcher Richard C. Hoagland in cooperation with Erol Torun, hypothesizes that gravity may not conform to known laws of physics, relative to its effects over vast distances, such as those involved in intergalactic separations.[12] According to Mr. Hoagland, hyperdimensional realms contain an enormous amount of 'free' or naturally occurring energy. Such a theory might also eliminate the necessity for the unknown and unexplained dark matter that cosmologists use to explain the theoretical 'missing matter' content of the universe. These findings share certain core beliefs with the Meta Model proposed by noted astronomer Dr. Tom Van Flandern.[13] Other researchers investigating such theoretical hyperdimensional realms include Drs. Bruce DePalma, Thomas Bearden, Michio Kaku, Brian Green, and Stan Tenent. The concept of such a puzzling multidimensional universe will be further explored within a later chapter of this writing.

Regardless of the underlying theory or explanation for the numerous confusing structures and enigmatic forces uncovered throughout the cosmos, their existence was apparently the result of the Big Bang event, the genesis of our physical universe. The 'how' has been the focus of study by the most learned men of every ensuing culture over the millennia, with explanations for the 'genesis process' eventually being pieced together from revelations uncovered bit by bit. The 'who' has been a point of speculation by theologians and philosophers since the earliest times. But the 'why' has never been fully revealed. Self-centered humanity would point to humans as the ultimate reason for the preeminent purpose underlying this marvelous creation event. Yet, humankind appears to be merely a minor afterthought, only emerging very recently by cosmic reckoning, roughly 13 billion years after the Big Bang initiation. Perhaps the real question should focus on why the universe formed 13 to 15 billion years ago, and not 20 billion years ago? Why not even 100 billion years ago? Were there perhaps earlier universes that preceded ours?

A 2001 report based on NASA data stated that supermassive black holes once dominated the universe more than 12 billion years ago.[14] That conclusion was derived from cosmic structures detected by the Chandra X-ray telescope from surges of erupted X-rays that continue to travel across the cosmos. Such emissions reflected the environment during the early formative periods of our present universe, and further suggest either a contradiction to our present theory of an ever-expansive Big Bang genesis, or perhaps represent remnants from a prior 'spent' universe.

Utilizing the most advanced technology, modern science can only now answer the most basic questions as to the nature and scope of our universe, along with Earth's place or humanity's role in that grand creation. Even so, the more we learn at our perceived advanced levels of attained knowledge, the more we realize that modern science is only now reaching parity with the most ancient beliefs and concepts put forth by the 'primitive' inhabitants of prehistoric Earth.

The theory, mechanism, and process emanating from the Big Bang event has required many centuries of empirical observations, scientific advancements, and cosmic discoveries, along with complex analytical thought and conjecture to reconstruct even its most basic and probable method of implementation that describes such a genesis event. Yet humanity's most archaic cultures essentially possessed the same descriptive narrative of that event, many millennia before our modern scientists. That would seemingly require ancient man to have observed the distant reaches of the cosmos in order to have ultimately arrived at the same descriptive conclusions.

A similar conundrum would likewise apply to all the astronomical knowledge possessed by numerous ancient cultures. Such knowledge would have required observation and record keeping by literate humans over at least tens of thousands of years, along with the invention and utilization of scientific tools and devices such as an ancient version of the Hubble Telescope, satellites, and space probes. Yet no physical evidence or record of such devices has ever been found that would confirm such hardware once existed during archaic times.

That absence tends to suggest those ancient cultures might have inherited or were given such information, rather than acquiring it through their own direct efforts and observations. Such knowledge probably would not have been fully understood or comprehended by the 'receiving' culture, and could have been subjected to distortion and misrepresentation, as those facts were handed down to subsequent generations. Yet numerous ancient accounts accurately describe the Big Bang event, paralleling levels of understanding recently achieved by present day humanity.

In fact, the concept and knowledge of outer space was well known to many ancient cultures. The vast regions of space were known as the cosmic waters or the cosmic ocean. Those 'waters' were often distinguished in olden manuscripts from the earthly bodies of water contained in our oceans and seas; either as the 'waters of heaven above the firmament' or the 'waters below the firmament.' The 'firmament' that divided the different 'waters' was never fully described or specifically defined, but it was believed to be a level of atmosphere that exists between terrestrial Earth and the 'void' of outer space.[15] The ancient Hindus spoke of this Upper Ocean or Universal Sea in the Puranas, stating that there were 'seven islands separated by seven oceans,' which surrounded and encircled the Earth.

Perhaps a preeminent example of ancient wisdom pertaining to cosmology is found in an often degraded, misunderstood, and controversial manuscript known as the *Book of Dzyan*. Arguably, that compilation may be one of the oldest texts of Earth. A Tibetan version of a Sanskrit translation, reportedly written on palm leaves, is believed to be its oldest extant form. Although that volume is ancient in age, it was merely one translation of many, from an even earlier original form reportedly written in *Senzar*. Supposedly, Senzar was the language of the gods and the script that was taught to the earliest adepts at archaic Mystery

6

Schools, where esoteric knowledge was imparted to them. When read with the understanding of modern science, the *Seven Stanzas of Creation*, also referred to as the *Cosmic Evolution* in the *Book of Dzyan*, displays remarkable parallels with our early 21st century theories of cosmology.

Perhaps no other ancient text details the unfolding process of the Big Bang event as accurately as the account contained in the *Book of Dzyan*. This is evident in Stanza III, Verse 6, (III.6.): "The ocean (space) was radiant light, which was fire, and heat, and motion (the expansive inferno from its energy release)." But other archaic texts are seldom so misunderstood as the *Book of Dzyan*, which has been described as one of the most puzzling and confusing manuscripts ever written by mankind. Realizing the possible distortions and confusion that may have permeated this work as it was translated and handed down over the ages by subsequent and less informed cultures, a slightly 'revised,' or more accurately 'updated' version will be reviewed. This version is based on the Sanskrit translations of the ancient Senzar text and commentaries, rearranged and redacted by this author with the following inserted clarifications.

The Seven Stanzas of *Cosmic Evolution* from the *Book of Dzyan*:

Book of Dzyan	Explanation
1. The Eternal Parent... slumbered once again for Seven eternities. (Stanza I. Line 1.)	The Creator allowed the past universe(s) to fully transpire without interference.

2. The last vibration of the seventh eternity thrills through infinitude. (III. 1.)

All remnants of the prior physical universe(s) had evidently expired.

3. The causes of existence had been done away with; the visible that was, and the invisible that is, rested in...the One Being. (I. 7.)

After all prior existence ceased, the Creator converted any remaining matter into pure energy. That force or energy was then absorbed by and contained within the Creator.

4. Darkness alone filled the boundless all. (I. 5.)
There was neither silence nor sound...(II. 2.)

Nothing existed except complete silent darkness...a 'clean slate' yet awaited.

5. The universe was still concealed in the Divine Thought. (II. 6.)

The Creator was contemplating and formulating the very nature and scope of the next world.

6. Time was not, for it lay asleep in the infinite bosom. (I. 2)
The hour had not yet struck; the ray had not yet flashed into the germ. (II. 3.)

The Big Bang event had not yet occurred.

7. Darkness radiates light. The ray shoots through the virgin egg. (III. 3.)

    The explosion of the Big Bang energy release created photons, the first particles, as 'light' emerged with the birth of our present universe.

8. The producers of form from no-form...the root of the world...rested in the bliss of non-being. (II. 1.)

    The quarks and leptons were produced from the one-time inferno environment, as a result of the Big Bang energy release.

9. Father-Mother [the Creator] spin a web whose upper end is fastened to spirit. (III. 10.)

    Elements produced from the Big Bang event were contained within the web or fabric of space-time. That invisible boundary separates the physical universe from the spiritual realm.

10. The germ is...the son of the dark hidden father. (III. 8.)

    The fundamental particles of quarks and leptons are the building blocks or seeds that the Creator intended.

11. Bright space, son of dark space, ...emerges from the depths of the Great Dark Waters. (III. 7.)

    Physical (bright) matter formed from the darkness of the Big Bang energy release throughout the dark 'waters' of outer space.

12. The luminous egg... spreads in milk-white curds...the root that grows in the depths of the ocean of life. (III. 4.)

The Big Bang birth expanded from gaseous cloud nebulas or nurseries, which do resemble 'milk curds'; forming the first stars, as well as all the later creations.

13. The root of life was in every drop of the ocean, and the ocean was radiant light, which was fire, and heat, and motion. (III. 6.)

The essence of life is everywhere, able to develop into specialized forms that can adapt to each different environment that might be encountered.

14. The Seven Sons were not yet born from the web of light. (II. 5.)

The 'Seven Sons,' the Ancient Ones, came later. They were not the 'Creator.'

15. This is thy present wheel. (VIII.7.)

This 'wheel' is our present universe, implying that there were other prior or earlier ones.

16. He builds them in the likeness of older wheels, placing them on the Imperishable Centers. (VI. 4.)

The Creator formed our universe based on the most successful prior universes. Favorable environments were located around the universe as sources or centers where life could flourish, reaching high achievement levels while obtaining vast knowledge.

17. The radiant essence becomes seven inside, seven outside. (III. 4.)

An essence of the seven prior universes is reflected in the present version, while the 'seven outside' (the Ancient Ones) were 'formed' at a later time in our present universe.

18. ...Listen, ye sons of the Earth, to your instructors - the Sons of the Fire. (IV. 1.)
Learn what we who descend from the Primordial Seven, ...have learnt from our fathers... (IV. 2.)

The Creator intended that later 'infant' races would be taught by earlier surviving species (the Ancient Ones). The Creator expected all subsequent emerging races would be guided by those wiser primordial patriarchs.

Chapter 2

Universal Spores & The Early Cosmos

Further statements contained in the *Book of Dzyan* indicate that our present universe may be the eighth one to have been created, as interpreted from Stanza III.1: "...The last vibration of the seventh eternity (universe) thrills through infinitude." However, it is not made clear what might have happened to those prior universes. They may have been destroyed by some cascading natural catastrophe or merely 'expired,' having expended their useful life span.

Perhaps such a natural demise may be the result of burnt-out or 'dead' stars, creating ever-expanding blackholes. Such 'gravity wells' might have eventually engulfed all remaining matter, leaving 'nothingness' in its wake. Or, the Creative Godhead may have ended the prior creations in order to construct a new, improved, or enhanced model. The existence of such prior universes may help to explain those structures found in our present universe that date to 15 billion years of age, contradicting the approximate 13.7 billion-year-old origin attributed to our present cosmos. Such formations may simply be the remnants of a prior universe that either overlapped with or was captured within a portion of our present universe during its earliest creation process.

One assumes that the subsequent universes were evidently based upon the essence of the previous ones, with galaxies clustered and dispersed in patterns similar to past cosmic plans. Such a conclusion can be derived from Stanza VI.4. in the *Book of Dzyan*: "He builds them in the likeness of older wheels (universes), placing them on the Imperishable Centers." Evidently subsequent universes somehow utilize the energy content resulting from the conversion of matter to energy within those prior realms. Stanza VI.4. of the *Book of Dzyan* states: "How does Fohat (the Cosmic Creative Force) build them? He collects the fiery dust...," perhaps a reference to the energy remnants from a prior universe.

The Creator may have conceived or envisioned into existence an endless sequence of universes, each conditioned by the character of its prior universe, working toward some Divine Plan unknown to humankind. Such a repetitive process may have been occurring prior to the creation of 'time,' or those creations may have commenced during periods so remote that human consciousness could not comprehend their infinite scope.

Similar levels of ancient cosmological comprehension can be found in numerous other texts. In Chapter V of *The Book of the Secrets of Enoch*, Enoch is shown: "...the treasure-houses of the snow...and the clouds whence they come out and into which they go."[1] This may refer to the countless number of glistening stars covering the vastness of outer space like snow, which are born in 'clouds,' the stellar nebula nurseries. Recycling is the eventual fate for stars, supplying elementary particles from which new nebulas are continually formed, and future stars are created.

The teachings of the Egyptian god Thoth contained in the Hermetic texts state: "For there were boundless Darkness in the abyss, and water, and a subtle spirit, intellectual in power, existing in Chaos. But the holy Light broke forth, and the elements were produced from among the sand of a watery essence."[2] Note that water consists of the elements of hydrogen and oxygen only, with hydrogen being the first element formed after the Big Bang genesis.

Numerous ancient Sanskrit records also contain astounding cosmological understanding, such as Creation Hymn 10.129. from the *Rig Veda*. A translation and commentary by Dr. W. Norman Brown, a professor of Sanskrit at the University of

Pennsylvania, identifies the Creator as *That One*. Professor Brown's commentary analysis of this controversial hymn is paraphrased in the following: *That One* existed first, not inspired by another, and spontaneously became reality. Nothing existed beside *That One*. There was only darkness hidden by darkness at the beginning. That which had the potentiality of becoming was hidden by a shell, and was born through the power of its own heat. *That One* became the first seed of mind, creating from desire. Forces were created, with potential below and emanation above. There were seed depositors, those gods who came later, after the creation of the universe by *That One*, the Creator.[3]

That descriptive translation and commentary seems to imply that a deliberate effort was undertaken to distribute life, or at least the dispersal of those elements that would later result in life formation. Modern science has concluded that the most fundamental primordial matter, the quarks and leptons that underlie subatomic particles from which stars and planets later formed, were created within the first fractional instant of the Big Bang event. Those same elementary particles comprise the nature of all things everywhere throughout the universe. Hence, all matter and life is made from these same basic quark and lepton particles, the essential ingredients of 'stardust.' Since everything in the universe is comprised of these same fundamental particles, perhaps things are not so different between the farthest remote reaches of our universe as we might first imagine. For that same reason, perhaps physical life may not be all that different elsewhere in the universe, especially where somewhat similar planetary conditions exist.

Scientists at CERN, the European Laboratory for Particle Physics, believe that they have confirmed the prevailing theory of the Big Bang genesis. A total of 350 scientists created a primordial 'soup' or plasma of subatomic particles that they think resemble conditions during the earliest moments of creation.[4] This unique plasma was observed to contain thousands of free-state quarks that quickly joined to form larger particles. It was concluded that similar 'creations' of fundamental particles occurred at the time of the Big Bang event. Those particles would have later combined to form more stable larger particles, around which gaseous nebulas eventually collected, ultimately resulting in the formation of stars. The CERN experimentation further suggests confirmation of our prevailing hypothesis that is used to explain the Big Bang event.[5]

Similarly, a 'primordial plasma' of complex organic chemicals, the suspected precursors of life, is incubated very quickly after the birth of a star. According to Sun Kwok, an astronomer with the University of Calgary, Canada, large organic molecules evolve within a few thousand years from chemicals in the cloudlike envelope surrounding certain stars.[6] Perhaps the universal phenomenon that underlies the composition of all matter shares a similar elemental basis in the formation of life. If so, it tends to suggest that life formation is not a unique process or event.

Such an original germ or seed, one responsible for the flora and fauna within a solar system, may also be universal in its origin. After dispersion of such spores throughout the universe, each 'seed' could evolve and develop independently on any contacted world; mutating, adapting, and conforming to the unique environment on each different world encountered. That would result in an independently unique species, or a variety of loosely connected lifeforms on different worlds.

Evidence suggests that such a universal spore or germ of life apparently existed shortly after the Big Bang birth of the physical cosmos; probably within the first several billion years of our infant universe, as stars and planets first coalesced. Such spores may be considered 'generic' by their ubiquitous nature, in a manner similar to the elementary particles of quarks and leptons that form the underlying basis for all material reality. Such spores might drift throughout space on the solar winds, or be transported on exploded debris of dead celestial bodies and rogue comets, or spread by deliberate acts of seeding by a surviving lifeform. By any means, such spores were evidently dispersed throughout the known cosmos, eventually finding homes on various existing worlds, as well as on new planets that formed many eons later.

Those spores that found homes on planets with suitable environments, ones conducive to nurturing, could then undergo their individual evolutionary process to create their own unique lifeform, based on the particular physical conditions and environment of each host world. Such basic life would then occasionally mutate in order to accommodate the numerous changes its host world would undergo over eons of time, thereby producing numerous different indigenous species from a single type of universal spore. Regardless of outcome, all life everywhere in the universe would thus be related through its primordial origin from that one common spore.

Numerous mythological accounts tend to confirm the deliberate seeding of worlds using universal spores. The Chinese claim that their 'first man' was born from an egg that their god Tien dropped into the waters of Earth from the heavens.[7] That suggests a certain understanding by primitive people that acknowledged some form of planetary seeding, with such spores delivered from outer space.

Such universal spores were not a one-time occurrence associated with the Big Bang event, but rather a continuous phenomenon. Earth's primordial history contains evidence of numerous mass extinctions that ended most planetary life. Yet new and varied 'replacement life' always formed afterward, and continues to form even during modern times. Such continuously produced new life is always directly affected or influenced by the ever-changing but then-current planetary conditions or environment, thereby shaping each unique creation based upon those existing local surroundings in which such fundamental underlying spores might presently be exposed.

The Urantia Book professes that planets and their animal population do not occur by freak chance, but rather from deliberate acts of 'designed creation' (seeding) by higher attained beings obeying a master plan.[8]   Once such seeding produces a lifeform with an ability to comprehend knowledge and demonstrate their capability for self-determination, certain nurturing 'overseer' beings known as Solitary Messengers reveal themselves and help guide those emerging species.   Such 'overseeing authorities' introduce their 'guidance' by stationing small groups of enlightened beings on those 'primitive planets.' Those beings then instruct and civilize the young inhabitants for eventual interaction with other worlds.[9]

Astrophysicist Sir Fred Hoyle of Cambridge University believes that the origins of life on Earth were imported from outside our solar system on massive interstellar comets.   That conclusion is contained in his book, *Lifecloud: The Origin of Life in the Universe*, a 1978 work co-authored with Chandra Wickramasinghe.   Their hypothesis states that fragments from those distant celestial travelers would have eventually visited our region of space and impacted Earth, along with most of our other planetary neighbors.   Such impacts would have consequently imparted those universal spores of life throughout our solar system, having been frozen and preserved in 'suspended animation' within each comet's icy composition.   Note that the normal temperature of outer space between stars, where negligible effects from radiant heating occurs, is -270 degrees Centigrade, an extreme condition that is quite capable of organism preservation.

Universal spores could have formed 'early life' wherever suitable landing conditions allowed. Astronomers concluded that more than 100 billion comets transverse through our solar system at any one time.   Those visitors reside mainly in two reservoirs, the Oort cloud and the Kuiper belt.   The Oort cloud forms a spherical shell around our entire solar system at a distance of about one light year.   Our periodic passage through gigantic molecular clouds and galactic spiral arms replenishes the Oort cloud with new comets and other masses, while the smaller

Kuiper belt is a flattened, concentric 'annular-band' formation that lies beyond the orbit of Neptune.

The amount of life-forming molecules observed in outer space suggests the seeds of life are everywhere. These building blocks of life are common in interstellar space, with eight new biological molecules found during 2006 within massive gas clouds that form stars and planets; bringing to 141 the number of different organic molecules found as of that date.[10]

Such wide spread dispersion of universal spores around the universe would likely assist or accelerate the formation of life throughout the cosmos. Such delivery might be the result of errant heavenly bodies such as comets and asteroids that contained the universal spore bacterium, impregnating or 'contaminating' numerous encountered worlds. Both Professor Fred Hoyle and Dr. Francis Crick, the eminent British biophysicist, embraced this concept, known generally as 'directed panspermia.' The 19th century mathematician and physicist Lord William Thomson Kelvin (1824-1907) also maintained a belief that life did not originate on Earth, but had drifted to our world as spores from remote regions of our universe.[11] It is also possible that such spore distribution could have been even more selective and deliberate, dispersed by earlier alien life that had eventually acquired intelligence and progressed to ever-higher advanced levels.

Where deliberate spore transmissions may have occurred, the process could have been performed in progressive, individual steps. Such stages may have depended on each planet's environmental development. The universal seed leading to primitive bacterial life may have been subsequently accompanied with more complex 'seeds' billions of years later, as planetary conditions become more ideal, perhaps even as a result or consequence of such earlier life. Our own earthly development tends to display such inexplicable evolution from one dominant species to another 'new or replacement lifeform,' such as the transition from dinosaurs to humans.

Considering this theory of a universal 'spore of life,' one common to all regions of the cosmos, the simple initiation of life on each different world would have naturally taken numerous different developmental paths on every impregnated planet. The earliest formation of bacterial life on Earth may well be the result of one or more of those spores finding their way to Earth 3.7 billion years ago. Humankind may simply be the result of continuous evolutionary forces and acute mutations caused by drastic climatic and environmental changes.

The Early Cosmos

As a result of knowledge acquired from deep space probes; the Hubble telescope; microwave readings; X-ray telescopes; high altitude data collections; and ground-based laboratory studies; a rough portrait of the early formative periods of our universe can be reconstructed. In the nearly nine billion years that passed since the Big Bang birth of the universe, prior to the formation of our own Solar System, an untold number of suns would have been born, lived their allotted span of existence, and died. Their expended remains were then converted and recycled into new creations over and over. Around those earlier stars were an even greater number of planets, moons, asteroids, and comets. Elementary life would have surely formed somewhere within that early cosmos. As one expands their perspective to accept alternate conditions under which life could evolve, it becomes apparent that a vast array of prior worlds existed that likely contained life in some manner or form. Such lifeform emergence would have been a continuous process since the earliest times, with new life constantly developing on at least a portion of subsequent planets, a process that apparently continues even during present times.

With reasonably stable environmental conditions occurring on at least a small percentage of the constantly created new worlds throughout the cosmos, ample time would have allowed early primitive life to evolve into more complex forms. Eventually a small portion of those earliest lifeforms likely would have mutated or evolved into some form of higher intelligent being during some adolescent age of our universe, creating their own form of civilization. It certainly would not have taken the Creator nine billion years to think of fashioning some form of organic sapient life into beings capable of inhabiting one or more of the many prior formed planets. Such worlds would have existed long before our solar system and planet Earth could have been a twinkle in the night sky of those inhabited planets, with their locations situated within far distant galaxies.

Those early beings may have had little in common with future creatures such as humankind, not only in appearance, but in multiple other aspects as well. That may simply be due to the fact that conditions within the universe during its infancy period were quite different from the later conditions of today. Numerous different lifeforms may have existed on those abundant and vastly scattered worlds, each remaining unknown to any of their other contemporary alien neighbors. Such creatures would have mutated and struggled with their survival over the ensuing eons, eventually becoming extinct with the demise of their sun, all without acquiring knowledge of any other worlds, or having had contact with those inhabitants. They lived, died, and were forgotten, never knowing of the vastly larger universe that they shared with other species on numerous different planets. Even the knowledge of their very existence and ensuing cultures would have evaporated with the demise of their worlds, perhaps never to be discovered by future generations of explorers and archaeologists from subsequently formed planets.

Eventually, such a dead-end cycle of birth and extinction would have changed. Progress and advancements would have certainly occurred on some of those worlds, eventually allowing civilization to ultimately occur. At least a few of those civilizations would have finally achieved space travel capabilities. Eventual exploration of other planets would have transpired, for any number of likely reasons. Those explorers could have simply been curious, wanting to know what might lie beyond. Others may have depleted their own planet's resources and ventured into space to find and secure such necessities from alien worlds. Overpopulation may have required some to seek colonization on other worlds, in order to ease their overcrowded condition. For whatever reason, space travel would have eventually occurred. Such travel may have also served as another method of conveying the universal seeds of life, augmenting or perhaps accelerating the 'natural' dispersion process of those spores throughout the universe.

Such a hypothesis possesses a certain degree of credibility. Probability would dictate that at least some of the early lifeforms would have evolved into sapient beings. With such a 'headstart' in developing their civilization, scientific knowledge and advancements would eventually also be the expected result, given sufficient time. One theory contends that discoveries will occur within a culture, predicated solely on their specific level of scientific knowledge, whether or not its people are actually seeking such a discovery. Thus, advancements simply become self-evident and obvious at various plateaus of development, even if they were not originally being sought.

As the capacity to obtain advanced levels of scientific progress expands, a civilization's ability to eliminate or cure most diseases would also seem a certainty, thereby extending the physical life span for such an advanced species. That scientific growth would likely also lead to overpopulation of their homeworld, prompting development of space travel in order to seek out 'expansion places' for colonization. Space travel would thus be a natural extension or evolution resulting from such acquired knowledge, once reaching certain higher levels of achievement.

Such primordial life in the early universe, coupled with their ability for intergalactic space travel, may account for or help explain many of the mysteries surrounding Earth's own ancient past. Mysteries such as anomalous advanced artifacts found embedded in geological strata during ages when no humans, primitive or otherwise, were thought to have existed. Or the human fossils that dated to eras long before their ascribed time period, along with the archaic megalithic stone structures that seemingly defy construction, even with utilization of modern land-based equipment. Such anomalies were disclosed and evaluated in the First Journal of the Ancient Ones, *Elder Gods of Antiquity.*

In addition to such physical artifacts, an equally mystifying component or factor is revealed from the very advanced cosmological understanding and knowledge possessed by Earth's ancient cultures. That knowledge is known from ancient texts and celestial alignments incorporated into many ancient monuments. Such advanced wisdom and capabilities allude to a legacy bestowed upon Earth by unknown beings during remote times. Those levels of scientific intellect and comprehension would not be self-evident commodities to an emerging species such as primitive humans. That is apparent from the discernible level of astronomical knowledge and application evidently possessed by numerous ancient cultures, a level that would have required the use of powerful telescopes, chronographs, and the application of advanced mathematics.

Additionally, those ancient human star watchers would have had to compile and document accurate observations of specific celestial occurrences over many thousands of years, all supposedly without the aid of written records. Their meaningful and analytical conclusions, evidently derived from such empirical observations, would certainly indicate a scientific methodology capable of predicting repetitive occurrences of celestial events, as well as plotting orbits of celestial bodies. Yet such capabilities and knowledge are vastly beyond the levels ascribed to those very ancient cultures by modern anthropologists and historians.

Chapter 3

Supplied Knowledge

Since it is quite possible that earlier extraterrestrial life could have actually evolved prior to the formation of Earth, such otherworldly creatures may have developed into very advanced beings that eventually became capable of traveling to our region of space. Such ancient beings may have visited our solar system and Earth during the remote past, perhaps before the emergence of humanity's earliest ancestors. Their continuing later visits could have imparted the high levels of knowledge that were apparently possessed by some of our oldest earthly cultures.

Such contact would further explain the numerous anomalous evidence and artifacts that simply do not correlate with the time period in which they were found. Still other explanations are also possible, such as an unknown civilization from Earth's far distant past that still remains lost to modern man. Whether such enigmatic relics, fossils, and wisdom represent the legacy from a long lost indigenous civilization of Earth, or knowledge and devices brought to Earth through extraterrestrial intervention, the astronomical and cosmological understanding of our oldest known ancestors was simply amazing.

Such archaic knowledge, as confirmed from ancient texts, reveals a refinement of thought and insight far in advance of levels ascribed to the times during which they originated. Such achievement seemingly could not have evolved from a primitive Stone Age culture without outside aid or tutor. The known level of understanding demonstrated by the accomplishments of the Cro-Magnons, along with the medical and scientific knowledge possessed by early Modern man, would have required human observation and subsequent recording of data over many millennia. Their ancient scientific knowledge, especially concerning cosmology, is only now being equaled by modern science. That level of comprehension is recognized as extraordinary, based on the time period during which it was conceived and incorporated by those ancient cultures. Such knowledge simply could not have been developed on Earth by humans through their own efforts without the use of sophisticated scientific equipment, which contradicts our present orthodox theories ascribing the evolution of *Homo sapiens* and their cultural progression.

That knowledge, along with the advanced inventions and finely constructed structures of ancient societies, can best be explained as inherited 'gifts' from a more advanced culture. Presumably, such advances could only be second-hand information, imparted as a legacy from some very ancient civilization or species that still remains unidentified and concealed to modern historians. Based on what little is known of early primitive life on Earth, all indications suggest that those legacies were not developed by indigenous inhabitants. Logic thus concludes that those advances, which were simply out-of-place for their cultural eras and time periods, were likely inherited commodities bestowed long ago upon our planet.

Most elements of the advanced Egyptian civilization were present from its beginning, indicating such components were not a development but rather a legacy. The oldest known archaic Egyptians were fascinated and mystified with their own enigmatic ancestors and their much earlier society. Archaic Egyptians highly valued anything that was considered to be 'old' by their then-present culture, a culture that itself is now regarded as 'ancient' by modern standards. But those ancient Egyptians collected the even older articles of their long ago predecessors as 'prized possessions,' as if to regain the glory or power from that earlier mysterious period of existence, a time perhaps still vaguely recalled in their memory and oral traditions.

That archaic era, ancient to the Egyptians of the earliest dynastic times, possessed a level of science that could only be categorized as 'magical' by the scientifically illiterate. Those earliest Egyptians were manipulators of great forces that evidently remained unknown to their later generations. Or perhaps they were able to create artificial environments in which natural laws of physics could be altered or controlled, allowing fantastic feats to be performed. The essence of their knowledge or science was subsequently either lost or shrouded in superstition, making it indecipherable to later generations; or perhaps it was gradually distorted, rendering it impotent.

Several competing theories attempt to explain this paradox, which was associated with those most archaic prehistoric humans. One speculative belief claims that such developments occurred from a vastly older 'lost' human civilization, one whose remains have yet to be discovered on our planet. Still others credit 'outside' conveyance of such knowledge by intelligent beings that visited our planet during remote epochs of Earth's history.

Such indigenous lost cultures of early Earth have speculatively been located in Antarctica, the Gobi Desert, and numerous island sites that are presently submerged under the seas. Yet adequate evidence of a permanent indigenous species that could have created such a culture has not been found. It could be expected that some major remnant of a prior great but lost Earth civilization would have been uncovered by now, if that was the true origin. But the mere fact that such an advanced lost civilization has not been uncovered does not negate its once possible existence. The locations of such sites may now exist in some of the most inhospitable areas of our planet, such as at the polar regions, places that may preclude their discovery until possible later climatic changes transpire on Earth to alter its topography.

Common sense would dictate that if indeed a much earlier human society existed, they would also have expanded their high culture to some land that was not completely destroyed, or not now essentially inaccessible. Such an isolated but reasonably accessible satellite site would seemingly reveal some evidence of their existence. But new exploration and research tend to discredit any trace of such an early human race and their high culture. Yet anomalous artifacts do occasionally turn up to indicate that some advanced intelligent beings did indeed interact with Earth during those long ago periods, at least as far back as ten million years.

However, such singular circumstantial evidence tends to point to a very limited exposure with Earth, usually encompassing an inadequate period of time for even a primitive culture to be developed, let alone a highly advanced one. Such limited or brief exposure more likely indicates a visitor to Earth, with little or no intention of permanent colonization. Such contact would likely be by explorers, monitors, guardians, or others reflecting similar motivational intentions. Perhaps such visits were conducted to evaluate the natural resources of planet Earth, while studying its potential for future development and habitation. Modern humans are striving to conduct similar such explorations or evaluations of our own celestial neighbors, especially Mars and Earth's moon.

Current scientific evidence tends to refute the lost ancient Earth civilization theory. According to a joint study undertaken by Duke University and the University of California at Berkeley, extinction of a species requires about ten million years to recover and produce anything resembling its original extinct species.[1] Such a conclusion was compiled by James Kirchner, a geologist with Berkeley, and Anne Weil, a Duke biologist, utilizing mathematical techniques developed for complex astrophysics computations, combined with the study of marine fossil databases. Their findings were published in early 2000 in the journal *Nature*.[2]

That ten million year 'time limit' associated with the rate of extinct species recovery is further based on the period of time it takes for the ecosystem to be rebuilt and sufficiently purge the devastating effects caused by its specific extinction-event. If accurate, such conclusions would require extinction of some lost 'early human' race to have been destroyed between 10.0 and 8.5 million years ago. Such a time frame is based on the earliest human ancestor, *Homo erectus*, which first appeared around 1.7 million years ago, or the earliest true human subspecies of *c*.400, 000 BC, the 'proto-Sapiens.' The proto-Sapiens is a term introduced in the <u>First Journal of the Ancient Ones</u>, *Elder Gods of Antiquity*, and is used in this text to identify the earliest but unnamed branch within our *Homo sapiens* lineage.

Yet the oldest circumstantial evidence of any human society only dates from three to one million years ago. Hence, some other rational explanation must exist. If not an indigenous species that sprang into existence on Earth through natural evolution, perhaps an otherworldly 'visiting race' was the source of such an early high culture. An advanced race of visitors would also be capable of fleeing Earth prior to the devastating effects of any impending cataclysm that would obliterate their culture, leaving only 'hints' of their prior presence on Earth.

If the source of such a diverse ancient legacy was extraneous to Earth, who were those benefactors? Most ancient legends tell of a time when only the olden gods were on Earth, prior to humankind's existence. Perhaps the earliest known extensive exploration of Earth is revealed from an apparent ancient global survey and mapping effort conducted sometime before 2.5 million years ago, evidenced by the ancient extant maps that reveal details of a fully ice-free Antarctic continent, a condition that last occurred around 2.5 million BC.[3] A subtropical climate is believed to have existed in the Antarctic prior to that time, one with abundant foliage of ferns and deciduous trees. Evidence of a suspected major Antarctic settlement during that time frame is

29

suggested,[4] along with traces of a smaller but similar settlement also at Earth's opposite end, near the Arctic North Pole.[5]

A more likely scenario finds otherworldly beings occupying our planet, either as temporary lodging while their homeworld purged the devastating effects of a planetary disaster, or as an unsuccessful attempt at a permanent colonization of Earth. The small quantity of anomalous artifacts associated with those settlements tends to indicate their very isolated nature and sparse integration with our planet, suggesting that any civilization associated with those sites was probably only temporary in duration. If such colonies were for the purpose of short-term housing of non-indigenous beings that came to Earth due to cataclysms on their homeworld, that would explain their sudden appearance, followed by their nearly total departure from our planet.

Such a theory would also explain the exceedingly rare but tangible evidence of anomalous humanoid fossils and artifacts found on Earth, such as the partial remains of several inexplicable *Homo sapiens* discovered in both Ethiopia and Kenya, Africa. Those fossils include a modern-appearing skull labeled "Number 1470" that was determined to be 2.8 million years old, which was found in 1972 by Dr. Richard Leakey in Kenya.[6] Further evidence is exhibited by shoe sole imprints found in the southwestern deserts of the United States,[7] as well as in the Gobi Desert.[8] Fossilized humanoid foot prints found in Nevada[9] and Tanzania[10] further confirm such visits. Those periods of otherworldly habitation may have ended when some natural catastrophe engulfed Earth. Massive Earth changes were known to have occurred between three million and 2.5 million BC, evidenced by the massive volcanic activity and lava flows dated to that time period that covered the entire Western United States,[11] which also formed many of the South Pacific islands, including Easter Island.

Chapter 4

Extraterrestrial Life

Some of the most intelligent people on Earth do not reject the existence of extraterrestrial beings, although they tend to doubt such lifeforms ever visited our planet. According to a 2001 *Parade Magazine* article, Stephen Hawking does not believe that Earth has ever been visited by any sapient extraterrestrial beings.[1] Carl Sagan believed that life must exist elsewhere in the universe, but was unsure if any otherworldly beings ever visited Earth. Marilyn vos Savant, who possesses one of the world's highest IQs, believes it likely that other forms of life exist in the universe, but also doubts that Earth has ever been visited by such extraterrestrial life, due to the lack of credible evidence suggesting such contact.

Dr. Vos Savant claims that we know our planet and its history very well, and thus would be knowledgeable of any evidence confirming such a visitation. But perhaps we only think we know our planet's history well, while ignoring the more obvious truth. Although the widely known and accepted 'factual knowledge' of a flat Earth at the center of the universe was promoted over many centuries, it never altered the true structural arrangement or nature of the cosmos. Such stated beliefs, regardless of their accompanying credentials, do not create factual reality.

Such perceived truths and knowledge emerge from personal beliefs, based on each individual's version and interpretation of facts to which they have been exposed. Most versions emerge from beliefs based on our limited knowledge of the physical

31

universe, derived through the perceptions of our five senses, as filtered through the process of mental classification leading only to a perceived understanding. The collected raw data are always 'contaminated' by personal and professional prejudice and bias, perhaps distorting, albeit honestly, one's version of the truth. Therefore, individual truths may not reflect factual reality, but merely one's own belief and bias.

The underlying factual reality is never altered or adjusted to agree with such incorrect beliefs, regardless of the intellect or credentials possessed by the believer. Facts and truths are always correct and constant, while beliefs are mere conclusions derived from opinions, hopes, and desires that may be altered by subsequent discoveries and obtained knowledge. Truth, whatever it may be, continues to be true if one embraces it or not, regardless of its partial agreement or its complete contradiction with any flawed theory or belief.

It is reasonably certain that otherworldly intelligent life does not presently thrive elsewhere within our own solar system, with the possible exception of Mars. Yet conditions on certain celestial bodies within our solar system may some day, in the far distant future, produce the basis for such life. That same possibility likewise provides the chance that life could have previously formed on a now-uninhabitable celestial body within our solar system, sometime during the remote past. NASA's 1989 Galileo mission, which reached orbital contact with Jupiter in 1995, passed close to that planet and three of its moons: Io, Callisto, and Europa.

The regularly erupting Io, Jupiter's large innermost moon, is the most volcanically active body in our solar system. Its harsh environment, ranging from 3,000 degrees Fahrenheit near its lava lakes, to 280 degrees below zero elsewhere, creates superheated geysers and vast sulfur plains. Its minimal atmosphere is virtually all sulfur dioxide, making humanlike life a remote possibility. Io reflects conditions going back to Earth's early years around two billion years ago, and may be a candidate for life development sometime in the far future.[2] Europa, the brightest object in our solar system and the fourth largest moon of Jupiter, possesses geological conditions within its slowly changing watery crust that could allow for life formation, even though its surface temperature hovers around 260 degrees below zero.[3] It is interesting to note that both of these potentially future 'living' worlds are also neighbors of the asteroid belt. That debris field contains partial remains of a terrestrial planet that is thought to have been similar to Earth. That world may have once also been home to the earliest formation of life within our solar system.

It is a certainty that other planets exist throughout the universe. Six newly discovered planets that orbit neighboring stars, located between 65 to 192 light years from Earth, were confirmed by the end of 1999.[4] All have been approximately the size of Jupiter, about 318 times Earth's mass. Another much closer Jupiter-sized planet was discovered in 2000 by the University of Texas' McDonald Observatory, orbiting Epsilon Eridani.[5] That star is very similar to our own sun, and is only 10.8 light years from Earth. Two other planets just slightly smaller than the size of Saturn, which is about 95 times Earth's mass, were also discovered and confirmed by March of 2000.[6] These smaller planets are also gas giants, orbiting stars more than 100 light years away. Their discovery was the result of new instrumentation added to the Keck telescope in Hawaii, allowing detection of planets that cause only minimal gravitational wobble to their host star.[7] Even with that updated capability, it would require future instrumentation to be 30 times more sensitive to detect smaller planets, such as ones the size of Earth.[8]

Hence, even though smaller terrestrial planets that might be similar to Earth have not yet been found, that does not mean they do not exist. Science has simply not yet advanced to the point where it would be able to detect those smaller worlds, but their actual existence has been implied by their effect on the already detected, larger neighboring gas giant planets. The leading group of planet hunters, the Marcy Team, is led by Geoffrey W. Marcy from the University of California at Berkeley, and includes noted astronomer R. Paul Butler, a scientist with the Carnegie Institute in Washington. That group believes smaller planets likely exist in those already detected systems, based on their present findings.[9] By 2005, just over 130 planets had been discovered outside our solar system.[10]

Now, more than 200 planets have been found through 2006, making it abundantly clear that extrasolar planets, which are known to exist in various sizes and types, may be quite numerous and common throughout our vast universe. Further, a solar system found around 55 Cancri, a star about 41 light years away in the constellation Cancer, contains at least five planets with stable orbits similar to those within our system.[11] This means that solar systems similar to ours are apparently not all that unusual among the billions of solar systems contained just within our own Milky Way galaxy.

Peter D. Ward, a paleontologist with the University of Washington, believes that a nearby giant planet, one similar to Jupiter, is essential for life formation to occur on neighboring worlds. It is thought that the presence of such a giant planet would both attract and absorb many 'killer' asteroids, preventing them from impacting its neighboring 'incubator' worlds. That would allow for the formation of life where suitable conditions existed, while also protecting it by absorbing life-ending celestial objects from destroying any existing or emerging life.[12] His observations were based on the then known 34 extrasolar planets discovered through the first quarter of 2000.

Dr. Ward concluded that all of the 34 'foreign' solar system planets had 'bad' Jupiters, those with wildly eccentric orbits that may actually enhance chance asteroid impacts with their smaller neighboring planets, rather than averting them.[13] Hence, he suggests that the probability for the development of extraterrestrial intelligent life, either past or present, may be small.[14] An increasing number of other scientists, including many astrobiologists and astrophysicists, express even greater doubts for finding intelligent otherworldly life, conceding the likelihood that only single-cell microbes might be found.[15]

Such pessimism is based on what this author refers to as the 'Goldilock's syndrome,' where conditions on every detected planet are simply never exactly correct or conducive for life formation. But life continues to be found on Earth in environments that are widely considered impossible to support any known form of life; yet such life actually flourishes in those extreme conditions. Perhaps evaluation of a mere 34 examples from the trillions of predicted planets might simply be an insufficient cross-section from which to derive such a 'decisive' conclusion.

Apparently NASA is also taking a new position regarding life elsewhere in the universe, one that differs with respected scientists such as Isaac Asimov and Carl Sagan. The topic of alien life elsewhere in the cosmos has been a long running debate. It may be presumptive to connect NASA's perceived new perspective regarding intelligent alien life in the universe with their well-publicized Martian spacecraft failures of 1999, and the discovery of numerous 'inhospitable' worlds outside our solar system.

NASA blamed the 1999 failure of its Mars Climate Orbiter on confusion arising from the combined use of both English and Metric measuring systems, utilized by two separate groups of scientists that worked on the project. Such a nonsensical excuse should be as big an embarrassment as the loss of the orbiter itself. Evidently our government and NASA believe the real cause of this failure would be even more damaging to their credibility than this embarrassing excuse. Less accomplished scientists and engineers have successfully and consistently worked concurrently with different or mixed standards without problems over many decades, as well as throughout entire professional careers. That is one reason why conversion tables are routine items seen at workstations and desks of most technical workers.

Through 1999, 16 of the 23 United States probes sent to Mars had failed, including the December 1999 Polar Lander failure. By 2005, over half of Earth's more than 40 international missions to Mars sent since 1960 have crashed, exploded, or were lost. Only Mars Pathfinder, the two Viking spacecraft, and the twin robotic explorers, Opportunity and Spirit, have successfully explored the Martian surface as of 2004.[16] Bad luck or mixed measurement systems would not seem to account for such a high failure rate. Perhaps other forces are involved, ones intentionally interfering with those missions. Perhaps those probes were perceived as a possible threat or an invasion of privacy, with ultimate secrecy or seclusion greatly desired by someone willing to actively maintain such covert status.

The perceived altered attitude adopted within NASA toward extraterrestrial life speculates that humans may be alone in our section of the universe, or perhaps even throughout the entire cosmos. Such an emerging opinion proposes that Earth's composition and stability are an extraordinarily rare occurrence. Further, other planets simply have radiation levels that are too high, while also possessing inadequate levels of chemical elements to ever allow life formation.

NASA's latest pessimistic outlook toward otherworldly life seems familiar to the Goldilock's syndrome, with every detected planet being too hot or too cold, too near the galaxy's dense center or too far away. Too young or too old, or too this or too that, always believing that only a very narrow window could possibly exist in which life could conceivably form. Yet life is found in the harshest of environments on our own planet. Life exists at unbelievable depths of the oceans, thriving under excessive pressures that would crush 'common life' as we know it. Other life flourishes around undersea vents at temperatures that would cook other known life.[17] Certain anaerobic life prospers by absorbing oxygen from contacted substances, rather than from the atmosphere. Apparently the temperature, pressure, and environmental extremes that might possibly support life, at least in some form, are much broader than professed by science. Life evidently is more adaptable than ever imagined.

Tiny bugs have been found in harsh Earth conditions that were previously considered impossible environments for life to possibly exist. Archaebacteria, the single cell transitional organisms between the primitive bacteria and the later ameba, seem to defy all other earthly life that flourishes only in the presence of water and sunlight, while requiring oxygen and organic carbon compounds for their survival.[18] Microbes such as the *Methanococcus jannaschii* live on the ocean floor around hydrovents, surviving in near-boiling water, while thriving on carbon dioxide.

Hence, lifeforms quite different from Earth-based physiology may thrive in conditions completely 'alien' to humans. Planets that once spawned life may eventually become too extreme to support its original life. But if that original life had sufficiently evolved into higher thinking beings, they might seek other compatible worlds on which to continue their existence and progress. Perhaps numerous homeworlds have been depleted by prior advanced lifeforms over the eons of time, followed by their routine migration to new environmentally compatible planets as needed.

Life Formation

Science has generally accepted the spontaneous generation of simple life during Earth's far distant past, followed by its evolution into higher lifeforms. That is the theory offered by Charles Darwin in his controversial 1859 book, *The Origin of Species*. More recent findings in molecular biology equate organic life with the complexity of: "...thousands of exquisitely designed pieces of intricate molecular machinery," according to molecular biologist Michael Denton.[19] Such complexity first became apparent with the deciphering of the double helix structure of the DNA molecule in 1953 by biologists James Watson and Francis Crick. The extent of DNA's vast complexity has been revealed from the human genome mapping project, with its first code compilation made in 2000, which was later released as a 'working draft' in February of 2001.

The complexity of the DNA molecule is astounding, with genes being only one portion. The gene is a chemical unit of atomic size that provides a pattern or code that determines the structure of an organism, part by part. Genes are stored in parts of the cell called chromosomes, which are very long DNA molecules containing many tightly-packed gene bundles. All human DNA is contained within 46 chromosomes, with 23 derived from each parent. The DNA molecule contains billions of codes from which trillions of cellular components can be made, resulting in numerous intricate assemblages. The human genome is the biological blueprint or sequence plan for the 80,000 genes that are derived from about 3.1 billion chemical base pairs that make up the DNA in each human cell.

Such unexpected complexity is reflected within all known organisms. That fact seems to contradict the theory supporting the spontaneous generation of life. Such a concept describes a number of chemical compositions that were merely mixed together or joined by chance within some energized environment that was conducive to life, thereby allowing animation of life from inorganic materials. From such early 'chance formation' that is credited with creating single cell chemical bacteria; higher lifeforms were believed to have emerged as products of ever continuing evolution. Due to the vast complexity of animated life, a random chance mixing of elements within some agreeable environment that was subsequently activated by some outside energy source was considered by Dr. Crick, "...to be a virtually insurmountable obstacle," according to biochemist and science author Michael J. Behe.[20] Other noted scientists are known to agree.

Using a super computer in the 1970s, Sir Fred Hoyle determined that spontaneous generation of even the simplest bacterium was a mathematical impossibility, while the generation of a complete human being was quite beyond comprehension. By

1981, Dr. Hoyle believed that life on Earth must: "...have been the product of purposeful intelligence."[21]

Conversely, other theories profess that humans are a special creation, genetically engineered by highly advanced extraterrestrials that imparted their own DNA upon Earth's lower lifeforms. But that would have still required the initial 'chance formation' of that advanced extraterrestrial form of life during some remote time period on their own alien planet. The same is true all the way back to the very first formation of animated life somewhere within the earliest primordial universe, shortly after the Big Bang event.

Hence, that concept provides further evidence that at least the very earliest lifeforms, either on Earth or elsewhere, were the direct preplanned result of the Creator, the author of the Big Bang genesis. Instructions for the formation of that very *First Life* were evidently encoded within the primordial DNA molecules that were forged from the energy release of that Big Bang event. Those molecules apparently became the universal spores from which all subsequent life would evolve, a purposeful result preplanned by the Creator. That germ of life may have been spread naturally, transported on the many asteroids or comets that subsequently 'contaminated' other encountered worlds throughout the universe.

This does not negate the possibility, even the likelihood, that such a universal seed was later also dispersed around the universe by the later intelligent 'biological products' that would have resulted from those earliest initial life formations. Such highly evolved creatures would merely be assisting the Master Plan that was conceived by the Creator. They may have accomplished their distribution plan by launching craft or probes containing such universal spores for their arrival on numerous distant worlds. Or, their delivery might have been more deliberate and selective, personally dispersing such bacterium spores to selectively encountered planets during their travels. Such an artificial distribution process would have merely supplemented or accelerated the intended natural formation of life around the cosmos. Such acts would then assure the continued propagation of that 'original seed,' in whatever form or manner each spore might take, depending on the evolutionary changes it would eventually encounter and endure over time.

Chapter 5

Life on Earth

Numerous theories attempt to explain the many mysteries surrounding the emergence of humankind's earthly ancestors. The prevailing scientific theory credits the process of natural evolution for the formation of intelligent life. Over a long duration of time, this process supposedly involved the linear progression of small mammals into monkeys, then into apes, followed by apemen, and finally culminating with humankind; a slow and deliberate evolutionary progression upward from lower lifeforms. Perhaps this process even originated with more elementary life that developed from universal spores, seeded within our solar system during the earliest primordial times.

If correct, the evolutionary process that apparently led to humankind's emergence started with the creation of monkeys and other early primates, which eventually led to the apes. Much later, the apes ultimately split into two branches, one of 'pure' apes and another of apemen called *Australopithecines*. Apemen continued to evolve through numerous subspecies into ever-higher creatures that were not quite human, but were a level above the apes. They represented the *Homo erectus* stage of humanity, which included the later crude *Pithecanthropus*.

That lineage was followed by a more modern version of a sparsely populated ancestor, the proto-Sapiens, which was perhaps the first branch in the *Homo sapiens* family. Those advanced beings were followed by a very primitive subspecies, the brutish Neanderthal man that was barely advanced from the earlier *Pithecanthropus*. The sudden appearance of Cro-Magnon man in the midst of Neanderthals is equally unexplained. Their extremely advanced capabilities and modern appearance tends to contradict known evolutionary principles. Their subspecies was then slightly 'tweaked' to produce Earth's current Modern man, *Homo sapiens sapiens*. All these changes occurred within about 20 million years, almost 4.7 billion years after Earth first formed.

Still other beliefs propose a much earlier natural evolution of humankind on planet Earth. Such an initial human emergence supposedly then built a high civilization, one reaching a very advanced level of achievement. That proficient but unknown archaic culture was later destroyed by some natural disaster, erasing all traces of that now extinct but presumed 'First Race.' Perhaps numerous earthly high cultures have perished through similar fates, remaining unknown to later humanity. Such a fate may yet await Modern man sometime in our distant future, obliterating all traces of our great culture, and once again leaving the planet without a dominate species.

But extant evidence contradicts that theory. A credible case can be made for progression from early hominid ancestors to apes, whose lineage eventually split into two paths. Progression to *Australopithecus* apemen, followed by numerous branches leading to *Pithecanthropus* is equally substantiated. But the supposed 'next generation' of a sudden 'modern appearing' species, an unnamed species identified in this text as the 'proto-Sapiens' that are perhaps best known from the Swanscombe man specimens, seems totally out-of-place and inexplicable.

Regression then followed that subspecies, producing the more primitive Neanderthal man, only to be succeeded contemporaneously by Modern man in the form of the Cro-Magnons; a path that simply does not fit with the evolutionary process, and may not be accurate. Genetic tests performed on DNA samples from preserved Neanderthal specimens lacked evidence for a true ancestral lineage with Modern man.[1] However, Neanderthals appear to be a normal evolutionary step from *Pithecanthropus*, traceable from the *Australopithecus* species; one that became an essentially dead-end branch of hominids that exhibited very little ancestry with true humans.

Modern mans' lineage seems to abruptly appear with proto-Sapiens by c.400,000 BC, only to die out by c.150,000 BC. After roughly 100,000 years of absence, perhaps its true successor suddenly appeared in recognizable numbers as the superior Cro-Magnon man around 43,000 BC; only to be closely followed by the new, slightly improved version of *Homo sapiens sapiens* around c.11,600 BC. That latest and still present 'model' was basically a 'refinement' of Cro-Magnon man, with a more efficient and slightly smaller size that was reduced from about 6' 4" down to an average height slightly over 5' 9". This truly Modern man branch also possessed a refined mouth structure that allowed more complex sounds to be produced.

Those minor changes make sense only if the latest version was intended to rely more on its intellectual resources and technology, rather than on brawn and size. But the lineage from proto-Sapiens to Cro-Magnons, followed by fully Modern man, contradicts 'pure' evolution; seemingly suddenly all emerging from nowhere, while progressing at an incredible rate. Just as mysterious are those few extant fossil specimens of an apparently Modern man, which roamed Earth during vastly remote ages before our species was thought to even exist. The best example being the previously mentioned 2.8 million year old modern Skull "1470" found by Dr. Richard Leakey.

Since no one was present when the first life appeared or formed on Earth, any proclamation about its origin must be considered only theoretical, not factual. The known oddities associated with evolutionary theories, such as whales having hipbones, tend to indicate that an incomplete understanding, or other additional influences, may be associated with this process. The expansion of a single theory to encompass all known elements may simply represent flawed logic. While evolution may account for certain species of animal life, it might not be the whole answer. Perhaps a specific ancestral strain of early prehumankind may have later mixed, or been manipulated to some degree, with an unknown humanlike being to eventually 'create' humans.

Such rigid thinking regarding humanity's origins appears similar to claims made by certain Egyptologists that the youngest pyramids are known to have been built by humans, hence all pyramids must have been built by man. Yet the very oldest pyramids were the best-built, largest, and most complex fabrications. Some are acknowledged as being beyond modern land-based construction capabilities, and would have apparently required aerial assistance.

Many later man-made pyramids seem to be merely 'poor copies,' inferior in both size and quality. That does not devalue or diminish the many great ancient achievements accomplished by humankind over the eons, through their own ingenuity, inventiveness, and determination. But, the many noticeable disparities between such structures clearly indicate that at least two different groups of builders were involved. Identification of the earliest group, based on the identity of the later one, is simply flawed logic, whether concerning humans or pyramids.

Another explanation favors divine intervention, where God created humans in His own image. Several questions emerge as to why the Creator would have waited more than 13 billion years after fashioning the universe to usher in intelligent life on some later-formed planet within a remote region of the cosmos. This belief also ignores prior lifeforms such as dinosaurs, which ruled Earth for hundreds of millions of years, long before the emergence of humankind.

Perhaps an overlooked argument against strict creationism, when viewed only from the perspective of planet Earth and its relatively recent formation within our universe, is the resulting implied insult it conveys upon the Creator. Such an implication suggests the Creator took almost 13 billion years to first conceive the idea to form sapient life in the form of humans, but was unable to produce a perfected species the first time, having to progress through numerous trials and errors producing various failed candidates. As previously stated, *First Life* may have indeed resulted from the Creationism process, but it was not on planet Earth. Surely the Creator would not have needed so many attempts to eventually produce a 'flawed' creature such as humankind.

Extraterrestrial intervention is yet another theory used to explain the emergence of ancestral humankind on our planet. Humans were either brought to Earth from some yet unknown world to colonize the planet, or an unidentified advanced otherworldly species performed genetic manipulations on existing earthly lower lifeforms to create the more advanced beings that later became *Homo sapiens*. Perhaps a combination of these two otherworldly scenarios occurred. Extraterrestrial life, or DNA from such species, may have mixed with indigenous Earth life to produce a hybrid human being. A further 'spiritual intervention' may have involved 'alien' souls incarnating into human vessels, for the learning opportunities such life-experiences might offer.

The truth pertaining to humankind's emergence on planet Earth may well be a mixture of all the above speculative theories and beliefs. The most logical thesis is the formation of the basic elements of life by the Creator, in the form of universal spores. Such seeds would possess the ability to develop into any number of living creatures. Some of those organisms would evolve into sentient life, with a certain portion further developing into intelligent life. A segment of that intelligent life would be destined to further evolve into enlightened, advanced thinking beings.

Those beings could then continue the work of the Creator within our physical realm. Such enlightened physical creatures could have perpetuated not only the universal seeding efforts, but also accelerated the developmental evolution of any encountered later emerging life through mechanical manipulation, thereby producing new functional species assuring continuation of the Creator's Master Plan. Whatever the true nature, origin, and purpose for the emergence of humankind, the known facts derived from meticulous work by dedicated paleoanthropologists and archaeologists have been reconstructed in the following brief chronology. This background data will then allow an informed evaluation of those developments that likely occurred on Earth during primordial times.

Earth Chronology

About nine billion years after the Big Bang event, planet Earth finally formed roughly 4.7 billion years ago, and 'solidified' into our world almost 800 million years later. Life developed quickly after that, probably within the first 200 million years or so,[2] sometime around 3.7 billion years ago. Those first organisms, the *heterotrophs*,[3] were primitive bacterial life classified as prokaryotes, which are cells that do not possess a distinct nucleus or a surrounding membrane. Between 3.5 and 3.4 billion years ago, those primitive cells mutated to form *cyanobacteria*, cells resembling rudimentary algae that subsisted on carbon dioxide. Those protoplant cells, known as *autotrophs*, were the forerunners of all future plants.

Between 3.0 and 2.8 billion years ago, that early autotroph vegetation clumped together over calcium carbonate deposits on the ocean floor to form structures known as *stromatolites*. Those organic mounds produced a by-product of oxygen that then enriched the surrounding waters as well as the toxic atmosphere of early Earth. Oxygen eventually accumulated in Earth's early atmosphere, forming minimal ozone that provided a limited protective shield from the sun's ultraviolet radiation.

Between 2.5 and 2.1 billion years ago, more complex forms of algae and bacterial slime then formed simple vegetation capable of true photosynthesis. Such life derived their sustenance from combining carbon dioxide with water, giving off oxygen as a by-product. As that vegetation spread, it produced ever-increasing levels of oxygen, resulting in an oxidizing atmosphere with an enriched ozone layer for further UV protection. Yet all these developments had still produced only unicellular life on Earth.

For some unknown reason, after more than two billion years of single cell life, a new type of cellular organism formed around 1.5 billion years ago, emerging as eukaryotic cells, which possess an organized nucleus and a distinct nuclear membrane. Such new life included the early protozoa and amoebae organisms of the *Protista* kingdom, the earliest proto-animal ancestors.

Eukaryotic cells also formed the first true plants, those multicellular green organisms of the *Plantae* kingdom. Continuing Earth changes further led to even more complex organisms that some classify as the earliest form of animal life, perhaps as early as 800 million years ago. That invertebrate wormlike creature possessed a soft-body, and was subsequently joined by the earliest jellyfish ancestors. They were followed by shelled trilobites, the first creatures with mineralized skeletons, which emerged around 570 million years ago to usher in the Cambrian Period.

By 550 million years ago, segmented worms, sea spiders, brachiopods, snails, and primitive crustaceans had emerged. The earliest primitive fish then appeared between 530 and 500 million years ago, forming the first known creatures with backbones. That era, which comprised the prolific Cambrian 'explosion of life' period, is believed to be the greatest diversification and expansion of life ever known on Earth, with evolutionary rates more than 20 times normal, according to research conducted at California Institute of Technology.[4]

After rock shield outcroppings from volcanic eruptions on the ocean floor had formed the primordial continental land mass now referred to as Panagaea, the ancient ancestors of the horseshoe crab temporarily ventured onto land to lay their eggs along its muddy shores sometime around 450 million years ago. That event was closely followed by the first known mass extinction around 430 million years ago, ending the Ordovician

Period. Earth's second Ice Age then ensued, perhaps as a result of whatever caused that mass extinction.

But life quickly rebounded, thriving on dry land with the first vascular plants about 425 million years ago. Over time, a primitive centipede and scorpion emerged, becoming permanent land dwellers around 395 million years ago. By 370 million years ago, certain lobe-finned fish, commonly known as tetrapods, had developed the ability to breathe air. They were the ancient ancestors of the first amphibians, which contributed to the number of creatures able to thrive outside the ocean. Early insects and ferns then added to the variety of life on dry land. Not long after, a second mass extinction followed some time around 365 million years ago.

Again, life rapidly bounced back with amphibians giving rise to reptiles about 320 million years ago. The earliest species of dinosaurs then first appeared between 250 and 230 million years ago, followed by the third mass extinction around 225 million BC, ending the Paleozoic era and killing an estimated 95% of all species. Even after such massive devastation, various animal species quickly emerged, including many new types of dinosaurs and early mammals. The fourth mass extinction then occurred at the end of the Triassic Period about 195 million years ago, as a result of a celestial impact. Birds formed about ten million years later, believed to be a branch or mutation from reptiles. The mighty dinosaurs continued to thrive until an asteroid impact ended their reign about 65 million years ago.

Much later, two other celestial impacts then occurred around 35 million BC, with one hitting Chesapeake Bay, while the second impacted Siberia, causing yet another mass extinction. As life slowly recovered, the new rulers became the mammals, with primates eventually assuming the lead role. Monkeys emerged about 30 million years ago, preceding apes within that lineage. The first true primates developed approximately 20 million years ago as the ancient ancestors of modern day lemurs. Primates then branched into three separate paths, two of monkeys and one of hominids, which included the various ape species and humans.

Various dead-end species of the earliest hominid ancestors died out, with all manlike apes vanishing by about eight million years ago, leaving only true apes. The apes then split into two groupings sometime between 6.4 and 4.4 million years ago during the Pliocene Epoch, forming both apes and a new apeman species.

Fossils of the oldest suspected ancestor of humans were found during 2000 in the Tugen Hills of Kenya in Northeastern Africa. Dubbed the Millennium man, this hominid species is officially classified as *Orrorin tugensis*, a creature about the size of a modern chimpanzee. It has been relative-dated to about 5.9 million years old, making it the suspected and presently oldest known relative within the human lineage. Since so few remains have so far been found, a more concise picture of this creature can not be developed. Fossils of a somewhat similar specimen, also the size of a chimpanzee, were found between July 2001 and February 2002 in the Djurab Desert in northern Chad.[5] Dated between six and seven million years old, the hominid skull of this genus, called *Sahelanthropus tchadensis*, shows a unique combination of both primitive and evolved traits.[6] These fossils are suspected to be possible ancestors within our human lineage.

The earliest 'confirmed' emergence of *Australopithecus* apemen, about 4.4 million years ago, was a major split within the hominid line, with at least five initial branches of evolution known to have occurred within that lineage. Certain inconclusive fragmentary remains, which can be dated to about five million years ago, are tentatively identified as possibly being an even earlier species of Australopithecine, but insufficient anatomical details exist to specifically classify those remains. About 2.3 million years ago the *Australopithecus* family further evolved into two additional branches. Those later Australopithecines branches were the first to use rock tools and implements; known from their stone tool factory found in the Rift Valley of Kenya, Africa.[7]

Around 2.1 million years ago a later branch of the Australopithecine family emerged that is identified as *Homo habilis*, meaning 'handy man,' so named due to their use of simple stone tools. Although this hominid is misclassified under the '*Homo*' genus, which refers to 'true man,' it was merely a transitional branch of *Australopithecus*. The earlier Australopithecine *Paranthropus* branch had used crude stone tools around 2.3 million BC, prior to *Homo habilis*. Hence, such a species within a new 'handy man' genus classification was probably unnecessary.

Our oldest traceable human lineage, the earliest extant near-man specimen, is the 1.7 million years old *Homo ergaster* genus that branched into *Homo erectus*, thereby ushering in the earliest 'men' that walked in a fully upright gate and stance. Certain paleoanthropologists combine all branches of *Homo erectus* into one group, the *Pithecanthropus*, its youngest branch. This group includes the Asian Java man that dates to about 675,000 BC; the European Heidelberg man that emerged around 500,000 BC; and the far-Eastern Peking man that first appeared about 450,000 BC. This genus, along with all its branches, became extinct sometime around 375,000 BC.

True Man emerged with the *sapiens* species by roughly 400,000 BC, although it is difficult to precisely identify their actual start due to the extremely fragmentary fossil evidence left by this earliest branch. This unnamed branch is identified within this text as the 'proto-Sapiens,' the one that preceded Neanderthal man, but are often incorrectly referred to as 'early Neanderthals.' Their brief coexistence with the earlier *Pithecanthropus* ended with that prior species' extinction sometime around 375,000 BC, shortly after the first appearance of this earliest *Homo sapiens*.

The oldest known specimen of proto-Sapiens is a lower jaw found in Kanam, Kenya, dating between 400,000 and 375,000 BC. Fragments of four similar skulls were found nearby in Kanjera, Kenya, dating to *c*.350,000 BC. Perhaps its earliest known European specimen is Vertesszöllös man from that same

time period, with later fossils of Swanscombe man dating to
c.250,000 BC. A yet unnamed 200,000 year old proto-Sapiens
jawbone specimen was found in July 2000 at a site in Southern
France by an international team led by Serge Lebel, a Canadian
paleontologist.[8]   Other remains include the *c*.175,000 BC
Steinheim man and the controversial Fontechévade man of
150,000 BC, believed to mark the end of this enigmatic branch.

Neanderthals emerged about that same time around 150,000
BC as a sparsely populated species at their outset, with increased
population numbers not occurring until around 115,000 BC when
they became quite numerous. They were followed by the abrupt
appearance of Cro-Magnon man by 43,000 BC, with some
indications dating back as early as 110,000 BC. That early
version of Modern man quickly dominated Earth as a far superior
species to the lowly Neanderthals, which could not compete with
that newcomer. The Neanderthals became a dead-end branch that
had mostly disappeared by 30,000 BC, although new findings
indicate a few lingered slightly longer, perhaps as late as 26,000
BC.

Neanderthal bones found in the Vindija cave of Croatia are
the youngest fossils of its species yet found, radiocarbon dating
to between 27,000 and 26,000 BC,[9] according to Fred Smith, an
anthropologist with Northern Illinois University.   This find
further reinforces the belief that mating, at least on a limited
basis, apparently occurred between the younger Cro-Magnon
subspecies and Neanderthal man. A modification or refinement
of Cro-Magnon man occurred with the emergence of *Homo
sapiens sapiens*, or truly Modern man, which first appeared about
c.11,600 BC. Those two closely related subspecies coexisted
until the Great Flood, the one associated with the Pleistocene
Extinction, which occurred around 10,500 BC.

Only truly Modern man survived that cataclysm, for some
unknown reason. That flood event is associated with many
enigmatic anomalies in Earth's history, mostly explained only as
'divine intervention from a higher source.' Even earlier anomalies

are found throughout Earth's past, ones that seemingly can only be ascribed to similar extraneous intervention with our world.

Such events add to the possibility that deliberate efforts might have been involved with the development of certain lifeforms on Earth. The inexplicable or sudden appearance of more complex life, at levels beyond expected evolutionary rates, can be observed with the appearance of protozoa and amoebas after billions of years of simple bacterial cells. Such anomalies were followed closely with the earliest animal life only slightly more than one-half billion years later. The enigmatic 'explosion' of life during the Permian Period then started only a quarter of a billion years later, while a later 'explosion' occurred during the Cambrian Period, which commenced about 570 million years ago.

Despite such a vast diversity of lifeforms, apemen did not emerge until well after another half billion years had past. But they were quickly followed with an archaic and inexplicable early ancestor of humankind only a few million years later. The first humans appeared only a little more than a million years afterward, a very quick and sudden occurrence when compared with the exaggerated time it took Earth to 'evolve' bacteria into an ameba. It would appear that Earth received some form of help with its development of certain species, at least during its more recent accelerated production of 'higher' indigenous lifeforms.

An attempt to uncover answers to such perplexing mysteries was explored in the First Journal of the Ancient Ones, *Elder Gods of Antiquity*. That book established a more detailed 'event chronology' from the Big Bang birth of the universe, to Earth's formation billions of years later. It then revealed the subsequent creation and evolution of life on our planet, highlighting the numerous mysteries, inaccuracies, misconceptions, and contradictions associated with the prevailing explanations put forth by academia and modern science.

Such discrepancies included the anomalous relics and artifacts that dated to times long before they were first believed to have existed, as well as the extraordinary ancient megalithic stone structures that would challenge even our modern land based construction capabilities. Additional mysteries also included utilization of advanced scientific knowledge and technology at levels of attainment that would have required use of modern equipment, exemplified by the medical and celestial wisdom that was apparently possessed by certain ancient cultures. Those same societies also recorded accounts of superhuman achievements performed by humanlike beings, which were documented throughout ancient texts. Such anomalies contradict accepted scientific doctrine, exposing attainment levels requiring abilities far beyond those ascribed for their time period.

Such lingering enigmatic mysteries required new insight and different conclusions to explain and encompass all that conflicting data, including the likely existence of much earlier sapient life within our universe. A new hypothesis known as the *Elder Gods* theory was introduced, which focused on extraterrestrial intervention as the probable explanation for early Earth's development, as well as similar involvement with our formation as a sapient species. The First Journal of the Ancient Ones, *Elder Gods of Antiquity* also provided the suggestive and supportive evidence necessary to validate the *Elder Gods* theory, revealing the surviving fragmentary evidence that remained from ancient times. That included advanced devices, megalithic stone constructions, and high scientific knowledge, along with recorded fantastic accounts of achievement supposedly performed by 'superhuman' beings.

Chapter 6

Elder Gods Theory

The unique *Elder Gods* theory is compatible with all the known facts of cosmology, archaeology, paleoanthropology, geology, and historic events of Earth's ancient past. It further accounts for the many anomalous artifacts that date to archaic times. This theory purports that soon after the Big Bang birth of the universe, perhaps after a mere two billion years or so, the first sentient life developed on some distant planet in a far away galaxy. Such an event occurred perhaps as the result of universal spores, long before our sun and planet had even formed. Over time, that earliest *First Life* might have even evolved into beings possessing higher intelligence.

Progress allowed their cultures to reach fantastic levels, only to self-destruct due to moral decay and their own inability to comprehend all the consequences of their actions. That same cycle of life creation, accumulation of knowledge, cultural growth, and scientific progress also produced similar high cultures of immense attainment on numerous other early planets. Just as before, despite their vast technological advancements, ethical problems ultimately threatened their cultures. Their advanced achievements eventually surpassed their ability to fully understand all the ramifications and consequences of their own inventions and actions, completing the now predictable continuing cycle of self-annihilation.

Eventually, one species of early *First Beings* finally altered their destructive behavior before reaching their point of no return, which ultimately ended this pattern of total annihilation. But they reversed their moral decay and survived past that previously established threshold of extinction. Moving into levels never before attained, they achieved peace and tranquillity through order and harmony. Their break in the repetitive cycle of past destruction was viewed as a reprieve, prompting that species of enlightened *First Beings* to devote even more resources to their own character and moral development. That produced an enhanced refinement previously unattained within their people, resulting in a thoughtful society that recognized and comprehended every potential consequence associated with all their actions and inventions.

Once this newly obtained level of enlightenment emerged from the early chaos, that *First Being* species then focused their energies, skills, and expertise on more altruistic pursuits. They rebuilt their previously 'degraded' world, allowing their new culture to develop into a higher level of civilization, one never before attained within the young universe. With an enhanced focus on self-responsibility and constraint, their culture advanced to greater heights through 'controlled' growth and planned accomplishments. Their technological achievements eventually included 'routine' interplanetary travel, which ultimately led to galactic capabilities; bringing them in contact with younger, more primitive species on far distant planets. The less developed lifeforms they encountered were always observed to be on predictable self-destructive paths not unlike the one previously avoided by that enlightened *First Being* species during their ancient past.

As galactic travels expanded to even more distant worlds, they encountered numerous other emerging races and observed the same uncontrolled growth, all lacking an understanding of the consequences caused by their chaotic actions. Those infant races would inevitably self-destruct, often taking other nearby planets with them, due to the far reaching scope of their own created demise. Such unspecified actions and perverse choices caused ominous imbalances and negative consequences within the early universe, disrupting the continuity of universal order, resulting in rampant chaos. The effects of such foreboding acts spread throughout the cosmos, with many worlds destroyed and numerous lifeforms lost.

Eventually, with ever increasing intergalactic travel capabilities, this *First Being* species encountered another species of beings that had also evolved during the earliest formative years of the universe. That second *First Being* species had also experienced its own reprieve from near self-created extinction, one that was also replaced with enhanced enlightenment and subsequent 'controlled' progress. By comparing their own backgrounds and observations of infant races on numerous planets each had encountered during their extensive cosmic explorations, both *First Being* species concluded that all infant races went through similar 'evolutionary' destructive phases. Those stages inevitably led to self-annihilation and perhaps even the destruction of their own solar system or galactic sector. Left unchecked, such chaotic actions might someday result in threats that would encompass the entire universe, including the *First Beings*.

It was further surmised that only in extremely rare exceptions could infant species evolve to higher levels of enlightenment, overcoming their innate propensity for self-destruction. Over time, those two enlightened early species eventually encountered different additional *First Being* races that had also survived self-annihilation; totaling at least seven distinct species of *First Being* 'survivors,' which existed at various locations throughout the vast expanse of our universe.

Together, those *First Being* species all agreed to form a collective alliance, one dedicated to civilize, educate, and control the growth of the younger infant races they would encounter throughout the universe. Accomplishment of such a goal would be achieved through adherence with an agreed upon code of conduct known as the *Cosmic Order*, one constructed and intended to create universal harmony throughout the cosmos.

Such a code was not viewed as merely a set of laws that were to be enforced by 'catching' lawbreakers. Such secular laws were considered to be secondary to this *Code*, which was more correctly a 'way-of-life,' containing both rights and responsibilities that were bestowed upon each emerging world. It was a universal paradigm intended to control the actions and developmental direction of primitive races, while teaching those younger beings ethical and moral 'core' values.

The Cosmic Order prohibited imparting any knowledge or advanced technology that might surpass the comprehensive abilities of each developing infant race. The criteria limiting such 'progress' required that every infant race must first be able to envision the ultimate and total effects resulting from implementation of all their advanced devices and processes. Any nonconforming technology would require containment within that planet's atmosphere, thereby limiting its effect on other worlds. Hence, only those planetary inhabitants implementing such unauthorized technology might be harmed, if any miscalculations might have been made.

Forced compliance using physical intervention was employed by the *First Beings* to contain any spread of chaos resulting from non-conformity with their code. Their Cosmic Order was to be the primary and fundamental commandment or rule, coming before and taking precedence over the laws of any 'member' planet. The *First Beings* pledged their life's effort and purpose toward implementing and maintaining strict compliance with their Cosmic Order once it was introduced to primitive societies, assuring harmony throughout the universe. In return, the *First Beings* would assist and impart knowledge to those infant races, in appropriate degrees, bringing civilization to those worlds while also educating their inhabitants.

The Cosmic Order became the foundation for universal harmony, as a prime directive intended to permanently alter the repetitive cycle of destruction within the physical realm. Its underlying alliance and mission may have even been the result of some form of direct contact with the Creator, the architect of our universe. Vague references in ancient texts imply that the *First Beings* may have somehow achieved interconnectivity with that Universal Consciousness, the Creator, and were ultimately commanded to oversee the physical realm. As the highest evolved physical lifeforms in the universe, the *First Beings* were essentially the only ones capable of shaping and changing the material world. Based upon their advanced attainments and accomplishments, their responsibility to be 'stewards of the universe' was conferred upon them.

Imagine the exponential difference in the technological attainment of the *First Beings* over that of later worlds, with their headstart of thousands, millions, or even billions of years. An earlier species would undoubtedly attain higher levels of technology than a later one, if essential developments were approximately progressive in their occurrence. Simply stated, with each level of higher attainment, more resources become available to obtain even more advancements. Hence, achievement levels seemingly would become exponential, finally reaching some zenith.

The previously mentioned contention asserting that such advanced inventions and scientific discoveries naturally occur when a species reaches a given level, even if they were not seeking such knowledge or invention, seems to indicate some divine preplanning that allows such self-evident developments. However, no implicit rule is known that requires a divine bond to exist between one's technological and spiritual development. A species may obtain great technical levels without achieving high spirituality. Conversely, a highly enlightened being may have little need or use for technology. The *First Beings* apparently had attained high levels of both.

The managed development of each encountered 'infant race' was accomplished by educating its populace and controlling what was taught, resulting in measured progress through regulated growth. Further advancements depended upon the achieved morality and maturity of each culture's values system. Such nurturing and assistance was not merely an altruistic act by a group of advanced and enlightened beings, but also an act of self-preservation. With successful efforts by the *First Beings* to thwart the innate trait of self-destructive behavior within infant races, their own existence and longevity could also be assured.

Those original surviving *First Beings* eventually became known as the *Ancient Ones*. They traveled the stellar regions throughout the expanse of galaxies, star clusters, and nebulas, where they spread harmony through adherence with the Cosmic Order to the emerging worlds that were encountered within those solar systems. The use of the descriptive term 'Ancient Ones' referred to their ancestral lineage or origins during the most primordial eras of our early universe, not their own individual chronological ages. The Ancient Ones were simply a united group of evolved beings comprised of different species that overcame the inherent cycle of self-destruction, and eventually achieved the highest levels of enlightenment.

Under unity within the Cosmic Order, the Ancient Ones were organized into groups with specific capabilities and functions. Where practical, such duties involved rebuilding devastated planets, including ones destroyed by the infant races themselves, for later habitation by other compatible emerging species that might be in need of a new homeworld. Another group seeded or colonized promising early solar systems. A third group civilized, educated, and monitored the growth of sufficiently mature races on each of the various developing planets. Each specific group was assigned a region of space in which to accomplish their assigned mission. Evidently those groups were normally comprised of a representative mix of different species, some perhaps even requiring the use of technical devices such as respirators or space suits within certain harsh environments or incompatible atmospheres of various alien worlds where they were assigned.

The desire to contact emerging races during their early developmental period required the group of 'educator' Ancient Ones to constantly travel throughout the universe to initiate such interaction. Periodically, those groups and duties would change, assuring that every region of the universe would be exposed to all seven different *First Being* species and their own unique cultures. That protocol provided diversity, assuring that no single species or civilization would forever dominate a specific sector of space. With all the different species adhering to the common set of laws and code of conduct embodied within the Cosmic Order, emerging infant worlds would not experience confusion during such periodic changes from one group to another.

The Ancient Ones' success in bringing civilization and the concept of the Creator to the infant races produced a sophisticated, knowledgeable, and enlightened following of 'students' that embraced the Cosmic Order. Eventually, the most enlightened representatives from those infant races were invited to join the 'missionary' efforts of the Ancient Ones, with those 'younger' assistants becoming known as the Helpers or Watchers of the Ancient Ones.

Initially, the Ancient Ones would determine the best method and lesson plan to educate and civilize each individual infant race, and direct that effort at its outset. Once acceptable compliance was established, the daily routine duties were then transferred to the Helpers. The Helpers became the ones that interacted most directly with the indigenous species on each encountered world. That allowed the Ancient Ones to contact many more planets, in their mission to spread the Cosmic Order. The Helpers were assigned to a specific planet partially based on their appearance, chosen for their similarity with the contacted race of beings that were indigenous to each world. That assured the best reception during first contact, minimizing any fear or violent reaction that might occur from the initial meeting between 'dissimilar' beings.

A near lack of written records confirming such contact would be normal, since the earliest intervention with infant races would have occurred during developmental periods when writing would not have yet existed, or was in its infancy and relegated to conveying only simplistic ideas. Any later 'revelations' or accounts concerning the specific nature of those earliest contacts and the resultant imparted legacies from the Ancient Ones would simply not have been necessary, due to the Ancient Ones' continued contact with those infant races. Their presence would have thus become merely a normal occurrence, as each infant race and its homeworld culture developed. That would be true for all emerging civilizations, unless an unusual event occurred, or some interruption in contact took place. That may well have been the case with Earth contact, and will be addressed in greater detail in the following chapters.

Chapter 7

Solar System Contact

Perhaps as much as seven billion years after the birth of the earliest species of Ancient Ones, the solar system containing Earth formed as part of the continuing expansion process of the Big Bang event. Eventually, our solar system reached a coalescent state, with conditions conducive for life formation. Due to the much later 'creation' of our solar system, it would be logical to assume that the Ancient Ones would have had some form of contact with it since its most formative primordial times. That first contact with our planetary system may have been billions of years ago, and would not have been any different than encounters with other emerging worlds.

Preliminary contacts with our early solar system most likely utilized unmanned probes, sensors, and exploration rovers. Their purpose would have been to monitor and perhaps nurture any developing lifeforms that might be encountered. That may have included seeding efforts on several 'chosen' planets, with differing lifeforms intended specifically for each individual world. Numerous early forms of life may have resulted, only to be destroyed by later natural cataclysms. Incubation of a successful long-term lifeform may have required numerous seeding attempts over the eons of time. Eventually, sustainable life within our solar system obviously flourished, thus allowing the process of natural evolution to then occur.

However, many indications suggest that the earliest intelligent life within our solar system developed first on one of the outer terrestrial planets, not on Earth. While planet Earth was an excellent candidate for life formation, its early environment would have been more hostile than that found on some of the outer planets, which would have condensed and cooled-off first, due to their more remote locations from our sun. All conditions being equal, an outer planet or moon would have produced a slightly earlier and more stable environment, one with a more moderate climate than that found on the inner worlds, which receive more intense solar radiation.

The initial indigenous intelligent beings within our solar system were likely a humanlike species that emerged perhaps as products of prior primordial seeding, developing through natural evolutionary processes associated with the unique environment provided by its host world. That species likely preceded any higher lifeforms on Earth by a substantial length of time, perhaps as much as 300 million years.[1] Such early solar system life formation most likely occurred either on our fourth planet, Mars, or our once fifth planet, Maldek. Maldek occupied the orbit between Mars and Jupiter during the earlier primordial times of our solar system. That orbit now contains the asteroid belt, the destroyed remains of planet Maldek, indicating its subsequent planetary destruction at some later date. It is quite logical and probable that this 'asteroid belt' planet would have developed life before any of the other terrestrial inner planets.

Considering only terrestrial-composition planets, not gas giants, those relegated to orbit at a greater distance from the sun would be theorized to have cooled and condensed first, creating environmental conditions suitable to sustain life; prior to similar developments on their 'inner orbit' counterparts. This theory is born out with indications that the fourth planet, Mars, developed bacterial life before that same occurrence on Earth, the third planet. This fact is derived from Martian meteorites that have impacted Earth. Magnetite, a crystallized magnetic mineral, was found in those rocks.[2] That material is similar to crystals that are formed by bacteria on Earth.[3] Hence, that cosmic evidence indicating microbial-formed Martian bacterial life is known to be older than any lifeform ever found on Earth. Moreover, those 'chance' meteorites that landed on Earth may not even represent the oldest forms of earliest Martian life.

As pointed out in the <u>First Journal of the Ancient Ones,</u> *Elder Gods of Antiquity*, the most likely planet to produce the earliest solar system life was Maldek rather than Mars. Such a supposition is based on its outermost position, and the fact that the quantity of later descendants from that original indigenous solar system species numbered only a few. For a highly advanced, successful civilization to be left with only a few descendants, such an outcome would suggest that their homeworld was completely destroyed, eradicating the vast majority of its people.

Evidence for such an asteroid belt planet has scientific backing. In a 1978 issue of the science journal *Icarus*, Tom Van Flandern, an astronomer at the U.S. Naval Observatory in Washington, D.C., presented a strong case that a planet once occupied the orbit of the asteroid belt.[4] He theorized its planetary destruction occurred about five million years ago, but could not conceive of a means capable of causing such a catastrophe. Numerous other scientists also hold similar beliefs, but date its destruction at widely varying times, with some as recent as 3000 BC.[5]

The scant knowledge of Maldek is derived mainly from mythology and meager geological evidence. Such rare scientific data have been extracted from the occasional meteorite fragments that have broken orbit and were subsequently captured by our planet. Approximately two pounds of an estimated 220 ton meteorite were salvaged from the frozen surface of Tagish Lake in the northern extremes of Canada's British Columbia province in January 2000.[6] Those fragments are considered by scientists to be the most pristine meteorite remnants from Maldek, the asteroid belt planet, and have undergone extensive study by Peter G. Brown at the University of Western Ontario in London, Ontario, Canada.[7]

Since those remains were collected soon after impact and kept frozen until examined, they are believed to be uncontaminated, portraying only the composition of its homeworld, not that of Earth. Commenting on those specimens, science reporter Paul Recer stated: "Preliminary tests made on the pristine rock found it loaded with organic molecules of the type that some experts have suggested could have been the original raw materials for the formation of life on Earth."[8]

It is known that Maldek was the same type of terrestrial world as the present four inner planets of Mercury, Venus, Earth, and Mars, inclusive of their satellites. All these planets exhibit a solid surface, with interiors comprising a stone mantle and inner iron core, rather than the gaseous composition of the outer planets. Maldek is believed to have been a medium to large terrestrial planet, larger than Mars and perhaps as large or even slightly larger than Earth. According to amateur anthropologist, author, and UFO researcher, George Hunt Williamson, Maldek had one natural satellite, a moon called Malona.[9] It definitely contained water, had an iron core, and a rocky mantle composition; facts derived from various impacting meteorite and asteroid fragments that have been recovered on Earth.[10]

Those fragments display a composition strikingly similar to our planet. The charred surfaces of those rocky chunks indicate that a great cataclysmic force was involved in its destruction. Analysis of those rock specimens revealed no 'foreign' substances or elements not also found on Earth, with an age of those specimens dated at 5.0 billion years,[11] making Maldek more than 300 million years older than Earth. Its earlier age provides a sizable period of time as a 'headstart' for more advanced life to have evolved on Maldek, before its similar occurrence on Earth.

When that earliest humanlike species within our solar system, either on Mars or Maldek, had advanced sufficiently to a comprehensive level capable of learning, the Ancient Ones made direct contact with their planet, introducing the Cosmic Order and assisting them with their development as a sapient species. The association was a most successful one. Those outer planet inhabitants, either of Maldek or Mars, progressed as a model civilization under the regulated guidance and tutelage of the Ancient Ones; developing into an advanced and highly accomplished civilization. They also became a moral and enlightened species by adhering to the mandates of the Cosmic Order. Due to their exemplary progress and growth in enlightenment, that humanlike species was eventually chosen to assist the Ancient Ones with their civilizing efforts. Those dedicated volunteers joined the group known as the Helpers or Watchers, and were assigned duties that involved other planets within our solar system, including Earth.

Most likely that outer planet was Maldek, an assumption used for expediency to develop the *Elder Gods* theory, although extant evidence is simply insufficient to determine if Maldek or Mars was their true homeworld. The outer planet humanlike beings eventually attained their own ability for space travel, allowing independent and separate exploration of neighboring worlds. They eventually constructed their own temporary colonies on several nearby worlds, including Mars and Earth. Their highly advanced but metered scientific and cultural growth matched their ethical development and adherence with desired core values established by the Ancient Ones. Due to such exemplary progress and development, their culture was deemed capable of choosing to formally join and follow the mandates of the Cosmic Order, an offer they eagerly accepted.

With the protection, guidance, and divulged knowledge provided by the Ancient Ones, those early humanlike beings rose to vast heights and accomplishments during the remote past, reaching levels far beyond those of 20th and 21st century Earth. With their increasing population, permanent bases were evidently established on Mars, a planet exhibiting similar environmental conditions to Maldek at that time. Martian resources were extracted, with continuous settlements established. Still later, explorations of Earth and its moon were made, with temporary settlements resulting periodically on those worlds. Since indigenous sentient life had formed on Earth by that time, those bases came under the monitored guidance of the Ancient Ones, recognizing the sovereign rights of each planet's indigenous creatures as the ultimate priority within their homeworld; as specified within the mandates of the Cosmic Order.

Such periodic visitations to Earth and its moon by the outer planet humanlike beings were made both through their own efforts, as well as through their routine duties as Helpers, as they accompanied the Ancient Ones on their surveillance missions. Earth may have also occasionally served as a temporary shelter for certain rescued species of other aliens that had survived a major global devastation or the destruction of their own homeworld, due to some natural catastrophe.

Indications of such periodic Earth visitations may be evidenced by the numerous anomalous artifacts that have been discovered that do not fit the time frame in which they were found, as previously referenced and detailed in the <u>First Journal of the Ancient Ones</u>, *Elder Gods of Antiquity*. Such discoveries include humanlike skeletal remains that definitely do not fit within the time period ascribed for development of indigenous life on Earth.

Due to the high achievement status of the humanlike beings on Maldek or Mars, they required little continuing direction and assistance from the Ancient Ones. Only occasional oversight contact was made with their advanced civilization, although the Ancient Ones did control their activities on Earth and their other developing colonies; assuring planetary independence on those worlds. In fact, around 1.7 million years ago, Earth may have posed much more of a concern to the Ancient Ones than the outer planet humanlike beings. The gentle *Australopithecus* apeman was undergoing replacement by the more aggressive *Pithecanthropus* species. That natural mutation and evolutionary direction of indigenous life on Earth was not a development entirely welcomed by the Ancient Ones.

As with all cultures, species, and worlds, cyclic changes periodically occur, which strain the capabilities of its affected people and perhaps even alter their very existence. That was the dilemma facing the humanlike beings on their homeworld where they were experiencing some type of planetary deterioration of their environmental conditions. In the First Journal of the Ancient Ones, *Elder Gods of Antiquity*, a speculative scenario was offered that focused on a chronic slow cooling of their planet's central core. The resultant symptoms included a loss of atmospheric gases, plus a diminished gravitational attraction and magnetic field with which to hold its ever-thinning atmosphere and protect it from cosmic radiation. As deteriorating planetary conditions continued to worsen on their homeworld, which is assumed as having been Maldek, a complex and highly scientific 'corrective measure' was devised and implemented by the humanlike beings to solve their global life-threatening problem.

The corrective measures that were implemented evidently involved some type of attempted modification to the planet's inner core, based on the known outcome of its total planetary demise. It is widely believed that only major internal disruptions within the central core of a planet could lead to such total global destruction. That leaves only speculative scientific possibilities, ones perhaps even beyond our present capacity to explain. No known ancient Earth records or myths allude to the specific nature of its cataclysmic demise.

One speculation offered in the earlier journal, *Elder Gods of Antiquity*, involved an effort to increase the planet's inner molten core temperature, returning it to a prior 'healthy' level, thereby restoring volcanism and a resultant reenrichment of all necessary gasses back into its atmosphere. That effort may have been undertaken in conjunction with an attempt to increase the rotational differential between the liquid and solid inner cores, in order to enhance Maldek's magnetic field for better gaseous retention within its ionosphere. The solution not only failed, but also caused the cataclysmic destruction of Maldek, resulting in the debris field we know as the asteroid belt.

The theory that a planet had long ago been torn apart by some unknown process was further substantiated by a number of facts detailed in the aforementioned *Elder Gods of Antiquity*. That book also identified the date of that catastrophe as sometime around 700,000 BC.[12] Such an event also marked the apex of the outer planet humanlike beings' civilization they had created, a culture evidently one to two centuries ahead of that reached by late 20th and early 21st century Earth. Such a cultural high point was destined to never again be obtained by its few survivors and their subsequent descendants.

The resultant vaporization of all the humanlike beings on Maldek, along with the death of many more on Mars, reduced their once plentiful species to merely a small number of survivors, probably totaling much less than one million. The few humanlike beings comprising that group of survivors would have been on the mothership of the Ancient Ones at the time of the accidental destruction, while others were stationed at their previously mentioned offworld bases. Those few remaining survivors left from this humanlike species were relocated to shelters that had been quickly reinforced by the Ancient Ones, at their colonies on Mars and the moon of Earth. The more inhospitable climate and environmental conditions of Earth, which was entrenched in a severe and prolonged Ice Age at that time, likely prohibited its use as a primary resettlement site.

The extent of such a cataclysmic force also disrupted the atmosphere of Mars, Maldek's closest celestial neighbor, partially tearing away portions of its atmosphere. That not only depleted large quantities of critical atmospheric gasses, but also disrupted Mars' magnetic field, creating numerous disorganized fields dispersed around the planet, rather than a stable one formed around its axis poles. That massive disruption of its magnetic field further diminished Mars' ability to retain its remaining diminished atmosphere. That same atmospheric erosion continues to this day, and may be similar to the earlier conditions that prompted the original corrective actions to be taken on Maldek. Although some humanlike beings were killed on Mars as a direct result of Maldek's destruction, a portion did survive. But Mars itself had suffered a fatal blow, resulting in a slowly dying planet, reminiscent of the problem originally on Maldek.

It is widely accepted that the environmental problems resulting from the partially stripped atmosphere of Mars were the result of a celestial event. The most likely cause would have been an asteroid-sized chunk of Maldek passing through the edge of Mars' atmosphere and into its lower stratosphere, as a result of the phenomenal destructive force that annihilated Maldek.

Although evidence suggests that such a huge meteorite did not directly impact Mars, perhaps partially due to the planetary 'repulsion mechanism' known as the Roche Limit,[13] at least some dismembered chunks apparently did strike its surface. Sufficient evidence concludes that Mars underwent a phenomenally intense but relatively brief bombardment of asteroids, producing thousands of craters and valleys on the Martian surface, mainly in its Southern Hemisphere. The Hellas basin, located in the southern region of Mars, is known to be the remnant of a huge asteroid impact.[14] Prior to that time, Mars' atmosphere had evidently been relatively robust.

Others speculate that a shock wave emanating from the catastrophic destruction of Maldek had initiated Mars' chronic environmental problems. Deep penetration of massive energy forces similar to an asteroid impact would have produced massive shock waves that reverberated throughout the Martian atmosphere, which passed around the planet. Perhaps a combination of both events actually occurred, with the effective result being roughly equivalent. Atmospheric percussion-wave impacts would reach Mars' surface, with some rebounding upward, while other waves would affect tectonic plate faults and pressure concentrations, causing magma to vent.

Such massive eruptions and gigantic pressure variations would have instigated sudden massive global climatic changes on Mars. According to researcher George Hunt Williamson, Mars' two moons helped readjust its unstable orbital condition caused by Maldek's destruction.[15] Along with Mars, reportedly four other planets were also affected. Mr. Williamson further revealed an ancient Chinese record that reportedly described some of those effects, which claimed: "In the tenth year of the Emperor Kwei, the eighteenth monarch since Yahou, the five planets went out of their courses (orbits). In the night, stars fell like rain. The Earth shook."[16] While this record may refer to the time period of Maldek's destruction and its aftermath, it certainly occurred long before the first emergence of the Chinese and their eventual Empire.

Initially, minimal damage was probably imparted to Mars' atmosphere, although high turbulence would have remained at the outer region of entry from either a gigantic asteroid or massive 'shock wave' energy forces. Evidently, the relatively low Martian gravity was simply insufficient to dampen oscillations remaining in those affected regions of the atmosphere. Vast disturbances would have likely continued to reverberate over an extended time period, eventually altering weather patterns. As a result of those gradually changed patterns, climatic conditions on the surface also began to deteriorate. The effects from the continuing atmospheric disturbances permitted the ongoing but slow bleed-off of atmospheric gasses into space.

Over time, the effects of Maldek's destruction resulted in very low atmospheric pressure on Mars, prohibiting most water from existing in liquid form on its surface. The prior surface water held in rivers, lakes, and oceans either vaporized; underwent a phase change into ice, mainly at the polar regions; or flowed deep into underground caverns, sinkholes, or aquifers. Other resultant damage included a slower planetary rotation; a greatly diminished and scattered magnetic field; irreversible harm to its atmosphere and ecosystem; and perhaps a slightly altered orbit. Such damage permanently and gravely altered the climatic weather patterns and subsequent living conditions on Mars.

Chapter 8

The Aftermath

Prior to Maldek's destruction, Mars was an inviting and livable planet. Authors John and Mary Gribbin, in their 1996 book *Fire on Earth: In Search of the Doomsday Asteroid*, wrote that planetary scientists Jay Melosh and Ann Vickery believed it was probable that Mars once had an atmosphere with about the same surface pressure as one exhibited by present day Earth, with a corresponding surface temperature somewhat above 32 degrees Fahrenheit.[1] That prior Martian atmosphere, one containing most of the same gasses as Earth, had since been torn away by repeated collisions with asteroids. Since Mars' low gravity was simply inadequate to contain the expanding cloud of vapor resulting from those major surface impacts, the regions of atmosphere affected by those vapor surges were ultimately lost, having been blasted into outer space.

The team of Samuel L. Windsor, an engineer, and Donald W. Patten, a geographer, made another connection with Maldek's destruction and its ensuing damage to Mars. They theorized that the asteroid belt planet left its orbit for some unknown reason and entered the Roche Limit of Mars. This team hypothesized that the destruction of the asteroid belt planet resulted in the physical and ecological damage known to have occurred on Mars, while the expelled portion of the invading destroyed planet then formed the asteroid belt between Mars and Jupiter. According to Messrs. Windsor and Patten, such an event occurred sometime between 15,000 and 3000 BC.[2]

However, contradictions with their theory exist. Its premise requires the asteroid belt planet to be much smaller than Mars, which itself is only about half the size of Earth. It also claims billions of years of orbital stability for that small planet until, for some unknown reason, it then invades the atmosphere and orbital space of Mars. It further purports that Maldek's numerous destroyed fragments were then expelled 'backward' toward Jupiter, rather than toward the greater gravity of the sun, thus creating the asteroid belt.

Consensus dictates a much larger planet to have once occupied the orbit between Mars and Jupiter, one at least the size of Earth or greater. That larger size would also assure a more stable long-term orbit, one not subjected to overwhelming gravitational disruptions by its gas giant neighbor, Jupiter. Based on a much larger planetary size, the greatly smaller Mars would have been destroyed by such a collision, rather than the proposed fate that supposedly befell the intruding and more massive asteroid belt planet. A smaller asteroid belt planet would also not account for the large volume of asteroids that still orbit between Mars and Jupiter.

A large portion of such a demolished planet would have been vaporized with its destruction, with about half the remaining fragments being propelled toward the sun and the inner planets, not generally 'backward' toward Jupiter, although the few unique Trojan Asteroids did follow just such a trajectory. The proposed event date of between 15,000 BC and 3000 BC for such a catastrophe, as estimated by Messrs. Windsor and Patten, should also display substantial evidence on Earth that could be dated to that time period. While Earth's Great Flood did occur between those dates, there is no evidence indicating a massive period of asteroid impacts that would have caused or resulted from such a cataclysmic planetary event.

The scant data known about Maldek suggests that it was quite similar to Mars. An ancient Nahuatl language myth states that the god Quetzalcoatl had a twin brother, Xipe Xolotl. This twin was a 'damaged companion,' also known as the 'Red god of the east.'[13] Such a statement is believed to refer to the neighboring planets of Mars and Maldek, with Mars suffering damage as a result of Maldek's ultimate destruction. The planets are associated as 'twins,' perhaps referring to their size, their similar environmental conditions, or possibly their inhabitants.

The Ancient Ones may not even know the exact mechanism of Maldek's destruction, or the specific cause of environmental deterioration on Mars, but the final situation prompted the Ancient Ones to intervene. Rescue efforts provided immediate food, shelter, and infrastructure support. Basic services were restored, utilities were repaired, and reinforced shelters were constructed on Mars to protect the survivors from the repetitive rain of meteorites and asteroid impacts upon that planet, the immediate fallout from Maldek's destruction. Those meteorite showers likely would have lasted for an extended period of time. During that bombardment, the once high Maldek culture that remained on Mars was evidently diminished to a much lower technological level, which reflected an equivalent mix of both 20th and 21st century Earth.

As things settled down after the cataclysm, focus would have been on providing a suitable and sustainable environment in which the humanlike survivors of the Maldek disaster could once again thrive and prosper. The partial loss of Mars' atmosphere restricted the amount of exposure the outer planet humanlike beings could tolerate outside their subterranean shelters and protective artificial enclosures on its surface, due to harmful cosmic radiation. The Ancient Ones provided much of the advanced technology for the Martian shelters, which included a reliable system for environmental control. At that time, Mars was a more hospitable planet than its current conditions, and also more compatible with the biological requirements of the humanlike beings than was Earth. During that time period, Earth was in the midst of one of its most prolonged and severe Ice Age glaciation, which was made even worse by the repeated meteorite bombardment resulting from the destruction of Maldek.

All those efforts by the Ancient Ones provided a livable environment, but one much below the prior high cultural level the humanlike beings had enjoyed on Maldek. The metropolitan structures and advanced devices that had been possessed by its prior high civilization at their Martian colony were evidently diminished with each subsequent generation, requiring continued repair for their utilization. Such persistent decline was due to both the dwindling population numbers required to maintain such systems, and a diminished scientific and technological ability of those survivors. Nearly all their top inventors, educators, scientists, and the vast majority of technically proficient people had been destroyed in the planetary destruction of Maldek. That left a void in the subsequent instruction of future students, resulting in a debilitating lack of scientific understanding of their ancestors' achievements. Nevertheless, the humanlike inhabitants of Mars still enjoyed a mix of 21st century technology, perhaps blended with a 19th century life style.

Later descendants of the few survivors of Maldek's destruction continued to regress rather than advance, focusing much of their efforts on basic survival needs, not on scientific and cultural advancements. Yet all around the Martian base were the remnants of the glorious high culture that was once the pride of their ancestors, a civilization that could not be fully understood or duplicated by an ever diminishing number of subsequent generation humanlike beings. Such cultural decline created a bitterness that was generally harbored by many of the surviving outer planet humanlike beings and their descendants. That bitterness eventually became a mental barrier toward any constructive effort to ever again regain their once great civilization.

Such resentment originated from the knowledge that the Ancient Ones had the ability and technology to virtually restore their once grand culture. But the Ancient Ones did not look upon recreating past accomplishments as a 'replacement.' They believed such restoration would create too rapid a rate of progress for mere descendants of a prior high culture. Such replacement would not assure that a corresponding 'ethical maturity' also existed, one that was necessary to fully appreciate the cultural concepts and consequences of actions emanating from such an advanced culture. The Ancient Ones viewed the survivors from the Maldek disaster as merely the beneficiaries of their prior ancestors' actions, an inheritance that included both good and bad consequences. The unwanted result from their prior ancestors' ambiguous 'corrective action' to fix Maldek's climate was just such a questionable legacy created by their prior civilization.

Although their ancestors had created an advanced culture, they had also established an accompanying 'learned and developed' value system that matured as they fashioned their many achievements. Simple outside replacement of those past or lost accomplishments would not necessarily impart the required wisdom and enlightenment to either comprehend or safely control all consequences associated with the use of such replacement devices and technology. Further concerns existed that the humanlike beings would come to expect subsequent rescue by the Ancient Ones from future problems they might create, if additional reckless mistakes and poor decisions should occur. Evidently the Ancient Ones had numerous prior experiences with similar natural disasters, ones that essentially exterminated the majority of inhabitants of other advanced species on different worlds. With added dedication, absent any help with 'cultural alterations' or 'enhancements' from the Ancient Ones, those same beings often came back stronger and better than before.

Many of the humanlike beings, primarily those at their main base on Mars, did not share that same philosophy, resulting in bitterness and resentment toward the Ancient Ones. Such negative reaction altered the highly ethical values that had previously been achieved by their species, changing their outlook into bitter cynicism. Over time, their bases on Mars and the moon of Earth drifted apart, differing greatly in both philosophy and development. The slow loss of atmosphere on Mars further exacerbated the schism between the Martian-based humanlike beings and the Ancient Ones. Any progress toward permanent recovery began to seem an impossible goal, with an estranged populace fighting for their very survival.

As time passed, additional effort was spent on crude repairs to the then badly worn and neglected high technology of their ancestors. Eventually those devices were abandoned, with the caretaker inhabitants no longer able to understand the principal or theory associated with their operation. A constantly increasing daily effort was spent to combat the slow but continuing loss of atmosphere on Mars over the ensuing years. Eventually, their stagnate Martian culture started to regress at a pace that exceeded the rate required to address daily problems. That regressive momentum eventually exceeded a point beyond reversal, one that the humanlike inhabitants did not recognize. Although the Ancient Ones had detected the eventual demise of the outer planet humanlike beings, they could offer no additional assistance, since the culture and its people had lost their self-determination and dedication to the concepts of the Cosmic Order.

The impatience of the humanlike beings with the Ancient Ones eventually turned to resentment, demanding direct 'replacement' of their lost civilization. They did not want to start over, although they knew what inventions and obtainment awaited them, based on their ancestors' achievements. Rather than viewing such insight as a positive influence, exposing the direction in which to proceed, such knowledge unfortunately only served as a detriment. The discouraged and despondent humanlike descendants of survivors from the Maldek disaster had forsaken all attempts to help themselves, expecting the Ancient Ones to fully restore their prior lost high culture. That was never the intent of the Ancient Ones, nor was it ever going to happen.

Chapter 9

Earth Evolution

Life on Earth had long been established by the time mass dissension and discontent had emerged as a prevalent problem throughout the Martian base. As revealed earlier, development of earthly life was shown to have been a slow and deliberate process, with humanity's earliest ancestors first emerging only within the last 99.96% of Earth's actual existence, making its occurrence an extremely recent and belated event. Yet the most rapid or profound hereditary developments and enhancements seemed to have transpired during the most recent phase of Earth's history, unlike earlier evolution or mutations that required billions of years to occur. The prior transformation from earliest bacterial life to crude mineralized-shell trilobites occurred over a period of three billion years, although that change still took place hundreds of millions of years before the first dinosaur. However, the sudden and inexplicable appearance of the different ancestral human species defies all conventional theories of evolution, mutation, and perhaps even creationism.

The *Elder Gods* theory provides answers for these enigmatic and persistent questions that surround humanity's origins. After the total destruction of Maldek and the ensuing efforts to stabilize its few survivors, the Ancient Ones realized that the long term viability of the Martian base was doomed, and the much smaller base on the moon of Earth was only a temporary one. Those facts eventually prompted the Ancient Ones to undertake a greater level of intervention, one involving the direct manipulation of the humanlike descendants' physiology. Such efforts may have even been in opposition with certain mandates of the Cosmic Order.

Action by the Ancient Ones, although belated, involved genetic alterations to the humanlike species. Those modifications were conducted to produce better adaptation with the deteriorating changes within the environment of Mars, along with the long-term intent for that species' future compatibility with Earth. The apparent continuation of the sparse population numbers associated with the humanlike species suggests that those manipulations might have even affected their birth rate, resulting in higher infant mortality, or possibly widespread sterility. Perhaps those alterations or genetic procedures were similar to the DNA experiments reportedly performed on Earth abductees by the occupants of UFOs during our modern times.

Those genetic alterations were initially undertaken to 'modify' the humanlike survivors' physiology to better withstand the higher radiation levels and diminishing atmosphere of Mars. The intent was to prolong compatibility with the deteriorating Martian environment, allowing time for the Ancient Ones to produce a viable mutated humanlike species capable of dual-habitation on either Earth or Mars. That would allow the species to continue in some form, at least on one planet, if not on both. All indications suggest a successful outcome of that project.

Those genetic modifications were introduced into both the humanlike beings, as well as in certain indigenous Earth species. An isolated group of *Pithecanthropus* apemen were evidently the recipients of that same 'shared' DNA material on Earth, while a more wide spread distribution was also introduced into the main populace of the humanlike descendants on Mars. The 'altered' *Pithecanthropus* parents and offspring were continually segregated on protected island locations or other isolated sites, so as not to interfere with a parallel evolutionary track of natural mutation. That assured the continuation of at least one branch of indigenous Earth life.

Eventually the subsequent descendants on Mars from the Maldek disaster no longer enjoyed that same dual option, with all inhabitants undergoing this genetic alteration. Such mandatory action was based on projections made by the Ancient Ones, calculating the remaining time that a life-sustaining environment would exist on Mars, which was projected to last for only a relatively limited time. Therefore, a successful genetic alteration permitting dual-world habitation became essential for the continued survival of that original outer planet humanlike species.

Use of the term 'humanlike' rather than 'humanoid' is intended to emphasize their ancestral commonalty with later humans, rather than merely portraying a common resemblance of physical form and characteristic features. Also, one can not simply call the original surviving humanlike beings 'human,' since they were a distinctly different genus. The term *pre-human*, referring to a species that came before humans, implies a being less developed than humans, when in actuality that earlier ancestor was decidedly more advanced. Their physiological differences from present humans was one reason why they could not merely be transported on the ships of the Ancient Ones to Earth for permanent relocation right after Maldek's destruction. But the biggest obstacle came from the Cosmic Order precepts, which gave the indigenous sapient species of each planet preference over all other lifeforms.

Ultimately, Earth was deemed to be the only viable planet on which to create a permanent homeworld for the ensuing genetically altered humanlike descendants. With the then imminent demise of the indigenous *Pithecanthropus* genus on Earth, a window of 'seeding' presented itself. By 400,000 BC, the Ancient Ones had introduced their latest version of engineered hybrids that were produced from recombinant outer planet humanlike DNA and indigenous earthly apemen.

According to numerous ancient Sanskrit texts, the source of humanlike DNA was evidently secured from the small base on the moon, a much more cooperative and compliant group than those on Mars. Evidently the earthly component of recombinant DNA material was extracted from the indigenous

Pithecanthropus species. The earliest candidates were first implanted with recombinant DNA only in small groups, allowing close monitoring of their resultant genetic and environmental compatibility. Later, an ancient African site was established in the now modern day Republic of Kenya, which is known from their 400,000 years old fossils found in that region. Still other 'trial' settlements were dispersed around the shores of the Mediterranean, primarily along the northwestern coastline now occupied by European nations.

That early humanlike candidate has been identified in this text as the proto-Sapiens, a branch of early human ancestors that included Swanscombe and Steinheim man in Europe. As predicted by the Ancient Ones, Earth's indigenous *Pithecanthropus* man disappeared around 375,000 BC, allowing the proto-Sapiens to claim exclusive rights to the planet. Their integration with Earth was ultimately a failure, since compatibility was never fully achieved, limiting that subspecies to become merely an anomalous dead-end branch throughout their quarter million year existence.

With the appearance of Earth's Neanderthal man around 150,000 BC, which was an actual indigenous evolutionary species from the earlier *Pithecanthropus* genus, the hybrid proto-Sapiens ultimately became extinct. The ensuing harsh climate of the Ice Age kept Neanderthals to only a few in number until a population explosion occurred around 115,000 BC, during an interglacial warm period. Hence, the window of opportunity to 'seed' an Earth devoid of its own indigenous species once again temporarily ended. However, geneticists have traced our human DNA back to a period roughly between 150,000 and 145,000 BC.[1]

Although that arbitrary origin is attributed to extreme Southeastern Africa, only sporadic evidence from isolated African and Near Eastern sites have been found. But a mere 100,000 years later, such a genetic line 'exploded' throughout Europe. Actually, this prevailing but perplexing occurrence actually substantiates the *Elder Gods* theory. It seems to prove that the nucleus of human DNA, evidently from the last proto-Sapiens, continued with subsequent ongoing experiments that involved genetic trials of a very limited size and scope. Such constrained 'lab-sized trials' would have left only minimal evidence, but absolutely no cultural remnants, while eventually producing a final perfected product in the form of the first Modern man, the Cro-Magnon subspecies. That is exactly what apparently happened.

Meanwhile, the humanlike species' struggle for survival on the Martian base overshadowed any real progress of their own. The moon base had long been abandoned, with all the humanlike beings relocated back to Mars to provide the additional 'manpower' to their diminishing numbers. The populace became resentful of the indigenous beings of Earth, and remained disillusioned with the Ancient Ones, who merely continued their genetic efforts to perfect a dual-habitable species. Around 43,000 BC, the Ancient Ones succeeded with their latest humanlike hybrid version, which became known as Cro-Magnon man. That 'created' genus may have included minimal Neanderthal DNA, providing the species with indigenous Earth status, thus satisfying the required compliance with Cosmic Order mandates. The new Cro-Magnons quickly dominated Earth, completely displacing the earlier fully indigenous Neanderthal man by 27,000 or 26,000 BC. Refinements continued on the genetically formulated Cro-Magnon species, ultimately leading to fully Modern man, *Homo sapiens sapiens*, around 11,600 BC.

During that same time, planetary conditions on Mars were livable, but were both severe and deteriorating. The atmosphere had become increasingly saturated with carbon dioxide. The slow heat loss from the ever-thinning atmosphere had ceased all planetary volcanism, including Olympus Mons, Mars' highest volcano at 88,000 feet. Its extremely weakened magnetic field no longer provided a shield against ultraviolet rays and lethal cosmic radiation, or a barrier to solar winds that eroded the surface of the planet. Hence, all life was relegated to subterranean shelters, abandoning the once impressive cultural centers located in its Northern Hemisphere. Those sites were last to be occupied, due to Mars' axis tilt, which produced a more moderate climate in the north than the one existing within its Southern Hemisphere.

The Northern Hemisphere had once been mostly ocean, with two land masses consisting of the Elysium Planitia in the Eastern Hemisphere and the Tharsis region in the northwestern quadrant of the planet. That once expansive ocean had an extensive shoreline with much construction. That ancient shoreline is still evident, with curved terraces running parallel to the shore, forming cone-like depressions at regular frequency. According to Brown University scientists that studied data from the Mars Global Surveyor, these depressions are mixed with rectangular troughs and straight-line grooves.[2]

Those formations are believed by some to be remnants of irrigation systems and agricultural terraces utilized by the humanlike colonists when prior environmental conditions allowed such activity. A section of land disturbed by those patterns clearly depicts a humanoid figure.[3] Those artificial excavations now comprise an area known as the *Noctis Labyrinthus*, the Labyrinth of the Night. Similar grooves are also evident on the Martian moon Phobos. Some of those radiate from craters, such as the series of uniform parallel rows of straight grooves that are found near Phobos' largest depression, its one mile deep by six miles wide Stickney crater.

Much of the Martian bedrock is volcanic basalt with a high iron content. That provided an abundant source of iron and steel for both the Ancient Ones and the humanlike beings. It is interesting to note that many ancient Earth cultures associated iron and iron objects with Mars, perhaps indicating specific knowledge of that planet's rich resource. The high occurrence of iron oxide in the Martian dust and rocks imparts the red color to its soil. That extremely fine ground cover has the consistency between fine sand and dust.

Massive dust storms still periodically occur, which are followed by a sudden and unusual turbulence within the Southern Hemisphere that propels tremendous quantities of dust into the Martian atmosphere.[4] The salmon-pink sky color is the result of large amounts of red dust particles being blown into the atmosphere by those frequent surface sandstorms. The powerful winds associated with those storms then carry dust to all parts of the planet. At the storm's conclusion, the settled dust then obscures the surface features of Mars. As a result of those frequent and massive sandstorms, a virtual cover-up exists. Numerous structures lay buried beneath that powder-like dust, obscuring most visual evidence that would confirm the existence of prior bases on Mars.

However, some evidence of that culture can still be found on the Martian surface, with numerous structures and monuments standing in mute testimony to that once great species of humanlike beings. Numerous artificial structures produced by their culture are found in an area known as *Cydonia Mensae*, a location in the northwestern quadrant of the planet. The Cydonia region comprises an area contained between eight degrees and 20 degrees north latitude, lying approximately between 30 and 40 degrees west longitude. The prominence of that region emerged from NASA's 1976 Viking 1 orbiter, when structures of apparent artificial origin were exposed. Such marvels of construction include a once magnificent city containing a massive fortress,[5] the much publicized carved Face of Mars,[6] and a massive monumental pyramid.[7] That tetrahedral structure, known as the D&M Pyramid, was named for its discoverers, Dr. Vincent DiPietro, an engineer and imaging specialist who worked with the Goddard Space Flight Center, and his colleague, Gregory Molenaar, a computer scientist. Other reputable professionals, including Professor Stanley V. McDaniel, have studied these enigmatic structures. He noted precise mathematical relationships of angles and dimensions, which were revealed in his 1993 publication, *The McDaniel Report*.

The noted scientific researcher, Richard C. Hoagland, has also extensively studied these structures of Mars, with findings detailed in his book, *The Monuments of Mars*. He is credited with detecting numerous anomalous shapes believed to be the remains of artificial structures, including the 'City' and the 'Fort,' both located near the D&M Pyramid and the Face at Cydonia. Mr. Hoagland described the city as: "a strikingly rectangular pattern created by numerous features at right angles...."[8] The Fort is the easternmost structure within this grouping, appearing as a straight edged edifice seemingly consisting of two huge walls, perhaps forming a triangle. Mr. Hoagland's research also included examination of the 27,000 additional NASA photographs taken by the Mars Global Surveyor spacecraft, released in late May 2000. From those delayed-release photographs, Mr. Hoagland observed anomalies believed to be numerous buried structures lying along the shoreline of Mars' once-existing ocean within its Northern Hemisphere.

Mr. Hoagland also identified what may be an abandoned aircraft lying exposed on a plateau in one of the Martian valleys.[9] Another anomalous image was discovered by Mr. Hoagland in photograph M0400291 taken by the Mars Surveyor, which he identified as a huge 'glass tunnel.'[10] That structure appears to be an artificially constructed flexible translucent tube that may have once been utilized for transport near or under the ocean. This tunnel is located about 200 miles northwest of Cydonia, in the region where the large northern ocean once existed. Mr. Hoagland estimates this enigmatic conduit to be about 600 feet wide by 5,000 feet long.

As conditions on Mars deteriorated, life went underground to take advantage of warmer temperatures and higher atmospheric pressure, with most of those subterranean shelter areas located along the equator. A possible remnant or indication of such structures may have been detected from an infrared image taken by NASA's Marnier 9 orbiter, which revealed a sunken central hublike structure with rectangular radial arms extending outward in all directions.[11] Such a layout is similar to the design of airport terminals found on Earth. It would have made an ideal structure from which 'public' utilities could serve closely connected working and living areas within an organized subterranean civilization.

Chapter 10

The Turning Point

Perhaps a turning point in the later history of Mars, and possibly the final frustration for the humanlike beings, was a major global cataclysm, not on Mars, but on Earth. Around $c.10,500$ BC, the Great Flood occurred, known from its aftermath association with the Pleistocene Extinction of that time. It caused the extermination of numerous species of flora and fauna on Earth, including Cro-Magnon man and most of its subsequent 'fully Modern man' version, *Homo sapiens sapiens*. The limited human survivors were those sheltered on the highest summits, and those few selected specimens that the Ancient Ones had removed from the planet. Those select humans, along with a wide array of plant and animal DNA material that had been extracted before the flood, were temporarily relocated to both the Martian and previously-abandoned moon bases of the humanlike beings, to wait-out the cataclysmic effects of that flood.

With the ensuing planetary devastation of most life, Earth was once again facing the probability of an indigenous species vacuum. Without a planetary heir apparent, the outer planet humanlike beings, which were now sufficiently compatible with Earth's environment, petitioned for permanent habitation of our then desolated world. For unknown reasons, the Ancient Ones denied that request, igniting the outer planet humanlike survivors' long simmering animosity toward the genetically engineered *Homo sapiens* and the Ancient Ones.

Not all of the outer planet humanlike survivors felt that same bitterness and impatience with the perceived slow recovery of their civilization. A substantial but minority number of humanlike descendants, including those that were Helpers, still strongly supported the slow growth policy of the Cosmic Order. But the malcontents, the majority of the Martian population, finally rebelled. They chose to break away from the Ancient Ones, but not necessarily from all the core beliefs of the Cosmic Order. The Cosmic Order strictly prohibited any hostile action that forced initial membership, retention, or continued affiliation, except to prevent the self-destructive acts of a world that would threaten others within the universe. All of the outer planet humanlike inhabitants then chose between either separation from the Ancient Ones, remaining with their fellow species on the Martian base; or leaving with the Ancient Ones, becoming permanent exiles from their present homeworld. After the individual decisions were made, the final split occurred, creating two distinct 'groups' of humanlike beings.

Ancient records allude to just such a split. As a result of that separation, the Ancient Ones relocated all 'loyal' outer planet humanlike inhabitants, those that chose continued alliance with the Ancient Ones, to the former base on Earth's moon. The breakaway outer planet humanlike dissidents were given full control over their sovereign world, their base on Mars. That included all the technology left by the Ancient Ones to run the numerous technical aspects of their world and their implements of defense and commerce. They became a sovereign world, completely free and independent from the influence of the Ancient Ones forever. To differentiate this group from their genetically identical loyal brethren that relocated to the moon base and remained aligned with the Ancient Ones, this text will refer to the rebels as the Breakaway Outer Planet Humanlike beings, the *BOPH* beings. The group living on the moon base will be referenced as the *Lunar Pitris*, Earth's ancient Patriarchs.

The Ancient Ones continued to monitor the Martian base, but without any intervention. On Mars, the BOPH survivors faced the prospect of fending for themselves without the assistance of the Ancient Ones. Those BOPH beings had hoped to quickly progress on their own, leading to space vehicles capable of traveling to Earth for their independent colonization of that planet after the Great Flood. They hoped to accomplish that migration before the Ancient Ones returned with their DNA 'salvaged seeds' to once again repopulate Earth with the *Homo sapiens sapiens*.

But the separation from the Ancient Ones involved greater adjustments and further empirical discovery in order to comprehend and utilize the technology left by the Ancient Ones. The utilization and maintenance of those devices thus became somewhat limited, since the scientific theory and aptitude underlying them were not fully understood by the BOPH beings. As those devices required repair, they became unserviceable to the BOPH inhabitants and were eventually discarded or abandoned, with subsequent generations losing that technology. Over time, some of those lost implements were ultimately reinvented, but at rudimentary and crude levels from their original versions. The BOPH dissidents' earlier goal of reaching Earth prior to the return of the Ancient Ones had ultimately failed.

As flood waters receded and Earth once again approached habitable conditions between 9600 and 9200 BC, the Ancient Ones returned with some of their loyal Helpers and the descendants of the pre-flood *Homo sapiens sapiens*. Much of the flora and fauna preserved through DNA specimens was then reintroduced to Earth. A small number of humans, including perhaps even some Cro-Magnons that had escaped to the higher mountainous regions, had survived the Great Flood. Their later descendants were the few wild primitives that inhabited the planet at the time of this return. With the reclamation and rehabitation of Earth underway, new settlement centers were established. They included the advanced cultures at Jericho and Jarmo in the Near East, as well as at Tiahuanaco in South America; naming just a few of the highly evolved cultural centers previously detailed in the <u>First Journal of the Ancient Ones</u>, *Elder Gods of Antiquity*. The Ancient Ones and their loyal humanlike Helpers continued their slow process of civilizing earthly humans. With colonies established for the restored human population, the Ancient Ones once again departed Earth, leaving their devoted humanlike Helpers to educate and watch over those fledgling humans.

Back on the Martian base, the BOPH beings finally obtained their goal of space travel, albeit much later than desired. Their early success was reminiscent of Earth's Mercury era space capsule program. Eventually, much more advanced craft followed, which were still an immense backstep in technology from the Ancient Ones' far superior intergalactic ships. This fact accounts for the mixed earthly evidence of some vastly advanced, futuristic technology possessed by the Ancient Ones during the earliest primordial times, followed by a 20th and 21st century technology found during later ancient times; a noticeable regression in technical abilities. Both distinct levels of technology were apparently later lost to subsequent human generations, with limited rediscovery and reinvention millennia later during our own 19th and 20th centuries.

The breakaway from the Ancient Ones had other consequences among the BOPH beings at their Martian base. Dissatisfaction with their leaders and the stagnant effort to improve the ever deteriorating living conditions on Mars had greatly increased. Conflicts finally erupted among the BOPH population, with some expressing their desire to rejoin the splinter group on the moon base; those still aligned with the Ancient Ones. The ruler of the BOPH beings on Mars temporarily contained such unrest by segregating the malcontents from society. But as their numbers grew, the dissension and dissatisfaction erupted into open rebellion. Eventually, the dissident group desiring realignment with the Ancient Ones fled to the lunar base in crude one-way ships. There, they reunited with descendants of the Lunar Pitris who previously chose to remain loyal to the Ancient Ones during the original schism. Perhaps this is the legendary event associated with the 'Fallen

Angels' account, wherein a third of those 'heavenly angels' changed allegiance and fled to another realm.

Some of the best BOPH scientists were among the exiles that fled to the base on Earth's moon. That fact caused major concern, suggesting that solutions to the problems with the Martian base would never occur, further worsening the discontent held by the few remaining BOPH beings on Mars. Their technology was not yet sufficiently advanced to reach Earth, fight a war, and escape Earth's much greater gravity for return to their homebase on Mars if necessary. But their space technology was sufficient to launch an attack on the moon base where the Lunar Pitris resided. It is believed that sometime between 6000 and 5500 BC, the BOPH leaders initiated a retaliatory attack on the moon base, although that attack might have taken place several millennia earlier. A brief war ensued, causing the annihilation of all Lunar Pitris, the humanlike beings loyal to the Ancient Ones. Such an event would become known as the 'War of the Olden Gods,' and perhaps the cause of the strange 'bombing-pattern' craters found on our moon. Life support equipment left for use on the moon, along with other 'new' technology supplied by the Ancient Ones since the schism, was plundered and taken back to the Martian base.

Further evidence of that attack may be found from modern thermoluminescence studies of Apollo 12 moon core samples conducted by Professor R. Walker at Washington University, located in St. Louis, Missouri.[1] Those evaluations revealed anomalies resulting from strange disturbances of a 'thermal nature,' thought to have occurred around 8000 BC, according to reports by Dr. Immanuel Velikovsky in the early 1970s.[2] An increased level of radioactivity in those samples was also detected, leading to the speculation that possible nuclear explosions occurred at that lunar site. However, the 8000 BC date for such anomalies may be off slightly, due to the lack of a sufficient lunar soil database, which could create significant errors in such subjective dating. Or, such samples may simply indicate a somewhat earlier date for this attack.

The subsequent reaction by the general BOPH populace over that attack was negative. It was viewed as wasting limited vital resources and efforts on warfare, rather than for the betterment of the homebase problems. Furthermore, the seized technological devices did not supply the environmental improvements sought by the rebel force. The BOPH leader was then replaced with a peaceful but ineffective ruler as a result. But after only a nine year reign, that 'king' was overthrown by a warlike ruler,[3] one who realized that the only future for the BOPH beings was to be found on Earth, since Mars was a dying planet beyond salvage. The dethroned ruler and his immediate family escaped the ensuing civil rebellion and sought sanctuary by fleeing to Earth,[4] landing in a region of Egypt about 5450 BC.

That visitor, the dethroned Martian king, was later identified in several mythological accounts as Alalu, known from both Hurrian and Hittite myths. A Hittite text recorded Alalu's escape from his 'throne in the heavens' to Earth, after his defeat by Anu, stating: "Alalu was defeated. He fled before Anu. Down he descended to the dark-hued Earth. Anu took his seat upon the throne."[5] Alalu did not remain in Egypt because of its low altitude location and excessive heat. Alalu and his family first relocated to Europe, where they formed the primitive settlement of Lepenski Vir in the mountains of Yugoslavia.[6] A final move was made later, settling in the cool mountains around Lake Van, the ancestral home of the Hurrians and other advanced Caucasoid trait people. Alalu may have also been the inspiration or origin for the earliest Fish or Water god worship on Earth.

Continuous developmental efforts by the BOPH beings resulted in spacecraft that became capable of reliably reaching Earth sometime between 5300 and 5200 BC. Initially, a small scout party arrived on Earth, lead by a person identified later as Enki from various myths. Their group initially remained passive and obscure, avoiding any unwelcome attention to their presence, while they awaited the reaction of the Helpers to their visitation. The Ancient Ones assigned to our region of space were not on Earth during that early arrival. They were visiting another 'emerging' planet where first contact was being established and efforts were being planned that would bring civilization to that world, carrying out the continuing Cosmic Order directive.

Since Enki and his small crew posed no immediate or apparent threat to the Helpers, their arrival invoked no initial concern. The Helpers did not contact the Ancient Ones to request their return, but decided instead to closely observe and evaluate the BOPH visitors' activities. Enki first located his home in Dilmun, his island paradise on modern day Bahrain in the Persian Gulf, where he established a following of humans under his tutelage, forming the start of what would later become the Dilmun Empire, the 'Land of the Gods.'[7] Enki maintained a low profile at his Dilmun retreat, causing no problems, so the Helpers eventually accepted his scouting party's arrival to Earth as an innocuous occurrence.

Around 5000 BC, the latest 'advanced' human settlements started to form around the fertile crescent of Mesopotamia, where a stone age culture was transitioning to the use of copper and clay implements. In c.4900 BC, the humanlike Helpers formed Eridu, a site in the far southern region of what is now Iraq, as their next primary human settlement.[8] That site was comprised of a mixture of different people, and even included some humans educated by Alalu at his mountain retreat near Lake Van. Eridu quickly prospered, with many 'firsts' introduced by its human population. That group, overseen by the Helpers of the Ancient Ones, expanded into surrounding lands, forming other small villages. Collectively, those societies formed the distinct Ubaid culture, as it later became known from one of its prime settlements, al'Ubaid.

Around that same time, technology had further advanced on Mars permitting a larger BOPH crew to be sent to our planet. Some descended to the surface, while others remained on their mothership, which was stationed in orbit around Earth to establish a more permanent presence. Such an occurrence is known from a confusing mythological record that stated such early gods had stationed 300 additional gods, the Igigi, in heaven (in orbit) to guard Earth.[9] The enigmatic reason why lookouts were necessary to guard Earth was never fully revealed in any extant mythological account. Apparently, the purpose of that sentinel act was to alert the BOPH beings of any potential or unexpected return of the Ancient Ones.

In the following years as more BOPH colonists continued to arrive on Earth, their increased presence slowly allowed implementation of their plan to exploit both the planet and its people. They established regional camps throughout the greater Near East regions from their cult center in Dilmun, where humans were taught and trained in more advanced levels of knowledge than the Helpers were allowed to impart to those humans under their guidance, due to Cosmic Order constraints.

Around 3700 BC, Earth culture underwent yet another transition from the Copper and Clay Era to the Bronze Age. Many records referred to the period between c.3800 BC and roughly 3150 BC as 'chaotic,' a condition possibly caused by the growing friction between the Lunar Pitris Helpers of the Ancient Ones, and the ever growing and influential BOPH colonists.

The successful Persian Gulf Dilmun culture eventually evolved into the Dilmun Empire, best known from its most advanced human graduates who were later called Sumerians.[10] The BOPH beings established themselves as regional supreme rulers over select groups of humans by revealing and utilizing their superior technology. They schooled humans in the written script, languages, and more advanced levels of science. By 3600 BC, the BOPH colonists started to relocate small groups of humans from the smaller regional sites of the Dilmun Empire, moving them into other existing human cultures already established by the Helpers of the Ancient Ones.

The first settlement to receive a few of those Dilmun immigrants was the thriving Egyptian culture in the Nile Delta, which was under the control of the humanlike Helpers of the Ancient Ones, who were known in that region as the Shemsu-Hor. That infiltration was soon followed by another migration around 3350 BC into the Ubaid culture at Eridu by the group of people that would later be known as the Sumerians, humans that were 'sponsored' by the BOPH colonists. The Sumerians would later dominate the Mesopotamian area by 3150 BC, forcing the remaining Ubaidians to flee into Egypt. Both of those original cultures were quite advanced by Earth's standards at that time, due to the efforts and guidance from the Ancient Ones' Helpers.

The metered-progress approach utilized by the Helpers in their efforts to civilize humans was contrasted by the unrestrained growth offered by the BOPH colonists. Without the prior safeguard restrictions on high technology that had been imposed by the Helpers, the rapid deployment of such advanced devices by the BOPH beings simply became more attractive to the humans. Hence, a human majority began to increasingly pledge their allegiance with the BOPH colonists over that of the Helpers, lured by the quick and easy path toward progress and promised riches. Without adequate safeguards assuring a slow introduction of higher technology, coupled with an adequate growth of ethical values that would assure its proper utilization, the knowledge and devices imparted by the BOPH colonists began to be misused by humans.

Although contact between the two groups of humans was competitive, it was purposefully kept peaceful. Around 3250 BC, the Ancient Ones returned for one of their routine visits to check progress on Earth. Although disconcerted by the orbiting mothership of the BOPH visitors,[11] the noticeable lack of violence raised no immediate concern. Since ancestors of the BOPH colonists had previously reached Earth millions of years earlier as a result of their own independent discovery and exploration efforts, the Ancient Ones recognized a certain validity to the BOPH visitors' claim of being true 'colonists.' The BOPH beings were familiar with the legal constraints and terms of the

Cosmic Order, and perhaps even used some of its own potential 'loopholes' to their advantage. Such maneuvering commenced an initially strained but subdued coexistence between all the participants; which included the Ancient Ones and their faithful Helpers, the humans of Earth, and the BOPH colonists.

That benign coexistence became strained with the *c.*3250 BC arrival to Earth of Enki's half-brother, Enlil, who assumed control over the BOPH beings' colonization of Earth.[12] Enlil's leadership resulted in excessive interference with human development, and was deemed a threat to the controlled rate of progress desired by the Ancient Ones. The two opposing doctrines divided humanity into hostile factions that eventually led to war. That conflict was identified in numerous ways throughout ancient texts, either as the 'battle between good and evil' or the war between the gods. Earth's first 'world war' was underway, one fought between the human supporters of the Ancient Ones and those favoring the BOPH colonists.

The result would seem to be quite predictable, but perhaps 'good' may not have necessarily overcome 'evil.' The BOPH colonists would appear to be no match for the far superior Ancient Ones and their humanlike Helpers. But this was a conventional war, which utilized humans as fighting pawns. Humanity was free to pick their allegiance with either side, but probably did not possess the ability or adequate facts to make an informed choice. The BOPH beings attracted the loyalty of a majority of earthly humans, a feat accomplished with the promise of a quick and easy path toward an advanced culture. That promise appeared more desirable than the restrained and incremental growth offered by the Ancient Ones, which also depended on the moral and spiritual development of humankind.

In an effort to increase the stakes in this 'war between the gods,' the BOPH colonists resorted to nuclear weapons, using the technology derived from both their own destroyed ancestors and the Ancient Ones themselves.[13] The BOPH warriors calculated that a few strategic nuclear explosions would appall the Ancient

Ones, making them believe the BOPH beings might devastate the surface of the planet, thus creating an uninhabitable world. Perhaps the BOPH colonists ultimately threatened extermination of all planetary life, if the Ancient Ones did not relent and leave Earth, knowing their adversary was prohibited from utilizing such doomsday devices under the mandates of the Cosmic Order. According to the edicts of the Cosmic Order, deadly force could only be employed to protect other worlds, but never against a rogue planet that was threatening only their own world or its secession from the Ancient Ones.

The decision by the Ancient Ones, advising the humans under their influence to suspend their hostilities with the warring humans sponsored by the BOPH colonists, had another cumulative consequence. Although it spared further loss of human life on both sides, and negated the devastation of Earth from further threatened nuclear attack; it allowed humans to democratically choose allegiance with either side. The majority of humans voted for an alliance with the BOPH colonists, rejecting the Ancient Ones. Such rejection by an indigenous species of an emerging planet required the Ancient Ones to cease contact with that world.

Due to the unique situation that compelled such a vote, a decision made well before the emerging humans were prepared for such a momentous choice, the Ancient Ones agreed only to a temporary period of exile, allowing for further human contemplation of their action. With agreement by both sides, the Ancient Ones expected further growth and enlightenment by the humans during the exile duration, while the BOPH colonists expected to increase their influential hold over the humans during that same time period.

As an altruistic act to save Earth and humanity, the Ancient Ones agreed to leave the planet and have no public involvement or influence over the development of humanity for an unknown period of time. The temporary exile also prohibited the Ancient Ones from influencing or coercing mass public opinion during their undisclosed period of absence from Earth. Many ancient records refer to that exile agreement as the 'separation of heaven from Earth.'

The time period involved in this separation may have been based on some celestial cycle, such as the arrival of a specific Zodiac Age, or may have simply been an indeterminate period lasting until the next unforeseen worldwide conflagration that would threaten Earth. At such a time, the Ancient Ones would again be allowed direct and open contact with Earth, permitting their efforts to assist any human survivors, as well as the descendants of the BOPH colonists. In the First Journal of the Ancient Ones, *Elder Gods of Antiquity*, it was speculated that this 'short' but indefinite period might be the time between 3113 BC and 2012 AD,[14] the beginning and projected end-time of an epoch or *Age* described by various advanced ancient cultures. If correct, perhaps the BOPH colonists believed that such a 5,125 year time frame would be a sufficient duration in which to secure the political support of humankind.

Such an exile agreement was a dual-fold decision by the Ancient Ones. First, it eliminated further physical warfare that threatened human life on both sides of the debate. Secondly, the temporary exile allowed the Ancient Ones a limited presence or opportunity with Earth, realizing that the infant human race had not matured sufficiently to make a truly informed decision in such an important choice for alliance with either side. The BOPH colonists embraced this agreement, believing they could attain an adequate level of technology comparable to the Ancient Ones before any planetary disaster would occur, negating the need for the Ancient Ones' assistance, or before the exile period expired.

After the Ancient Ones departed Earth, the BOPH colonists quickly established themselves as 'gods' over the human population and took absolute control over the planet. Such domination was made possible by their superior knowledge and weaponry, as well as through their many loyal supporters, which comprised the vast majority of the human population. However, many of the humanlike Helpers of the Ancient Ones chose to remain on Earth, a planet that they had come to consider as their home, although the Helpers had far fewer human followers than the BOPH gods. That imbalance allowed the unchecked spread of the BOPH gods' influence, and their subjugation of early Earth cultures in dynastic Egypt, ancient India, and China, as well as throughout the Middle Eastern civilization centers of Mesopotamia.

The BOPH gods also realized that the then-current human development was insufficient to have made such an important decision concerning allegiance with either side. With focus toward the day when the temporary earthly exile of the Ancient Ones would end, the BOPH gods chose to tightly control the human population, thereby making it difficult for humans to achieve future enlightenment. For that reason, the BOPH gods ordered the suppression of most knowledge, in an effort to promote only their desired doctrine and chosen result. Only the relatively few humanlike Helpers of the Ancient Ones that had stayed on Earth after the exile were then left to spread the real truth and higher levels of enlightenment to humankind.

The quick growth and advancement promised by the BOPH gods ultimately benefited only a select few humans, such as the loyal pawns that would do the bidding of the BOPH gods while reigning over their fellow humans as dictators. Most progress, knowledge, and technological advancements became more restricted and restrained under the BOPH gods than the open-but-regulated growth previously offered by the Ancient Ones. Recognizing the known technology that existed 5,000 years ago, it is apparent that earthly cultures should be much more advanced than they are today, had it not been restrained by the 'liberators' of the Ancient Ones' constraints.

Chapter 11

Confirmation

The *Elder Gods* theory, which exposes an enlightened and advanced group of *First Being* species known collectively as the Ancient Ones, provides tangible explanations for all of Earth's many mysteries and archaic anomalies. Further, it does not contradict any factual evidence, or other known data. Its premise is based on much more than mere supposition and guess work. It is predicated on strong physical evidence and other material indications that support this theory. Further corroboration is derived from ancient records and esoteric texts, when those documents are reinterpreted with the perspective of modern scientific knowledge and understanding.

Some of the best supportive evidence can be found in the ancient Sanskrit texts of India and Tibet, as well as the very oldest records of Egypt. The lack of similar supporting texts from other archaic cultures will be explained, along with reasons why some records exist and others do not.

Perhaps the main reason for the survival of a substantial portion of Tibetan records was due to their protected and hidden status over the ages, during times when texts were subjected to numerous destructive acts. Those historic acts of destruction were revealed in the First Journal of the Ancient Ones, *Elder Gods of Antiquity*, where the continuous elimination of 'contrary' records was fully documented. Dedicated monks, many fleeing from the Aryan intrusion into India as early as 3000 BC, had removed and subsequently hid numerous Tibetan annals within the Himalayan Mountains. The oldest records of India, those written in Vedic, an early form of Sanskrit, were recorded prior to the Aryan influence backed by the BOPH gods. Such a takeover of an existing early human culture, one strongly influenced by the Ancient Ones, was similar to the intrusion upon the Ubaid culture in Mesopotamia by the Sumerians who were also sponsored by the BOPH gods in Dilmun.

Unlike the Ubaidians who eventually deserted their sites at Ur, al'Ubaid, and Eridu by c.3150 BC, leaving Mesopotamia in exclusive Sumerian control, the indigenous Dravidian culture of India did not leave. Their original advanced but controlled culture, one spawned by the Ancient Ones, was merged with the Aryan influx. Thus, much of their beliefs, knowledge, and texts that existed before the Aryan influence continued to remain intact. Those records were later slowly distorted, partially suppressed, selectively redacted, or revised with numerous additions; in an attempt to incorporate and reflect only the influence of the Aryan BOPH gods. However, those actions sometimes produced a confusing mix of truth and fiction, which was often contradictory.

Conversely, the wholesale exodus of the original mixed Ubaidian people from Mesopotamia left a thriving culture that was converted into a Sumerian society, one without a prior extant written record that would have required such conversion, modification, or suppression. The few known fragmented Ubaid records had been carved in wood, which deteriorated or decayed over the ensuing years. Thus, only vague and fragmented oral traditions existed from the prior Ubaid culture, since their original versions were no longer handed down to subsequent generations. Hence, the ensuing Sumerian culture was free to literally write the initial and earliest records of that region, ones that were directly influenced by the BOPH gods from their onset.

But a merging and blending of the existing and new cultures of India had retained a portion of its olden record prior to the Aryan influence. A similar occurrence also took place in ancient

Egypt where the Ancient Ones' influence, which was spread by their humanlike Helpers known as the Shemsu-Hor, was later displaced by the followers of the BOPH gods. The confusing and sometimes contradictory recorded history of archaic Egypt thus reflects the blending of those two cultural influences. But a much different fate befell many of the earliest esoteric records of Tibet and India, which were preserved in numerous hidden mountain lamaseries and subterranean crypts known as *guptas*, the guarded archives of the Tibetan monks. Such an effort preserved the archaic wisdom and secret knowledge as originally written, without later distortions or editing.

The archaic records from many ancient cultures referred to the Ancient Ones only by their numerous epithets, the same epithets the BOPH gods later usurped. Therefore, not all citations referring to the Ancient Ones were fully purged. Rather, those 'elder gods' (the Ancient Ones) were simply first 'demonized,' and then later 'defeated' by the BOPH gods, according to the later revised and expanded versions of those prior records.

Perhaps the epic Sanskrit *Rig Veda* provides some of the best confirmation to support the *Elder Gods* theory. A summery of that epic work, as it pertains to the *Elder Gods* theory, is provided in the following synopsis: In the beginning, before Earth was formed, there were beings called *Asuras* (the Ancient Ones), meaning the 'living power.' Some of the earliest records also referred to those divinities as *Suras*, reflecting a significant change in stature that will be further addressed later within this writing. Those beings were revered as the *elder gods*, the ones who possessed the greatest powers and magic. According to one account, Danu, a feminine deity that was associated with 'restraint and bondage,' was one of the highest ranking Asuras.

Her status as a female leader parallels the Egyptian belief where the goddess Isis assumes leadership duties after the death of her husband Osiris, the previous leader and teacher of Egypt. It further relates with the universal Mother Goddess theme, one that originated long before the Great Flood of *c.*10,500 BC.

Mother Goddess veneration continued as a main focus until *c.*3500 BC, a fact confirmed in the research and writings of Maria Gimbutas, a scholar of mythology. Her book, *Gods and Goddesses of Old Europe 7000 BC - 3500 BC*, stated that the Mother Goddess remained the dominate divinity during the time span of her book's title.

Much later in the *Rig Veda*, the Asuras were degraded as evil beings or demons, although no clear explanation is provided for such a change. One of those later 'demons' was Vritra, who was called a Danava, meaning a descendant of Danu (a Helper or Watcher), the 'personification of restraint.' This repeated reference to restraint and bondage referred to the slow and regulated growth mandated by the Cosmic Order, enforced by the Ancient Ones and imposed on all infant races. Still other olden beings associated with the Asuras were called Adityas (the Breakaway Outer Planet Humanlike beings, the BOPH gods), who were the descendants of Aditi, a feminine deity who personifies release or non-restraint. The Adityas represent the 'good' deities of the *Rig Veda*, led by their chief, Varuna, a BOPH god. It is made clear that the Adityas were not actual descendants of the Asuras, but were a different 'race' (or more correctly 'species,' specifically the outer planet humanlike beings). Those beings were described as a 'younger race' than the Asuras, although they considered the Asura to be their 'ancient ancestors.'

The Adityas were also called devas, the term used to denote the original children of heaven and Earth. But earlier accounts recognized the Dawn Usas (aka Ushas, or simply 'Dawn' or the 'Dawns') as the original cosmic children, a term that was later associated with the Adityas. Later still, the Adityas simply became known as 'the gods.' The Adityas chose Indra as their champion to defeat Vritra and the Asuras. At the onset of that conflict, there was only deadlock. Then power was generated from heaven, using devastating weapons unleashed from the sky (or outer space) by the Adityas, which threatened the very existence of life on Earth. With the use of such 'mobile fire' (the nuclear weapons), the 'hearts of the Asuras were pierced.' Note that the Asuras were not killed, but merely 'heartbroken' and disappointed, their 'hearts pierced.' That passage evidently refers to the threat made by the BOPH beings, promising to destroy all planetary life on Earth if the Ancient Ones did not relinquish and leave the planet for some unknown time period.

That threat led to the 'retreat' of the Asuras, initially separating Earth from the bonds of heaven. The agreed upon departure and temporary exile of the *elder gods* caused the Waters of Heaven (freedom) to flow for humankind, according to the *Rig Veda*.[1] The constraints or bonds previously placed on humanity's rate of growth were thus ended, with progress no longer limited or restricted by the prior Cosmic Order mandate requiring a corresponding level of ethical growth and spiritual enlightenment within humankind. The Adityas (BOPH gods) then filled that void in heaven, caused by the departure of the Asuras.

Beside the direct references to the *elder gods* (signifying the *First Beings* known as the Ancient Ones), their galactic code of conduct and unified governance throughout the universe, the Cosmic Order, can also be found in the *Rig Veda*, as well as numerous other ancient records. A modified form of the Cosmic Order was evidently still embraced by the successful BOPH gods, one in which they held the ultimate authority over the direction and rate of progress that was allowed for mortal humankind. According to Ptahotep, an Egyptian high priest: "Great is the Cosmic Order, for it has not changed since the time of Osiris...."[2] The Aditya gods of India also retained a similar concept, with the *Rig Veda* again providing documentation for the BOPH gods' implementation of the Cosmic Order.

It was the duty of Varuna, the leader of the Adityas, to oversee Earth from heaven for any violations of the laws of the *Rta*, the (modified) Cosmic Order. Such an act supposedly then rejoined heaven and Earth once again, as long as humankind obeyed the laws of the Adityas. Such obedience to the BOPH gods and their laws allowed Earth, and perhaps our solar system, to be put into a state of 'order and harmony,' but not necessarily with the entire universe. In other words, the war with the Ancient Ones was ended, but not necessarily its underlying conflict.

The *Rig Veda* is an explicit account that both suggests and supports the *Elder Gods* theory, one in which the Ancient Ones retreated from Earth as a benevolent act to prevent any further harm befalling humankind. Their absence allowed a younger 'divine' race, the BOPH gods, to then demonize the Ancient Ones and usurp their past achievements. The temporary exile from Earth was a selfless act by the Ancient Ones to save humanity. However, the Ancient Ones did insist that their associates, the humanlike Helpers, be allowed to remain on Earth.

That concession allowed the Helpers to continue their efforts to civilize, educate, and guide our infant human race. It also permitted an opposing faction of the 'younger divine race' (the outer planet humanlike Helpers) to offer humanity a different perspective or 'rival version of the truth,' one competing with the regime of the BOPH conquerors. Such an ongoing effort was in preparation for the future return of the *elder gods* to Earth. Their return will allow humanity to ultimately choose allegiance with either the Ancient Ones, or continue with the present status under the influence of the BOPH beings, the one that they had established after *c*.3150 BC.

The oldest archaic Egyptian records seem to confirm that the Helpers undertook such a mission. However, even those records were tainted with later distortions. Although the Ancient Ones never claimed to be gods, they were considered divine beings, lifeforms that had attained a higher level of enlightenment, who were apparently assigned their mission by the Creator. Only much later were they incorrectly called gods by subsequent generations of misinformed humans. The same distortion also applied to the Lunar Pitris, the humanlike Helpers.

One of the most prominent Egyptian Helpers was a teacher known incorrectly as the 'god' Thoth (the Greek god Hermes).

The name 'Thoth' was likely a specific title or position, rather than a single person. Later scribes such as Manetho recorded Thoth's teachings, but his three volume work, *Aegyptiaca*, is also lost. However, portions of that text are known from excerpts used by later historians such as Josephus during the first century AD, and the ninth century Georgio Syncellus, with both writers providing some fragmentary record of Thoth's prior teachings.

The incomplete record of Thoth's writings, known as the *Thoth* or *Hermetic Fragments* (also the *Trismegistic Literature*, the *Corpus Hermeticum*, and the *Collectum Hermeticum*), were highly revered by the early Christian Church Fathers. Those teachings also formed the central elements within the Gnostic belief. During more modern times, Professor G.R.S. Mead's early 20th century publication, *Thrice Greatest Hermes*, was also based on those fragmented remains.

Researcher and author Murry Hope's interpretations of Volume III of that work revealed that the 'Old Ones' (likely referring to the Ancient Ones), 'whose origins were not of this world,' were the wise spirits who descended from heaven to teach mankind, and then returned to their original home among the stars.[3] But Thoth's fragmented record also indicated that the influence or power of those older, wiser beings was later usurped by a younger race (believed to be the BOPH gods) through the use of force.[4]

Another portion of Thoth's teachings is a Greek fragment called the *Kore Kosmu* (aka *Kosmou*), written in Alexandria around 100 BC, and commonly translated as *The Virgin of the World*. It has Isis telling her son, Horus [the younger], the origin of their descent to Earth. It states that Isis and Osiris were sent by the 'Universal Orderer' (perhaps the Cosmic Order) and 'Architect'[5] (likely the Ancient Ones), that they might help the world, for all things needed them.[6] This Hermetic fragment further revealed the results of that visit by Isis and Osiris, stating: "…'Tis they who cause the savagery of mutual slaughtering of men to cease. …'Tis they who gave to men laws, food, and shelter."[7]

The impact of Isis and Osiris' visit to Earth further claimed: "...'Tis they who were the first to set up courts of law; and filled the world with justice and fair rule. ...'Tis they who searched into the cruelty of death, and learned that though the spirit which goes out longs to return into men's bodies, yet if it ever fail to have the power of getting back again, then loss of life results. 'Tis they alone who, taught by Hermes in (the Creator's) hidden codes, became the authors of the arts, and sciences, and all pursuits which men do practise, and givers of their laws."[8] With Isis and Osiris' mission successfully completed, the *Kore Kosmu* concludes: "...And having done all this...were thereupon demanded back by those who dwell in Heaven...."[9]

That account is similar to the Gnostic tale of Sophia who descends to Earth in order to assist humankind. In fact, a great deal of substantiation for the *Elder Gods* theory can be derived from Gnostic beliefs, one of the earliest sects of the Christian faith. Some in the Gnostic sect believed that the souls of humankind were completely alien to Earth, belonging to a different celestial realm. Gnosticism was partially based on secret wisdom and hidden mysteries of a divine or higher realm, reportedly divulged directly by Jesus.

That esoteric knowledge included a belief in an original unknowable divinity, the Creator, along with several levels of lesser divinities. Certain of those lesser divinities, referred to as *gods*, were sent to Earth by the Creator or an intermediate group of 'higher powers' (perhaps the Ancient Ones). Valentinus, one of the chief Gnostic proponents, further clarified the distinction between the various levels of divinity. He identified the head of the lesser gods as, "the king and lord who acts as a military commander, the one who gives the law and judges those who violate it,"[10] referring to the Chief God that ruled over Earth. Valentinus believed this commander king was Yahweh, the God of Israel. Some Gnostics also believed that an element (perhaps referring to DNA material) from those 'lesser' divinities, who either 'fell' to our world or were sent here by the Creator, was later combined with a degenerate mortal lifeform to produce humans.

The Hopi clan of the Pueblo Indians holds a similar religious belief. It claims that beyond (or perhaps before) our present known universe are six more universes (or galaxies or solar systems),[11] producing a total of seven 'worlds' marking our 'Road of Life.'[12] This Road of Life describes levels beyond those found on Earth, which are reached through higher enlightenment. The superhuman *kachina*, the Helpers and Guides to the Hopi, had attained that higher level of enlightenment. A level even higher than that of the kachina was obtained by the *Sotuknang* (believed to be the Hopi's concept of the Ancient Ones). An even higher realm exists above the divine level of the Sotuknang, which is identified as the indefinable and incomprehensible domain of the Creator.[13]

From those higher levels of enlightenment, both the Sotuknang and the kachina then assisted lower forms of life on their evolutionary journey wherever they were needed throughout the universe.[14] Beings such as humans, occupying lower levels of existence, could be elevated to higher enlightenment by obeying the *Laws* and conforming to the pure and perfect pattern laid down by the Creator (believed to mean adherence with the Cosmic Order).[15] An integral part of Hopi religion was obeying the dictates of their supreme authority, the sacred *mongko*,[16] which was the Hopi's 'Law of Laws,' perhaps their understanding or version of the rules of the Cosmic Order. This Law, the sacred mongko, contained three dominant factors or aspects; namely: respect, harmony, and love.[17] It further included the act of claiming the Earth for the Creator.

Such knowledge and enlightenment, which was imparted by the Helpers such as Thoth, was apparently understood and accepted by most pre-Flood humans, as well as their later descendants such as the earliest Egyptians. Such fundamental ancient wisdom included vast cosmological knowledge of Earth and the universe, along with a metaphysical understanding of the Creator, as well as the Laws of the Cosmic Order. The suppression and distortion of that knowledge over the millennia can be clearly detected, suggesting the true extent to which truth has been distorted or concealed from humanity since *c*.3150 BC by the BOPH gods and their followers.

Some early cultures of North Africa, such as the Bambara and Bozo, also believed that their olden ancestors had lived with and were taught by beings that were reportedly similar to the Helpers.[18] Many have a connection or familiarity with the star Sirius. They further profess the belief that many stars (star systems) were populated with intelligent life, which were not always humanoid in their appearance.[19] Author Murry Hope divulged that the Dogons and Tutsi tribes of North Africa, as well as the related Ammonites, had long retained strange esoteric beliefs.

The Ammonites were an ancient Semitic people who existed between the 13th century and the sixth century BC, occupying the region between the Syrian Desert and the Jordan River of present day Jordan. Their principal city was located on the site of modern Amman, Jordan. According to Biblical accounts in Genesis, the Ammonites were the descendants from the son of Lot, and were closely associated with the Moabites. The mysterious Dogons of Mali in North Africa claim an ancestry with the Ammonites.

Additional related tribes included the Ta, Tedas, Tuaregs, and the Garamantes. The Garamantes are a tribal people from the North African oasis of Djerma in the Fezzan region of the Sahara, an area in Southwestern Libya with a number of oases. The ancestors of the Tutsis may have been the Tuaregs, also from the Fezzan, during the time of the great Triton Sea when floodwaters had forced the indigenous people to seek sanctuary in the mountain peaks. The Triton Sea was the ancient inland lake that once covered the Sahara valley, which was formed by the Great Flood. A wide mix of people possessing strange beliefs and exotic customs inhabit that greater mountainous region of North

Africa, which also contains the world's largest desert. The Ammonites and other diverse but related tribes of that region contend that their ancestors were taught the *Hekau*, the 'words that move,' by a group of beings that watched over their tribe.[20] They also claim that their earliest ancestors married and had children with those ancient teachers (evidently the humanlike Helpers of the Ancient Ones).

The Ammonites, Dogons, and the Tutsi tribes believe they descended from the 'Ones of the Shining Faces' who left their footsteps upon the mountains of stone by the tone uttered from their mouths. They were the *Ones* who created 'The Mountains' of perfection in the North, who later moved east to the mountains by the sea, with others going back to the Source in the Heavens.[21] Their leaving caused great sorrow for earthly humans, according to tribal edicts and histories.

According to ancient oral traditions, the earliest distant ancestors of those three tribes had originally lived with the 'Shining Ones' in their ancestral lands.[22] Later, those Shining Ones went into hiding or exile, while those tribal ancestors prophesied: "...the coming of the wild ones who shall cause the name of their leader the one of evil to be heard throughout the Holy Land as God Itself...."[23] In turn, they would: "...succumb to the Shining Ones, [who] though in hiding still (perhaps the agreed exile), shall join to our people once more and cause a new age to begin."[24] The term 'hidden Shining Ones' refers to the Ancient Ones and their mutually agreed period of exile, prohibiting public contact and direct influence over the humans of Earth. This same event, or a very similar one, is described or implied within other legends and oral traditions retained by numerous ancient cultures, and is generally known as the 'separation of heaven and Earth.'

115

Chapter 12

Separation From Heaven

Accounts preserved by many ancient cultures contain references to some profound occurrence that created a separation between heaven and Earth. That specific act of separation implied an opposition or competition, perhaps even a discord between two ideologies. Such an indication of an inherent dualism between two contrasting or opposing sides appears to be a basic belief since remote times. Numerous oral traditions and legends of many ancient cultures speak of two different groups of supernatural beings, usually in opposition or conflict with one another. The Zoroastrian religion of ancient Persia is credited with the formal inception of such dualism. Their concept of both a good element (personified by the ancient Persian god Ahura Mazda) and an evil element (the god Ahriman) became the basis for similar subsequent dualistic beliefs.

The ancient titans opposed the Greek gods. The Hebrew Nefilim and Christian angles are in opposition with the devil and his demons. The Hopi clan of the Pueblo Indians professes that the good kachinas are in opposition with the evil *Soyoko*. From an archaic earthly perspective, such dualism contrasts the Ancient Ones with the BOPH gods, with the humanlike Helpers of the Ancient Ones later continuing that struggle.

Such an ancient event was associated with chaos, either as some type of discontent or as various forms of conflict that led to open hostilities. Actions causing those various separations usually resulted in some form of exile 'punishment.' A vague Egyptian vignette links such chaos with the Children of Rebellion (aka Children of Impotence) who were also associated with the primordial parents of humankind. A similar version can be found in the Babylonian *Enuma elish*, which stated that the 'primordial parents,' Tiamat and Apsu, bore offspring that later destroyed them, splitting Tiamat into two parts.[1] Such an act is metaphorically explained as the separation from a revered source, thereby creating two opposing factions. In India, the gods were ordered: "To throw off the burden of earth...."[2] That action caused conflict that: "Between the gods and the Asuras there arose a great feud over the sovereignty of the universe...."[3]

The *Rig Veda* also confirms a similar separation. The Hindu god Indra's killing of Vritra, the serpent-demon son of the goddess Danu, who is equated as being Tiamat's equivalent, separated the Earth and sky from the heavens and released the waters that then flowed for man.[4] Such flowing waters represented freedom from the constraints imposed by the Ancient Ones. The *Rig Veda* further discussed the cosmic battle that was associated with separating heaven and Earth,[5] an act also referred to as 'measured apart.' That event was associated with Indra or Varuna who used a 'pillar'[6] to maintain such separation, creating two world-halves[7] that resulted in a basic two-part universe consisting of an earthly region and the upper dwelling place, which required a three step process for its completion.[8] That three step process is referenced in Hymn 1.154.3, stating: "Vishnu...who alone with but three steps measured apart this long, far-reaching dwelling-place." Some speculate that such a three step process referred to three domains: the earthly region, the massive expanse of outer space (the heavens), and an unseen spiritual realm.

The ancient Egyptians defined the 'divine world' as encompassing anything that could not be directly perceived by the physical senses or explained by humankind's rational reasoning, with heaven being 'the realm above Earth.' The heavenly roof was made from metal and supported by specific divine objects, the zam-supports,[9] which were located at its four corners, creating the foundation between heaven and Earth. Later, that foundation was 'torn asunder,' separating heaven and Earth. Some have speculated that the 'metal roof of heaven' was a huge mothership of the Ancient Ones, with the zam-supports serving as the mechanism by which both ascent and descent from heaven (the ship) could be facilitated from Earth. Reportedly, those divine supports or conduits were religiously guarded. They were accessible to only a very few select humans, but were regularly used by the gods to maintain contact with Earth.

The act of 'separation from heaven' is attributed to a number of different heroes from many cultures. The earliest account of this event is found in Sumerian records, per the fragment known as the *Myth of Enki and the World Order*, which stated: "In the days of yore, when heaven was separated from Earth...."[10] Other Sumerian records indicate that Enlil was the god who separated heaven from Earth, claiming Earth for himself. Additional accounts are discussed in Hesiod's wars of the Titans, as well as in the Puranas, which describe the Great Wars in heaven. The 6th chapter of the *Huai-nan-tzu*, a Taoist text of the second century BC, reveals that in very ancient times, heaven and Earth were split apart.[11] The Chinese goddess Nu-kua, the consort of the god Fu-hsi, helped repair that rift to some degree, partially restoring some harmony.

Further accounts referring to the separation of Earth from the heavens are found in the Bible, as well as in specific myths where a dragon, Leviathan, or serpent was defeated. Archangel Michael and his angels prevailed in their fight against the dragon, casting out and forcing the demon to leave the heavens. This is similar to the theme describing the 'fallen angels,' when Lucifer and his hosts, a third of the heavenly population, were evicted from Heaven. The Mayan *Chilam Balaam* describes a time when "a fiery rain fell, and ashes fell...And their Great Serpent was ravished from the heavens."[12] *The Urantia Book* also relayed a similar dissatisfaction or discontent with the regimented 'universe administration' dictates of its Joint Council,[13] reportedly the celestial planetary governance or guidance committee overseeing the universe.[14] A resultant split occurred due to the desire for greater freedom of choice and self-government, which also meant exclusion or isolation from that Joint Council administrative bureaucracy.[15]

The god Thoth reportedly taught Egypt its ancient wisdom. Much of that knowledge was blended with certain beliefs from the Essene sect of the Jewish faith, thereby creating the Gnostic doctrine, one of the earliest sects of the Christian faith. Other competing Christian sects later banded together to form the early Church during Constantine's reign, and regrettably declared the Gnostic tenants to be heretical, persecuting this doctrine. But the Gnostic belief is more in agreement with the true understanding of spiritual evolution, since it professes that all souls are 'morally equal,' although existing at differing degrees of enlightenment. The distinct level of one's enlightenment then determines the morality (or lack thereof) behind each act committed, taking into account whether each deed was performed due to a lack of understanding, or from intended malice. The active and passive elements of dualism, exposed within the nature of good and evil, comprise the essence of the Gnostic *Ogdoad*, the ensuing balance or harmony thought to be required in the physical world.

Author Timothy Wyllie's interpretation of Gnosticism is a somewhat depressing realization of Earth in opposition to the better judgment of older, wiser beings in the universe.[16] Such opposition was designed to seal off certain knowledge, as well as any contact with a higher divine realization, a notion similar to one expressed in *The Urantia Book*. Such accounts may be references to the schism between the Ancient Ones and the BOPH gods over control of our planet, resulting in Earth's separation from contact with its prior heavenly source of guidance.

In the mid-twentieth century, the noted French mythologist, Mircea Eliade, stated: "...the myths of many peoples allude to a very distant epoch when men knew neither death nor toil nor suffering...."[17] He further wrote that: "...the gods descended to

Earth and mingled with men."[18] Mircea Eliade revealed that during such times, men could evidently travel or ascend to heaven with ease. As the result of some unknown ritual fault, communications between heaven and Earth were interrupted, causing the gods to withdraw to the highest heavens.

According to the oldest known Chinese text, the *Shu ching* (*Classic of History*), a troublesome antediluvian race called the Maio (aka Mao, Miao, Mao-tse) existed during the reigns of Yao and Shun. They were originally described as having existed back in the time when man was: "…joined in body to Heaven and Earth, united in spirit…in harmonious oneness…."[19] Reportedly, their race eventually became evil, 'lacking in virtue.' In Book 17 of the *Shan-hai ching*, those same Maio are described as 'winged' human beings, living in the extreme northwestern corner of the world, while a later text described the Miao as having wings, but unable to fly.[20]   The Maio, who reportedly came from the heavens, caused such disorder that the chief god, Shang Ti (aka Lord Chang-ty, the Divine King), ordered their extermination. Shang Ti then: "charged Ch'ung and Li to cut the communication between heaven and Earth so that there would be no descending and ascending."[21] After that ancient act, discord ceased and order was ultimately restored on Earth.

A later account in the 4th century BC Chinese text, the *Kuo yu* (aka *Kuo-yiu*), has King Chao of Ch'u, who reigned from 515 to 489 BC, inquiring about that olden account discussed in the *Shu ching*, which 'separated heaven and Earth.' He wondered, asking his minister: "If it had not been thus, would the people have been able to ascend to Heaven?"[22] Clearly some form of separation occurred that apparently resulted in global exile, which was then recorded by many ancient cultures.   That same separation and exile was somehow also associated with universal harmony.

The concept of exile is an interesting one. Historians date the process of exile as a penal policy around the 8th century BC, during the first Chaldean reign over Babylonia. But Sumerian and Akkadian accounts had described exile as a known punishment during much earlier times. Author Zecharia Sitchin relays the story of the god Enlil's banishment as his punishment for raping a female.[23] That punitive exile was lifted when Enlil married that same woman, Ninlil, 'negating' his crime and atoning for his actions. Exile also played a role in the history of Alalu, who was overthrown as king by Anu after a nine year reign. Rather than execution, Alalu was exiled from the kingdom and fled to Earth.[24] That kingdom was identified in the <u>First Journal of the Ancient Ones</u>, *Elder Gods of Antiquity*, as the base on Mars that was occupied by the humanlike beings that had survived the destruction of the asteroid belt planet, Maldek. A more familiar exile was the Biblical pre-Flood banishment of Cain after killing his brother Able. Ancient texts further state that exile as a punishment method emerged at the beginning of time, when humans were held to a certain code of ethical conduct by the gods, possibly referring to the Cosmic Order.

Perhaps the most remarkable expulsion was the agreed upon temporary exile of the Ancient Ones around *c.*3150 BC, perhaps in the year 3113 BC, the date that marked the Mayan calendar's *Long Count* that initiated a New Age. Most ancient calendars were cyclic in function, tracking either the solar or lunar cycles. The *Long Count*, being a chronological one, was different. It measures the passage of time from some significant event, until the specific end of that event or Age, marking a time that would then signify the emergence of yet another New Age. Other ancient cultures share nearly that same date or time period, signifying that such a date was of some major importance. The *Kaliyuga*, the present Age of the Hindus of India, further reflects that same approximate starting time; calculated as having commenced in the year 3102 BC.

In the *Vishnu Purana*, the hero Krishna discusses the destruction of the race of Yadu, the Yadavas, stating: "When I have annihilated the race of Yuda, I will proceed to the mansions of the immortals. The tyrants that oppressed the Earth...have been killed. When I have taken away this great weight upon Earth, I will return to protect the sphere of the celestials."[25] A similar archaic record from Egypt, the previously mentioned fragment known as the *Virgin of the World*, seems to confirm the exile portion of the *Vishnu Purana*. It states that God commanded: "Depart, ye Holy Ones...nor yet in any way attempt to innovate, nor leave the whole of this world without your active service."[26] The god speaking evidently was the leader of the BOPH beings then on Earth, the humanlike god that was identified as Enlil in Mesopotamian texts. Yet, the eventual return of those 'Holy Ones,' the Ancient Ones, is also apparent. Such a return is often connected with a specific passage of time, when humanity would have likely achieved greater enlightenment. Hence, exile and its 'end' has also been linked with the coming of a New Age.

A related future-return belief describes the Second Coming of the Messiah. Yet such an occurrence is portrayed as an apocalyptic event, something ominous and dreaded, a rather strange foreboding of what should be a glorious occasion. Such apprehension may actually be referring to the return of the Ancient Ones, per their agreement made sometime between 3150 and 3100 BC. The BOPH gods would apparently want to create the idea that such an event would be foreboding, a dreaded event that humankind should fear.

Portraying the return of the Ancient Ones as a dire event would be similar to the practice of the winning side demonizing their defeated opponent after a war. The *c.*50 BC *Testaments of the Twelve Patriarchs* (aka *Prophets*) forewarn of an age of salvation when two messiahs will appear. Yet only one could be the 'true' messiah. Later Christian texts warn of Christ's return, an event also accompanied by an anti-Christ. Such warnings of an impending event containing the dual elements of good and evil, both offering salvation, was apparently intended to influence the outcome of that future occurrence. A time when two potential leaders, one presumably representing the Ancient Ones and the

123

other the BOPH gods, would require humanity to finally chose permanent allegiance with only one of those opposing sides.

Chapter 13

The Eradication Plan

More explicit evidence that might prove the existence of the Ancient Ones, their Helpers, or their fateful conflict with the BOPH gods simply appears to be lost. Such an outcome is the result of an organized campaign by the BOPH gods to eradicate all trace of the Ancient Ones from Earth. That covert effort involved the distortion, suppression, editing, and redacting of archaic accounts, along with the wholesale destruction of ancient texts and records. Similar major record alterations and destructive actions were known to have occurred throughout Earth's historic past. A chronological review of some major destructive occurrences was presented in the First Journal of the Ancient Ones, *Elder Gods of Antiquity*.

That revision of Earth's historic events started with the earliest written records, which date back to *circa* 3500 BC. However, most of those records were merely financial dealings or administrative documents, not narratives. It is known that between 90 and 95 percent of the Sumerian clay tablets consisted of commercial records or business transactions.[1] Not until about 2200 BC did myths, legends, and heroic narratives such as *The Epic of Gilgamesh* first emerge. Hence, very few texts would have existed prior to the separation and exile of the Ancient Ones around *c*.3150 BC. Therefore, only a few prior records would have existed that could have accurately portrayed the Ancient Ones, the humanlike Helpers, or their mission on Earth.

Generally, emerging worlds would have recorded very little information concerning the altruistic Ancient Ones, by the very

125

nature of their mission. Their most extensive and direct involvement with any newly contacted infant race would have occurred during the very earliest formative phase of each world's cultural development. Most likely, those infant races would not have yet self-evolved to a level producing a form of writing. Naturally, a substantial period of time would be required to impart such skills before useful written accounts would eventually ensue. Since written records would not yet have occurred during the earliest periods of contact, an accurate or detailed accounting of events would simply not exist. Further, descriptive abilities would have been quite limited or simplistic during those earliest formative periods, most likely resulting in merely pictorial representations, symbolic notations, art scenes, or cave and rock drawings. While such depictions do suggest encounters with unusual beings, they unfortunately provide very little insight or additional specific details of their underlying meaning.

Later, as each contacted world progressed toward true civilization, a majority of interactions would have been conducted through intermediaries, such as the Helpers of the Ancient Ones. Hence, most written and oral accounts would have described those Helpers, not necessarily the Ancient Ones. In the case of ancient Earth contact, nearly all references to the Ancient Ones were later eradicated by the BOPH gods, essentially removing their very presence from Earth history. That eradication plan was implemented in several phases over distinct historic periods, in order to shape a desired impression and produce an intended goal for a specific purpose.

During the following years after the temporary exile of the Ancient Ones, the initial phase of this eradication plan was implemented in an effort to distort perceptions and memories of the Ancient Ones, by demonizing those *elder gods* as evil entities. Since memory of those divine beings existed in the recollection and minds of humanity, it was not possible to simply 'deny' their existence. Rather, such demonization was intended to sway public opinion and perception, assuring the BOPH gods' future control over Earth and its human occupants. Such portrayal of the *elder gods* as 'evil' is evident throughout most ancient texts and religious beliefs.

The early Persian Genii (the Ancient Ones) were originally described as wise and helpful, but were later called the 'Dark Ones' to diminish their status. The Ancient Ones were further portrayed as Satan, a Leviathan, evil spirits, demons, devils, or the numerous other 'dark forces' described in human lore and legend. It is interesting to note that religious accounts generally only report the defeat, not the death of the 'serpent,' or any of the other related names assigned to the Ancient Ones and their Helpers, the enemies of the BOPH gods. However, we are repeatedly warned that the devil constantly remains at hand, ever watchful over humankind while awaiting its opportunity for contact.

One of the most revealing records indicating such rewriting of actual history is found in the *Rig Veda* where the Ancient Ones are referred to as the Grand Asuras of Heaven, who in the beginning were the only 'Living Power.' According to the Vedic scholar, Professor Wendy O'Flaherty, the Asuras were initially described as the 'elder brothers' of the Aryan gods, the oldest and wisest ancestors, who possessed the greatest power and magic of all the gods. Only later were those *elder gods* demonized as dark deities and transformed into 'enemy demons,' the evil dark divinities of ancient times.[2] That degradation from good-to-evil was further distinguished by a name change from Sura to Asura in some of the oldest esoteric texts of India, as referenced earlier. The Suras were considered to be the earliest and brightest gods, but ultimately became the Asuras only when arbitrarily 'dethroned' and degraded by the much later Hindu Brahmans.

Other records reflect similar degradation of their 'elder divinities.' Siberian Shamans relate accounts of a prior race that possessed great knowledge, but threatened rebellion against the 'Great Chief Spirit.'[3] In Egypt, Ani, a royal scribe of Thebes around 1450 BC, recorded an even more descriptive narrative that was based upon very ancient temple accounts. Vignettes relating to Chapter 17 of the *Papyrus of Ani* refer to the 'War in Heaven and Earth,' stating: "...the Children of Impotent Revolt...that night of battle...into the eastern part of heaven, whereupon there arose a battle in heaven and in all the earth."[4] Due to the BOPH gods' revisionism plan and the sometimes puzzling nature of *The Book of the Dead* and the *Papyrus of Ani*, certain records can be interpreted as implying that the 'Children of Impotent Revolt' apparently had succeeded in their 'impotent' effort, actually 'winning' that war, or at least that specific battle.[5] That account of the 'War in the Heavens' seems to parallel the 'defeat' of the Ancient Ones around 3150 BC.

Perhaps Hesiod, the 8th century BC Greek poet and orator, was one of the first philosophers to actually recognize this eradication and demonization plan of the BOPH gods. Hesiod often contemplated the future role of the gods, as he considered the nature and exploits of the earlier 'golden race of (beings),' thought to be a reference to the Ancient Ones and their much earlier influence on human civilization. Hesiod stated: "But now that fate has closed over this race, they are holy demons upon earth, beneficent averters of ills, guardians, of mortal men."[6] Hesiod seems to imply that the transition of power from the 'olden gods' (the Ancient Ones) to the younger gods (the BOPH gods) was merely a natural evolution; as was the degradation of those prior gods, which would normally be the process associated with such an evolutionary transfer.

Such demonization may have even continued into modern times, with governmental denial of UFOs and extraterrestrial life, although such official disavowal seems to be diminishing to some degree. But that perceived change might simply reflect a revised approach suggesting that otherworldly beings could be 'evil entities,' awaiting their moment to attack and take over Earth to enslave its people. Such an inference, if regularly stressed and repeated, could create an intended negative impression toward the

Ancient Ones; in anticipation of when they are once again allowed to make open contact with humanity, after the expiration of their temporary exile.

Over time, as human memory of the Ancient Ones diminished, the second phase of such an eradication plan emerged. That involved a deliberate suppression by the BOPH gods of nearly all accounts and records of the Ancient Ones. With nearly total suppression of the Ancient Ones' existence, the only accounts allowed to be known were negative ones. Although very little direct reference and evidence is specifically known of the Ancient Ones, Earth's oldest records, myths, and legends provide the best informational sources alluding to those beings. The records and efforts of their humanlike Helpers are the only other source, but those were equally suppressed.

The intent to suppress the existence and deeds of the Ancient Ones became widespread once the influence of the BOPH gods had become firmly entrenched on Earth. Evidence of this phase of the eradication plan can be detected by 2000 BC, from the alteration of prior records and the obvious deletions of most references to the Ancient Ones. Such an effort to revise history further spread to various religious sects, where their doctrines and records were also distorted. That suppression can be detected in numerous ancient accounts that either hint at the truth, or openly state its manipulation. According to Robert Graves in his 1958 book, *The White Goddess*: "The Essene initiates, according to Josephus, were sworn to keep secret the names of the Powers who ruled their universe under God...."[7] Seemingly, this is a reference to the Ancient Ones, and their true position within the divine hierarchy of the universe.

According to certain Gnostic beliefs, the lesser god of Earth, the *demiurge*, was identified as Yahweh (aka Iao, Ildabaoth, and Ialdabaoth), the being also identified as the God of the Old Testament by others.[8] The Gnostics further believed that this 'false god' made every effort to keep humanity immersed in ignorance, by focusing on physical desires and material goods, thus keeping the truth hidden from humans. Yahweh reportedly even punished some of humanity's attempts to acquire knowledge and truth. For this reason, the Gnostics did not associate 'God the Father' of the New Testament, the father of Jesus, with the God of the Old Testament. Further, the Gnostics also did not believe that the Godhead (the Creator) had ever taken human form. Hence, neither Yahweh nor Jesus could actually be the true supreme Creator.

As human memory of the Ancient Ones dissipated over the ensuing centuries, the next phase of the eradication plan focused on the usurpation of all past accomplishments made by the Ancient Ones, claiming those achievements as accomplishments of the BOPH gods. That also included usurpation of the *Grand Plan* orchestrated by the Creator, the divine intent to utilize the simplest basic particles to continually build ever more complex creations. That usurpation by the BOPH gods had them actually taking credit for the creation of the universe and all it contained.

Those claims contribute to the inconsistency, contradictions, and discrepancies evident in many ancient texts; caused by a younger race taking credit for all the prior accomplishments of a much older race. The vast bulk of our ancient folklore depicts the lives, events, and times of the BOPH gods, rather than the true exploits of the Ancient Ones, although the Ancient Ones never claimed to be 'gods.' That fact partly accounts for some of the confusion often found in many archaic records that may not accurately identify which 'gods' were actually being discussed.

Further confusion emerged as some later 'gods' even usurped past accomplishments of earlier BOPH gods. The Egyptian god Amen gradually usurped the attributes accorded to many prior gods, while the Babylonian god Marduk took credit for every accomplishment claimed by all prior gods.[9] Still more confusion ensued when the BOPH gods further became known as the Anunnaki, the Elohim, the Archons, the Nefilim, the angels, and the various heroes known from Earth's mythologies. Such usurpation was an ongoing process, and was also practiced by the human collaborators of the BOPH gods. That group included the elite high priests, kings, lords, governors, ancient ensi, and other human leaders appointed by the BOPH gods.

Some of the ancient altered texts became so garbled they were rendered unintelligible, due to the contradictions and confusion that resulted when the BOPH gods were substituted in place of the Ancient Ones. Such a vague and mostly confusing reference is found in *3 Enoch* (aka the *Hebrew Book of Enoch*) in a proclamation made by three angels to the 'Lord of the Universe,' the ruler of the home planet of the gods. Those angels implored the Lord not to create humankind, using Enoch as an example, stating: "Said not the Ancient Ones [First Ones] rightly before Thee: 'Do not create man'!"[10] But the Lord of the Universe, the 'Holy One' did anyway. Certainly such a statement did not reflect the actual Ancient Ones, the *First Beings*, asking a BOPH god not to create humans. Further, such a request was made using a specific human example, namely Enoch, thus producing a very strange request not to create a species that was already created.

Perhaps that 'contradictory record' actually pertained to a much older account, when the 'olden' outer planet humanlike beings, prior to their own breakaway from the Ancient Ones, implored the Ancient Ones not to genetically 'create' humans. Such a request might have been made in an attempt to preclude the formation of a new indigenous species that would have sovereign rights to planet Earth, a world coveted by the humanlike survivors of the Maldek destruction as their intended future homeworld. With later transposition of 'gods' for the Ancient Ones in existing records, and the demonization of Ancient Ones to 'lesser' or 'lower' beings, those substitutions could produce such confusing passages as the previous example from *3 Enoch*.

Further study of ancient Sumerian, Akkadian, Egyptian, and Babylonian texts reveals a startling contradiction. While highly technical devices were possessed and utilized at will by the BOPH gods, they did not appear to understand their full potential or the theory behind their operation. Those same texts also described most gods as being illiterate, except for a very few such as Osiris, Thoth, Horus, and Enki. Certain literate 'gods' are thought to have actually been Helpers, rather than BOPH gods. An advanced civilization of godlike beings that are capable of interplanetary space travel is inconsistent with a culture of generally illiterate people.

The fact that only small portions of inhabitants within such a culture were literate tends to indicate that their technology was probably inherited, most likely from their ancient ancestors, not self-developed. Such a conclusion seems to suggest a break or disruption in the progress of their culture, perhaps from a later relocation due to a destroyed homeworld. It could also indicate technology and devices that were either loaned or provided to them as a legacy from an outside source, such as the Ancient Ones; rather than being developed and built by their own society.

A somewhat similar break or disconnection can also be detected in some of the most ancient written records of Earth. Such an interruption or abrupt change is evident in many Sanskrit texts, including the *Rig Veda* and *The Mahabharata*. The most notable instance is the early accounts of the Asura (Ancient Ones) and their wondrous powers, as contained in *The Book of the Origins*, a chapter and Minor Book in *The Mahabharata*. The noted Sanskrit scholar, Professor J.A.B. van Buitenen, alludes to a break in its narrative when the story is changed or altered, stating: "And then *The Origins* begins a second time with a prose chronicle that has scarcely more than a nodding acquaintance with the previous one."[11] This seems to indicate the degradation of an original mythology that was later replaced with a new one, which included some portion of the original, incorporating and embracing certain olden accounts within the new, but with changes.

A similar scenario is found in ancient Egyptian accounts concerning the Ennead, the genealogy of their gods, the Neteru. *The Cosmogonic Concept of Heliopolis* (aka *The Lineage of*

Horus) describes the transfer of power from the early Great Gods to the Neteru, then to semi-divine beings, followed by 'heroes' and the pharaonic dynasties. Commenting on this record, Dr. Rudolf Anthes, a professor of Egyptology, stated: "Furthermore, the whole composition gives the impression that there was a break in the middle of the tale."[12] Such observational analysis of the ancient records of India and Egypt suggest those 'narrative breaks' were the result of the BOPH gods usurping the influential deeds of the prior Ancient Ones, thereby altering those accounts.

Rather than completely purging the very existence of the Ancient Ones from oral traditions and written texts, an act that would have also remove their legacy (the 'gifts' bestowed upon the humans of Earth); some texts were simply rewritten. That became the subsequent method enacted as the next phase of the eradication plan by the later descendants of the BOPH gods. Such wholesale plagiarism in the rewriting of ancient records was evident throughout their edited versions, which omitted, redacted, and distorted any remaining mention that might allude to the Ancient Ones. Later additions made to the Egyptian *Book of the Dead* clearly reflected this new phase of writing, which commenced shortly after 1600 BC with the advent of the pharaonic 18th dynasty.[13] By 1500 BC, this method was widespread throughout the numerous cultures under the influence of the BOPH gods; producing their version of archaic history, which was recorded in their ancient texts known to later generations.

But not all texts required editing, since certain cultures exclusively reflected the dictates of the BOPH gods from their start. Those texts also tend to be the most consistent, without the usual contradictions found in other ancient records. The hieroglyphic notation of the Egyptians and the cuneiform script of the Sumerians were claimed to be gifts from the gods, not inventions by man. Therefore, 'misuse' of those 'gifts' was prohibited, allowing the BOPH gods to exert maximum control over that form of communication in cultures they controlled.

Perhaps the least confusing texts are those from Sumer and Akkad. That may be the result of those cultures being essentially controlled by the BOPH gods since their inception, as was the case with Akkad, or from very early periods of development, as experienced in Sumer. To find any confusion, it is necessary to go back to the prior Ubaid culture within that region. Even then, contradictions arise mostly in the form of confusing relics and practices, not from written records. Many later ensuing cultures were also influenced from their onset by the BOPH gods after 3100 BC, exempting their subsequent records from any 'necessary revisions.' The only source of truth after that date emerged from the efforts of the humanlike Helpers that stayed on Earth after the exiled departure of the Ancient Ones.

Professor Samuel Noah Kramer noted that only rarely do the myths of Sumer and Akkad involve struggles for power between the gods. The rare exceptions are not depicted as bitter, vindictive, or gory conflicts; but merely as struggles for power or prestige.[14] Generally, the Sumerian gods chose to avoid human contact, considering humans to be their slaves. The same was true for the later gods of Egypt. No Egyptian mythology told of any human intrusion into the world of the gods, unlike the later Greek myths. Still, most all pre-dynastic concepts survived within the later Egyptian religion of the unified 'Two Lands of Upper and Lower Egypt,' although much alteration and usurpation of past accomplishments contained in the pre-dynastic texts slowly occurred over time; a result of the eradication plan of the BOPH gods. The same is true with the classical Sanskrit epics and records that were written prior to the Aryan intrusion into India, but later underwent alteration under the direction of the Aryan gods (the BOPH gods).

Hence, the earliest narratives referring to the BOPH beings can be found in the garbled and somewhat confusing mythological accounts and religious beliefs of Earth's ancient civilizations. Those texts used numerous designations to identify the ancient BOPH gods of various cultures, calling them the

Anunnaki, Nefilim, angels, the hosts of heaven, or the Great White Fathers to name just a few. A modern version of those same tales, updated to reflect humanity's present knowledge of advanced technology, is contained in Zecharia Sitchin's entertaining Earth Chronicles book series. That collection seems to mainly describe exploits of the BOPH gods, but apparently after the Ancient Ones had departed Earth. Those accounts reflect the altered records made by the Anunnaki, the younger BOPH gods, after they claimed credit for past deeds made by the Ancient Ones; further demonstrating the true success of the BOPH gods' eradication plan.

Only minimal evidence of the Ancient Ones can now be found scattered throughout written records kept by ancient human historians. Due to the success of the BOPH gods' eradication plan, nearly all knowledge and accounts pertaining to the Ancient Ones were eventually lost. Merely a few remaining vague references and fragmented records yet remain from which to partially extract a sketchy picture of these very advanced 'divine beings.'

The Ancient Ones may best be identified from their many epithets, their numerous 'titles,' and their associated activities that were described by or connected with those designations. Their existence and presence on Earth is evident by the advanced devices and megalithic structures they left; as well as through more intangible evidence, such as the knowledge they imparted to the early indigenous inhabitants of Earth. These represent merely a few of the known legacies of the Elder Gods. In order to develop a more explicit understanding and concept of the Ancient Ones, the subsequent chapters will expose what little documentation is known of these beings, along with specific contributions they bestowed upon our species, planet, and solar system.

Chapter 14

The Seven Sons

The Ancient Ones represent the unified group of *First Beings*, the original intelligent lifeforms that emerged during the earliest eras of our present universe, shortly after the Big Bang event. They represent beings of different species and appearances that evolved independently on seven different planets scattered throughout various regions of the cosmos. They were the 'exceptions' within the early universe, having survived their species' inherent propensity for self-destruction. As survivors, they mastered the sciences and natural laws, rising beyond normally obtained levels to unprecedented heights of achievement, reaching the pinnacle of obtainment within the early universe. Such a lofty level of attainment evidently separated them from the 'lower' lifeforms, allowing them to become the highest enlightened beings within the physical realm, having also mastered a spiritual or metaphysical discipline attuned to the cosmic forces of the universe.

Each individual species of Ancient Ones eventually met their otherworldly counterparts, and joined together in an effort to assure harmony throughout the universe. Together, they possessed the greatest collection of knowledge and wisdom, with mastery over most physical laws. Their collective alliance was known from an ancient Tibetan text as the *Tridasa*, meaning the hosts and the multitudes,[1] perhaps influencing the later Hindu concept, the *Trimurti*,[2] which combined the elements of three gods into a unified trinity. The basic regulation or dictate adopted by those seven diverse species of *First Beings* was commonly referred to as the *One* or the *Cosmic Order*. The Cosmic Order was a simple code of conduct consisting of basic rules, laws, and regulations universally applied throughout the cosmos. That united group of *First Beings*, who initially formed and oversaw this alliance, were known collectively as the Ancient Ones. They occasionally were referred to in the singular as the Ancient One, which apparently reflected their single united-group status. Other ancient texts also referred to them as The One; with the Ancient One, The One, or the Ancient Ones all referring to the same group of beings.

These distinct and unrelated species had evolved to become highly enlightened beings, all following a fundamental objective, unmoved by emotions or feelings. The Ancient Ones were altruistic and pragmatic beings, neither benign nor malevolent, who were filled with conviction of purpose while promoting strict adherence with their Cosmic Order. They established that code of conduct in order to produce and maintain universal harmony. That same code also allowed knowledge and civilization to be bestowed upon emerging worlds, in exchange for a regulated or metered rate of growth, one dependent upon the enlightenment and ethical morality of each 'infant' world contacted. The Ancient Ones deployed and implemented their agenda in a similar realistic and pragmatic manner, with no preconceived expectations or bias. Knowledge was also dispensed in that same method; merely conveying information without any intent to influence the recipients of such data, thereby allowing an informed decision based on free will choice.

Such methodology apparently implied their firm conviction with their ideology, philosophy, and knowledge, which they imparted to the infant races that were contacted. Such conviction of purpose displays a confidence that might have resulted from being entrusted with the duty to oversee the universe, perhaps even as a mandate or command coming directly from the Creator. That possibility is vaguely implied by certain stanzas in the *Book of Dzyan*,[3] as well as in several other ancient texts, especially records from the earliest archaic periods of Egypt. Such a personal mandate, perhaps one received directly from the Creator, elevated those primordial entities to the level of 'divine beings' in physical form, those possessing the highest levels of enlightenment.[4]

While these seven lifeforms had emerged within diverse and far reaching sectors of our early universe, certain vague archaic statements tend to indicate that those *First Being* 'survivors,' each from their separate worlds, may actually reflect only four distinctly different species or lifeforms. But adequate facts simply do not exist to make a final determination on this aspect.

Obscure ancient references were made to four distinct groups known as the Dioscuri, the Cabiri (also Caberi), the Corybantes, and the Samothracian deities; races that reportedly were the 'first to build a ship complete,'[5] perhaps referring to a space craft. These terms may refer to the earliest *First Being* species, or the first four worlds to unite under the Cosmic Order mandate. Later, these four 'races' were changed into minor gods or demigods, with the Phoenician historian Sanchuniathon claiming those groups were the offspring of Thoth's uncle, Sydyc (aka Sydyk).[6] Additional references to these four 'powers' will be discussed further in Chapter 18.

However, the seven original homeworlds of those surviving *First Beings* may additionally represent the underlying sources for all life in the universe, either through their own seeding acts, or by their direct relocation of lifeforms from planet to planet. Thus, all species in the universe might be based on or from those original seven sources, the seven worlds that were commonly considered to be the 'sacred planets' during ancient times.[7]

Such surviving primordial beings evidently included feline entities, insect-like creatures, a reptilian or amphibious species, and humanoids of both large and small stature. The shear notion that intelligent beings could evolve from reptiles or insects is no more absurd than humans evolving from primitive mammalian creatures. An intelligent, self-aware reptilian being would thus

139

be related as closely to a lizard as a human would be linked to a lemur. A few of these species may have even reached a quasi-physical state of existence, perhaps able to inhabit both the ethereal and physical realms.

Descriptions of such different beings are readily evident throughout ancient records, with their seven individually distinct homeworld origins perhaps explaining the often-contradictory depiction of 'alien creatures' described throughout various accounts of different ancient cultures. Such beings were often reported to wear very simple attire without any jewelry or frivolous adornments, although 'devices' were described as being carried in many instances. Their clothing was usually described as resembling a functional jumpsuit or plain tunic, usually of a single metallic-appearing or reflective solid color, with either type of garment being worn by all members within their group. The Ancient Ones apparently emphasized function over show, and durability over comfort or luxury.

Numerous accounts state that one race of the Ancient Ones came from 'cloud ships' or 'cloud-borne chariots.'[8] Those beings were described as having a golden tint, or a brass-colored 'suntanned cast' to their skin. Eyes were slightly slanted upward, covered by very thick eye lids, with very thin lips the same color as their skin.[9] That description is not unlike modern accounts of the little gray alien beings associated with the present UFO phenomenon. The paintings of the oldest Egyptian gods tend to reflect a similar depiction, as do certain ancient rock drawings.

Due to the previously mentioned suppression and editing of ancient records, which redacted nearly all mention of the Ancient Ones, such beings can now be known only from indirect mention and veiled inferences. An examination of the few extant texts that tentatively identify the Ancient Ones will provide a better understanding of these descendants of the universe's *First Beings*. Those ancient references are typically in the form of descriptive titles or epithets, such as the records of the Egyptian god Thoth, in which they are referred to as the Seven Governors.[10] The

Ancient Ones were known by a wide variety of names, including the Primordial Seven and the Seven Sons.[11] Such terms simply refer to the seven surviving *First Being* species, the earliest progeny that existed during the most primitive eras of the universe. Those *Ancients* were the "first begotten, born from chaos and the Primordial Light" (the 'flash' from the Big Bang event).[12]

Other epithets referring to the Ancient Ones include the Primary Seven or the Great Seven.[13] According to Stanza V.1. of the *Book of Dzyan*, they were: "The Primordial Seven, the First Seven Breaths of the Dragon of Wisdom...." Another ancient Sanskrit fragment states: "The Seven Beings in the Sun are the Seven Holy Ones, Self-born from the inherent power in the matrix of Mother substance."[14] Beside the sun, other celestial bodies were also considered sacred, such as the seven stars of the Pleiades, which the Hopi Indians revered. The Hopi believed the seven stars that comprise the Pleiades symbolized the 'Harmonious Ones, the stars that Cling Together.'[15] Professor M. J. Dresden, who taught Oriental Studies at the University of Pennsylvania, noted a similar belief, referencing fragments from the cosmological portion of an ancient Persian myth written in the Sogdian language. That passage stated: "The twelve constellations [of the Zodiac] and the seven planets they made rulers over the whole Mixed World...."[16] Such a statement evidently referred to the seven homeworlds of the Ancient Ones, situated within a universe populated or mixed with a number of different species.

As late as the Middle Ages, the constellation Ursa Major, the Great Bear, was known as the 'Abode of the Seven Sages.' In India, Ursa Major's seven stars were known as the Seven Rishis.[17] That constellation contains the Swastika (aka the fiery wheel or cross), the ancient celestial formation that was associated with the administration of Divine Wisdom and Divine Rule, as well as the beings that came to teach such knowledge. *The Secret Doctrine* stated that the ancient Egyptians associated those same stars with the Seven Elemental Powers and the Mother of Time.[18] Reverence toward the Mother of Time (aka Mother of the Revolutions) focused on the constellation's northern quadrant where the 'Goddess of the Seven Stars first gave birth to time.'[19] Apparently, such archaic beliefs were references to the alliance of the seven *First Being* species that comprised the Ancient Ones. However, other ancient texts establish similar beliefs with Ursa Minor, the Little Bear. *The Mahabharata* associated Ursa Minor with the ancient supernatural divinities known as the Seven Seers.[20]

Hieroglyphic notations found engraved on the walls of the Temple at Edfu (the modern day Idfu) in Upper Egypt, credited its building's construction as the work of the Seven Sages.[21] Those records are perhaps best known from the excellent work of Professor E.A.E. Reymond, author of *The Mythical Origin of the Egyptian Temple*. The wisdom of the Seven Sages was a recurrent theme, revealing their great knowledge to be their special gift. The Seven Sages were additionally associated with the Egyptian *First Time*, the *Zep Tepi* (also *Tepi Zep* and *Tep Zepi*), a vague and remote time when gods ruled over a divine paradise on Earth. No additional mention of these Seven Sages is known from other Egyptian records, beside their tribute at Edfu. However, that group of beings is thought to be the same as the Seven Rishis found in India, as well as the seven Babylonian *Apkallu* that lived before the Great Flood,[22] the divine beings credited with building the great walls of Uruk, the sacred city of the gods.

The Ancient Ones were also known as the *Sephiroth*; the Builder gods; 'Builders'; or the 'Creators,'[23] an epithet not to be confused with the *Supreme Creator*, the Source of All. They were the Builders, the first constructive forces,[24] the 'builders' of the inventions, infrastructure, and knowledge that was brought to each of the different emerging worlds within the universe, 'creating' the cultures and civilizations on those planets. They were called the Great Builders and the Heavenly Architects in the esoteric texts of other ancient societies.[25] Sanskrit records state: "...Narayana (aka Caisha), the Seven-headed Intellect, the Creator (Builder) of all things throughout the universe, created man[kind], and placed [bestowed] within his body a living, imperishable spirit [soul]...."[26] Those Seven Builders were called the *Prajapatis* in other esoteric Sanskrit records, which also directly associated them with the Lunar Pitris.[27]

The process of imparting civilization and building productive cultures may have occurred on some 'divine' schedule. A Senzar commentary elaborating on certain passages within both the *Book of Dzyan* and the Puranas claimed that at the beginning of every cycle of 4,320,000 (unidentified units, perhaps years or other similar cyclic revolutions), the Seven great gods descend to establish the new order of things and give the impetus to a new cycle.[28] However Berosus, a Babylonian high priest, referenced Chaldean records that mentioned similar 'divine' cycles that only encompassed a period of 432,000 years.

Another passage associated with such cycles stated: "The Mighty Ones perform their great works, and leave behind them everlasting monuments to commemorate their visit, every time they penetrate within our [atmosphere]...."[29] The efforts performed by such Builders during their 'divine cycles' apparently included the enigmatic megalithic structures of Earth that confound archaeologists and historians. One of those groups of Builders was known collectively as the *mitimas*, which were associated with the Island of Titicaca in Lake Titicaca, according to oral traditions.[30] That group likely referred to both the Ancient Ones and their Helpers. Only later did the *mitimas* travel onto the mainland where they also built the megalithic city of Tiahuanaco on the southern shore of Lake Titicaca. Such commentaries suggest that the Ancient Ones were the true builders of those exquisitely ancient enigmatic structures of Earth.

Certain vague Senzar commentaries also allude to the possibility that those 'building' efforts were at the direction of the Creator. Commentary passages in the *Book of Dzyan* infer possible communication between the Supreme Creative Force and the Ancient Ones, a development that would have occurred during the early epochs of the universe after the Big Bang genesis. Much later writers also recorded other references to such possible contact. Clement of Alexanderia (aka Clemens Alexandrinus), an early initiated Father of the Church, wrote: "...these Heavenly Architects (the Ancient Ones), emanate from the Great Supreme Infinite One, and evolved the material universe from chaos."[31] Similar verification is found in the writings of Valentinus, the religious philosopher who discussed the power of the Great Seven, the ones *called* to bring forth this universe after [the Big Bang creation].[32]

The most archaic Sanskrit texts, including the *Book of Dzyan*, state that there are three main groups of these Builders, with each group divided into seven subgroups.[33] The first group rebuilt the universe after the self-destruction caused by the numerous non-surviving early *First Beings*. The second group brought civilization to the many infant races, as they emerged on their respective homeworlds throughout the universe. The third group seeded desolate celestial worlds to assure the continuation of later lifeforms.[34]

Passages from fragmented records attributed to the Egyptian god Thoth stated: "...the *Old Ones* (the Ancient Ones), whose origins were not of this world...were the wise spirits who descended from heaven to teach mankind, and later returned to their home among the stars."[35] Thoth further stated that prior to the beginning of all things, there existed a Dark Mist, a boundless chaos. Within that darkness, from the Great Mother (the Creator), every seed of creation came, which included the birth of all cosmic formations. Thoth also referred to the intended steps involved with the process of evolution, stating that initially there were lives devoid of sensation (perhaps referring to bacteria), and from that came lives possessed of intelligence.[36] According to the Phoenician historian, Sanchuniathon, that latter life was called *Zophasemin*, the 'Overseers of the Heavens,'[37] perhaps an explicit reference to the Ancient Ones.

The *Guardians* was yet another descriptive term used to indicate the Ancient Ones' role in civilizing emerging races. References to this group of teachers, which existed before the Great Flood, can be found in numerous ancient texts. The extra-Biblical *Book of Jubilees* elaborated upon those generations soon after the Great Flood. One of those accounts stated that Kainam, one of the later relatives in the lineage of Noah, found an inscribed record on a rock that was written before the Flood. That petroglyphic record contained 'the teachings of the Guardians.'[38] That same term is also found in Central America where it was used to describe the god Votan as a 'descendant of the Guardians,'[39] according to Mayan traditions. Similar descriptions included the Guardians of the Sky, the Holy Guardians, and the Brilliant Guardians.

Those same Guardians were further associated with Mars. Researcher and author Brinsley le Poer Trench reported that the earliest belief associated with Mars was its original role as the Guardian of the Solar System, not its association with war.[40] Likewise, its original 'sword' was the Sword of Wisdom,[41] not one of conquest. The Sword of Wisdom (aka Sword of Knowledge) reportedly cut through the dark cloud of ignorance, imparting knowledge.

Additional epithets of the Ancient Ones included the Great Ones, the Overseers of the World, the Rulers of Darkness, the Orbs of Wisdom, the Perfect Ones, the Senior Ones, the Transfigured Ones, and the Seven Sons of God. The Egyptian *Book of the Dead* refers to the Ancient Ones as the Masters, the souls of Osiris, and the Authors of Truth.[42] The Ancient Ones were also known as the Watchers over their many architectural achievements, but that term likewise referred to their Helpers, the enlightened 'infant race' of beings previously tutored by the Ancient Ones. Many of those enlightened Helpers or Watchers became the heroes of mythology and legend, the ones that became the early rulers, regents, or leaders of those contacted worlds.

They will also be discussed in more detail later in this writing.

The Shining Ones

The Ancient Ones were often described as shining, radiant, or brilliant; leading to their epithet as the Lords of Light or the Shining Ones. Perhaps the term *Shining Ones* was the most commonly used ancient reference to the Ancient Ones. Researcher and author W. Raymond Drake revealed that ancient Sanskrit texts made references to the 'Shining Ones on high,'[43] perhaps referring to their status aboard their mothership. Mr. Drake also stated that such beings were described in ancient India as 'golden gods.' In both the *Shi-Chi* and the *Han-Shu* texts of China, commentaries were recorded that referred to a 'gold-colored heavenly man.'[44] Chinese poetry written between 241 and 223 BC in the Chou (aka Ch'u) Court of Southern China, revealed a 'god of Radiant Splendor' that soared around the sky in his dragon chariot. That god lived in the House of Life where he was supreme within a group of gods known as *Di*, a pantheon that populated various regions of China along with the First Ancestors.[45] Similarly, Japan's Amaterasu, the mother of all the later gods, was described as a shining goddess of the sun.[46] Craft used by such gods were generally described as gleaming, golden ships.

Many of the oldest texts found in different ancient cultures also mentioned the Shining Ones. Chapter 134, section 15 of the Egyptian *The Book of the Dead* states: "...O ye Shining Ones, ye Men and Gods...." Many other testimonials mentioning the Shining Ones are also found in *The Book of the Dead*. Chapter 124, section 17, states: "I speak with the Shining Ones," while Chapter 78, section 14, proclaims: "I am One of those Shining Ones who live in rays of light...." From Chapter 125, section five, another passage states: "The holy Rulers of the Pylons (the four corners of the Earth) are in the form of the Shining Ones...." A similar epithet is found in *The Secret Doctrine*, where Osiris speaks of: "...the Seven Luminous Ones who follow their Lord, who confers justice."[47] The Shining Ones were described in other ancient Egyptian records as the Kings of Light, 'the gods whose forms are hidden.' They reportedly had blazing faces with two red eyes, enabling them to see at night, perhaps an archaic description of infrared night vision goggles. However, such beings eventually 'departed in wrath.'[48]

In Chapter 18 of the Egyptian *Papyrus of Ani*, references are made to: "...the Seven Shining Ones...the Holy Ones who stand behind Osiris,"[49] while further questioning if those beings are the 'ones beyond the constellation of the Great Bear in the northern sky.' According to renowned Egyptologist Sir Wallis Buge, numerous other ancient accounts also claimed that the celestial gods regularly appeared from the northern skies.

One of the most comprehensive Egyptian records that reveals the existence of the Ancient Ones is contained in the previously mentioned temple records of Edfu. The *Edfu Texts* reveal the existence of a group of wise beings known as the 'Shining Ones,' and specifically linked the *Shemsu-Hor*, the humanlike Helpers in Egypt, with those same Shining Ones, which were also known as the Lords of Light. Those texts also mention the 'Senior Ones,' evidently a reference to the 'elder gods' status of the Ancient Ones. The temple records from Edfu state: "...the Senior Ones who came into being at the beginning, who illuminated this land [the island Homeland of the Primeval Ones] when they came forth unitedly...."[50] Such a statement apparently and concisely identifies the Ancient Ones, and their 'united' educational and civilizing efforts, which are contained within the mandates of the Cosmic Order.

In olden Sanskrit accounts, the Ancient Ones are similarly portrayed as the Seven Sons of Light. Similar epithets are also found in the *Book of Dzyan*, where Stanza II.1. revealed the Ancient Ones to be: "The Builders, the Luminous Sons," while Stanza VII.1. referred to them as: "The mind-born sons of the first Lord; the Shining Seven." The *Book of Dzyan* also cites such

147

luminous beings as the Lords of the Flame and the Lords of Light.

Such Shining Beings are also mentioned in numerous religious texts. According to the *Book of Job*, the Bible originally called Lucifer the Son of Light, while Isaiah referred to him as the 'bright star of the early morning' and also as the 'Luminous Son of the Morning,' calling him Lux.[51] One definition of the name 'Lucifer' is the *Shining One*. Lucifer was apparently the highest divine being in heaven under the Creator, prior to his 'defeat and exile' from heaven. He was reportedly the first Archangel, older and higher than Yahweh. After his 'fall,' he was demonized by the Church and equated with Satan, the devil. Such action parallels the eradication plan implemented long ago by the BOPH gods. But this is not meant to imply that such an association with the devil, or pure Evil, should ever be considered a good thing; or as an actual association with the Ancient Ones, simply due to their demonization by the BOPH gods.

References to the Shining Ones are also found in *The Book of the Secrets of Enoch*. Chapter I, verse 6, states: "And there appeared to me two men, exceedingly big, so that I never saw such on Earth; their faces were shining like the sun, their eyes too were like a burning light...." Chapter XIX further described these beings as: "...seven bands of angels, very bright and very glorious, and their faces shining more than the sun's shining." The luminous condition of these 'glorious ones' may have been artificially created. In Chapter XXII, verse 9, Enoch is anointed with an ointment that "is more than the great light...like sweet dew, and its smell mild, shining like the sun's ray, and I looked at myself [Enoch], and was like one of His [the Creator's] glorious ones." Further, the term 'shining' may have an entirely different meaning in modern times, than its use during archaic times. Such a different meaning is implied in Ecclesiastics 8:1, which states: "...a man's wisdom maketh his face to shine"; perhaps equating knowledge with radiance.

The Eskimos claim that their ancestors were transported by great white birds from their homelands, which had been devastated by a flood, assisted by beings with shining faces who came from the stars.[52] Traditions of the Haida natives of British Columbia, Canada, describe 'wondrous beings' that arrived in flying machines shaped like discs.[53] According to W. Raymond Drake, those natives noted a distinction between the Great White Fathers (the gods) and the Shining Ones (the Ancient Ones) who merely accompanied them.

Island folklore and oral traditions reflect several migrations to Easter Island. The earliest inhabitants were an unknown antediluvian race known as *The Others*, who were survivors of the First Race,[54] and reportedly "possessed a superior knowledge of an entirely different world...one that existed amongst the stars."[55] They were described as very big men, but not giants, yellow in color, with long arms, great stout chests, huge ears, pure yellow hair, and hairless <u>shining</u> bodies. They occupied the island long before the next successive inhabitants.[56] Their tale is reminiscent of the previously mentioned Dogons and Ammonites that believe they descended from 'the Ones of the Shining Faces' who went 'back to the Source in the Heavens,' but promised to return and once again join with their faithful human followers.[57]

According to French scientist and author Jacques Bergier, accounts describing beings similar to the 'Shining Ones' continued into later times, with contact extremely active from 1000 to 1500 AD,[58] when it peaked or perhaps merely became better known with the early manifestations of Freemasonry during the 13th and 14th century. It is noteworthy that the Freemasons once called themselves the 'Sons of Light' and observed a calendar based upon a 'year of light' that began around 4000 BC. In the 19th century, the Freemasonry historian, George Oliver, stated: "The ancient Masonic tradition...says that our secret science existed before the creation of this globe and that it was widespread throughout other solar systems."[59]

People in the Middle Ages were believed to converse with luminous beings as naturally as they would with travelers from a foreign country. Those meetings inspired curiosity, but never evoked fear. Such creatures were always described as a species different than humans, wearing garments of light, and claiming to be 'messengers.' Reports claimed those messengers often met with Rabbis to debate the Jewish *Cabala*, discussing the nature of God and Earth's scientific knowledge. Those 'creatures of light' reportedly came to teach humankind, claiming they knew the Guardians of the Sky, but specifically stated that they themselves were not Guardians.[60]

The frequency of such visitations diminished as time passed. In the 17th century, reports in Europe were scarce, while none were reported during the 18th century.[61] The Japanese reported that similar luminous beings reappeared near the end of the 18th century,[62] while contemporary Native Indians of California had also described the arrival of 'luminous' humanoids, claiming that they often paralyzed humans with the 'aid of a small tube.'[63]

Chapter 15

The Serpent Symbol

Similar to the linguistic epithets that were utilized to denote or identify the Ancient Ones, a logo or symbol was also used, one that resembled a serpent shape. That ancient 'serpent logo' was extensively used to identify its wearer, or the bearer of such a symbol, as a representative of the *Tridasa* alliance, which spread the Cosmic Order. Such a logo, perhaps one similar to the *tilde* symbol, apparently resembled a serpent. The tilde symbol ~ is the squiggly or wavy line used as a linguistic diacritical mark to aid in word pronunciation. A comparable symbol is also used in mathematics to mean 'similar to,' or to indicate general equivalency. Humans could easily mistake such a symbol for a snake, leading to its connection or association with a serpent.

The Ancient Ones, as well as their followers, were often referred to as the Serpent People or the People of the Serpent. Originally, the serpent shape was the common symbol of wisdom throughout ancient cultures, while the much later Gnostic Christian sect equated the serpent with the Divine Instructor. According to *The Secret Doctrine*, the Gnostics acknowledged a wise and benevolent serpent, calling it: "...the Messiah of the Naaseni, whose symbol in heaven is Draco (the Dragon),"[1] unifying the serpent and dragon. Many ancient drawings depict snakes, serpents, or a related hybrid creature known as a dragon.

Such creatures were also consistently depicted with wings, apparently indicating their ability to fly. Other related images depicted a human upper torso ending with legs that transformed into snakes, creating a half-human, half-reptilian being intertwining those two species. Similarly, the previously mentioned Egyptian 'Sons of Light' were associated with the 'Serpents of the Clouds,' directly connecting those two epithets with a single entity, the Ancient Ones.

A modern connection to the snake symbol is found with the pale, short-stature humanoid 'aliens' that reportedly have large heads with almond-shaped eyes. Those beings are commonly called *Grays*, and believed to be otherworldly occupants of modern UFOs. They are often described as wearing a light-colored uniform with an insignia that consists of a coiled snake or serpent in the center of a Valentine-shaped heart.

Early South American explorers reported seeing numerous serpentine monsters depicted on statuary and plaques. Such drawings were found in the ruins of many ancient cities, exemplified by the figure of a flying dragon that was found near Chimbote in Northern Peru. Since the earliest times, the headstream of the Amazon was called the River of the Serpent, the symbol of both the Earth Mother and the Ancient Ones. The god of the Nahuatl natives, Quetzalcoatl, reportedly arrived in a vessel displaying a serpent that was carved on its bow. That god was also reported to have worn a gold band around his forehead, which was likewise in the shape of a serpent. Such adornments may be the reason he was named "the feathered (as in flying) serpent."

Legends claim that Quetzalcoatl was accompanied by a group of master builders, musicians, astronomers, mathematicians, and artists. They imparted laws; instructed humans to live moral lives; educated humans in the sciences and agricultural practices; and recommended a vegetarian diet rather than eating meat. That cautionary advisory may have been due to the simple lack of refrigeration during that time period. Without refrigeration, the spoilage of meat products would have posed serious risks of illness and disease.

The serpent symbol was also associated with a great white father called Saiyam Unicob, who was accompanied by a group of Helpers. Those white Helpers were known as the Adjusters, due to their ability to compensate for errors in the natives' calendar reckoning, and make realignments to sacred sites for observing celestial events. Kukulkan, a later bearded white god, then assumed those duties; developing the arts, sciences, and the governing system of the Mayans. The Quiché Mayans of Central America also associated the serpent or its symbol with their group of white gods led by Votan, according to the *Popul Vuh*. It is often believed that the name 'Votan' referred to a group of beings rather than an individual person, even though a specific being named Votan was sometimes characterized as the grandson of Quetzalcoatl. Such a person or group of superhumanlike beings 'taught many wondrous things' while living with the Mayans over a very long period of time. Upon their death, they were venerated as high priests, not gods.

The Mahabharata discussed the ritual killing of snakes that reportedly occurred shortly after the Big Bang event. It involved females of two different egg-laying species, one of snakes and the other of birds.[2] Perhaps some of the destructive actions involving the *First Beings* were not all self-inflicted, but may have also been the direct result of warfare between different worlds. References to such reptilian and avian species are numerous in ancient texts and oral traditions.

An African Ivory Coast tribe known as the Dans retain an oral tradition pertaining to their First Ancestors, a race of beautiful bird-humans that possessed great scientific knowledge.[3] On Easter Island, depictions of humanoid beings with hook-beak bird's heads are found around the Orongo village and nearby rocks. Numerous Birdman carvings were also found on the island, which were linked with an earlier race of beings that once inhabited that land. Similar Birdman cults or beings were also evident at Tiahuanaco and within the Chimu culture of coastal northern Peru, as well as from artistic pottery depictions made by the Peruvian Moche culture.

Sanskrit records are full of references to the People of the Snake or the Serpent People, sometimes simply called the Snakes. References are made throughout *The Mahabharata* to the Snakes, a mythical race of semi-divine serpentine beings that mostly dwell in the nether world, but are able to assume any form.[4] Other Sanskrit texts reveal that the Serpent People were a non-human race of wondrous beings that possessed immense cosmic wisdom.[5]

As previously stated, numerous ancient mythologies and oral traditions refer to the gods who descended from the heavens as the Dragon or Serpent People. One Hindu allegory pertaining to the Seven Headed Dragon is thought to refer to the Ancient Ones, with each head representing one race of the seven different species of *First Beings*.[6] As the symbol of the Ancient Ones, it is no surprise that the BOPH gods would later demonize that serpent symbol, portraying it as an evil entity or force, ultimately associating it with the devil. Such universal denigration of the serpent into a symbol of evil was a common theme in oratories, epic narratives, and drawings from ancient times. Such demonization is prominent in numerous olden accounts, evidenced by the serpent tempting Adam and Eve in the Garden of Eden, or the snake that stole the secret of immortality from Gilgamesh.

The use of the dragon as the national symbol of China seems to conflict with its later efforts to defeat all dragons. As mentioned earlier, many religious beliefs refer to the defeat of a dragon or serpent, such as Leviathan, Lotan, or other similar demons that were often depicted as 'seven-headed fiends.' In Revelations 12:3, the seven-headed monster of evil that emerged from the sea, perhaps the 'cosmic sea of outer space,' symbolized the evil to be vanquished by God. Such a creature was described as "...a great red dragon, having seven heads...and seven crowns...." A cylinder seal identified as "Number 14" from the Sumer and Akkad Kingdom, which dated to the 3rd millennium BC, depicts heroes vanquishing a seven-headed serpent monster.[7]

Numerous other cultures depict a serpent with seven heads, which were often described as heads of intellect. In parts of India, that serpent was called both Caisha and Narayana; while in the Yucatan, it was called Ahac-chapat. In other areas of India, along with Cambodia, it was named Naga, which was also the name of an earlier race of people in those territories. The Naga, Uigur, and Carian people, along with certain Mayan cultures, had uniformly depicted a similar 'unadorned serpent' known as Khanab.

The Greek Apollo overcame the serpent Python, while the Hindu Vishnu overcame Anatha (aka Ananda), the Naga serpent. Horus (Ra in other accounts) is also depicted as piercing the head of the serpent Aphophis. The serpent monster, Apep, was vanquished after its head was first pierced; its face split into two halves; with its head ultimately fatally crushed on its own land where it was dismembered. The god Aker helped defeat Apep using the 'darts of his beams,'[8] perhaps referring to a laser or photon weapon. Apep was assisted by his serpent 'fiends' Nekau and Tar, which were also defeated along with him. According to the Egyptian *Book of the Dead*, Fohat was identified with Toum, the Divider of the Earth, who also separated the universe into seven zones. Both Fohat and Toum were known as the "Great Ones of the Seven Magic Forces (who)...conquered the serpent Apep."[9]

Such manipulation, inversion, and reinterpretation of the ancient serpent symbol eventually degraded into the emblem representing evil, ultimately becoming associated with the devil. Such serpent demons were further described as participating in aerial battles in heaven. The rival groups that fought for Chinese rule were reportedly assisted by celestial beings utilizing fantastic weapons described as 'Dragons of Fire.' Those Chinese conflicts reportedly occurred in remotely ancient times, during the Age of Miracles. Researcher Peter Kolosimo reported that Chinese professor Tchi Pen-lao had dated such an 'Age of Miracles' to *c*.43,000 BC.[10]

Many ancient tales describe quarrels, discord, and even outright warfare between the gods. The Norse mythology known as the *Battle of the Flames* described struggles fought for control and supremacy over Earth's inhabitants. Stanza VI.6. in the *Book of Dzyan* cites similar battles fought for space. Perhaps dominion over Earth, as well as over other worlds, may have once been sought by extraterrestrial beings, through open acts of interplanetary warfare.

Religious Parallels

Still other references to the Ancient Ones can be detected in numerous archaic religious texts. The previously divulged demonization, suppression, usurpation, and editing done at the direction of the BOPH gods also affected most of those sacred records. While every religion contains an element of truth, their basis beliefs have also undergone certain changes over the ages. Such acts hid the very existence of the Ancient Ones, transferring their divinity to later mortals that then claimed all the prior achievements of the Ancient Ones as their own.

Many modern versions of those earlier religious beliefs have retained little of the original philosophy, teachings, and inspiration of their initial founders. Author and occult researcher, Eklal Kueshana (pen name of Richard Kieninger), suggested that Confucianism is one exception, remaining close to its founder's intent. Religion is primarily concerned with humankind's 'purpose' while on Earth, as well as with one's ultimate fate or destiny. Its offshoots, often consisting of cultists and fanatics, have unfavorably tainted many religions, alienating numerous people that might have benefited from their original covenants and ideology. The ensuing altered doctrines, upon which many of our modern religions operate, strive to keep humanity in bondage based on their misleading beliefs, which are often rooted in their desire to assert firm control over others. Salvation does not simply occur after we undergo the process of corporeal death, it must be earned by each entity. It is never attained merely through faith alone, but also requires some form of ongoing committed effort from each individual.

A universal element found in most religious records is the number seven, perhaps signifying the seven species comprising the Ancient Ones. The number seven is prominent in the Bible, the *Vedas*, and numerous other ancient religious texts. The Great Seven were the ones called to bring forth this universe after Arrhetos [the Ineffable], referring to the Big Bang creation.[11] According to Valentinus, the Gnostics knew of the powers of the Great Seven, "the self-evolving beings from the one Causeless Energy."[12] The Egyptian god Thoth referred to the Seven Governors as "the spirits which guide the operation of nature...and the animated atoms [of Life]...."[13] In Plato's *Timaeus*, Proclus quoted Iamblichus, stating: "The Assyrians have not only preserved the [270,000 years]...the whole apocatastases and periods of the Seven Rulers of the world."[14] This 'seven ruler' concept may have inspired the ancient custom of grouping divine kings into seven great dynasties, a belief tradition held by numerous advanced ancient cultures.

In certain Hindu texts, the Ancient Ones were also known as the *Saptarishis*,[15] the Seven Rishis of the Stars, whose Helpers were subordinate angels or messengers of the Rishis. The Hebrew mystics associated with the *Cabala* called the Ancient Ones the 'Seven Pillars of Wisdom.' In other ancient esoteric texts, the Ancient Ones were referred to as the Primary Seven, the beings that self-evolved from the one causeless Force (the Creator). The Ancient Ones were apparently also the model from which the Zoroastrian Seven Amshaspends were formed, although that concept underwent much distortion and change by the BOPH gods who ultimately usurped that prior group's title.

A similar evolution evidently occurred with the name *Archon*, which also changed over the years. Originally, the term apparently referred to the Ancient Ones, as evident from the writings of Basilides, the early 2nd century AD Christian mystic and Gnostic writer whose thoughts were similar to Aristotle. He wrote about the 'Great Archon,' the Head of the World that broke forth from the Seed of the World (perhaps referring to the universal spore). The Great Archon was also known as 'Lord and Ruler,' as well as the *Intelligent Architect*, who set about to create the world after the upper world (the universe resulting from the Big Bang event) was formed by the "No-being God" (The Creator).[16]

The Creator predestined the Great Archon (the Ancient Ones) as part of the original Master Plan. That was apparent from Basilides' claim: "The creation being finished, there arose out of the seed a 'Second Archon,' designated as the Hebdomad."[17] It remains unclear if he was referring to a second generation 'divine group,' such as the Helpers of the Ancient Ones, or a separate species (or 'son') of the Ancient Ones, one not associated with the coalition that formed their Cosmic Order. However, he also referred to a 'Third Sonship,' which was further described as the Spiritual Men left here to guide and perfect the souls inhabiting developing worlds.[18]

Other ancient records also reference the Archons, such as the writings of the Egyptian god Thoth, collectively known as the Hermetic Writings. Those records discuss the Seven Rulers of Fate, the Seven Rulers of the Spheres, and the Seven Planetary Rulers; referring to them as the powers of Harmony and the Archons of the Seven Planets, who are also credited as the source of humankind's evil tendencies.[19]

According to the Gnostic record derived from the Nag Hammadi texts, the Archons (aka Archontes) were Rulers or gods. A passage in the *Apocryphon of John*, a part of the Nag Hammadi record, stated: "And the Archons created Seven Powers for themselves, and the powers created for themselves six angles for each one until they became 365 angles."[20] Later, the Archons were generally equated with the Elohim, the Fallen Angels; while later still the term 'Archon' simply became a common reference to any high Athenian magistrate or ruler.

Similar usurpation of the Ancient Ones' epithets also permeated many extra-Biblical texts, where the Elohim, the humanlike beings that were either the trusted Ancient Ones' Helpers or the BOPH gods, were occasionally described as the 'Genii of the Seven Planets.' However, the Genii were also identified as 'the Sons of Light,'[21] clearly referring to the Ancient Ones. Although the 'Genii of the Seven Planets' epithet was later usurped by the BOPH gods, its original use referenced the Ancient Ones and their seven distinct homeworlds, which olden accounts described as 'sacred planets.'

Many ancient cultures believed that the universe was 'set-in-order' through a certain mathematical formula and corresponding musical patterns. Specific references made about 'the seven planets that rule the destiny of mortals' stated that such worlds possessed a harmonious motion with "...intervals corresponding to musical diastemes."[22] According to ancient Sanskrit commentary, 'diastemes' evidently referred to certain harmonic lengths of musical strings. But it may also be an ancient inference to String Theory, a speculative supposition offered by our modern astrophysicists. That concept will be discussed in greater detail later in this writing. Still other accounts evidently pertained to constellations or specific star systems where early life had first evolved, along with an inherit trait for self-destruction, which was apparently overcome through eventual obtainment of higher enlightenment levels.

This speculative 'seven planet' conclusion is based on extrapolations from ancient texts, suggesting seven original homeworlds for the seven distinct species of *First Beings*, which later collectively formed the *Tridasa* coalition that then created the *Cosmic Order*. This is derived from Stanza VII.1. in the *Book of Dzyan*, which refers to the 'First Lord' as the Shining Seven, the Builders: "They, who watch over thee, and thy mother Earth." Other references in Stanza V of that text also refer to the Seven Sons, and discuss the Primordial Seven. Such notations refer to the seven primordial self-born gods, the species that survived to their next level of enlightenment without the assistance or aid from 'outside influences,' because they were the first, existing before such help was available.

The *Cabala* makes reference to 'the seven other revealed inhabited worlds,' further collaborating this speculative assumption. Those seven worlds may also represent the sole sources from which all life in the universe emerged, either through their seeding efforts, or direct relocation of lifeforms from planet to planet. Another epithet, the Seven Great Logoi, reportedly embodied every possible manifestation of physical life, those that were capable of existing within the known material universe.

The *Book of Job*, believed to be one of the oldest works in the Hebrew canon, speaks of the making of Arcturus, Orion, and the Pleiades. Job referenced the 'sweet influences of the Pleiades,' the 'seven stars beyond the Bull,'[23] which are somehow connected with certain mystic principles of nature, especially with sound. The Hindus of India used the rising of the Pleiades, which they called *Krittika*, to regulate their months and years. Another reference to a vague location or homeworld of the Ancient Ones is found in Isaiah 13:5, "They come from a far country, from the end of heaven, even the Lord...."

Actual locations of the seven homeworlds of the Ancient Ones remain unknown, but certain repetitive mention and popular focus on specific celestial bodies might provide a clue. A somewhat contradictory passage in Professor Mead's book, *Thrice-Greatest Hermes*, may refer to the homeworlds of the Ancient Ones. That passage states: "Each of the [Seven] Planetary Spheres is a complete World containing a number of divine offspring, which are invisible to us, and over all of these Spheres the Star we see is the Ruler."[24] Apparently all but one of the original solar systems containing the Ancient One's homeworlds are so distant (or now extinct) they can not be seen on Earth, except for one that is evidently visible. That observable solar system seemingly contained the planet where the then present 'Ruler over Earth' (or perhaps over the Cosmic Order coalition) originated.

According to Enoch, the constellation from which our first ancestors came was the star Altair.[25] Great attention was also focused on the Sirius, Orion, and Bootis star systems. The center of our region of the universe was thought to be at Alcyone, the brightest of the seven stars of the Pleiades. Specific tales from antiquity actually state that divine visitors to Earth had their home within the Pleiades. Subsequent South American natives believed that the earliest ancient Peruvians were descendants of the gods from the Pleiades. According to Peruvian legends, the Pleiades were considered to be the 'Celestial Gates' of heaven. Additionally, a later Mayan tradition actually claimed that 400 of their youths had returned to the Pleiades.[26]

The Boötes constellation was also a focus of much ancient interest. One of its stars, Epsilon Bootis, was called Izar, while its largest and brightest star, Alpha Bootis, was called Arcturus. Some texts specifically state that Arcturus was the home of the gods. Islamic texts of the *Annunciation* reference Archangel Gabriel as being directly associated with the star Arcturus. Other stars that were of specific interest to archaic cultures included Vega, Castor, Antares, Aldebaran, Capella (the goat star), Betelgeuse, Regulus (the King's star), Rigel, and Fomalhaut.

Another candidate, but from more modern times, includes Zeta 1 and Zeta 2 Reticuli, the binary star system in the constellation Reticulum. Betty and Barney Hill, the famous couple that claimed to have been 'abducted' by a UFO in 1961, reportedly identified that system from star charts revealed by their 'host' aliens. This system is visible in the Southern Hemisphere of the celestial vault, between the two bright stars Achernar and Canopus. Some also associate the Zeta Reticuli system with the 'gravity-defying' spacecraft that are supposedly housed at Area 51, the reportedly secret government research complex located in the Nevada desert. At least one informant, supposedly a former employee at the secretive Area 51 base, divulged that such 'gravity wave generating' craft either came from Zeta Reticuli, or were based solely on their technology;[27] perhaps indicating its status or reputation as some sort of recognized cosmic UFO Motor City, but apparently without company recalls, union strikes, or fuel economy mandates.

In 1960, Project Ozma was formed to search for extraterrestrial signals using radio telescopes. The program first focused on Epsilon Eridani and Tau Ceti; star systems about 11 light years from Earth.[28] According to Dr. Frank Drake, the program director, intelligently coded signals were recorded from the Epsilon Eridani system on the first day of operation. However, other reports claimed those signals were of Earth origin, upon which the project was abruptly termination shortly later, after only 150 hours of cosmic searching.[29] Russian astronomer, Joseph Shklovsky, reasoned that Epsilon Indus, Tau Ceti, and Epsilon Eridani are likely candidates to support intelligent beings, based on his theory requiring a minimum distance of ten light years between civilizations, a belief also held by American scientist, Professor Robert N. Bracewell.[30]

The oral traditions of early natives in New Zealand, Lapland, and the Americas all describe visitors from the stars, often alluding to seven different stars or constellations as their sources. The Hopi clan of the Pueblo Indians revered the *Choochokam*, the seven stars of the Pleiades, a celestial region that also inspired great interest among numerous other olden cultures. Despite not knowing the exact locations of the seven homeworlds of the Ancient Ones, the younger emerging worlds they contacted and ultimately brought into the Cosmic Order are evidently countless in number. *The Mahabharata* talks of such planets and their inhabitants, stating: "Infinite is the space populated by the Perfect Ones and gods; there is no limit to their delightful abodes."[31]

Chapter 16

The Creator

The concept of physical creation and its author, The Creator, apparently permeated the traditions and beliefs of numerous ancient cultures. Archaeological evidence suggests that early humans possessed a basic belief in some form of Higher Power from which everything emanated. That source is known as the Creator, an unseen Entity that remains formless and incomprehensible.

Our universe is too structured and orderly to have simply occurred from some random act. Examination of the intricate process associated with the Big Bang event seems to confirm the likelihood of its orchestration by a higher intelligence. The resulting universe is believed to be part of the infinite domain of the Creator, which comprises everything from the smallest particle to its very largest one. Its physical boundary apparently encompasses the Big Bang point of origin, while extending outward in every direction to the farthest edges of our cosmos. Yet the Creator apparently existed before such a vast physical universe began, so the Creator's domain must also extend beyond or 'outside' this material world, perhaps to some unseen spiritual realm.

Modern anthropologists have noted a metaphysical spirit as an underlying element within humanity's most ancient beliefs, one that also included a superior order to which all matter in the universe is subjected.[1] Some believe that all physical particles will ultimately be reabsorbed by the Creator, with everything reverting back from which it came, perhaps also eliminating the physical realm in the process. Since the Creative Force is able to be in all places simultaneously, there would never be a reason for the Creator to take physical form, an act that would impose limits on the Limitless. Hence, the physical domain appears to be merely a transitory one.

Moreover, the earliest detectable spiritual concept held by primitive humans, as related to their mortal existence, reflected a belief in only a finite animation of the physical body. That belief was also accompanied by an inference that some non-physical life force was further associated with each entity. That unseen commodity, which some ancient cultures called the *Inner Man*, continues to exist after physical death through the human *soul*, inhabiting an unseen realm for at least a temporary period, before some rejuvenation or transformation process again occurs. That ancient concept is the very essence of the modern reincarnation belief. A later corruption of this very basic concept apparently occurred through its degradation and distortion by later human clergy, which created numerous imagined after-life 'lands' of either a paradise or an atrocity, to which the deceased entity would then inhabit.

An old and revered document from Gnostic esoteric belief, the *Pistis-Sophia*, stated: "The Astral Ruler(s) of the [universe] created [souls] from [Its] own substance…endowing the monads (all animated soul-bearing creatures) with a spark of the Divine Light,"[2] the very substance of the Creator. Hence, the Creator's essence apparently permeates all matter throughout the universe. Yet such a Creator is incomprehensible to physical beings, and therefore can not be fully understood or described with tangible terms. Further, humanity does not yet fully understand its own nature, and therefore may be presently incapable of truly knowing the Creator. As an incomprehensible entity, the Creator can not be described or named. Such a limitation has been accepted down through the ages, as expressed by Lao-tzu in 604 BC when he stated that the Creator is the *Nameless*.[3] But such a fundamental ambiguity and anonymity also allowed certain

beings with personal motives to falsely identify or name the Creator for their own purpose.

From the earlier review of the ancient *Cosmic Evolution* that explained the Big Bang event recorded in the *Seven Stanzas of Creation* from the *Book of Dzyan*, it was clear that the Creator was not one of the Ancient Ones. The Creator was perhaps an ethereal entity of pure energy, the designing Architect that planned our physical realm. The Creator apparently brought about our material realm as a deliberately planned result of the Big Bang energy release. This all-powerful Entity was known by many different archaic names, such as All-Maker, The Supreme, The One, or The Source. However, the use of the term *God* is a relatively later occurrence, and may have started as a descriptive designation referring to superior physical beings that are above humans, but below the divine level of the Creator.

Still later, the meaning of the word *God* came to represent the unseen highest authority within that collection of superior physical beings, and even later began to signify the Creator. The use of such nomenclature invokes an image of a physical being, which may be erroneous. Pure energy would need neither shape nor vessel to exist, and would be more restrained in any physical form than in its pure energy state. Since the Creator apparently existed before the Big Bang event, such an Ultimate Essence would appear to be beyond any physical reality or form.

Archaic texts clearly differentiate between the Creator and the Ancient Ones. The olden commentaries accompanying the *Book of Dzyan* stated that the Creator was: "...the Initiator, ...sitting at the threshold of Light...from within the circle of Darkness"[4] who conceived and implemented the Big Bang event from which the universe was created. The seven self-born primordial 'gods' (the seven species of Ancient Ones) then resulted from that original Big Bang event initiated by the Creator. But thereafter, everything else essentially relied upon the efforts of those *Primordial Seven*, the Ancient Ones, the Builders of that 'created' physical universe.

While the Creator conceived and initiated the Big Bang event to form the physical realm, it was the Ancient Ones who were the actual 'Builders' of the worlds within our universe. These Builders 'created' the civilizations, cultures, inventions, and collections of knowledge (albeit with the probable inspiration or perhaps specific revelations from the Creator). These Builders of the universe were also known as the Universal Mind, referring to their common mindset and unified mission, one perhaps somehow ultimately directed or inspired by the Creator.

The Cabala seems to confirm this belief, stating that the Creator did not produce a 'finished' world, only the fundamental elements from which material worlds would eventually form after many millions of years.[5] Once such 'raw' worlds were formed, it required physical life forms to actually build those worlds into useful and productive places. This does not imply that such a designed process was not the original intent of the Creator, one in which all the necessary pieces were provided to subsequently produce the resultant numerous and pre-planned creations.

Some may question if the Creator was unwise in working only on the 'minor details' leading to the Big Bang genesis, while leaving the important formative work to the 'secondary forces,' the Builders (the Ancient Ones). Recognizing the limited human understanding of the complexity behind the genesis event, it is now apparent that no physical being could have envisioned its infinite number of variables, or supplied the required natural laws and formulas to regulate such an ensuing massive and intricate grand process. Only the Creator was capable of such a task.

The Ancient Ones may have had direct contact with the Creator during some early formative period of the universe, as part of an overall Master Plan. A confusing passage made in Stanza IV. 2. of the *Book of Dzyan* states: "Learn what we who descend from the Primordial Seven... born from the Primordial Flame [the Sons of the Fire], have learnt from our fathers." This passage has been interpreted by some to conclude that certain later generations of Ancient Ones were told that their ancestral

'Primordial Seven' forefathers might have once received instructions directly from the Creator. Colonel James Churchward alluded to an ancient Naacal tablet from India that referred to the Forces (presumed to be the Ancient Ones) that 'came directly from the Creator,' after which the tablet stated: "...and when this was accomplished, they (apparently the Ancient Ones) were given charge of the physical universe."[6]

Those 'first' Ancient Ones may have agreed to undertake, or been charged with the task and duties of continuing the work of the Creator within the physical world; spreading civilization, order, and knowledge throughout the universe. Other vague Sanskrit references allude to such an imparted assignment, as does Valentinus, the Greek religious philosopher who claimed to have been privileged to esoteric knowledge and teachings associated with Jesus. Valentinus discussed the powers of the Great Seven, evidently the Ancient Ones, who were "called to bring forth this universe"[7] after the Big Bang genesis. The Ancient Ones may further be undergoing a learning process themselves, exploring all varieties of intelligent life and different perspectives offered by each distinct lifeform and their various cultures within our vast universe.

As the Creator's 'instruments' within the physical world, the Ancient Ones implemented the Creator's Will and Master Plan for the universe. They taught infant races that the spirit or soul of each physical entity never died, and was released after the death of its material vessel, returning to the Great Source, the Creator. Between each mortal life there was a veil of darkness. Material life was intentionally short, allowing rejuvenation of each individual essence to continue and eventually complete its character perfection by learning all things and acquiring enlightenment.

At that point when each entity's deficiencies were fully corrected and all knowledge was learned, reincarnation of such a perfected soul would only be to participate in those duties of the divine Ancient Ones, spreading harmony and knowledge to others. Such a Master Plan involves many reincarnated lives along such a continuing journey to eventually reach perfection, though not always within the same species, or on the same planet.

It may have been the Creator who assigned the Ancient Ones their task to instruct all the infant races. Their duties were to civilize aspiring emerging cultures they encountered, educating their populace, and instilling ethical and secular values within their character composition by teaching 'right from wrong.' Such duties were called 'circular errands' in ancient Sanskrit texts, referring to tasks that never ended. When an infant race became civilized and brought into self-sustaining compliance with the Cosmic Order, the Ancient Ones' work would once again start over with another emerging world elsewhere within the universe.

Such duties were performed by the Ancient Ones, according to the *Rig Veda* in 10.90.14, which states: "...they (the gods, meaning the Ancient Ones) set the worlds in order." Note the plural use of the word *worlds*, referencing the fact that planets beside Earth were also provided with order. *Rig Veda* hymn 6.55.1 also relates the importance of Order (Rta) by "sending the charioteer of Order to carry the unharnessed [chaotic] child to be joined." Perhaps this is a reference to the Ancient Ones as the Charioteer, spreading the Cosmic Order to emerging worlds, referring to inhabitants of those planets as 'chaotic children.'

Evidently not all the *First Being* species had followed the commands of the Creator. A significant minority, apparently one-third of the *First Beings*, who evidently were all from a single species of *First Beings*, disobeyed the Creator's wishes. Stanza VI.5. of the *Book of Dzyan* states: "...the sons are told to create their images, one-third refuses...two obey." This rebellious *First Being* species evidently also refused to cooperate with the alliance of the Ancient Ones, the Cosmic Order. That insubordinate species is identified from other vague passages as the *Destroyers* or the *Devourers*, and will be discussed in greater detail in a subsequent chapter.

168

It must be stressed that the Ancient Ones were not considered 'gods.' They were categorized as 'divine beings,' referring to their position as emissaries directed by the Creator to carryout the Divine Plan. The term 'divine,' meaning "of the Creator," signified the highest level of physical life within the universe, sent by the Creator to express Its will (ethereal entities have no gender). Later, the term was used to denote all beings above humans, but below the level of the Creator. That expanded concept of divinity then encompassed the humanlike Helpers of the Ancient Ones, and hence also applied to their 'distant cousins,' the BOPH beings. Once the BOPH beings enacted the temporary exile of the Ancient Ones from Earth, they elevated themselves to the higher level of 'gods,' a level above all other physical beings on Earth. Further degradation of the term ensued, referring to any loyal associate of those 'gods' as 'divine beings.' Such beings later became known as the Anunnaki, Igigi, Nefilim, genii, angels, and numerous other 'divine' terms.

The oldest records of humanity only used the term 'Creator' when referring to or describing the sole Supreme Being of our universe. The Ancient Peruvians called the Creator of the world Pachacamac, signifying: "He who animates the universe."[8] The personification of physical gods emerged after $c.3350$ BC, due to a lack of differentiation between the Creator and those later physical beings that displayed superhuman abilities. That marked the transference of divinity from the ethereal to the physical realm, although the one and only Creator would never have a reason to confine Its essence within a physical vessel. Many extant ancient texts that retained their original composition, those not subjected to later revisionist alterations, clearly concede that such physical gods could not be the Creator, the ultimate Supreme Entity. References contained in Christian Gnostic texts are perhaps the most specific statements reflecting this fact, and will be examined in the next chapter.

The Ancient Ones themselves revealed that 'The Supreme' was the Creator, an entity that they did not refer to as 'God,' but only as *The Creator*. The term *God* simply appears to be a much later classification devised by humans or some other physical beings, with its actual meaning altered or augmented numerous times over the ages. Perhaps its later evolution was mortal humankind's attempt to explain and elevate certain physical beings to a higher level of adoration or power. The Greek term *dios*, meaning god, was derived from the Sanskrit word *div*, meaning shine or bright. It is likely that this descriptive term initially referred to the Ancient Ones, based on their epithet as the Shining Ones. While the Ancient Ones were divine beings, they were neither gods nor The Creator, and never claimed such status.

The concept of a universal Godhead was first reported in the *Pyramid Texts*, with the oldest extant reference dated to *c*.2500 BC, one believed to be a reaffirmation or 'copy' of an earlier record from *c*.3100 BC; although its origin definitely dated to predynastic times, before such written records. This cosmogonic concept is known as *The Lineage of Horus*, which reveals a group of nine gods called the *Ennead*, which includes: Shu, Tefnut, Geb, Nut, Osiris, Isis, Seth, Nephthys, and Horus. But this lineage also revealed a tenth god, Atum. According to the *Pyramid Texts*, Atum is the Very Old One, the One, the Oldest One, the Lord of All, the Great One, and the Primeval One. Atum was born before heaven, Earth, the gods, humans, or before anything else came into existence. Atum means "the one who has been completed by absorbing others."[9] Atum was also the concept of the first living beings, the *Divine Ones* from which the genealogy of the gods emerged. Such a definition implies that those divine ancestors were not gods themselves, but their later lineage or descendants apparently became gods. Other specific references to the Creator appear throughout the *Pyramid Texts*, stating that the Creator was "He whose name is not known,"[10] the highest entity throughout the universe.

Previous mention was made of Professor Rudolf Anthes' observation that the composition of the *Pyramid Texts* gave the impression of a break or interruption within the middle of its

170

writing. The first portion was an account of divine beings, while its second section is a story of humans and the influence of a sole deity, Osiris, on their earthly lives. From that composition, later texts expanded on the influence of the 'gods' over the lives of mortal humans. Those records and accounts, which were recorded during later times, contained the most inconsistencies, alterations, and contradictions. Such a break tends to indicate numerous combinations of separate accounts or changes made to an earlier original record. That interruption could help explain the *Pyramid Texts'* description of two different entities being combined into one being. Those two entities are believed to be the Creator and the Ancient Ones. Additionally, the perceived 'break' in that text would likely signify the assumption of power or change of influence over Earth by the BOPH gods, which was appropriated from the Ancient Ones after their temporary exile.

Chapter 17

Personified Gods

God eventually became the term used by later humans when referring to the Creator. After a long duration, during which the Supreme Entity was known only as the Creator, the terms God and the Creator became interchangeable, referring to the same Divine Entity. Sometime between those two distinct periods, a physical god or group of gods reigned over Earth. Most ancient accounts record periodic changes in either this sole God or in the leadership over a group of gods. Yet, those records seemingly still suggest a distinct difference between God and the Creator.

The personification of those 'divine beings' was in the image and likeness of humans, or *vice versa*, depending on one's perspective. Humans were even thought to be descendants of those divine beings, producing myths stating that mankind was created by various acts of the gods or God. Numerous other myths proposed that man was formed from the dust or clay of Earth. The idea that humans were brought into existence from clay first appeared in Egypt around 2000 BC, as an act by their creator god, Khnum. Later, that same concept again emerged within the Old Testament of the Hebrew Bible.

The abstract principle of a sole Universal Deity, a supreme Godhead, is a concept or belief in an entity without finite form. Even with such an unknowable aspect of God, most philosophers and many theologians believe that a limited knowledge of God is possible. The basis for such speculative but conceptual comprehension may arise from mystical experiences, revelations, visions, or from a 'sense of presence.' Perhaps renowned mythologist Joseph Campbell best defined the concept of God, describing God as a metaphor for a mystery that absolutely transcends all human categories of comprehension or thought.[1] Thus, God became a creation of man, shaping God into humanity's notion of what a Supreme Entity or Higher Power should be.

But the Creator was never a male or female of any specific race or ethnicity, nor a physical form of any particular species. Sanskrit texts refer only to an 'image' of God, not a descriptive depiction. Thus, any specific physical description or gender conferred upon the Supreme Being undoubtedly referred to a 'lesser' divinity or god. By any name, there is only one Creator. But the term 'god' could be personalized, becoming either gender, or assuming any form; while being known by any number of different names, or perhaps even as a number of different species.

The early Hebrew understanding of God was anthropomorphic. While their interpretation made God a living being, it also limited God, as did the contractual covenants binding Him with His people. Any personification or physical manifestation of God within the finite order of the universe would always limit that Higher Power. But such personification is evident throughout many ancient texts, in which the gods were depicted as physical beings. Those gods lived among the humans of Eridu, Sumer, Akkad, Ur, and other Mesopotamian city-states. Similar occasional appearances by humanlike physical beings identified as gods or God were also reported in Egypt, Canaan, Turkey, and other Near Eastern countries.

The chief deity or leader of those physical gods would also change periodically, with replacement by another physical being. He was Yahweh of the Hebrews, Marduk of Babylonia, Ra of the Egyptians, Ahura Mazda of the Persians, or Zeus of the Greeks. Although those chief gods were apparently not the Creator, they later evolved into a universal Godhead, the true nature of the Creator. That evolution was similar to the manner in which a flat-Earth belief did not alter the reality of a spherical world, just as the many variants of past gods, by any name, did not alter the factual nature of the real Godhead, the Creator. Whatever the evolutionary path taken from primitive god to Cosmic Godhead, the Judeo-Christians and Muslims, along with many other major religions, ultimately arrived at the universal reality and true nature of the Creator.

That evolutionary path had one notable exception with the Hindu belief of India. According to the *Vedas*, Hinduism taught belief in only one Supreme Entity, the Creator (Brahma), right from its start; along with lesser divine beings or deities that had obtained a higher enlightenment level, possessing greater abilities than those of mortal humans. Brahma was always the absolute reality from which all else flowed, an unseen Creator beyond comprehension or description. The great Hindu gods Vishnu, Shiva, Indra, and the goddess Devi were believed to be emanations or 'creations' of the Creator, Brahma. However, certain Hindus did believe that the Supreme Entity, the All-Father, was a trinity comprised of Vishnu, Shiva, and Brahma. Although a few temples were erected to honor Brahma, no personification of this Creator God is known, and therefore, no Hindu myths concerning a physical manifestation of Brahma have ever been found.

A similar belief can be detected within the Christian Gnostics' concept of an original but unknowable divinity, the Creator, along with several levels of 'lesser divinities.' Valentinus described the Creator as the "...[Root] of the All, the [Ineffable One who] dwells in the Monad. [He dwells alone] in silence...since, after all, [he was] a Monad (a single unit), and no one was before him...."[2] The Creator was the 'God beyond God,' referring to that latter God as the lesser god of Earth. Such a god of Earth was believed to be a lesser divine being that served as the instrument of the higher powers.[3] Those 'higher powers' were below the supreme level of the Creator, but above the lesser god of Earth. Valentinus further clarified the distinction between such levels of divinity, stating that the lesser god reigns as king and lord, acting as a military commander, who gives the law and judges those who violate it; referring to the chief god who ruled over Earth. Valentinus believed that 'commander king' was the God of Israel, Yahweh.[4]

Mormon doctrine describes God as a physical humanlike being that interacted with humans on Earth around c.2500 BC. That God was a being of the same form from which humans were fashioned. Although later Mormon commentators interpreted that specific humanlike being to have been Jesus, that would require Jesus to have appeared in physical form about 2,500 years prior to His actual birth, thereby disaffirming Him as the truly begotten human Son of God.

Still other personifications of the Supreme Being involved a gender change. Numerous accounts, perhaps even a majority, refer to the Creator, as well as a certain leader of the Ancient Ones, as being female. The Nazarenes, an early mystic Christian sect with doctrines similar to Gnosticism, professed that Earth's various evolutionary or creative stages were the result of interventions by a female divinity or spirit, the Spiritus (believed by many to be the Mother Goddess). She was further described as an evil power and influence over Earth. They knew of various different phases, levels, or versions of humans; believing that the newest or latest man, the ones created by or from the Lunar Pitris, was inferior. They believed that such an inferior version did not possess a divine soul, meaning they were not 'heavenly men.' Such a belief may have reflected the BOPH god's demonization of the Ancient Ones and their earlier 'creation' of humans, prior to the widespread interbreeding of the BOPH beings with those later humans.

The Creator was often given feminine personification, as stated in Stanza VII.1. of the *Book of Dzyan*: "Behold the beginning of sentient formless life. First the Divine, the one from the Mother-Spirit...." Another feminine reference is found in Stanza IV.4, which referred to: "the Divine Mother of the Seven," meaning the source of the Ancient Ones. A very similar statement is found in the Egyptian *Book of the Dead*, which states: "...in the great mother, all the gods, and the *seven great ones* are born."[5] The *Trimorphic Protennoia*, a Gnostic text from the Nag Hammadi documents, quotes the Divine Mother stating: "I am Protennoia the Thought that dwells in the Light...she who exists before the All...I am the Invisible One within the All."[6] Such female attributes assigned to the Creator may have been the impetus behind the ancient practice of Mother Goddess veneration.

The Hindu Virgin, Kanya-Durga, was one of the most ancient goddesses, perhaps a prototype for many of the later Mother Goddess cults. She was believed to be the same goddess referenced in the *Sibylline Books*.[7] A form of universal restoration was associated with the return of this virgin goddess. Perhaps such a notion refers to the return of the Ancient Ones, after some passage of time or future conflagration. If indeed the earliest representatives or perhaps the majority of Ancient Ones on Earth were females, they may have been the inspiration for the term 'The Mother of Invention.'

Perhaps the Mother Goddess (aka Great Mother or Earth Mother) was the earliest venerated figure on Earth. Evidence of such reverence first appeared in the early Stone Age Gravettian cultural epoch around 24,000 BC, and continued uninterrupted to at least 3500 BC, with later revivals persisting into modern times. Evidence of such adoration has been found throughout Europe and the Near East, and was believed to have been the focus of worship by the Indus Valley culture. Mother Goddess figurines were also found in Baluchistan, Elam, the Balkans, Egypt, Mesopotamia, Cyprus, Crete, and the Cyclades, all dating from those region's earliest known periods; and later between 2000 and 1200 BC throughout more widely scattered areas. The Indian Mother Goddess was not Aryan in origin but pre-Aryan, and is different from any other female deity within the *Rig Veda*.[8] In modern non-Aryan Southern India, the Mother Goddess is still highly venerated.

Robert Graves stated in his *The Greek Myths* that ancient Europe did not have gods, only the Great Goddess or Mother Goddess. Perhaps that goddess became the Greek Hestia of the Hearth, whose symbol was the omphalos (navel-boss), a conical white mound symbol found at Delphi. The Sumerian Mother Goddess was Belili, the creator of the world, with Bel becoming her subsequent masculine version.[9] The original Belili later became known as the Babylonian Tiamat. The historian Berosus identified this female goddess as Thalatth. She was reported to have been from "one of the seven planets of the ancient world,"[10] evidently meaning she was an Ancient One. Sesha, the Seven-headed Dragon, may have been Tiamat's equivalent within the Hindu belief. Each of her seven heads was said to represent a 'race' or species of the original *First Beings*. Ananta, the Serpent of Eternity, became her later version.

Another equivalent to Tiamat is evident in a Pelasgian Creation myth where Eurynome, "the Goddess of All Things, rose naked from Chaos."[11] She created the seven planetary powers (believed to be the Ancient Ones), setting a Titaness (goddess) and a Titan (lord) over each. According to Hopi belief, when Earth was first created, it was created 'female' as our Mother Earth. Sotuknang, apparently an Ancient One, was then appointed to be Earth's earliest tutelary deity, and was instructed to make Mother Earth become fertile.[12] Later, that Hopi name (Sotuknang) became the term used to refer to all the Ancient Ones.

The Australian Aborigines associated their female divinities with the Pleiades, a practice common among numerous other ancient cultures. Those divinities were often considered emanations of the Moon Goddess, or otherwise closely linked with Earth's moon. The Peruvians viewed the moon as the mother of their people. Barbara Walker, author of *The Woman's Encyclopedia of Myths and Secrets*, noted that early Persians believed the moon to be the source of the 'blood of life' from which real children were *produced* (not necessarily born) on

Earth. The moon was further thought to be the source of all the magical powers possessed by females.

The ancient Ugarit Text "Number 77" details the marriage of Yarih, a personification of the moon or a Moon god, with Ningal, the Sumerian lunar goddess.[13] Yarih is often compared with the Hebrew Yahweh or His ancestors. This seems to reinforce the Sanskrit belief that humans descended from the Lunar Pitris, the outer planet humanlike species. During the most ancient times, in certain parts of the world, the moon was referred to as the 'Mansion of the Fathers.'

One Indian female deity was the Infinity Goddess Aditi. Aditi was the mother of Mitra (aka Mitravaruna), one of her twelve Zodiacal sons. Mitra is believed to be the Persian god Mithra, who had a much earlier version as a female deity. Herodotus supplied confirmation to that belief, stating that the Persians had a prior Sky Goddess called by the similar name of Mitra. Aryaman was another son of Aditi and was the eponymous ancestor of the Aryans. The Persians transformed Aryaman into Ahriman, the Great Serpent of Darkness, the enemy of Mithra. A special female deity was the goddess Anahita. She was: "...the goddess of the sacred waters (perhaps the celestial 'waters' of outer space); her dwelling place is amongst the stars."[14] She was described as a slender maiden, with white arms adorned with bracelets, indicating she was likely either a humanlike Helper or a BOPH goddess.

Numerous other inferences to a female Creator can be found in Sanskrit texts, the Gnostic Gospels (aka the Nag Hammadi Texts), and 'mixed' citations within the Hebrew Bible that refer to God in female terms. Since the Creator has always been an entity of pure energy without physical form, personification of the Creator is both irrelevant and frivolous. Ostensibly, any gender reference would infer a physical or quasi-physical being. Additionally, those 'mixed' gender references, which were used to describe the God of Earth, often changed from one section of a specific text to another. Such repetitive interchanges between genders seem to suggest a periodic replacement or change from one physical deity to another god of the opposite sex.

By evaluating the many different names assigned to God, as well as God's variously conflicting physical descriptions and numerous gender changes, one may conclude that such an entity could not represent the true Creator of our universe. The Creator would have obviously existed before any such subsequent physical being or beings. From rigorous cosmological study, an understanding can be deduced that space, time, and matter had a simultaneous origin, which emanated from the Big Bang event. That event, referred to as a singularity by physicists, had a finite point within the history of our universe. Certain religious beliefs further profess a concept in which the Creator Itself became the universe, with all physical components within our cosmos representing an individual portion of the whole, all comprising the essence of the Creator.

Those beliefs have been attacked, based on the knowledge of a finite point in time during which the universe came into existence from the energy release of the Big Bang event. Such a belief implies that the Creator therefore did not exist prior to the formation of the universe, since the Godhead is conceived to be the universe. But as previously suggested, the Creator apparently is not exclusive to the physical realm. Although capable of interacting with the material world, the Creator is ultimately non-corporeal and ethereal, incorporating a spiritual composition as Its core reality, one that is outside our known space-time continuum and evidently beyond human comprehension.

Modern cosmologists assign a fixed starting point for the formation of our universe, calculated to be 13.7 billion years ago. Some question the Creator's existence before that event. But chronological 'time lines' and time itself appear to be commodities that have consequences only within the physical world. It is defined as the temporal dimension of the fabric of space-time, the boundary encompassing and promoting the expanse of physical reality. Time may simply not exist outside that 'enclosure,' thus exempting non-material elements from having a finite beginning or demise, or any susceptibility to time-consequences outside our physical realm.

Commodities such as pure energy, human souls, and the Creator appear to be substances and forms that exist beyond our material world. Therefore, the presence of those commodities prior to the Big Bang event would not have depended on the existence of a physical universe, thus permitting an autonomous and eternal reality. Moreover, certain ancient references allude to prior universes before our present one, seemingly indicating the existence of the Creator before our present (or latest) Big Bang event. Therefore, arguments over the Creator's existence prior to our specific genesis are simply irrelevant.

Chapter 18

Cosmic Order

The Cosmic Order evolved as a result of the spiritual enlightenment attained by the 'surviving' *First Beings*, perhaps at the direction of the Creator. This mandate or commitment involved the creation of harmony and order from chaos. That effort was undertaken and accomplished by the Ancient Ones' dedication to their mission of guiding infant races toward peaceful coexistence and enlightenment. That intervention was implemented to prevent possible destructive actions before they might occur. The intent was to spare later infant races the degree of loss and suffering that the *First Beings* had wrought upon themselves and the early universe, prior to a few of those earliest species ultimately gaining the necessary wisdom to overcome their own self-destructive paths. The *Rig Veda* seems to confirm that task in Hymn 10.154.4, which claimed that the fathers (the Ancient Ones) had reached high levels of attainment and were: "Those who first nursed Order, who had Order and made Order grow great...." The *Rig Veda* further stated in Hymn 10.90.14: "From [various parts of the gods, the Ancient Ones] came the earth...thus they set the *worlds* in order." Note the plural use of the word 'worlds,' suggesting that other inhabited planets exist within our universe.

It was from the unification of those seven enlightened primordial *First Being* survivors that subsequent developmental intervention with emerging infant races occurred. The Ancient Ones based their actions on the recognition that all primitive lifeforms would eventually progress through virtually identical evolutionary stages, culminating in inevitable self-created common problems. Such destined failures seemingly resulted from a sharp disparity between the scientific development and the ethical growth attained by those infant cultures. Such a gap indicated an inability within those civilizations to recognize or comprehend all the potential consequences of their actions. Such reckless disregard for the repercussions of their acts eventually led to chaos and destruction. It was further concluded that only a small portion of primitive lifeforms would ever succeed in overcoming such inherently destructive behavior on their own, thereby negating any meaningful progress toward higher enlightenment and cultural growth. Even with those few exceptions where that self-destructive trait was overcome, some of those infant species ultimately reverted back to their prior damaging ways, leading to the inevitable extinction of their cultures.

A pro-active approach was undertaken by the Ancient Ones to break that repetitive cycle of chaos and destruction that threatened the well being of the universe. They implemented a strict but simple code of conduct, allowing infant races to achieve higher levels of enlightenment, one reflecting altruistic motives rather than the self-centered desires possessed by 'doomed' chaotic societies. This code of conduct required civilizations to envision all possible outcomes any invention or action might have on the universe, realizing all acts have permanent consequences on everything within the physical realm. Such a code became known as the Cosmic Order, which stated that the rights of a species ended when they infringed upon the rights of other lifeforms, and the universal well-being of the cosmos as a whole.

There is ample evidence that Earth was introduced to this Cosmic Order during remote epochs. Cornelius Loew, a Western Michigan University professor, concluded that ancient civilizations apparently believed that a sacred 'world order' existed, a cosmic order to which humans must be attuned.[1] That universal order seemingly permeated every level of their reality.

Such a conviction was also associated with the tradition of divine kingship. Helena Petrovna Blavatsky revealed in *The Secret Doctrine* that one common theme throughout ancient Sanskrit texts was the belief that the entire universe is guided, controlled, and animated by an endless series of hierarchies comprised of wise and exalted beings, each having a specific mission to perform. These beings are the agents and messengers of the Law of the Cosmos, the 'great law of continuity that rules the universe.'[12] This prevailing *One Law* governs the physical universe and is also associated with karma, which is known as the Immutable Law of Retribution.

The Cosmic Order, which was also known as the *Great Order* or *Universal Reality*, was a common belief with the Greeks, Hindus of India, Egyptians, Chinese, and Native American Indians. It was known by numerous names within each separate culture. Ancient tablets from Sumer and Akkad stated that the *Me's* were the divine laws that governed the universe.[3] Ancient Persian mythology stressed that all deeds were to be done in accordance with a 'righteous order,' referring to a belief called *Pairi*, which designated a way-of-life that was in harmony with the cosmos. The Hindus knew the Cosmic Order as *Rta*, as referenced in the *Rig Veda*.[4]

A divine 'law and order' was evident with the earliest texts of Egypt, and was identified in their *Coffin Texts* as *Maat*.[5] Maat regulated all the cosmic, political, and social laws within the universe, as well as the righteousness of each individual. It was the ultimate divine creative power allowing order and harmony to ultimately ensue from full compliance with its mandates. This concept was even personified by the Egyptian Goddess Maat, and was further objectified as 'sustenance,' the 'food' upon which we live.[6] The very spirit of Maat permeated all matter and life in the universe, creating balance. On Earth, that balance was known as the *Mekhaat*, the Great Scales.[7] Egyptian records also indicated that implementation of this 'perfect balance' had been achieved at Ayan.[8] Ayan was a place immediately north of Memphis, at the site of the modern day village of Mit Rahin, about ten miles south of Giza. Ayan was also the division between Upper and Lower Egypt, the regional separation believed to have started around 3850 BC.

According to the Hopi *Myth of the First World*, before that 'first world' only the Creator, Taiowa, existed in the nothingness of endless space. The Creator then created the finite from the infinite, the inception of a lifeless universe. The Creator then created Sotuknang (the First Being, an Ancient One) to carry out His plan for life in 'endless space' (aka Tokpela). The Creator then charged Sotuknang (the Ancient Ones) to: "Go now and lay out these universes in proper order so they may work harmoniously with one another according to My plan."[9] Later, the use of the term 'Sotuknang' came to mean all the species of *First Beings*, when referring to the Ancient Ones.

An integral part of Hopi religion was their sacred *mongko*, their 'Law of Laws'[10] which was perhaps their understanding or version of the Cosmic Order rules and mandates. Their mongko law contained three dominant factors consisting of respect, harmony, and love; the unifying aspects from which order could ensue in all facets of life. It was the supreme symbol of spiritual power and authority, the pure and perfect pattern established by the Creator. Similarly, the Iroquois Indians followed the Great Law, which governed rules and duties associated with a life style that centered around hunting. One aspect of that law prohibited the confinement of animals.

The *Word* or the *Logos* of the earliest Greeks became their *Law*, and was also known as the *Order*. It was considered to be a divine metaphysical force, producing the order and regularities in nature, including the physical or natural laws that governed the pattern and direction of all matter in the universe. Harmony resulted from such an order, which was the connecting force between the Creator and the physical world. Elements of the Cosmic Order can also be found in the Judeo-Christian records. The *Testaments of the Twelve Prophets* even refers to Yahweh as the God of Order. Mormon doctrine states that there are Governing Stars, the ones that reign over all the planets that belong to the same *Order*.[11] Kolob was named as one of these Governing Stars, and is believed by the Mormons to be the homeworld of God.[12]

The Urantia Book describes a Mortal Ascension Plan that is overseen by the Joint Council of the 'universe administration.' That assembly is supposedly a form of celestial government that oversees emerging inhabited worlds. It attempts to ensure that such infant races are guided through their development by more enlightened helpers.[13] *The Urantia Book* professes that once a lifeform is capable of self-determination and possesses the ability to learn and comprehend knowledge, their overseers, those higher enlightened beings, then reveal themselves. They then directly assist that emerging species by stationing a small group of teachers on that 'primitive' planet; to guide, instruct, and civilize its inhabitants for eventual interaction with other worlds.[14]

The concept professed by *The Urantia Book* has supposedly also been perceived by at least one remote viewer, researcher Courtney Brown of the Farsight Institute of Atlanta, Georgia. He believes that a Galactic Federation exists in 'subspace,' a form of United Nations for all the evolved extraterrestrial species within our universe.[15] This council is a governmental group that functions as caretakers, overseeing the interactions and resultant consequences from a number of inhabited worlds. This group's main focus is survival and evolution, according to Dr. Brown. This Federation is an altruistic one, but not a strong central authority. Rather, it is an organized collaboration of species, homeworlds, and groups. While it evidently does not solve problems, it does give guidance when asked.[16] It supposedly is not the only confederation, with other non-related galactic organizations existing in other parts of the universe, according to Dr. Brown.[17] Perhaps all such groups are linked through a common purpose, such as the Cosmic Order.

The concept of the Cosmic Order is believed to be entwined or intractably linked with the Initiator of the Big Bang event. That connection emerged from the use of the term *Holy Being* to describe the Creator. That same 'Holy Being' terminology was also widely used during ancient times to describe the ultimate authority or reality within the universe. Many archaic beliefs associated that 'reality' with some type of cosmic order, an abstract entity or force that permeated every region throughout the universe. That ancient concept spawned the later Greek belief in a cosmic destiny, which was thought to be superior to the dictates of even the highest gods of Earth. In Chinese religion, the 'Holy Being' is conceived as an 'impersonal order.' In Taoism, the 'Holy Being' is the rhythm of the universe. Confucianism professes that its 'Holy Being' is the 'moral law of heaven,' while pantheism links such a 'being' with World Order.

It was previously indicated that the Ancient Ones might have been charged with executing the Creator's Master Plan, putting them in charge of the physical universe to fulfill that mission. Such an assignment consisted of bringing civilization to the infant races, educating them, and implementing universal laws to govern and guide those worlds. The Cosmic Order was evidently that set of laws. The intent of such a mission was neither benevolent nor malevolent, but more of a preventative measure to negate needless destruction and chaos brought about by emerging worlds. The Cosmic Order may possess a universal rule that limits the degree of intervention by a superior race toward an infant one. Such constraint may allow only guidance and instruction, without direct intervention in cultural development, with its sole safeguard merely containing any and all non-conforming behavior solely within the cosmic boundary of such an offending planet.

Breaking the Cosmic Order essentially meant isolation from other worlds and exile from the Ancient Ones. That meant a loss of planetary protection from possible attacks by the *Destroyers* or other invaders from independent 'rogue worlds.' It also eliminated any contact and cultural exchange with other infant worlds within the Cosmic Order. It further ended the gifts of civilization and knowledge from the Ancient Ones, including their assistance with invention, progress, and moral and ethical development. It meant a solitary existence, depending solely upon that planet's own resources and talent, without sharing in the assets of other worlds.

Ancient records further indicate that the species of Ancient Ones overseeing each emerging world would change from time to time. That would explain the differing archaic accounts describing various species of Ancient Ones as amphibious humanoids, reptilians, or insect-like beings. The periodic changes within the Ancient Ones' group overseeing each world was perhaps connected with a celestial phenomenon or cyclic advancement. It may have involved some timed or measured movement through the twelve Zodiac Ages, which was linked to the Cosmic Order as referenced in the *Rig Veda* 1.164.11: "The twelve-spoked wheel of Order rolls around and around the sky and never ages." The exploration, education, and civilizing efforts of the Ancient Ones are evidently perpetual. Such labors were a continuing and ever-expanding venture deemed necessary for the spread of the Cosmic Order throughout the universe. That undertaking further substantiates the previously mentioned cycle known as 'circular duties,' the tasks that never end.

References to the Cosmic Order are evident in numerous archaic religious texts. In Chapter IV of *The Book Of The Secrets Of Enoch*, Enoch is brought before the 'elders,' the "rulers of the stellar orders...who rule the stars and their services to the heavens...." Chapter XIX describes those elders as "seven bands of angels," defined as archangels who "make the orders, and learn the goings of the stars." Chapter XXVII discusses the act of creating the universe, revealing the formation of seven circles...and the seven stars each one of them in its own heaven...." In Chapter XLVIII, the seven heavenly circles comprised the appointment of 182 thrones, perhaps regions of space that have been brought under the alliance of the Cosmic Order.

Researcher and tireless archaeologist, Colonel James Churchward, detected this universal Cosmic Order from ancient records found in India and Mexico. The first was a set of sunbaked clay tablets known as the *Naacal Tablets*, which had been in the possession of an unnamed college temple in India. Those records were translated with the assistance of a high priest from that same temple. They reportedly were written in the glyphic symbols and characters of the Naga or Naga-Maya script, a dead language that supposedly predated Sanskrit. The second set of records are known as the *Niven Tablets*, which were uncovered near Mexico City, Mexico, by William Niven, a mineralogist and archaeologist from Austin, Texas. Those records consisted of more than 3,000 stone tablets containing unfamiliar symbols of an unknown origin and meaning.

Colonel Churchward occasionally combined data from the *Naacal Tablets* of India with the *Niven Tablets* of Mexico, based on his assumption that both records came from the same origin, the long lost ancient Pacific Ocean continent of Mu. Therefore, the specific underlying source of the information used by James Churchward for certain references made within his writings are occasionally difficult to identify, or at times impossible to determine.

Colonel Churchward continually referred to a specific original or primordial 'creation' of the Creator as the *Sacred Four*, the *First Four* Great Commands,[18] although he also acknowledged that a total of 'seven commands' actually existed. This seems to suggest his acknowledgment of the Ancient Ones, albeit an unintentional one. Colonel Churchward later 'changed' those four 'commands' into 'forces.' However, such references may have simply referred to an earlier time period within our universe when only four species of *First Beings* had united, prior to offering membership into the Cosmic Order to other subsequently 'encountered' *First Being* species.

The *Naacal Tablets* describe the *Sacred Four*, the Law Commands from the Creator that ordered harmony from chaos throughout the universe. Those four basic or fundamental immutable laws were expected to be observed everywhere within the physical universe. Such a conclusion appears to be a direct reference to the Cosmic Order, although Colonel Churchward evidently interpreted that Order or set of laws to be 'forces,' the Four Great Primary Forces, ones he believed were issued directly by the Creator.

Colonel Churchward quoted translations from those ancient texts, which described a specific restoration of order, stating: "...and when this was accomplished, they were given charge of the physical universe."[19] This is seemingly a reference to the Ancient Ones being directed by the Creator with the task of establishing and maintaining order from chaos throughout the universe. James Churchward also referenced an unidentified legend that stated: "By command of the Creator, the Sacred Four are establishing Law and Order throughout the universe."[20]

James Churchward thought that an ancient concept of Order was a universal belief among the archaic cultures of Earth. He referenced the Naacal records of India, which claimed that the *Commands* (the Ancient Ones) were ordered by the Creator to evolve law and order from any chaos found throughout the universe. Upon completing their initial task, they (the Ancient Ones) were given charge of the physical universe.[21] Colonel Churchward noted that those Great Primary Forces, as referenced in ancient religious teachings, were associated with the Builders, one of the many archaic epithets that specifically identify the Ancient Ones.

Colonel Churchward noted a similar reference to that same Divine Law decree, which had been carved on the *Niven Tablets*, in a series of glyphs contained on Tablet No. 339. That tablet implied that the Forces (the Ancient Ones) were the 'mouthpieces' of the Creator. Additionally, the Creator may occasionally speak through the Ancient Ones, conveying the wishes and desires of the Nameless One (the Creator). That stone tablet depicted the Creator (as a circle symbol) commanding (with a tongue symbol) the Ancient Ones (as a butterfly symbol) to spread the sacred Law and Order (symbolized as two antennas) throughout the universe (an elongated circle symbol).[22] Such a portrayal is an ingenious yet simple method in which to relay the concept of a benign and beneficial creature, the butterfly (depicting the Ancient Ones), being charged with the task of spreading (pollinating) the Divine Order (by flying) throughout the universe.

The Cosmic Order appears to be the basis for all the following later commandments and laws that were bestowed upon Earth. It further appears to be the source from which numerous religious beliefs likely emerged. Evidently a modified form of the Cosmic Order continued to be embraced by the ensuing BOPH gods, which was evident with the Vedic *Rta* of the Aditya gods. Their slightly modified form of 'order' was one in which the gods held the ultimate authority over the direction and rate of progress allowed for mortal humankind.

It was the duty of Varuna, the leader of the Adityas (the BOPH gods), to oversee Earth from the heavens for any violations of the laws of the Rta, the (modified) Cosmic Order. That suggests the BOPH gods apparently established their later laws by retaining some of the same nomenclature that was in use prior to the Aryan intrusion into India. According to the *Rig Veda*, observance of the Rta once again caused heaven and Earth to rejoin after their prior separation. But that 'union' would continue only as long as humankind obeyed the laws of the Adityas. That supposedly allowed Earth, and perhaps our solar system, to be put into order and harmony, but not necessarily with the rest of the universe. Accounts from numerous other ancient cultures describe a similar 'oversight' by the gods, who exercised strict control over their followers through enforcement of the *Me's*, the Maat, and the various other names given to those laws.

By 2300 BC, certain other accounts complained that humans had to comply with a divine decree that no longer exemplified true order, or even continued to exist on Earth. However, God would still judge all human deeds as to their compliance with the rules contained in that original divine order. A basic tenant of reincarnation emerges from this ancient belief, one that is often misinterpreted by many religions of the world, and thereby retained as a misconception by many people. That misconception is the 'judgment' by God of the actions committed by the deceased.

The earliest form of this belief emerged from the Egyptian notion that their god Osiris conducted that judgment. But the true Egyptian belief professed that all deceased humans reverted back to their original composition, the spiritual form of Osiris, meaning the ethereal construct of the Godhead Itself. Hence, it was 'Osiris judging Osiris' upon mortal death, or 'self-judging-self.' This refers to each individual entity judging their own actions, since they are the only one able to know the true intent behind all their own actions.

This correctly means that each individual entity, when in spiritual form after the physical death of their most recent vessel, reviews or 'judges' their own just-expired life to determine the lessons learned and what remaining deficiencies still await correction. Such a process further exposes all the missed opportunities that went unused, which wasted one's most recent chance to correct their remaining character deficiencies. Such personal assessment of failed opportunities, as well as appraisal of the gains and accomplishments made during the most recent life, helps guide each entity along their path of perfection for reunification with the Creator. It is ultimate 'judgment' by the one committing those actions. Truth would always be a product of such self-evaluation, since we can not lie to our self. Each individual would know the true motive behind all their past actions. Such actions were either a deliberate act or an accidental one, performed with the intent of being either hurtful or helpful. Therefore, 'Osiris judging Osiris' merely refers to the act within the spiritual realm wherein every entity judges their own past deeds.

Chapter 19

Evil & Good

The Ancient Ones' acceptance of the Creator's dictate to implement harmony within the universe by spreading the Cosmic Order was apparently not embraced by all the *First Beings*. One *First Being* species or their homeworld evidently did not participate within that coalition. According to the *Book of Dzyan*, a rejected 'Eighth Son' was missing, as revealed in Stanza IV.5: "...the Eighth left out." A specific notation indicates only one *First Being* species, the eighth and only one, was excluded, per Stanza IV.6, line 2: "The Rejected Son is One." Perhaps that eighth *First Being* world initially joined, disagreed over policy or directives, and later resigned their alliance or participation. Or maybe they simply chose not to become involved with the other *First Beings* right from the start, thereby allowing them to pursue very different interests. Perhaps they had a tendency toward less altruistic pursuits, preferring to be a 'rogue species' preying on 'lower' lifeforms, and thus were purposely excluded from the alliance of the other seven species.

It is believed that this Eighth Son is the 'evil' group of *First Beings* that are referred to as the *Destroyers* in Stanza VI.6, line 2, of the *Book of Dzyan*, which states: "There were battles fought between the Creators (the Ancient Ones) and the Destroyers...." Other ancient Sanskrit records revealed that the Destroyers were the 'worst enemies' of the 'Creators' (the Ancient Ones).[1]

Previous mention of the Destroyers in Chapter 16 of this text indicated they comprised a large group of *First Beings*, perhaps accounting for one-third of the total number of 'surviving' *First*

Beings. Although first reported in the *Book of Dzyan*, the account of a one-third defection of early 'divine beings' from some 'accepted' Order may have been the basis for the later Judeo-Christian belief associated with the 'Lucifer Rebellion.' In that conflict, Lucifer was defeated by God's forces and driven from heaven into exile, taking one-third of the 'fallen angels' with him.

While this Destroyer species is outnumbered by the other combined altruistic *First Beings*, it should be recognized that their efforts are evidently focused on more malevolent pursuits. Such proclivity toward evil would seemingly have focused much of their efforts on the perfection of more potent and lethal weapons than those possessed by their more idealistic counterparts, the Ancient One, who chose to concentrate their efforts on civilizing infant races found on emerging worlds throughout our universe.

Such pursuit by the Destroyers would seemingly result in their superiority with the 'Dark Side' and the negative elements of life, allowing their perfection of more destructive weapons. Hence, their weaponry would be expected to be more potent than those developed by a species intent only on spreading harmony and order. Despite the Destroyers being physically outnumbered by their larger 'opposing' but benign group of Ancient Ones, they apparently represent a major threat to the Cosmic Order coalition.

The ancient Hermetic Writings, referring to those religious and esoteric records attributed to the Egyptian god Thoth (the Greek god Hermes), seemingly address the destructive potency of the Destroyers. That record referenced the Ancient Ones as originating from: "Nature...brought forth a wonder...the Concord of the Seven, who...[were made] of Fire and Spirit."[2] Conversely, another passage that apparently referred to the Destroyers was also contained in those writings, which seemingly indicated their superior power over the Ancient Ones, stating: "The Powers who are above the Nature (i.e. superior to Nature's Ancient Ones)...belongs unto the Eighth."[3] Even considering their smaller number of constituents, the Destroyers may well possess superior destructive power. Therefore, the Destroyers may represent a genuine obstacle to the mission and efforts of the Ancient Ones, and perhaps a real danger to their very existence.

The Phoenician historian, Sanchuniathon, ostensibly supplied another vague reference to this 'dark' *First Being* species, making a distinction between the Seven Sons of Sydyk (apparently the Ancient Ones) and their 'eighth brother,' *Esmun* (aka the *Eighth*).[4] This Eighth Son or Brother, the Destroyers, may have sought emerging infant races to aid in their malevolent pursuits, or perhaps conquered otherworldly species, forcing them into servitude as subjugated affiliates of the Destroyers. Their marauding travels throughout the cosmos would have been in direct opposition to the Ancient Ones pursuits, disrupting the spread of the Cosmic Order. Disputes, confrontations, and battles surely would have ensued between these two groups.

Vague records refer to such hostilities, where the Ancient Ones are called 'The Seven Fighters' and the 'Holy Ones and their armies.' The battles referenced earlier from Stanza VI.6. in the *Book of Dzyan* were 'battles fought for space.' Numerous references indicate those battles were a continuous cycle of victories and defeats fought over the 'oldest planets,' with each side gaining control over disputed worlds for lengthy periods of time, only to revert back to their opposition. Such battles for control of infant races may still be occurring in far away galaxies.

There are limited indications that the Destroyers may have even visited Earth. Sanskrit texts name Mara as the God of Darkness and Death, 'the Fallen One,' linking him with the Destroyers. According to Greek scholars, the Hebrew *Abaddon* (the Greek *Apollyon*) was the Destroyer, the minister of death and the author of havoc on Earth. That entity was also translated as Satan or the devil. Its Greek equivalent was a *Titan*, while the comparable Chaldean being was *Sheitan*. Perhaps it was not merely those individual beings that once visited Earth, but rather a group of like-minded beings, the Destroyers or the Eighth Son, those rebellious *First Being* 'renegades.'

Other ancient texts may also allude to such a race of Destroyers, calling them Devourers;[5] beings that live and thrive at the expense of other life. One 'Devourer' was identified in ancient Egyptian texts as the 'Chimera-like monster,'[6] described as a creature having the head of a lion and the body of a goat that transformed at its rear portion into a snake or dragon. Other Egyptian records associate the Devourer with Apophis, the Serpent of Darkness, while also calling the 'amemet-beast' the Devourer. The Egyptian *Book of the Dead* stated that the Devourer was also known as the Weary One,[7] while the distinguished Egyptologist, Sir Wallis Budge, identified the Devourer as Amam.[8]

The *Rig Veda* referred to the Devourers as the Raksases, often associating them with the Asura (the Ancient Ones). However, Vedic scholar Dr. Wendy O'Flaherty concluded that the Raksases were definitely not one of the Asuras.[9] But their frequent association in Sanskrit texts may be traced to their Primordial Parents, Pulastya and Pisacha, with Pulastya being identified as a Son of the Creator, one of the First Progeny,[10] apparently identifying him as a *First Being* (perhaps the 'Eighth Son' species). In modern times, the term 'devourer' is used to identify those anaerobic organisms that absorb oxygen from contacted substances, rather than from Earth's atmosphere.

Disclosure of an 'opposition' *First Being* species could be further interpreted as the universal element of evil, or the negative side of existence. Perhaps negative elements are merely a natural result of free will choice granted by the Creator. Lifeforms such as humans are thus allowed to choose the wrong things, although appropriate consequences are always also involved. Evil is frequently the chosen commodity, perhaps due to its appearance as the easier or quicker path.

The commodities of good and evil comprise dualism, which was a basic tenant within many religious beliefs. A prominent early example of such dualism emerged in ancient Persia, with the Zoroastrian belief that the Creator produced two mighty beings endowed with abilities and powers nearly equal to those of the Creator. One, Ahura Mazda (aka Ormuzd or the Greek Oromasdes), remained faithful to the Creator, and represented all that was good. The other, Ahriman (the Greek Arimanes), rebelled against the Creator and became the 'author of all evil.'

However, ancient Egyptian texts greatly predate the Persian concept of 'good and evil.' From a fragment relating to the Egyptian land of the dead, the god Osiris professed: "The wayfarer who crosses millions of years, in the name of One, and the Great Green (primordial water of Chaos) the name of the other."[11] Olden commentaries suggested that this 'proclamation' referred to the two forces of good and evil within our universe, one representing restraint and discord, with the other begetting knowledge and progress. Although the archaic term 'Great Green' was often used to refer to the Mediterranean Sea, it also meant the great expanse of the Cosmic Ocean, that vast expanse of outer space.

The *First Being* species identified as the Destroyers may be known from their many deeds. Universal references to evil dark forces are abundant in texts from all cultures. Gnostic texts recovered within the Nag Hammadi documents relate that the Great Flood of Noah was not a punishment from God, but rather the 'work of the forces of darkness' as punishment for humans establishing an advanced scientific and spiritual culture.[12] It was also an attempt 'to take the light' that was growing among men. Gnosticism believed such 'darkness' could not triumph on its own, requiring the willing help from complicit races to achieve the destruction of the 'light.'

Perhaps the evil influence or 'dark force' of the Destroyers might have a foothold on Earth. Humanity has always displayed atrocities carried out by both massive groups and individuals alike, those demonstrating an affinity toward the darkness of evil rather than the light of good. Author Graham Hancock concluded that the universe is infinitely mysterious, and may well contain some monstrous cosmic intelligence that feeds on negativity and darkness, one nourished by unspeakable tragedy. Perhaps such an evil supernatural force or entity to which Mr. Hancock alludes is one similar to the 'pure evil' referenced in Gnostic Texts.

Other references are more benign, or perhaps the evil associated with the Destroyers can be counteracted or neutralized when paired with elements of good. Such balance is evident in the Egyptian concept of the Ogdoad. The Ogdoad was the group of eight gods of Hermopolis in Middle Egypt (present day Eshmunein), stemming from 'primeval beginnings.' They were looked upon as the elements of the primeval chaos, out of which the sun rose and order was made. The Ogdoad is conceived as: "...the eight first living beings who appeared on the flaming isle of the Primeval Beginning,"[13] evidently a specific reference to all eight *First Being* species, the Seven Sons and the Rejected Son, shortly after the Big Bang event. They were also known as the *heh-deities* that were associated with the original four pillars that supported the foundations of heaven and Earth, later changed to eight supporting gods.[14] A characteristic of those eight primeval deities was their duality, including representation as both male and female, always in pairs. Their representation as the foundation of the world may be a reminder that both good and evil or order and chaos are ever present, but can ultimately be balanced or counteracted.

Contacted younger worlds may have been beneficiaries of some primordial agreement between the Ancient Ones and the Destroyers. Vague references infer that some archaic treaty may prohibit an opposing group's subsequent intervention with an emerging world once one of them made first contact. Such a treaty apparently establishes a protective territorial boarder around a member planet or region of space, prohibiting contact with that world by its opposition.

Such an agreement would be similar to modern nations claiming surrounding air space and territorial waters around their geographic borders, claiming those zones as protected domains. It would seem logical that such a protective system might exist.

Considering Earth's natural resources, materialistic wealth, and abundant work force; some malevolent alien high civilization seemingly would have plundered our planet by now, if not for an observance of some posted 'territorial protective limit' that apparently implied a certain risk or some other threat of reprisal.

The departure of the Ancient Ones from Earth, brought about by the conflict with the BOPH beings around $c.3150$ BC, may have put such an 'off-limits' boundary in jeopardy. Or, perhaps a temporary protective edict still exists that guards Earth while the Ancient Ones are in exile. Only a very few modern UFO reports, along with an equally small number of olden accounts, describe contact with alien beings as violent, abusive, or confrontational. Some encounters may have resulted in capture without release, or perhaps even death. Those encounters are quite different from more commonly reported abductions that involve physical examinations and DNA extraction, with a later safe return to Earth without any permanent injury. The Destroyers, their direct associates, or perhaps an independent rogue world could be the source behind those few reportedly negative extraterrestrial encounters. Certain rogue worlds may have even been planets previously contacted by the Ancient Ones, which subsequently chose to remain autonomous. Others may be independent explorers or 'pirates' plundering vulnerable worlds for their resources.

An indication that such a protective zone may still be in place around Earth can be inferred from the fact that very few of the many UFO encounters have been malevolent in their nature. Further, the intermittent frequency and short duration of those few aggressive contacts suggests an implied respect or fear of the Ancient Ones. But if the tenuous ties with the Ancient Ones are ultimately broken by a majority of humans after their future reestablishment of contact with Earth, our planet might expose itself to open invasion from the Destroyers or other independent rogue worlds. Yet another alternate possibility might be the reemergence of modern descendants of the BOPH gods, from their suspected behind-the-scenes influential positions within world governments, perhaps in an effort to once again openly control humanity.

The Counterpart

The Ancient Ones and their Helpers act as a counterbalance to the evil Destroyers and others of their kind, maintaining harmony and order throughout the universe. The previously mentioned term *Watchers* alluded to both the Ancient Ones as well as their Helpers, those assistants chosen from the evolved races of younger worlds. The ones most important to Earth, a group integral to the *Elder Gods* theory, were the outer planet humanlike beings from within our solar system. It was that species of humanlike beings that later underwent genetic alterations to accommodate environmental conditions on Mars and Earth. A portion of those genetically mutated beings, the Lunar Pitris, lived on the moon base and became the reported ancestors of earthly humans.

But a dissenting group within that same species comprised the Breakaway Outer Planet Humanlike (BOPH) beings, the ancient gods of Earth. Early archaic records identify those BOPH gods as Overlords, a fitting description based on their actions after the Ancient Ones had departed Earth in temporary exile. Certain ancient texts also state that those Overlords were the ones that destroyed the 'divinely established order,' perhaps referring to the Cosmic Order.

Those humanlike beings, either Helpers or BOPH gods, were the mythological or legendary characters that eventually became the rulers, regents, and leaders of ancient Earth, as well as the rulers on other contacted younger worlds. They were also the generic 'patriarchs' associated with numerous archaic cultures. They included the Hindu Pitris, the Sumerian and Akkadian Igigi and Anunnaki, the Judeo-Christian and Islamic angels, the Hebrew Nefilim, the mystery cult leaders, the ancient gods, the

Urshu, the Great White Fathers, the Dawns, and the Heroes or Mighty Ones of Earth's ancient civilizations.

Ancient records discuss the Heavenly Twins (aka Primordial Twins or Gemini Twins), one figure or symbolic sign of the Zodiac. Such twins were traditionally depicted as two comparable beings (or groups of beings) that were somehow also 'different.' The Gemini Twins represented an original 'Heavenly Race of Man' that later divided into two parts. Those two groups of affiliated beings both distributed similar knowledge, teaching the arts and sciences, but in different ways. One Twin reportedly arrived in a ship called Argo, which was associated with the Ark, perhaps referring to their return after the Great Flood.

The Egyptian monk, Panodorus, stated that the *Egregori* descended to Earth in 'ancient times before calendars existed' and became known as the Watchers or Angels.[15] Later, such humanlike beings were separated into two different classifications of angels. According to author W. Raymond Drake, early Hebrews discerned those two classes as 'those above,' referring to the *Elyonim*; and 'those below,' meaning the *Tachtonim*.[16] The Tachtonim may have specifically referred to the Helpers, with the term 'those below' meaning those 'below humans,' demonizing them as 'fallen angels.' Or, it may have differentiated between the humanlike beings 'on high,' those BOPH gods residing on their mountain top retreats; and the lowly Helpers, who lived among the 'common' humans. Other explanations may include a distinction between humanlike beings in the heavens, perhaps on their spacecraft above Earth, such as the Sumerian and Akkadian Igigi; and those below on the surface of planet Earth, who were called the Anunnaki.

The benevolent Helpers of the Ancient Ones changed from time to time, either as a result of death or by rotating into a new assignment, which required replacing them with a new Helper to continue their efforts to educate and civilize infant races. Such assignment changes might also reflect a 'graduation' by those students to their next level, or the introduction of a new discipline, such as a change from artistic pursuits to study of the sciences. Either a course change or a graduation may have required a new 'specialist' Helper, one more versed in teaching the new assignment. Evidently an extended period existed on Earth when the lead Helper was a female. That may have led to the ancient emphasis on feminine deities such as Isis, who carried on the work of her predecessor husband, Osiris. Numerous other prominent female leaders were recognized in archaic accounts as being the highest governing power during their time period.

It is interesting to note that over the years those superhumanlike beings, both the Helpers and the BOPH gods, slowly decreased in number, eventually disappearing completely from public view. Those beings then became 'invisible,' reportedly existing only as 'spiritual beings.' Such a transition may also be detected in the name change from Helper to Watcher, perhaps indicating humanity's perceived change in their composition from a physical to a spiritual being, as an unseen entity 'watching' over humans.

In the case of the Helpers, that may have been due initially to the difficulty caused by the Ancient Ones temporary exile from Earth, resulting in an inability to provide new or replacement Helpers over time. Or, it may be due to the decision not to put any replacement Helpers in danger, due to the animosity that existed between the humanlike Helpers and the BOPH gods. Equally intriguing is the lack of a continuous influx of BOPH gods to Earth from their Martian base. A number of possibilities exist to account for that outcome, such as an unknown calamity befalling their few remaining brethren on Mars before they could be evacuated to Earth, or perhaps simply a lack of resources to convey all those remaining immigrants to our planet.

The eventual transfiguration of the Helpers and the BOPH beings into 'invisible' or spiritual entities can be noted in certain ancient texts. The *Atharva Veda* mentioned four scribes called the Lipika (aka the Recorders), the 'spirit' immortals that were celestial beings.[17] They were 'the Hosts of Heaven who ascend and descend,' the ones also called Watchers.[18] They were considered to be of spirit-form only, the first entities manifesting from thought-form will, which inhabited the Arupa, the Formless World. This may be a reference to the spiritual realm where our soul might reside after the death of our physical vessel or body. The Rupa, the first infant race of the World of Forms, came after those spiritual entities, which also included the Builders (the Ancient Ones).

However, the Lipika were also described as the 'sons' of the Divine Sons (sons of the Ancient Ones). Those 'sons of the Ancient Ones' most likely referred to the enlightened infant race beings that became known as Helpers or Watchers. That would suggest that the Lipika were at one time physical beings, and not just spirit-form entities. The Lipika apparently also included the numerous beings known as gods, the ones that brought civilization to various parts of the ancient world, according to certain legendary accounts.

The early predynastic Helpers of the Egyptians were known as the Shemsu-Hor, the 'Followers' of the god Horus. They conveyed the teachings of Horus, bringing enlightenment and civilization to Egypt starting around 3800 BC. Like the 'elder gods,' they also suddenly disappeared sometime around 3150 BC.[19] Later, the Shemsu-Hor became great exalted spirits, much like the Sanskrit Lipika, perhaps reflecting the hidden nature of those Helpers after 3150 BC, or merely their transition into their new function as Watchers. Or conceivably, such absence was their final demise, having been exterminated by the new dynastic BOPH gods. Perhaps the cherished memories of those prior benefactors lingered with subsequent Egyptians, allowing their eventual reinvention as 'invisible guardians' that would still watch over their society as spirit-form beings only.

The Zuñi and Hopi clans of the Pueblo Indians held a similar belief in a spiritual 'watcher.' Those guardians were known as the *kachina*. The kachinas were originally physical humanlike beings, reported to be of a Caucasoid race, sent to give help and guidance to each clan of human survivors of the Great Flood. Those beings physically lived among the early Hopi. The kachinas were reported to have come from a "long, long way"; either from neighboring stars, planets, some mysterious spirit world, or from constellations too distant to be visible on Earth.[20] They were not considered to be gods, but rather intermediaries or messengers sent to Earth by a Higher Source to assist humankind.

Eventually, the kachinas no longer lived directly with the Pueblo natives. That may have been the consequence of a battle during a distant time when the kachinas and their descendants were reportedly killed-off while protecting the Hopi. Before their demise, they promised to continue their assistance as spiritual or ethereal beings, whenever summoned by the Hopi through ceremonial means. Each year, the 'spirit kachina' would help the Hopi by bringing blessings from other stars, worlds, and planets. Such a belief is contained in the Hopi legend of the *Red City of the South*,[21] believed to refer to the citadel of Palatkwapi. That citadel has speculatively been associated with the Mayan temple at Palenque, in the Mexican state of Chiapas. Others have hypothesized that the immense walled ruins of Casas Grandes in Chihuahua, Mexico, resemble the Hopi descriptions of Palatkwapi. Further south into the Andes, one can find similarities that also connect Palatkwapi with the Ancient Peruvian ruins of Machu Picchu and Cuzco.

Regardless of Palatkwapi's actual location, oral traditions claim that the last physical humanlike kachinas died defending that citadel during an olden enemy attack, thus allowing the ancestors of the Hopi to escape into the darkness and restart their migratory search for their promised homeland. Another version states that not all kachinas died, with a few escaping to a certain high mountain site after saving those Hopi ancestors, although they no longer allowed the Hopi people to ever again see their physical bodies. In either version, special note was made that it was not yet time for the physical humanlike kachina to depart for "their far-off planets and stars,"[22] likely indicating that some preplanned period of time remained before their eventual departure.

Such a tradition or oral history seems to parallel the Judeo-Christian belief in angels, the 'messenger assistants' of God. Those beings were also originally physical creatures, but later existed only as a spiritual composition. The otherworldly origin of physical angels is stated in Jude 6: "And the angels which kept not their first estate, but left their own habitation...." Some believe this refers to their homeworld in the spiritual realm, from which they materialize into our physical space-time world, but it could also refer to their arrival from another planet. Evidently little distinction existed between those 'physical' angels and humans. Hebrews 13:2 in the New Testament advises that many humans may have encountered angels without being aware of that fact, apparently indicating that no discernible differences existed between their appearance and that of mortal humans.

Enoch reportedly described the arrival of angels to planet Earth sometime between $c.18,000$ and 13,000 BC, according to certain sources.[23] Those angels were described as physical beings that watched over humans, but were not of this world. They were called God's Sanctified Ones, His Mighty Ones, and also the Watchers. According to the *Book of Enoch*, the Watchers were a specific group of angels assigned to watch over Earth. The earliest ones were: "...created from above; from the Holy Watchers was their beginning and primary foundation."[24] Later ones, the fallen Nefilim, were born on Earth. They were the ones: "...which shall oppress, corrupt, fall, contend, and bruise those upon Earth."[25] According to Chapter 10 of the *Book of Jubilees*, the Watchmen (aka the Watchers) were the fathers (ancestors) of the later Nefilim. That statement seems to imply a distinction or change between two similar groups of physical superhumanlike beings. One apparently consisted of the Holy Watchers, the Helpers of the Ancient Ones, while the other group was composed of the Nefilim, the BOPH gods.

The Watchers were also known as *Azazel* (aka Azael, Azaeil, or Azarel) in the Bible, the Hebrew *Cabala*, and numerous other extra-Biblical texts. They were the intermediaries between Divine Beings (evidently the Ancient Ones) and humans. The name has also been used to refer to six different beings, each believed to be the leader of their group of Helpers at various different times on Earth. According to the Hebrew Talmud, the *Law of the Azazel* are laws that the intellect of man can not understand. Later, according to the *Cabala*, Azael was a 'fallen god' who came to Earth during the time of Tubal Cain. Chapter 10 of the *Book of Jubilees* also introduces 'evil demons that led astray the sons of Noah, deceiving and destroying them.' Yet no biblical reference mentioned demons prior to the Great Flood. Scholarly studies of legendary demons and monsters that are mentioned throughout history reveal their description and actions to be similar or virtually identical to reported modern encounters with occupants of UFOs.

Clement of Alexandria understood that the term 'sons of God' referred to angels. The early Church fathers and olden rabbis both believed that 'fallen angels' and demons were separate and distinct entities. Angels, along with 'fallen angels,' were initially physical humanlike beings. But the nature of demons was different, since they were considered to be disembodied spirits seeking embodiment. Humanity now perceives angels only as spiritual entities, except for an occasional television series or bad Hollywood movie in which they are personified by assuming physical human form.

By all accounts, using any of their epithets, the Helpers primary function was their role as teachers, imparting both knowledge and civilization. The Ammonites, a Semitic people that inhabited the land of present day Jordan, contend that their earliest ancestors married and had children with those teachers. Most cultures retain a memory of divine beings that lived with and taught their earliest indigenous ancestors. According to the extant Egyptian fragment, *The Virgin of the World*, Geb and Nut,

208

the parents of Isis and Osiris, were sent by: "...the Universal Orderer (the Cosmic Order) and Architect (the Ancient Ones)...that they might help the world (Earth), for all things needed them."[26] Those Helpers, along with their humanlike brethren, were the ones responsible for peace among humanity. They also created laws and justice; provided food, shelter, and medical treatment; and taught knowledge, spiritual beliefs, and the arts and sciences. When all this was accomplished, they: "...were thereupon demanded back by those who dwell in Heaven...."[27] That passage is a concise description of ancient enlightened beings imparting civilization to an infant race, while also instructing and educating those 'emerging humans.'

Similar beings are found in the religious traditions of ancient Africa. Beside that region's predominate practice of ancestor worship by its indigenous tribes, common pantheons of deities modeled after kinship groups are also known. Author and anthropology professor Dr. Ralph Linton noted that messengers or helpers sometimes conducted certain transactions for those deities. Those humanlike representatives reportedly possessed supernatural abilities and often operated as the gods' intermediaries when dealing with humans. In many cases, the natives sought the favor of those humanlike intermediaries more than that of their gods.

Since the related species of BOPH beings were the 'distant cousins' of the humanlike Helpers of the Ancient Ones, a physical description can be compiled from accounts that described both groups of beings. A certain type of statue found in Syria, Ubaid, and Sumer is called an Eye-Idol. These figurines exhibit domed heads displaying distorted features, including extremely large eyes. Some represent deities, such as the limestone statues of the god Abu and his consort, found in the ruins of Eshnunna. Others represent worshipers in veneration of gods, such as those found amid the Nintu Temple at Khafajah.

Other depictions of 'unusual' appearing humanlike beings can be found from certain artistic stone bas-reliefs displaying extremely fine detail, such as the alabaster reliefs found at Nimrud. They depict humanlike beings with wings, along with extremely large and elongated fingers and toes, and a muscular physique revealing decidedly different underlying skeletal bones in their arms and legs. Another example that depicts divine beings with distorted features, especially cranial deformities, is found in Egypt with Akhnaton and his family.[28] Additionally, early Peruvians practiced a cranial deformation known as *Saytu Uma*, where skulls of 'chosen infants' were tightly bound in order to produce a flattened sugarloaf-shaped head as the child grew, which reportedly resembled the heads of their gods.[29]

From all accounts, the humanlike helpers were white or fair skinned, with large bodies and large heads displaying suspected cranial distortions that would be considered a deformity when compared with human physiology. All were very tall, at nearly seven feet, with light, flaxen, or blond hair and blue or gray eyes. One ancient account, which involved Osiris and Isis, dealt with an encounter in Thebes where a human traveler described Osiris as being: "…of enormous stature and he seemed more than mortal."[30] They evidently wore only long black or white robes, sometimes decorated with red crosses, and usually carried a device similar to a walking staff. Their heads were often covered with a helmet-like device or other protective gear.

According to author Murry Hope, those unusual humanlike beings were of a Type A blood group with its appropriate genetic markers, mainly based on identified specimens of the Egyptian Shemsu-Hor and early dynastic royal mummies.[31] DNA dating to at least 5000 BC was taken from human remains found in a brackish lake that formed over a deep sinkhole known as Little Salt Spring, a site between Sarasota and Fort Myers in Florida, which also revealed a similar composition.[32] The Type A blood group is usually associated with individuals having blue eyes and fair skin, traits unusual for those specific ancient locations, and extremely rare for population distribution patterns in any period, further indicating the remains were of an ancestral group mostly unknown within the New World. But the fossil remains of the Shemsu-Hor discovered by Professor Walter Emery might possibly represent the best definitive extant evidence of these humanlike Helpers on our planet.

Many of the physical traits associated with the Shemsu-Hor might have been evident within the later Egyptian pharaoh Akhnaton and his family, especially the deformed cranium feature. Much has been written about the odd physical appearance of this 14th century BC pharaoh. Numerous drawings depicting him and his offspring clearly reveal their anomalies, which have been confirmed from examinations of the mummified remains of his children, according to Dr. Immanuel Velikovsky. Perhaps such deformities resulted from reintroduction of genetic material taken from the humanlike Helpers of the Ancient Ones, stored for later artificial insemination with select indigenous humans. Or, it may simply reflect human mating with one of the later descendants of the few Helpers that remained on Earth after the c.3150 BC departure of the Ancient Ones.

Perhaps not all Helpers were primarily humanlike. The combined mythological records of Norse Mythology are known as the *Eddas*, which comprise two collections. The oldest texts are poetic verses dating back to 1056 AD, while the second set of records was written as prose, dating to 1640. Beside the Norse gods, the *Eddas* mention another class of beings, the 'white spirits' or Elves of Light. Those beings were said to be inferior to the gods, but possessed great power, a description very similar to the Asuras, the 'elder gods' referenced in the *Vedas* of India.

Those unusual beings were described as exceedingly fair, more brilliant than the sun, and clad in delicate garments that were shimmering or translucent.[33] They came from a country called Alfheim, a domain of the sun god. They were distinguished by their knowledge of the mystic powers that existed in nature, and reportedly always acted kindly to humans.

They were the most skillful craftsmen with wood and metal, producing Thor's hammer and a gigantic ship called *Skidbladnir* (perhaps a spacecraft) that could house all the deities and their many implements, and yet be 'folded' so as to be unseen.[34] The Dark or Night Elves were their evil counterparts. They were described as ugly, long-nosed dwarfs of a dirty brown color, who would only appear at night. Their exposure to light reportedly would change them into stone, so rumors claimed they lived in dark subterranean caves and hidden chasms.

Chapter 20

Purpose & Activities

It must be emphasized that specific references to the seven member *Tridasa* alliance of the *First Beings*, as well as their mission to spread the Cosmic Order throughout the universe, is a very rare occurrence in most archaic records. The previously documented identity suppression that was undertaken to eradicate most traces of that extraterrestrial group allowed the BOPH gods to take credit for nearly all past deeds that had actually been accomplished by the Ancient Ones and the legacies they left on Earth.

However, close examination of an array of ancient records exposes a few obvious references to that specific group and their alliance. But even those sparse indications tend to be only vague references that were either left unchanged, or otherwise eluded alteration by the later revisionists and editors. Only through the recognition of certain key epithets that indirectly identify the Ancient Ones can the true identity of individuals described in those records be established.

Some of the most revealing sources are found in ancient Sanskrit records, especially the *Rig Veda* and the underlying texts that comprise *The Secret Doctrine* written by Madame Blavatsky. That may have been due to the fortunate sequestering of many of those documents by devoted monks during olden times, concealing them deep within their lamaseries from both revisionists and later book-burners that destroyed many other ancient texts.

213

The most archaic Egyptian texts are also an excellent source of evidence attesting to the existence and deeds of the Ancient Ones and their coalition. Some of those oldest records are reflected in the *Pyramid Texts*, which were engraved on the earliest ancient edifices, thus making them more resistant to revisions by later cultures. Archaic stelae and obelisk records, which often represented 'restored' or subsequent copies of much earlier records, also provided some insight into the many activities of the Ancient Ones.

The Sumerian records, as well as those of the Akkadians, were unique exceptions. Most of their original texts survived the numerous mandated acts of destruction ordered by later religious and political regimes, due primarily to their 'natural' concealment within buried ruins that awaited their archaeological discovery millennia later. But the revisionist BOPH gods presided over the original versions of those writings from their very inception. Thus, it was never necessary for those texts to undergo alteration, since they originated as already 'distorted' accounts.

However, such records do represent perhaps the best descriptive narratives of the early BOPH colonists. Only the most archaic accomplishments and deeds of those narratives required clarification, realizing the perpetrators of those glorious deeds were the Ancient Ones, not the younger BOPH gods who ultimately took credit for them. One of the best examples of such blatant appropriation of prior achievements is found in the Babylonian *Enuma elish*, in which the BOPH god Marduk takes credit for all accomplishments since creation.

Despite the BOPH gods' expansive plan to eradicate all trace of the Ancient Ones, it is still possible to extract a meaningful understanding of that enlightened group and their cosmic mission. It was previously stated that the Ancient Ones were divided into three principal groups, according to archaic Sanskrit records. One group could be described as construction experts. A second coalition consisted of 'missionaries' that civilized and educated the infant races. The last grouping was that of the 'explorers.'

Each grouping was expected to carry out their designated specialty, but was also allowed to engage in duties typically assigned to other crew divisions as a 'secondary mission,' or whenever an unscheduled need or emergency might arise. Those three groups were further divided into seven subgroups according to Sanskrit records, although few details of those subdivisions are known. Other indications suggest that those 'main' and 'subgroups' were comprised of a representative mix of different *First Being* species.

It is likely that certain species would have exhibited superior skills or achievement in specific disciplines or areas, and would probably reflect the 'majority species' that comprised certain subgroups specializing in their area of expertise. Further indications allude to a rotating or cyclic period being associated with each mission or specific group of Ancient Ones. Upon such a cyclic expiration or task completion, each group-mix and duty assignment would change, thus assuring that all species would be versed in the functions of every principal and subgroup. The following summary will further explain the specific functions of the Ancient Ones' three primary 'working groups.'

The Architects

The first grouping, the 'construction experts,' was originally given the task of rebuilding the universe after the self-destruction caused by the other non-surviving *First Being* species. Evidently massive destruction and losses resulted from the chaotic, unregulated actions of those early lifeforms. Perhaps the demise of the reported 'seven prior universes' was the result of similar unchecked advancements, which had defied previous ineffective regulatory efforts and controls. During our present universe, it is conceivable that some attempted repair work would still have been insufficient to salvage the most devastated worlds, likely losing certain species of flora and fauna and perhaps some unique natural elements forever.

Thereafter, this group of Ancient Ones, known as the Builders or 'Creators' in numerous ancient accounts, concentrated on the resultant destruction caused by the technology and inventions of later emerging species. Such 'advancements' had exceeded their ability to envision all possible consequences of their implementation. This group's other tasks involved rebuilding basic life sustaining necessities and infrastructure on planets that had endured a natural calamity. Such reconstruction was usually provided only for total planetary destruction, regardless if caused by a natural terrestrial disaster or from a celestial cataclysm such as an asteroid impact.

Such intervention provided life saving and life sustaining aid, but not complete replacement of a planetary society's prior technology and innovations. Through empirical experience, it was deemed unwise to fully restore a culture to its prior level, since the ensuing society may not possess the moral maturity to deal with such 'replacement.' Likewise, such civilizations might actually expect future bailouts if additional catastrophes were to occur, thus neglecting to adequately provide for such possibilities or eventualities. Empirical experience may have indicated that a determined and dedicated species could bounce back with increased resolve, thereby creating an even greater replacement civilization than their prior destroyed one.

A related duty of this first group involved relocating survivors of global cataclysms from their devastated homeworld to another temporary planet. That would have involved the mass evacuation of their planet, with transportation to and from a temporary 'shelter' world, along with design and construction of living quarters and life support equipment on such a shelter planet. It also required debris removal and replacement of essential planetary services and key physical structures back on the damaged homeworld. Such projects could have involved years of constant work, despite the advanced levels of technology possessed by the Builders. Similar work would also commence after the total destruction of a homeworld, which necessitated finding a suitable 'replacement' planet, with required preparatory work performed on that new world prior to any permanent relocation and habitation by those rescued survivors.

Construction by these Builders usually involved the use of massive stones, building long-lasting structures that were durable and functional. Such megalithic stones were utilized because the technology to handle them existed, and the use of such massive blocks allowed quicker construction completion. Records also state that monuments were erected to commemorate their visits to emerging planets, perhaps explaining the many enigmatic ancient structures on Earth. Construction methods of the Ancient Ones involved an intelligent utilization of nature, with integral subterranean chambers excavated from both earthen and bedrock strata, creating naturally-moderated temperature environments. Such simplistic designs, mostly devoid of non-functional ornamental features, displayed the rustic aesthetic beauty of nature, with the blended use of natural textures and colored rocks.

Providers of Civilization

The second group of Ancient Ones consisted of 'missionaries' that civilized and educated the newly encountered emerging infant races. This group was known as the 'Bringers of Civilization' throughout ancient texts. Such activity would commence when reports from probes, monitoring stations, or scout ships determined that an emerging race had reached a level of development sufficient for 'First Contact.' Such indicated maturation allowed the initiation of civilizing efforts, intended to both educate the inhabitants and impart within them a moral value system, one leading to ethical character development and acceptance of responsibility.

These 'Workers of Wonder' would first establish a rapport with the indigenous population, slowly building trust and acceptance. The Ancient Ones often had only minimal contact with the infant races they encountered. They may have been shy or apprehensive of mass contact with other species, fearful that such encounters might lead to confrontations, choosing to have direct meetings with only a few indigenous beings where the circumstances and environment could be controlled. Of the few ancient accounts that apparently detailed such contact with humans, one described a being of short stature dressed in a brilliant white tunic, surrounded by six very tall humanlike beings that dealt directly with that primitive group. Evidently, most contact with an infant species was conducted through intermediaries such as the Helpers, as direct operatives and representatives of the Ancient Ones. The Ancient Ones normally remained in their spacecraft to observe the outcome. Once the Ancient Ones had established their plans for civilization and progress had been established, the Helpers then transacted virtually all daily duties and decisions.

Professor William Howells asserted that the conversion of humans from their savage or feral state to a civilized existence was a learned process. Such civilized behavior is not an inherited or genetic characteristic, but a result of culture, which was taught by one person to another.[1] The innate traits of selfishness and greed, especially when associated with basic necessities such as food and shelter, are natural instincts that must be suppressed and replaced with learned 'civil' behavioral traits. In essence, such transformation must be taught. Civilization can not emerge until sharing between its members occurs, along with acceptance and tolerance of others within their society. Observation of animals in the wild prove that such changes do not occur through evolutionary advances alone, although glimpses of 'civilized behavior' are exhibited by certain species within the narrow scope of their immediate family members. Even such rare behavior does not extend to the larger society of the animal group in which they live. Competition within their circle is fierce, although each group blindly unites when threatened from outside their pack.

The Ancient Ones, with input from the Helpers, created 'lesson plans' tailored to the specific needs and conditions of each encountered homeworld. Schools would eventually be established to impart certain knowledge and instruct trade skills, all within a metered growth environment that would guide the progress of technological achievements within each society. This was accomplished through select small bands of natives, segregated from the general populace as control groups, usually on a small island retreat or some remote difficult-to-access location. Once a specific timetable and plan was customized for each planet, the Helpers of the Ancient Ones assumed the mundane daily duties. The Ancient Ones would then depart to initiate the next First Contact with another emerging world, where this process would again be repeated.

The Helpers of the Ancient Ones were then left with the responsibility to implement and oversee the mission. Such Helpers were themselves 'graduates' of similar training and education that had been provided by the Ancient Ones upon their own infant world in ages past. Some of those otherworldly graduates had been chosen to join the Ancient Ones as Helpers, assisting in their continuing work on other contacted planets to spread the Cosmic Order throughout the universe. Certain Helpers were specifically chosen as intermediaries for each different emerging world, predicated solely on their appearance, one that most closely resembled the physiology of the infant race being contacted. After each group of indigenous students graduated, they were then sent from their remote, isolated training centers in all directions, to spread their newly acquired knowledge and skills to their yet untrained brethren throughout their own world.

Subsequent students were then selected from the general populace of the emerging world to commence the next training class. Those schools or academies of learning were esoteric ones, imparting knowledge only to select initiates that would follow the constraints and intent of the regulated discipline offered through the Cosmic Order. The *Cabala* referenced these celestial academies, stating that they were where 'revelations from above were received.[12] As young graduates left their respective academy in numbers sufficient to cover the entire planet, the Helpers' duties changed to those of a monitor, overseeing the progression of their 'graduated' students. When a working majority of inhabitants were indoctrinated within the initial program, the Helpers-turned-Watchers then went public, commencing the next phase of education. Those Watchers would commonly become the leaders, regents, or kings within their societies. From those positions of power, they could effectively implement any remaining civilizing efforts, while overseeing the continuing education and growth of the community.

The Ancient Ones recognized the importance of having each indigenous infant race actively involved in their own destiny at an early stage, allowing them to shape and mold their own future by setting priorities important to each individual culture. Self-determination for each contacted infant race was the ultimate goal, but it was also recognized that a species could not make such choices until they were provided the tools and abilities to evaluate all options, and understand all the possible consequences that could result from their own actions.

The Ancient Ones carefully monitored the delicate rate of regulated progress, controlling all knowledge dispensed, so as not to overwhelm the ethical and spiritual capability of its people. This allowed basic knowledge to be taught while also instructing correct use and application of such data. As knowledge was absorbed by an emerging culture, a moral and ethical value system was also introduced to its people. Its ultimate acceptance and actual implementation then determined the rate and degree of further allowed growth for each individual populace.

Such character development went beyond merely a conditioned compliance with established rules. Moral and ethical integrity incorporated the most appropriate approaches to life, and subsequent interactions with others, by employing the proper and correct manner in which to conduct one's actions. It reflected the necessary wisdom to perceive and reject those desires that could adversely effect the common good of other inhabitants, while controlling urges, desires, ambitions, and appetites within all facets of life. Such maturity went beyond will power and discipline, creating a mind-set allowing a balance within life that led to further enlightenment and growth. Heavy reliance on fundamental religious principals was utilized to implant such a basic system of core values and moral integrity within the cultural framework of each infant race.

The metaphysical spirit that was apparent in ancient cultures involved a belief in a superior order to which all matter in the universe is subjected. The very existence of such spiritual contemplation, and its ethereal connection or influence upon the physical world, is puzzling on its own. Such a concept is not readily self-evident, or one a primitive species would stumble across during their daily routine duties of securing food, shelter, and clothing; all while attempting not to become 'food' for other creatures. Such a primitive life style does not inspire self-evaluation or philosophic searches within an individual. Hence, just as with the emergence of civilized cultures, religion and spiritual concepts also appear to be imparted commodities; a direct legacy of the Ancient Ones.

Apparently, when the character development of a species paralleled their advances in knowledge and technology, more complex religious tenets were also introduced. Indications suggest such concepts included the revelation of an unseen Creator, the ethereal non-physical Entity that evidently produced the physical world from nothingness. The concept of producing 'something from nothing' would have been difficult to convey, so perhaps the Helpers used the process of female birth as an example. Such personification of the creation event, one linking the Creator with a fertile female, may be the basis from which Earth's oldest religious icon, the Mother Goddess, emerged. That may also account for the numerous religious references that also described the Godhead in female terms.

221

The elevation of females to a prominent cultural position may have emerged from such primitive goddess worship, as well as from her reproductive ability, although other explanations may also exist. Perhaps it was a female Helper that first bestowed the gifts of civilization and knowledge to primitive people, thereby imparting a level of reverence to all other females by such an association. Perhaps a majority of 'civilizing' Helpers that were used to educate infant races were females, similar to later times when school teachers predominantly were female. Labor division by gender has been a common tradition. Olden Andean cultures selected beautiful maidens to become skilled workers. Such chosen women, called *Nustas*, received special training as artists, weavers, cooks, and practitioners of elaborate religious rites and ceremonies.[3] They then became instructors to the rest of their population.

On emerging worlds, all progress and growth was allowed only in incrementally small steps or stages, so as not to overwhelm its populace. Such custodial nurturing by the Ancient Ones was intended to establish a universal foundation for fundamental ethical conduct, which was expected to become an ingrained response within all infant races. Such an implanted behavioral response provided the basis for an entrenched innate aptitude within each infant race, which established the desired level of comprehension allowing ever-higher attainment of enlightenment.

Such oversight helped to assure the security of the universe by reducing the risk of an infant race, one that might lack the necessary wisdom or ethical maturity, from eventually achieving detrimental levels of technology that could endanger the cosmos. Such safeguards discouraged emerging worlds from pursuing quick technological growth that could lead to self-destructive behavior, conduct that could ultimately also destroy the universe. Complex knowledge and advanced technology was imparted only as societal levels of responsibility increased within each emerging species. That occurred when an awareness of all consequences associated with their actions clearly emerged within the greater populace.

As revealed in the First Journal of the Ancient Ones, *Elder Gods of Antiquity*, control is one expectation that is desired from implementing any religious belief. Such control over another person's actions was intended to create a desired routine within a regulated life, one that included a basic value and moral system. The spiritual belief in an omniscient Creator produced an environment in which one's actions were constantly observed. As a society realized that civil laws were only effective when 'prohibited actions' were caught through enforced observations, it was concluded that an even more expansive constraint of undesired actions could be achieved through religious belief. When religion is introduced into a society, its inhabitants tend to reflect those behavioral traits that are desired, based on the belief that an unseen Higher Power is always watching every action of each individual.

Intervention by this 'civilizing group' of the Ancient Ones also went beyond the intangible levels associated with their educational and missionary efforts, and included the imparting of an advanced knowledge of art, music, government, law, science, religion, and ethics. It also involved some tangible gifts associated with those duties, such as the construction of permanent structures including governmental centers, communal housing, monuments, and sanctuaries used as 'educational temples.' Some of Earth's earliest institutions are found among the ruins of Malta and Tiahuanaco. Those schools or training centers went beyond merely relaying facts and data. The Ancient Ones knew that 'stand-alone' knowledge without practical application served no meaningful purpose. Imparted knowledge must also have an economic function as an underlying objective, thereby providing a productive result or outcome. Hence, their learning academies also taught trade practices and life-skills necessary to elevate each species to ever higher pursuits, allowing its recipients to create working, vibrant, autonomous, and self-sustaining cultures.

Those colleges taught techniques and procedures designed to instill the concept of commerce and meaningful work duties, which created self-reliance and self-determination within the community. The creation of such an economic system that engaged all members within its society also provided purpose and a productive use of their time and energy. Such a system required both a number system and a written script for accounting purposes. Many ancient cultures specifically stated that writing was a gift from the gods. In addition to such notation systems, devices and tools were also introduced into cultures that had achieved acceptable progress, allowing them to engage in such basic commercial 'arts' as metallurgical pursuits, complex construction techniques, and the process of weaving various fibers into fabrics. Perennial gifts such as the grains of barley, wheat, corn, and other food commodities were also provided according to ancient accounts, along with the introduction of advanced agricultural procedures and practices.

Evidence of such scientific farming applications date to the earliest times, as exhibited by the Tiahuanaco culture. That inhospitable site succeeded in raising specialized and hybrid crops utilizing unique farming terraces, a trait common with many advanced ancient cultures. The Tiahuanaco culture developed *guanats*, the horizontal wells formed from cutting the sloping hillside ground to access subsurface water, in conjunction with an ingenious irrigation canal system that diverted Andean river waters onto farming fields and terraces, converting the arid wastelands into rich agricultural areas. Such complex farming practices rival those techniques taught by our modern universities.

Such introduction of skills, bestowment of gifts, and imparted knowledge and instruction of all necessary fundamental concepts, as well as many advanced practices and work techniques, implanted the seeds for unlimited future greatness. Such intervention left nothing to chance, providing infant races with the tools, training, and guidance to become great societies, as great as their efforts and dreams might take them. That spirit of community negated the negative aspects associated with the closeness of group living, such as theft, greed, and covetousness; which are certainly unwanted traits for any species that may potentially someday obtain the ability for space travel. An ulterior motive or goal of the Ancient Ones was for each infant race to eventually become a contributing and productive member of the cosmic community within our universe. Such contact with emerging worlds may have also been reciprocal, providing necessary raw materials for other more evolved 'younger' races, as well as for the needs of the Ancient Ones.

The introduction of civilization and social skills to emerging worlds was further intended to impart a basic uniformity throughout the cosmos. Its intended purpose was to spread familiarity, which should not be confused with conformity. No desire existed to create programmed drones conforming to a common pre-established format. Rather, the aspiration was to establish a degree of uniformity within the practices and customs of all species, a form of universal 'similarity.' That was in anticipation of infant races eventually achieving their ability to travel in outer space, thus allowing encounters with other lifeforms. Where familiar or universal rituals would exist between worlds, contact involving such basic 'sameness' would permit better integration between different species, without seeming so 'alien' to each other. Since time immemorial, similar 'shared practices' on Earth have transcended most cultural differences, providing a common basis upon which to build an initial connection between strangers.

As expansive as such a civilizing process was, it observed finite boundaries. In keeping with Cosmic Order precepts, the minimal amount of intervention necessary to influence the emerging worlds was used in their 'calculated' or metered growth development. Such regulated compliance was never forced on emerging races, although force was used to contain any noncompliant actions that would threaten other worlds. Perhaps such lack of interference is most apparent within the secular laws of ancient cultures. Specific references carefully state that God gave the moral and ethical laws, but required humans to write their own civil law code. The Hebrew God, Yahweh, reportedly gave Adam and Noah a set of seven laws, the Noachide Laws (aka Noachian Code), which included a mandate to establish a civil rule-of-law, which also included a formal court system. According to the *Book of Exodus*, when God inscribed the Ten Commandments (the Moral Laws), He further issued a similar edict instructing Moses to also write a set of secular laws to govern the Hebrews.

The Explorers

The third grouping, the Explorers, seeded the myriad number of desolate but 'potential' worlds eventually encountered by the later Ancient Ones. The concept of a universal spore was addressed in prior chapters, comparing it with the elementary particles of quarks and leptons from which all other substances formed. In similar manner, all life may have ensued from a universal spore of life, which adapted, evolved, and mutated into distinct and unique lifeforms predicated on the conditions of each host planet on which they were seeded.

Such spores may have been deliberately seeded by subsequent advanced beings following a master plan, a contention expressed in *The Urantia Book*. A divine aspect was further associated with such universal spores, as disclosed by the previously referenced Gnostic *Pistis Sophia*. Recall that it claimed the Creator 'created souls from Its own substance,' thereby endowing all animated creatures that possess a soul with a 'spark of Divine Light.' Thus, the essence of the Godhead is believed to permeate all such life, everywhere in the universe.

Those emerging worlds with primitive developing life were evaluated for long term potential through periodic monitoring.

Such life could have either resulted from earlier artificial seeding by prior Ancient Ones, or by 'natural' distribution of spores that were transported through space by comets and asteroids. While the spontaneous emergence of planetary life can not be considered a true legacy of the Ancient Ones, the later subsequent contact with that life was their donation to the process initiated by the Creator. Such oversight would also involve the relocation of fauna and flora from one planet to another. That may have been a safeguard against species extinction, the 'thinning' of a species as in population control, or the conservation of limited resources. Ongoing genetic experiments, selective breeding, and hybrid grafting/germination would have been conducted by this group in order to maximize each planets' resources and the potential of its unique indigenous lifeforms.

The multiple reports of modern day UFO sightings in which extraterrestrial visitors are observed collecting plant and animal specimens, as well as 'abducting' humans, may indicate such monitoring and experimentation still exists. Genetic alterations may be an effort to create a species compatible with a specific planetary environment. Such efforts could be a continuing seeding mission, or an attempt to repopulate a dead or dying planet. Perhaps the intent may be to create a hybrid species capable of dual habitation on multiple worlds. It would be likely for such attempts to emerge from efforts to save a unique species from extinction. The early periods of Earth may have been integral in such a process, temporarily housing certain otherworldly beings awaiting relocation back to their rebuilt homeworld, or perhaps even to a 'new' planet.

One could categorize this third group of Ancient Ones as the custodians or caretakers of the universe. Duties also included their role as enforcers of the Cosmic Order as its 'celestial police,' patrolling for both internal and external threats while exploring within their assigned regions of space. In that capacity, the Ancient Ones would subdue out-of-control infant worlds on the verge of possible self-destruction. They might ultimately

227

eliminate such worlds if its self-destructive path was determined to eventually endanger or adversely impact other neighboring planets or adjacent galactic regions. Their duty as an 'enforcer' was evidently also a defensive one, through which they protected 'helpless' infant worlds.

Some of those conflicts would have involved aggressive acts by the Destroyers, the 'Eighth Son' of the *First Beings*. Other hostilities could have involved invasions by rogue worlds, those independent planets not affiliated with either the Destroyers or the Ancient Ones. Such extraterrestrial conflicts could be motivated by the rich natural resources of an emerging planet, or by a desire to enslave its inhabitants, forcing them to join in raids on other worlds as conscripted soldiers. As previously speculated, infant worlds the Ancient Ones first contacted, prior to any other outside contact, may somehow be perpetually protected against the Destroyers and the independent rogue worlds. Vague references found in archaic Sanskrit documents seem to indicate some sort of beacon or warning system may have been implanted as protection over such planets, indicating their safeguarded status by the Ancient Ones.

Perhaps such notification was accomplished by some sort of buoy marker in space, a 'do not enter' zone around a planet. Stanza V.6, line 2, in the *Book of Dzyan* may allude to just such a marker, stating: "It is the ring [orbit] called 'Pass Not' for those who Descend and Ascend (those capable of space travel)." Other Sanskrit records refer to a circle of 'pass-not,' the 'Ring Pass-Not,' a 'World-Ring,' or simply the 'Rings.'[4] A similar vague reference is also contained in the fragmented records of archaic Egypt, where the term 'ring-pass-nots' was also used.[5] Such an identification system may encompass an entire solar system, or perhaps even a sector of space, proclaiming that region's alliance with a specific group. It can not be known with any certainty if the temporary departure of the Ancient Ones from Earth sometime around *c*.3150 BC may have disrupted or suspended such planetary protection for our world.

Evidently, protection from attacks by either rogue worlds or the Destroyers was assured as long as each member world continued to obey the precepts of the Cosmic Order. Such an association should not be interpreted as becoming possessions of the Ancient Ones. Rather, such an alliance would be an agreement to observe and follow the mandates of the Cosmic Order, with certain expected benefits in return. Therefore, a planet's sovereignty would not be relinquished by its alliance with the Cosmic Order, or the protection provided by the Ancient Ones.

Sufficient documentation from ancient texts of most cultures, along with the sacred history accounts of many religions, indicates that a war or wars took place in vastly olden times. Those conflicts were reported to have been waged by two groups of olden gods, or between Good and Evil, or God and the devil. The oldest records identify those heroes by their epithet, the Seven Fighters,[6] an obvious reference to the Ancient Ones. Those same records seem to indicate that infant races may have also been employed in the battles, referencing the "Holy Ones and their armies."[7] Additional references found in both Sanskrit and Chaldean records called the Hosts of Heaven the *tsabaoth* (aka *tzbaut*), which referred to both the crew and the army of the 'sky ship of the Upper Ocean.'[8] These hosts were often analogous with the *Shboh*, meaning "The Seven." Chapter XVII of the *Book of Enoch* reveals armed soldiers within the midst of the heavens (of outer space), in the service of the Creator. Evidently those 'fiery troops of great archangels' were headquartered on the 7th heaven, according to Chapter XX in the *Book of Enoch*.[9]

Hostilities between the Ancient Ones and the Destroyers were specifically mentioned in Stanza VI.6. of the *Book of Dzyan*: "There were battles fought between the Creators and the Destroyers, and battles fought for space." Note the plural form, Creators, used in this account. That clearly refers to the Ancient Ones, the 'creators' of civilizations on emerging infant worlds, not the Supreme Creator of all. Numerous other references state that those battles between the Ancient Ones and the Destroyers were a succession of victories and losses, both maintaining and relinquishing control over some of the oldest worlds, with victorious outcomes over such disputed planets enduring over lengthy periods of time.[10] Those conflicts over disputed planets are likely still occurring somewhere within the greater universe.

Interaction or direct intervention with an infant society did not imply an allegiance with the Ancient Ones. Every emerging world is considered to be independent, with full sovereign rights. Any decision to join the Cosmic Order is allowed only when the inhabitants of those independent infant worlds became sufficiently advanced, both ethically and mentally, to be capable of making such an important but informed choice. While such voluntary alliance required compliance with the constraints and restrictions of the Cosmic Order, it also provided many benefits derived from the imparted knowledge and nurtured enlightenment bestowed from such an agreement with the Ancient Ones. Rejection of that alliance allowed any sovereign world the freedom to attempt indigenous growth and progress at their own desired pace without restraints, but also without the assistance and guidance of the wiser Ancient Ones. Rejection of the Cosmic Order did not guarantee that an independent world would not later be restricted or even destroyed in the future, if that world's independent actions should threaten other outside worlds.

The Ancient Ones would not view the eradication of all lifeforms from an entire world that would threaten the well-being and continued existence of innocent neighboring worlds or some region of the universe as a malevolent act. Rather, it would be deemed necessary 'surgery' for treating an ailment. The removal of a malignant tumor or diseased organ from a patient's body is deemed to be the correct and beneficial course of action. The similar forceful eradication of a destructive lifeform, one in a position to threaten and destroy others, would reflect the necessary loss of some to save many. As the highest evolved beings in the universe, the *First Beings* understand the principal involving the sacrifice of a few for the good of the whole.

The elimination of a rogue world that could be projected to someday disrupt the well-being of neighboring planets, solar systems, and galaxies, would be deemed 'expendable' in the best interest of the universe as a whole. The primary mission of the Ancient Ones was to create order and insure universal balance and general harmony, by providing an environment in which infant races could potentially learn, advance in enlightenment, and eventually perfect their spiritual component. Such a process minimizes an infant race's inclination toward self-destructive behavior that could also adversely affect other worlds.

While these three groups or divisions of Ancient Ones had their specialty, each group was sufficiently accomplished to undertake tasks beyond their specific area of expertise, overlapping or expanding their duties where necessary. Undoubtedly, the three groups would operate outside their specialty on numerous occasions, with each group being sufficiently proficient in all other disciplines to allow completion of whatever task that might arise, without summoning extraneous specialized assistance. Such 'discipline overlap' would be required, for example, after regional disasters such as tidal waves, hurricanes, or tornadoes; natural disasters that might occasionally affect only a portion of the contacted planet.

Such overlap could also explain those subtle differences found in the construction of megalithic structures built in various regions around Earth. While the Ancient Ones and their Helpers built those structures, they reflect different 'specialists' working during each of their cyclic-planned 'rotational periods.' Hence similar structures, but with subtle differences, were built over various times, after 'replacement groups' had taken over ongoing responsibilities from their prior counterparts. Still other structures may have been the result of 'overlapping duties' brought about by necessity, perhaps due to natural disasters. Conceivably, a 'civilizing group' might have rebuilt or replaced

231

certain edifices destroyed by regional cataclysms, rather than waiting for the group of Architects to return to Earth to complete that work.

Chapter 21

Imparted Wisdom

Although written records expressly disclosing the existence of the Ancient Ones or any other extraterrestrial visitors are extremely rare, other forms of inferred substantiation can be detected. Archaic cultural evidence consisting of advanced devices and fantastic constructions reveal obtainment levels much higher than those ascribed by historians and orthodox archaeological beliefs. Such tangible evidence, along with other documented inferences of high scientific comprehension during ancient times, implies that such advanced knowledge and skills were imparted gifts rather than self-realized achievements by human cultures. Many of those anomalous artifacts, along with the amount of ancient scientifically advanced knowledge, were explicitly stated to be gifts from the gods, thus providing further indirect verification supporting otherworldly contact with Earth during its remote past.

The Secret Doctrine alludes to those legacies, indicating that such a process involved: "...seven divine dynasties...the seven primitive and dual gods who descended from their celestial abode...teaching mankind Astronomy, Architecture, and all the other sciences that have come down to us."[1] Professor George F. Creuzer, a late 18th-early 19th century German scholar of ancient religions, claimed that humanity's earliest knowledge was originally relayed from enlightened beings to emerging races. He specifically stated: "From the spheres of the stars wherein dwell the gods of light (apparently the Ancient Ones) that wisdom descends to the inferior spheres."[2] Other archaic records throughout the ancient world seem to confirm this legacy from the stars.

The time frame involved in that early instruction of humanity was during the presence of the Ancient Ones, long before Dynastic Egypt. This belief is confirmed within the writings of the *circa* 400 AD Egyptian monk, Panodorus, who stated: "Now, it is before that time (the Egyptian times of Menes, before *c*.3150 BC), that the reign of the seven gods who rule the world took place. It was during that period that those benefactors of humanity descended on Earth and taught men to calculate the course of the sun and moon by the twelve signs of the Ecliptic."[3]

However, certain tangible gifts as well as some indirect legacies that were bestowed upon ancient Earth may not be adequately recognized, or perhaps not yet made public, with some of those greatest legacies still remaining unrealized or hidden. Such unknown but 'intended' beneficial gifts would seemingly include the vast quantity of advanced scientific knowledge that the Ancient Ones had collected over their many prior eons of existence. Yet that wisdom apparently still remains concealed or lost, perhaps buried deep within some undiscovered ancient ruin or deliberately withheld from humanity.

Certain undiscovered ancient knowledge, which apparently was intended to be shared with our species, might still remain concealed, perhaps awaiting the eventual return of the Ancient Ones. Persistent rumors from numerous ancient cultures seem to hint at an all-encompassing 'Book of Knowledge,' one that contained the acquired wisdom of the Ancient Ones. Those rumors indicate that such a long lost written record supposedly contains all past knowledge. That encyclopedia of wisdom has been identified by various different names over the ages, including the *Tonalamatl* (Book of Fate), the *Records of One*, the *Great Book*, the *Serpent Text*, and the *Book of Gold*, to name merely a few titles.

Those texts were reportedly prepared with the intent of being shared with emerging races and their cultures, in an effort to save them the pain and misfortune the ancient compilers of those records had to endure in order to assimilate their wisdom. Those lost records reportedly contained secrets pertaining to the origins of humankind and the universe. Most references cite an unknown age before the Great Flood as the time frame when those records were compiled.

The previously referenced pre-flood record that was inscribed on a rock, as reported in the extra-Biblical *Book of Jubilees*, reportedly contained the 'teachings of the Guardians.'[4] That petroglyphic record was thought to also be connected with the pre-flood patriarch, Enoch, who was given similar knowledge by the archangel Pravuil (Uriel in another account) that filled 366 books.[5] That wisdom was then shared with Enoch's sons, who were expected to spread that information around the world. Prior mention was also made to Votan, the great white god of the ancient Mayans whose emblem was the serpent, thereby associating him with the Ancient Ones. Votan reportedly was a "descendant of the Guardians"[6] who imparted knowledge and civilization to the Mayan people.

Numerous other advanced cultures from antiquity expressed similar beliefs, using either the serpent or the dragon as their symbol of wisdom.[7] The Gnostics equated the serpent with the Divine Instructor, who was the: "Good and Perfect Serpent, the Messiah of Naaseni, whose symbol in heaven is Draco."[8] Similarities are apparent with the beings that were known to the ancient Assyrians as the Seraphim, which were associated with the 'Serpent Men, the Dragons of Wisdom.'[9] Those Serpent Men (aka Serpent People) were known in esoteric records as 'a non-human race of wondrous beings with immense cosmic wisdom.'[10] They descended from the stars to teach humankind, and were also known as the Dragons.[11] In ancient China, the word 'dragon' signified "the being who excels in intelligence," according to *The Secret Doctrine*; claiming that the Dragons of Wisdom were the instructors to Earth's first civilization.[12] Throughout antiquity, dragons were held as symbols of Eternity, Secret Knowledge, Wisdom, and Immortality.[13]

Many widely separated and diverse ancient cultures thought that a hidden repository of 'lost knowledge' still existed somewhere in one or more locations. Such a concealed 'Hall of Records' was believed to have preserved the entire wisdom and knowledge of a prior lost civilization, perhaps similar to the previously mentioned Book of Knowledge. Actual locations of those hidden archives have been speculatively associated with such sites as the Temple of Poseidon in Atlantis and the Hall of Records within the Great Pyramid. Other sites included the Chamber of Archives within the Cholula Pyramid, and a lost temple known as the House of Darkness, which was reportedly located near a Guatemalan river.

According to the Egyptian *Kore Kosmu* (aka *The Virgin of the World*), before the god Thoth returned to heaven, he wrote 'secret writings of divine knowledge that contained the teachings of Osiris and the holy symbols of the cosmic elements.' Such records were known as the *Holy Books*, which Thoth had 'blessed,' thereby making them 'free from decay' throughout all of eternity.[14] According to the goddess Isis, Thoth deposited those sacred books in a secret place. Such a belief tradition goes back to at least the 3rd century BC with *The Book of Sothis*, an account that some attribute to the Egyptian historian, Manetho.[15] That same text was later also referenced by the 9th century AD Byzantine historian, Georgios Syncellus. Those accounts are reminiscent of the Biblical patriarch Enoch's lost 366 books of divine knowledge.

Further reference to such imparted knowledge was made by the Roman historian, Ammianus Marcellinus (330-400 AD), who wrote that underground galleries were built, along with the Giza pyramids, in order to preserve the records and knowledge of past ages. He further stated: "There are also subterranean passages and winding retreats, which...men skillful in the ancient mysteries ...constructed in different places lest the memory of all their sacred ceremonies should be lost."[16] The *Westcar Papyrus* also indicates that ancient wisdom was stored in some secret chamber concealed [in the Great Pyramid].[17]   The *Coffin Text*, in "Spell 1080," claims that secret 'sealed teachings and things of Osiris' were hidden in the desert sands;[18] while "Spell 1087" from that same text indicates that other written material from Heliopolis was also hidden in the desert.[19]

According to the Arabian historian al-Masudi, King Surid, the son of Salahoc, reportedly ruled Egypt about 300 years before the Great Flood.   Surid reportedly intended that all Egyptian wisdom and knowledge, including their vast understanding of different arts and sciences, to be committed to the written record and then sealed in the Great Pyramid to preserve that knowledge from the impending flood destruction.   Reportedly, Surid's stated purpose was: "...for the benefit of those who could afterwards comprehend them."[20]   It should be noted that the Great Pyramid is generally recognized as having been built after the global deluge of *c*.10,500 BC.   Therefore, the Great Pyramid was evidently not in existence during the time of Surid to store such wisdom, although some other equally impressive structure that was later destroyed might have been.

Such knowledge was reportedly imparted by divine beings during the remote past, although no public acknowledgment claiming such a find is known.   However, the polished outer limestone casing stones of the Great Pyramid did contain some inscriptions, according to many archaic reports; with confirmation by Herodotus who personally saw those writings during his visit to Egypt.   Reports indicate the inscriptions evidently consisted of more than 10,000 words.[21]   Yet, no extant record of that composition is known to have survived into modern times, although an unknown secretly hidden record may exist somewhere, since reports state that copies made 'in a number of languages' existed as late as the 14th century AD.[22]

The Sphinx and Giza pyramids have consistently been linked with or suspected of housing a collection of Ancient Wisdom.   At least one of those chambers may exist under the Sphinx.   A seismic study was conducted on the subterranean bedrock of the

Giza plateau between 1992 and 1993, by the United States geophysicist Dr. Thomas Dobecki. Results indicated the possible presence of a large rectangular crypt beneath the front paws of the Sphinx.[23] Apparently the chamber was artificial, due to its reportedly squared-corner construction.

Ancient Wisdom is often linked with the oldest megalithic sites, which display some of the most compelling evidence indicating ancient visitations by otherworldly beings. Such sites were distributed around the world, indicating their common or centralized origin from a single source. With most of those structures erected long before 1500 BC, the basic intellectual requirements necessary to plan, orient, build, and utilize those precise megalithic complexes were clearly beyond the capabilities of their Mesolithic and Neolithic cultures. The oldest sites were some of the most challenging, and certainly could not have been conceived and constructed by primitive Stone Age humans alone.

Some of those ancient megalithic structures are still beyond the land-based construction capabilities of modern civilizations, and would have seemingly required some type of aerial assistance during their building process. The level of engineering science that would have been required for those sites clearly exceeded the abilities assigned by modern historians to those ancient humans. Even if a single genius such as Albert Einstein was involved during conceptual layout, that person would have died prior to completion of such structures, since some complexes were built in several phases, perhaps over many centuries.

Those sites, their layout, and their eventual construction all reflected preplanning, requiring detailed calculations for the precise alignment they exhibited. Accuracy of their mathematical and celestial orientation would have required the collection of raw data over tens of thousands of years observing cosmic events. Any useful results would have then required certain intricate deductions from the complex cosmological movements derived from those empirical efforts. Such efforts would have also required written records to document and detail their findings.

Yet those sites predate any known written script by many millennia. That dilemma could indicate its status as 'inherited information' from an older and wiser source, one probably not of this world.

The celestial orientation of those ancient sites has spawned recognition of the science of astroarchaeology, also known as archaeoastronomy. The father of 'modern' archaeoastronomy is considered to be the British astronomer Sir Joseph Norman Lockyer, who wrote *The Dawn of Astronomy* in 1894. The slight alignment imperfections measured during modern times may not reflect construction errors, but rather natural celestial changes that have occurred over extremely long periods of time. Some experts believe the slight variance detected in the alignment of the Great Pyramid is due to the gradual movement of Earth's axis, rather than any error in its original construction. If correct, certain structures could be much older than ever imagined.

Astronomy was a common science embraced by even the most archaic civilizations. Some Sumerian cuneiform tablets detail the location and orbit of one of the outer planets in our solar system; the four largest moons of Jupiter; and the knowledge of certain moons of Saturn. Such wisdom would require the use of telescopes thousands of years before their invention by Galileo.

It is known that the manufacture of both glass and mirrors dates to Sumerian and Egyptian antiquity. Ancient concave mirrors, which rival our modern parabolic reflectors, were found in La Venta, Mexico, dating to 1400 BC.[24] Optical lens ground from rock crystal were discovered among the temple ruins at Nineveh and also at Nimrod.[25] Another ancient lens was taken from a tomb in Helwan, Egypt, along with others found in Libya, Ecuador, and Mexico.[26] The ancient inhabitants of Sicily reportedly used a magnifying instrument that they called a *nauscopite* to view the coast of Africa.[27] The olden description of that device clearly reveals a telescope, long before its introduction by Galileo.

Ancient astronomical knowledge would have also required the use of accurate timepieces such as chronometers, in conjunction with early telescopes. The *Brihath Sathaka* and other olden Sanskrit texts reference microsecond subdivisions of time called *kashtas*.[28] Ancient anomalous advanced devices, including complex geared calculators, confirm that both the required advanced tools and components, along with comprehension to utilize them, once existed that would have allowed the design and construction of megalithic structures. The cosmological knowledge that existed during Earth's earliest civilizations can only now be discerned as 'advanced,' based on modern discoveries and theories. With such complex understanding and abilities demonstrated by early primitive cultures, it is likely that such knowledge and skills were not self-conceived, but rather imparted to ancient humanity as a legacy from an 'outside source.'

Another stunning example of advanced ancient knowledge can be found within its medical expertise, which vastly exceeded olden obtainment levels ascribed by modern scholars. In the Western world, Egypt is considered to be the origin of medical science. Egyptian records state that Imhotep was the first and greatest doctor, and also the first architect and engineer. Imhotep is reported to have lived during two different time periods, the first around 4500 BC, and the second during the reign of Pharaoh Zoser, *circa* 2650 BC. His medical skills reportedly included the regrowth of severed limbs, and even the resurrection of the dead.

Evidence of the extent of Egypt's medical knowledge is reflected in written discoveries. The *Edwin Smith Papyrus*, named after its discoverer, is considered to be the world's oldest known medical textbook, containing modern approaches and logical treatments. Another medical text is the *Ebers Papyrus*, which details surgical procedures and pharmaceutical treatments. Another medical papyrus from Egypt's 11th Dynasty prescribed what would now be known as penicillin,[29] some 4,000 years before its discovery by Dr. Alexander Fleming. Alcmaeon, a Greek student of Pythagoras, was familiar with the circulatory system and performed the first human dissection.[30]

Ancient India also possessed advanced medical knowledge. Surgical manuals dating from the 8th century BC were included in the *Atharva Veda*, which contained detailed and specific transplant techniques.[31] Another text, the *Sushruta*, which was also based on Vedic knowledge, lists diagnosis for 1,120 diseases, and also details surgical procedures.[32] Doctors of ancient India understood the functions of the circulatory system, the nervous system, metabolism, and how specific characteristics are transmitted through heredity. Advanced medical knowledge is also contained in an ancient Chinese text, the *Nei Ching* (*Book of Medicine*). Its modern diagnosis and treatment plans reportedly date to 2650 BC.

Approximately 800 clay tablets taken from Ashurbanipal's vast Assyrian library dealt with medical subjects. The ancient Peruvians performed a brain surgery procedure, known as trepanation, as far back as 500 BC. Dr. Roy L. Moddie wrote in his *Studies in Paleopathology* that no ancient culture anywhere in the world had equaled the surgical skill and knowledge practiced by the ancient Peruvians.[33] Their archaic advanced culture was reportedly proficient in amputations, excisions, bone transplants, cauterization, and other highly evolved procedures.

Other evidence exists to indicate that advanced ancient cultures also understood and utilized electricity. Earthenware jars with iron rods set inside copper cylinders sealed with pitch, were used as dry cell batteries in the ancient Near East.[34] Such devices may explain those numerous objects that dated to 2000 BC, which had been electroplated with gold or silver over their base metals. An ancient Sanskrit text of India, the *Agastya Samhita*, even contains instructions for constructing electric batteries.[35] Furthermore, one Egyptian papyrus depicts a device appearing to be a Van de Graaff static electricity generator.[36]

The Danish inventor, H. C. Oersted, first understood the basis principals of electricity in 1820. Thomas Edison then used that knowledge to eventually develop the incandescent light bulb in 1871. Yet tomb paintings and wall reliefs found in the Egyptian Temple of Hathor at Denderah, Egypt, unmistakably depict huge five feet long light bulbs, complete with filament and braided wire connectors attached to what appears to be a transformer; all held in position by a large high-tension insulator.[37] The object resembling an electrical insulator that was illustrated in those paintings was a common Egyptian symbol or depiction known as a *Tet* (aka *Tat* or *Tattu*), which was also called a *Djed* pillar.[38] According to Egyptologist Sir Wallis Budge, those objects were made only from wood (an insulator) or from gold (a conductor).[39]

Ancient legends tell of flying gods in celestial chariots, boats, and discs; but primitive cultures supposedly did not possess any technical knowledge or understanding of aviation and aeronautics. Yet airplanes, jets, rockets, and craft resembling modern day UFOs were clearly depicted in archaic times. Numerous wooden models of glider airplanes have been found in Egyptian tombs.[40] Analysis of those model craft have revealed aerodynamic designs ideally proportioned for flight.[41] A similar evaluation of the design and proportions of a small 1400 BC solid-gold object resembling a delta-winged aircraft, which is on display in Bogota, Columbia, was also determined to be airworthy.[42] *Aeronautics*, a later scientific text of India authored by Maharshi Bharadwaja, was reportedly based on ancient Sanskrit manuscripts that detailed archaic aircraft construction and the 'secrets' of aviation.[43]

The manufacture of such flying machines, along with numerous other complex devices, would have required advanced manufacturing techniques, including sophisticated metallurgical skills. Substantial evidence of advanced metallurgical knowledge has been found in the ruins of certain ancient cultures. That evidence included artifacts made from high alloy steel, aluminum alloys, wrought iron, bronze, and cast platinum. Also found were dies and molds that were capable of producing advanced parts, which were cut directly into stone cliffs.

Other anomalies include ancient maps depicting accurate land mass locations and relative positions, further revealing the legacy of knowledge bestowed upon Earth by the Ancient Ones. Those maps suggest that some ancient cultures had a much greater knowledge and understanding of geography, logistics, and spatial layout, long before any subsequent society was thought to possess such abilities. Those olden charts accurately show details that can only be graphed from an aerial perspective, yet they were made during times when aircraft supposedly did not exist. Those maps show accurate delineation of land masses in their relative position, while also correlating with landmarks and other features. Such charts further suggest the likely existence of extremely archaic written records, which were apparently known to the olden cartographers, but were evidently lost to later cultures.

Perhaps the 1513 AD *Map of the World* by Piri Reis is one of the most perplexing. That map depicts the eastern coastlines of both North and South America, including the entire profile of Brazil. It further detailed the layout of the South American interior, showing the Andean Mountain range and unexplored waterways including the Amazon, Orinoco, Parana, and the Uruguay rivers. This remarkable map featured the contours of Antarctica without its two mile thick ice cover, virtually fitting the known continental contour determined in modern times. As with many olden maps, the Piri Reis chart reflects a knowledge and ability to correctly determine latitude and longitude positions, evidenced by the correct alignment of the continents, although such modern survey skills were not mastered until the 1700s. Such charts also employ sophisticated map projection techniques that require high level mathematics.[44]

However, glaring inaccuracies were also evident. Although this map depicts both southern continents distorted and elongated, sinking downward and away as if viewed from space, the representation does not fully fit with modern day space photographs. Further, the South American continent is drawn about 900 miles shorter than its true length, and appears to join the South Pole. The size and placement of certain interior South American features are also distorted.[45] However, Piri Reis reportedly had referred to himself as 'a poor copyist' who merely reproduced archaic maps that were originally made during ancient times, claiming no part in the basic survey data used in their layout.

Perhaps an even more astonishing map was drawn by Glareanus. Its rough form was contained in a 1482 book, the *Ptolemaeus Cosmographia*, and updated in 1510 by Glareanus, a Swiss scholar also known as Heinrich Loris. This map depicts Greenland, Iceland, and both North and South America. It accurately shows both coasts of the Americas, and correctly depicts the actual shape of South America, including its southernmost portion as a 'tip,' detached from Antarctica and the South Pole. However, once again there were also inaccuracies, such as an erroneous size attributed to Africa.[46]

Many European maps were copies of earlier charts from second century AD cartographers, such as the *c.*120 AD work by Marinus of Tyre and those of the olden classical geographer, Ptolemy of Alexandria (aka Claudius Ptolemaeus). Ptolemy was the second century AD director of the Alexandrian Library, perhaps his main source of data used for much of his works including *Geography*, which charted the known world of his time utilizing a similar system of latitude and longitude. His *Map of the North* depicted Sweden with remnants of the glaciation from the last Ice Age, which had disappeared by 9600 BC. The Zeno brothers of Venice, Italy, specialized in Icelandic and Arctic maps, producing similar maps in Europe. A 1380 AD Zeno map accurately shows Greenland without its ice cover, reportedly based on very ancient data when Greenland had a temperate climate.

Philippe Buache, a French geographer, published a map of Antarctica in 1737 that showed the precise subglacial topography as it would appear if absent any glacial ice. Yet that continent has not been without ice cover for over two million years, although certain small areas enjoyed a short ice-free period about 125,000 years ago. Further research conducted by Professor Charles Hapgood calculated that the source map used by Buache to construct his chart apparently dated to the end of the fifth millennium BC.[47]

Other remarkable maps depicting the coastal contours of the Antarctic continent without its ice cap were drawn by Gerardus Mercator in 1538, along with another by Ptolemaeus Basilia that exhibited a 1540 date. The Mercator map also included accurate details of the West Coast of South America before its more extensive exploration decades later. These maps are thought to have been derived from even older works, such as those of the Greek scholar, Eratosthenes, who drew a map of the world in the shape of a sphere to within 1.3% of its true diameter around $c.250$ BC. The majority of similar ancient maps were based upon vastly older source charts, handed down from some unknown time and origin. They allude to their existence as an ancient legacy from an unknown benefactor, most likely the Ancient Ones, produced sometime during Earth's remote past.

Chapter 22

Education & Mystery Schools

Ancient texts reveal a refinement of thought and insight far advanced from the levels typically associated with the primitive times in which they were written. The remarkable knowledge possessed by ancient cultures simply could not have evolved solely from Stone Age men, without outside help or tutor. Laws, critical thinking, and civilization are not commodities that naturally occur. Rather, the opposite appears to be the common pattern. Normal traits of assault, theft, selfishness, and many other 'undesirable' characteristics, as defined by most civilized societies, are survival instincts found in primitive or feral lifestyles. Domestication necessitates sharing, compelling peaceful coexistence within an organized society, and ultimately requires some form of instruction from teachers. But who were those first tutors and civilizers?

The *Elder Gods* theory attributes ancient Earth's inexplicably high level of wisdom, which was evident in many archaic cultures, to outside intervention from extraterrestrials. Such advanced knowledge was dispensed to small, selectively chosen human groups, often sequestered at protected locations. The Helpers, under the guidance of the Ancient Ones, administered that ancient schooling. In the earliest times, those sites of learning were the 'ceremonial caves' used as meeting places by the Cro-Magnons. Their magnificent rock paintings and engravings have been found in over 200 caves, with heavy concentrations in Spain and France, which date from *c.*35,000 to 10,500 BC. They were not merely aesthetic efforts that occupied time, or activities to entertain their fellow clan members. Rather, such artistic creations reflected a true mastery of perspective, proportion, detail, and great preplanning; traits that are also necessary to conduct engineering analysis and design, as well as investigative study and scientific research.

More sophisticated academies naturally evolved from those earliest operations. Knowledge and truth were then imparted in measured amounts appropriate with the achieved comprehension and enlightenment levels of the students. Those later efforts involved the gathering of selectively chosen indigenous people that were then segregated from their general populace in isolated areas. Those sites were often small but fortified island retreats, or complexes in remote mountainous regions. Many of those locations became known as the Land of Paradise, or the Garden of the Gods. Certain schools were also known regionally as 'Atlantis,' a generic name used to describe those places of higher learning over the ages.

Remains of such colleges can be found within the massive stone 'temples' on the islands of Malta and Gozo, on high Andean plateaus at Tiahuanaco and Machu Picchu, and the archaic Egyptian temples at Saqqara and Abydos, to name merely a few. Substantial evidence suggests Tiahuanaco was likely one of the earliest schools, based on its elaborate collection of stone heads that displayed different facial features of human physiology, representing all racial types; perhaps as a study aid or learning tool. Celestial oriented sites also existed to observe and document cosmic events. Such isolated and mostly inaccessible regions assured privacy for its 'selected students,' offering protection from the 'common public.' As cultural progress also ensued, such learning centers expanded their curriculum to ever increasingly advanced studies and skills.

Such ancient learning and apprenticeship centers are commonly referred to as 'Invisible Academies' by modern researchers. Many of those early colleges were not specifically known or apparent from extant ruins or hard evidence, but rather are implied by their resultant effects or influences in introducing inventions, skills, and analytic knowledge to primitive civilizations. Such accomplishments seemed to appear without evidence of any earlier instruction or prior development phase, however someone must have initially introduced those advanced abilities.

Those ancient colleges were further 'invisible' by their very nature of operation. They were not public institutions, where any local resident could simply apply for admission and attend classes. Rather, students were carefully selected by the 'teachers,' undoubtedly a process based on a diverse but exceedingly strict criteria. The chosen humans were expected to become the future instructors and leaders within each of their own communities upon graduation. Their education went beyond any level of private schooling, operating within a strict level of esoteric secrecy, divulging knowledge only at requisite times when the students were deemed ready.

Various temple records further allude to these ancient esoteric academies, ones that generally remained hidden from the public. Egyptian records associate the *Akhu* with their secretive, invisible academies. The term *Akhu* referred to beings identified as the Shining Ones or the Venerables, epithets that are associated with the Ancient Ones and their humanlike Helpers. According to fragments preserved from Thoth's teachings, Egypt was once considered to be "the teacher of Mankind,"[1] and further stated that Thoth: "...succeeded in understanding the mysteries of the heavens [and to have] revealed them by inscribing them in sacred books which he then hid here on earth...."[2]

A passage in the *Kore Kosmu*, which reflected Thoth's teachings, stated: "And I, [Thoth] will make mankind intelligent, I will confer wisdom on them, and make known to them the truth."[3] According to Professor G.R.S. Mead, another fragment based on Thoth's teachings, known as *The Sacred Sermon*, revealed pre-flood humanlike beings who were "devoted to the growth of wisdom."[4] Their educational task was later transferred to the demigods, the products from unions between a 'god' and a mortal human, who then continued that tradition. Those specific teachings were stated to be "of divine origin,"[5] intended to balance, unify, and bring harmony to humans. That reflects the intent of the Cosmic Order to bring civilization to emerging worlds.

Later, additional accounts indicate that the teachings and secrets of the gods were carefully handed down by their loyal associates, such as the Followers of Horus (aka the Shemsu-Hor), the Egyptian group of humanlike Helpers assisting the Ancient Ones. But those 'followers' also established numerous institutions of learning around the world, which were known by various different names. The origin of those colleges in Egypt is most often associated with Heliopolis, thousands of years before the emergence of dynastic pharaohs. That city even remained as one of the later great centers of learning in Egypt under the BOPH gods.

Graduates from such academies were strategically dispersed among the mainland population as 'missionaries,' to spread the knowledge and truth those students had been taught. Due to such efforts, civilization was more rapidly and widely dispersed, while utilizing only small regional sites for those Invisible Academies. That plan allowed tight control over what was being taught, thereby moderating or controlling the rate of advancement and progress within the general human populace. Such academies represented a continuing process, one that was updated with fresh and ever expanding subject matter; exposing ever-higher knowledge dispensed in metered doses, based on the comprehensive abilities and ethical growth of each society.

In much later times, those institutions, or their 'modified' successive academies, came to be known as the Mystery Schools. Those colleges were worldwide, and were usually administered and taught by the high priests that imparted esoteric knowledge, which was often derived from their sacred temple documents. Those records reportedly reflected knowledge and data acquired over several millennia, which was usually handed down through strict oral tradition until its incorporation within the temple's preserved sacred record.

Other academies were also known as the Halls of Mysteries, such as the Egyptian mystery schools associated with the Sphinx Temple at Giza, or the 'Invisible College' at Heliopolis. Such ancient universities imparted an esoteric knowledge known as the Sacred Wisdom Science. The very composition of that dispensed ancient knowledge reflected its status as imparted facts, not wisdom derived or postulated directly by ancient humans through their own observations, examination, or contemplation. Such wisdom apparently initiated from a more highly informed source, which then imparted that knowledge to less sophisticated beings. The combined vast knowledge of the Ancient Ones would have encompassed every conceivable topic, as well as the wisdom to reveal only certain levels of knowledge to a developing species; a level dependent upon their obtained 'maturity' of thought and degree of enlightenment.

Throughout Egypt and Mesopotamia, the term 'good and evil' referred to 'all things' or 'everything.' Hence, the Tree of Good and Evil meant the Knowledge of Everything. That may have been the basis for the Biblical Tree of Knowledge in the Garden of Eden, from which the devil, in serpent form, tempted Adam and Eve. However, the serpent was the ancient symbol of knowledge and wisdom, as well as the logo of the Ancient Ones. Such an association indicated that the Ancient Ones possessed all the knowledge of the physical universe, knowledge that the BOPH gods apparently did not want humans to know, thereby demonizing its source.

Several explosive periods of discovery and knowledge can be detected throughout historic times. The oldest acknowledged phase is the 'Chaotic Period' that occurred roughly between c.3800 and 3150 BC, mentioned by numerous cultures including the Egyptians. That conflicted period reflected the competition between the humanlike Helpers of the Ancient Ones and the increased number of BOPH colonists, both vying for support and loyalty of earthly humans. The next era occurred between 2100 and 1500 BC, an unusual period when many formative events happened. A number of natural disasters ensued during that time period in Egypt, India, the Indus Valley, and the Mediterranean; including the volcanic burial of Santorini in Greece. The time near the end of that period may further reflect the historic turning point when the BOPH gods finally achieved full domination over the remaining Helpers and their few human followers.

Indications suggest that a majority of those 'defeated Helpers,' the later descendants of the original Helpers that remained on Earth after the Ancient Ones' temporary exile around 3150 BC, then went into hiding after 1500 BC to spread their teachings secretly until the return of the Ancient Ones. Such an occurrence may also reflect the time when those 'guardians' or Helpers became 'invisible,' beginning their existence only in spirit form.

The last 'enigmatic period' occurred between 800 and 300 BC. In particular, the interval around the end of the 7th century and early 6th century BC was a remarkable time of intellectual discourse and deep spiritual awakening. It was the time of the Greek Anaximander, Thales, and Pythagoras; the Buddha in India; Zoroaster in Persia; the Egyptian Pharaoh Necho II; Confucius and Lao-tzu in China; and numerous Jewish prophets. It would appear that a coordinated effort was undertaken during that period to impart and spread great knowledge, understanding, and a spiritual awareness around the world. The impetus behind such a movement is unknown, but speculation suggests that an influx of replacement humanlike Helpers possibly arrived on Earth during that time, prompting just such a renewed expansion of enlightenment and knowledge.

Some of the lost writings of Sanchuniathon, the 12th century BC Phoenician historian, are known from the records of Philo of Alexandria (c.25 BC - 45 AD), the Jewish Hellenistic scholar. According to Philo, Sanchuniathon stated that Taaut, an instructor before the Great Flood, was the first to record written knowledge on Earth.[6] Later, the earliest Egyptians after the flood then knew that instructor, or perhaps his replacement, as Thouth (aka Taautus). The later Hellenistic Egyptians of Alexandria called their similar instructor Thoth (aka Thoyth), while the Greeks referred to him as Hermes.[7] Other olden sources seem to support a similar contention of such a 'perennial teacher.'

The respected theosophical scholar, Professor G.R.S. Mead, extensively researched esoteric Gnostic beliefs and wrote *Fragments of a Faith Forgotten* during the early twentieth century. According to Professor Mead, the Gnostics believed that the founders of all the great Mystery Schools were either gods or select 'human initiates' taught by the gods.[8] Those gods were the civilizers and teachers of infant races, believed to be souls belonging to a highly developed humanity that possessed knowledge of natural powers learned from prior-perfected beings not of Earth origin. Their impressive Mystery Schools, which became prevalent throughout many parts of the ancient world, were taught by some of Earth's greatest scholars. It was generally believed that those teachers gradually withdrew from Earth as 'maturing' humans developed the faculty for higher reasoning, and were deemed to be strong enough to function independently.

Professor Mead's earlier three volume work, *Thrice Greatest Hermes*, was also published at the start of the twentieth century. It was based on the scant fragments from Manetho's writings, which were rooted in and derived from facts revealed by the Egyptian god Thoth (the Greek Hermes). Professor Mead concluded that there were several beings known by the name 'Thoth' over the ages. The original Thoth (aka Taaut or Taautus) represented the first priesthood of the pre-flood Egyptians, while a second Thoth (aka Thouth or Thoyth) came much later after the Great Flood, when he reintroduced that earlier priesthood to the Egyptians during his subsequent but unknown time period.

Reportedly, the second Thoth formed the archaic Mystery Schools,[9] and preserved the ancient 'great knowledge' by recording it 'in the sacred language of the gods.'[10] Evidently that was also the source of knowledge that Manetho then accessed millennia later. The name 'Thoth' may have eventually evolved into a title or position, perhaps encompassing the duties that are now assigned to or associated with the term 'teacher,' and thus represented a series of different beings who served in that function over the ages. According to G.R.S. Mead, the Thoth Mystery Schools had three levels of students, or three grades of initiates, which included mortals undergoing instruction; the *Intelligences* achieving higher enlightenment; and the Beings of Light who have become one with the light (the Creator), reaching divine status.[11]

Similar to Thoth, there were numerous different beings known as Horus. It is likely that one of those younger Horuses continued Thoth's missionary work, forming a later priesthood. Still later, that priesthood then became known as the Shemsu-Hor, the Followers of Horus. The still later *Tat* priesthood under dynastic-rule, the one that included Manetho, reflected the influence of the BOPH gods that distorted the original teachings of Osiris, Thoth, and Horus. That much later priesthood accessed the knowledge included in Thoth's records, but were apparently unable to fully understand the advanced scientific nature of his writings, or the science behind them.

Evidently the teaching tradition associated with Mystery Schools was continued by the BOPH gods to at least a limited degree, often by merely taking-over existing academies previously established by the Ancient Ones and their Helpers. Those institutions sponsored by the BOPH gods commonly encompassed the art of writing, mathematics, architecture, science, and astronomy. An essay compiled by Samuel Noah Kramer from scattered fragments identified an early Sumerian mystery school, believed to have been located in Erech. It was called the E.dub.ba, the House of the Inscribed Tablets, Sumer's principal academy for scribal arts.[12] Many of its records were inscribed on lapis lazuli tablets. The House of Learning was a continuation of that academy, or perhaps a competing school. It was dedicated to, or perhaps run by, the Sumerian Goddess of Wisdom, Nisaba.[13] Yet it is interesting to note that very few of the Sumerian gods could read or write, usually assigning that task to humans.

Mystery Schools were prevalent throughout most parts of the ancient world, for the purpose of introducing knowledge, art, and civilization to the infant races. One of the most respected centers was the College of Anu in the ancient city of Heliopolis (about six miles northeast of Cairo). It was established sometime before 2500 BC, with the much later high priests of Heliopolis being renowned for their knowledge, having gleaned much of their information from the olden royal temple records. It was apparently one of the prior academies that had been established by the Ancient Ones that taught the 'Wisdom of Horus,' which stressed astronomical study. Diogenes Laertius determined that the celestial observations of the Egyptians dated back to c.49,190 BC, based on astronomical data and calculations believed to have been recorded over a period of 48,863 years before Alexander the Great.[14] Other scholars, such as the 5th century Latin writer, Martianus Capella (c.400-439 AD), also concluded that the Egyptians had studied the cosmos for more than 40,000 years.[15]

Hathor's temple at Denderah was a sanctuary for the Osirian Mysteries, a Secret Wisdom School that taught science to the ancient adepts. According to author W. Raymond Drake, the Zodiac carved in its temple ceiling is believed to portray a cosmic star configuration that existed around 90,000 BC, based on the arrangement of the astrological symbols depicted.[16]

According to Dr. Velikovsky, another academy, the House of Life, was built near Akhet-Aton where scribes were trained and esoteric wisdom was taught.[17] Akhet-Aton was midway between Thebes and Memphis on the eastern bank of the Nile, at the site of modern day el-Amarna. In India, archaic Sanskrit records indicate that Kapila founded the Sankya School, while Vyasa founded its Vedanta School. Author Eric Norman revealed that the Brahmanical chronology stated that the Vedanta of Vyasa was first mentioned in 10,400 BC.[18] While that record may have alluded to an early school of that date, it could not have been the one of Vyasa, who lived around 3000 BC. In addition to the Near Eastern and Asian locations, Polynesia and Peru also operated schools for select members of their tribes. Additional schools have also been found on the islands of the Marquises and the Maori, as well as on Easter Island.

Colonel James Churchward stated that the Naacals were 'Masters,' trained in the ways of civilization and knowledge, who traveled extensively to spread the wisdom of the Ancients. The Naacals formed colleges in each contacted community to impart their knowledge to the general public. Some Naacal records were reportedly written in a language called *Neferit*, thought to be associated with the language of the gods, with certain documents known as *Neferit Records*.[19]

The Brahmins were the Aryan high priests sponsored by the BOPH gods. They cultivated the sacred language that was called *Hanferit*,[20] perhaps one similar to *Senzar*, but with the BOPH gods as its source. The Brahmins displaced the Naga, the later version of the prior Naacals; with both groups believed to have been Helpers of the Ancient Ones. The Brahmins reportedly knew of the Ancient Ones, who they called *Genii*, and claimed the knowledge of the Naga as their own wisdom. Their esoteric doctrines, the *Upanishads*, are meant to overcome ignorance through revelations of secret cosmic knowledge believed to date from *c*.600 BC. The *Upanishads* are roughly equivalent to the Vedas, as the *Cabala* would be to the Old Testament of the Bible. Still later Mystery Schools included or evolved into esoteric societies such as the Egyptian Hermetic Brethren, the Pythagorean Society, and the Greek Eleusinian Mysteries. The Tibetan Yogis and monks, the Persian Magi, the followers of the Jewish *Cabala*, and the initiates within secret levels of the Gnostic faith further spread this form of ancient wisdom.

One of the most renowned academies was taught by the Greek genius, Pythagoras (*c*.582-*c*.507 BC). The young Pythagoras traveled extensively, visiting Egypt where he was taught by Oinouphis and other priests at Heliopolis. He then traveled to Persia where the Magi tutored him. He later went to India for training by the Brahmins. He settled in the Greek colony of Crotona in Italy, forming a mystery school to teach the sciences. Pythagoras required all candidates entering his school to have previously studied the sciences, mathematics, astronomy, geometry, and music. He believed in a well-ordered and harmonious universe, one capable of being understood by humanity. He stated that the world was called forth from chaos by sound or harmony, and was constructed according to the principles of musical proportion.

Pythagoras described such a relationship as the 'music of the spheres' or the harmonies of the universe;[21] a concept believed to refer to the proportional orbits of heavenly bodies circling a central star. That belief formed the basis for ascribing harmony as the result of vibrations in equal times, with discord as the outcome from its opposite state. His theorems, mathematical prowess, and achievements are historic, forming the basis for much of our modern mathematics. The mystical concepts associated with Pythagoras' teachings later evolved into a religious belief.

Religion emerged as a natural evolution from the Mystery Schools, made possible by the expansion of knowledge imparted through those institutions. Such spiritual enlightenment acknowledged a realm beyond the physical, recognizing a small component of the Creator as being contained in all sentient life, evidently referring to an immortal soul. Such a belief reflected an understanding that all life shared a common heritage with some universal spore, much the same as all matter shares its common composition with elementary quarks and leptons.

It was believed that such a single common origin united all sentient life with some universal cause, perhaps through each soul. The underlying intent was the perfection of the intangible element known as character, the essence of each entity. The assistance provided by the Ancient Ones to the emerging infant races within our universe may be in keeping with their commitment made to the Creator. Perhaps that assistance was considered a form of repayment for knowledge the Creator had imparted to them, with utilization of that knowledge intended to also help others; or it may simply be their altruistic belief in the reverence and potential of all physical life.

Expansion of religious thought also spawned philosophic contemplation. That emergence was wide spread throughout ancient Greece, Persia, and India. A number of notable Greek philosophers exemplified that profound and enlightened movement. Plato considered Socrates to be the ultimate philosopher. It was Socrates who taught Plato the doctrine that the soul is able to explore its own nature, because it is illuminated with consciousness. Plato propagated the conviction that the soul participates in the eternal power that orders the cosmos. According to Plato, the Godhead strove to direct the actions of man to bring them into harmony with some Cosmic Symphony, believing that man must work in harmony with the higher powers.[22]

The Athenian statesman, Solon, is credited as the first to interpret the premise that humans are directly responsible for order or discord, with human actions linked to a universal cause and effect relationship. The Greeks believed that 'causality' was the same, whether in nature or from the actions of men. Solon believed justice to be an inseparable part of the divine world order, and believed that all injustice would eventually be punished. The Greeks further believed in a cosmic 'compensatory reaction' against all human transgressions, reaffirming the 'cause and effect' principle, which they claimed existed throughout the universe, perhaps referring to karma.

Elements from the basic teachings of the Ancient Ones and the Cosmic Order are evident in subsequent cultures over the ages. A continuation of the slow and deliberate rate of growth in revealed knowledge, one mandated by the Cosmic Order and the Mystery Schools, is found in the Hopi religious belief. The Hopi clearly professed a cultural concern, one that recognized that a little knowledge could be harmful if not used correctly. The Hopi realized that their knowledge pertaining to the pattern of physical creation was incomplete, a condition they referred to as 'half-vision.'[23] They were concerned that any use of their knowledge, without knowing all the facts and pertinent details, could cause harm or damage.[24] Hence, they continually endeavored to obtain all truth and knowledge that would lead to 'full vision,' a condition known as *Soyal*.[25] That condition required elevation of the human consciousness to its highest enlightenment level.

The concept of Soyal enlightenment further involved the use of a sacred rod or magic wand, as the embodiment of the esoteric knowledge that was brought from their prior Third World, the one ended by the Great Flood.[26] That belief is represented in their ritual Flute Ceremony, which symbolizes the existence of that now lost, but ancient power. According to author Frank Waters, many Hopi esoteric beliefs became quite distorted over time, which has resulted in a connection with witchcraft and the occult. Such interest is credited with spawning the emergence of witches and sorcerers within all modern day Hopi clans.

An offshoot or perhaps an evolution from the early mystery schools was the priesthoods and brotherhoods that kept alive the esoteric knowledge imparted by the Ancient Ones. Brotherhoods formed as organized associations to garner all knowledge pertaining to the 'truths of existence,' thereby preserving a continuing history of humanity. They also attempted to identify and analyze the successes and failures of different cultural civilizations that had been developed by earlier societies. Besides imparting knowledge and implementing the cosmic order, another 'expanded' purpose of these secret societies was to guide and protect Earth and its inhabitants.

The later Brotherhoods that were organized by the Helpers of the Ancient Ones remained active in distributing the great truths entrusted to them for the advancement of humankind. Yet, not all similar organizations were as benevolent, with those formed by the human followers of the BOPH gods usurping that same esoteric wisdom for their own personal benefit, while striving to keep such knowledge hidden from the 'common people.' Perhaps those disreputable societies once affiliated with the BOPH gods have continued to suppress esoteric truths through numerous nefarious means for more than 5,000 years.

Mystery schools continued at least into the 3rd century AD, as evidenced by the first School of Neoplatonism, reportedly founded as early as 193 AD by Ammonius Saccas (*c.*175-250 AD) in Alexandria, Egypt.[27] Over the ages, apparently all those organizations degraded or diverged from their intended purpose, distorting the esoteric knowledge they possessed. The much later and 'lesser' mystery schools and their loose 'affiliations' promoted those distortions as profound truths, often without even realizing their error. Eventually all esoteric academies and their secret wisdom abruptly ceased or became hidden. As those mystic societies and secular organizations slowly degraded into lodges, fraternities, fellowships, and other similar clubs formed by humans; many became merely centers of political idealism, business alliances, and social cliques.

Such transformation could have had many causes. Perhaps it was a natural consequence of the Ancient Ones' exile from Earth, which disrupted their conveyance of knowledge to humans. Even though some Helpers had been left on Earth to continue that mission, they may have eventually relented to competing efforts by the BOPH gods who were not interested in sharing that advanced knowledge. Or the Helpers may have simply reached the pre-set levels of imparted knowledge authorized by the Ancient Ones at the time of their departure into temporary exile.

Yet numerous examples of human genius have been detected since remote times. Many 'new' inventions seemingly emerged 'before their time,' or were discovered from subsequent archaeological finds. Speculation suggests that periodically certain 'gifted' individuals might have obtained access to some lost esoteric knowledge, allowing them to devise or reconstitute past advanced inventions and devices. Genius innovators such as Pythagoras and Archimedes are well known examples, while others are more obscure, but no less accomplished.

Archimedes of Syracuse (287-212 BC) produced extraordinary inventions such as a complex system of levers, pulleys, and grips for lifting massive weights; advanced versions of the screw pump; and solar refraction weapons capable of creating fires from a great distance. Many of his inventions were war related, a practice that continued throughout history. His inspiration is often thought to have occurred during his time as a student within the massive Library of Alexandria.

Similar lost prior knowledge also seemed to reappear around 1453 AD after the fall of Constantinople, the last repository of ancient Eastern esoteric records and culture. An occasional reemergence of esoteric or advanced wisdom would resurface periodically throughout later times. Periods of such reemergence defy explanation, with some speculating that hidden ancient texts of knowledge may have been found, allowing access of that 'lost wisdom' to select humans. Others suggest that the higher level of enlightenment and spiritual evolution of humanity has allowed additional knowledge to be revealed. Such periodic occurrences of phenomenal growth in knowledge and individual genius have been historically documented throughout the ages.

The legendary institution known as the Invisible College might have been a continuation of the Mystery Schools. French scientist and author, Jacques Bergier, reported that around 1660 the Invisible College decided to "reveal to the world a certain number of secrets"[28] through the Royal Society of Science, reportedly an organization that the Invisible College subsequently created as a charter from Britain's King Charles II in 1662.[29] That release of secrets was reportedly a discriminatory one, with some secrets deemed too dangerous to be revealed. That mysterious college is speculated as having also inspired the later organization founded by Cardinal d'Este in 1700, which was called the Academy of Secrets, perhaps the first 'modern' academy of science.

Jacques Bergier further contends that around 1730 AD an unknown ancient source of data became known to a select few men. He called that collection of wisdom *source X*, which was thought to be an advanced level of knowledge dealing with physics and chemistry.[30] Those esoteric secrets are credited with inspiring a few well-known men to produce their contemporary inventions and scientific breakthroughs. By 1810, that *source X* repository seemingly vanished, with a noticeable decrease in discoveries and inventions over the ensuing century.[31] Numerous researchers have attempted to compile lists of inventions that were deemed to have appeared 'prematurely' or 'before-their-time' between 1750 and 1800. While those lists are numerous, no uniformity exists among them, due to the subjective nature of such a task.

Chapter 23

Concept of Religion

The previous chapter exposed the concept of religion as one of the many legacies bequeathed to humanity by the Ancient Ones. Religious thought is not a self-discovered or naturally occurring commodity, especially for primitive people. The pursuit of countless other necessities would have preoccupied primitive humans, rather than such an introspective sojourn that speculated on the nature of the universe created by a Higher Power, and perhaps contemplation of humanity's place within that physical domain. Thus, the abstract commodity of religious or spiritual thought would appear to have been 'introduced' into human culture, rather than self-conceived.

Presumably, the more-expected primitive result would have been an instinctive emergence of superstition, symbolism, and fear or phobias; commodities known to have existed among some early primitive human groups. Much later those illogical but instinctive concepts, or their variations, were combined with certain aspects from ancient esoteric spiritual teachings that had been previously revealed by the Ancient Ones. That subsequent formation resulted in occult practices and corrupt religious theories often associated with many ancient cultures. Becoming widespread, such corrupted teachings distorted the truth and wisdom contained in the spiritual doctrine the Ancient Ones originally imparted.

It could be concluded that the altruistic Ancient Ones had apparently mastered a spiritual science attuned with the cosmic forces of the universe. They approached situations in a strictly realistic and non-emotional manner, introducing and implementing their agenda without any preconceived expectations or bias. They performed their 'civilizing' tasks in that same uniform and methodical manner. Apparently a similar approach was also used when they presented knowledge of the natural world to each infant race they encountered, providing those recipients with all the data necessary to make informed and ethical decisions. That methodology would imply their conviction with the factual validity of the knowledge they imparted. Such certainty suggests that the advanced knowledge they imparted might have been supplied directly to them by the Creator, an implication found in vague and perplexing statements from various ancient texts, including certain Gnostic and Sanskrit records previously mentioned.

As civilization was imparted to the earliest humans at select sites such as Eden, Dilmun, Amenti, E.Din, and the legendary Atlantis, the Ancient Ones also preached an adherence with their code of conduct, the Cosmic Order. As humans progressed in metered steps toward more advanced levels of civilization, their educational training was then expanded to include spiritual realization and philosophy. Those higher pursuits introduced or exposed a comprehensive ethical and moral value system, building a foundation for later religious beliefs.

Just as civilization is not an obvious or inborn commodity within any primitive group, the principles of morality and ethical values are concepts that also require instruction. The notion of compassion, honesty, and assisting others are traits inherently at odds with the survival instincts possessed by most fledgling creatures. Such characteristics must always be taught. Virtue and high technology are not necessarily intertwined. A rigidly controlled society that possesses advanced devices and technology would qualify as being civilized, yet could also be devoid of a true value system. While the infusion of ethics and morality into a primitive society is not a self-evident occurrence, it does require its introduction and tutoring to occur during a more mature phase of development, since a 'minimal prerequisite' foundation or basis must first exist.

One outgrowth from the pursuit of higher human thought was the emergence of religious teachings. The Ancient Ones evidently taught a continuation of each individual consciousness after physical death, as its ascension through or into a different non-corporeal dimension, where each individual consciousness reintegrates or mingles with other similar entities or lifeforces. Within that realm, subsequent physical existences are chosen, ones that would provide further learning opportunities from which each individual entity may grow in enlightenment, perfecting their own character development or composition in a progressive step by step fashion. Thus, the seemingly vast and overwhelming task of perfection is spread over as many physical lives as might be needed, without the pressure of failure dissuading that pursuit.

Such a concept is recognized as the belief in reincarnation, which also inspired the notion of immortality found in most archaic cultures, a doctrine that was often misunderstood and distorted by subsequent societies. It is now generally accepted that only the immortal soul or spirit, the essence of each individual, survives the physical death of its containment vessel or body. When that soul finally sheds all deficiencies and faults after numerous lifetimes, ultimately obtaining a state of perfection, it can then reunite with the Creator in the spiritual realm.

Reincarnation emerged independently throughout many diverse parts of the ancient world. Its concept was an integral part of the body of knowledge known to early humanity as the *Ancient Wisdom*. Reincarnation spawned the transmigration or metempsychosis belief that was observed by early Egyptians as well as the Hindus, where its belief first emerged in Northern India along with the concept of *karma*. Karma is the inevitable sequence of events that emanate from each and every physical act, forming consequences from those actions that then ripple throughout the entire universe. It is often simplified as a universal reward or punishment concept or mechanism.

The reincarnation belief professes a personal immortality leading to the perfection of each individual essence. A similar concept is also embraced in pantheism, a belief that identifies the universe with the Godhead, while further linking world order with that same Supreme Entity. Its doctrine asserts that the Creator is the transcendent reality that brought forth the universe and everything it contains. It also professes the notion that the entire universe is God, and therefore any perfected commodity within that domain could eventually obtain Godlike status.

Recognition of the reincarnation concept may emerge through personal introspection and self-awareness, revealing a duty to perfect each individual's essence. That individual perfection allows eventual reunification with the Creator, with reincarnation the process through which such perfection may be obtained. Its concept is thought to have been imparted by higher evolved beings, although others profess enlightenment of this concept through the inevitable evolution of knowledge that has emerged in fragmented form, from bits and pieces being exposed over years of inquiry. Perhaps its existence emerges from a combination of both forms of revelation.

Reincarnation recognizes the relationship between self and the Creator, with both entities comprised of the same energy. Thus, the Creator can experience physical aspects of the universe through Its creations, with love and acceptance as its underlying theme. Hence, the love of self translates as the love of everything. Since all things in the physical world are parts or separate elements of the Creator, that Supreme Force can experience every aspect of life through each of Its infinite creations. Numerous interpretations of this theme are evident, with many religions believing that all physical life and objects are creations from the very substance of the Creator, or are fragments of the Creator, with every creation representing an individual portion of that Original Source. Such fragmentation of the

Creator is believed to have occurred at the first moment of the Big Bang event. Further evolution of each created element involves its perfection toward a central point, with an ultimate return back to its source of origin.

Unification with the Creator requires an infinite expansion of perception, producing an ability to perceive the whole. That reunification would result in the fusion or joining with its origin. Such attainment always requires preparatory efforts through many lifetimes of fault and deficiency correction over an expanse of time, eventually producing the desired individual perfection. It is through this continuing process of learning, correcting, and development of character that allows us to eventually perceive and love beyond our individual self.

One would expect the oldest recognized form of religious belief on Earth to be the one imparted by the Ancient Ones. Its concept would therefore be reflected in the earliest spiritual or metaphysical beliefs exhibited by primitive humans. That fundamental underlying element is detectable as the belief in reincarnation, and continues to remain the process embraced by many modern followers as the mechanism for human immortality. Such a concept seemingly would not be self-evident to primitive people, and would thus indicate its imparted status, one derived from more enlightened beings. Later, numerous misunderstandings and alterations distorted this spiritual belief. Another book by this author, *Reincarnation...Stepping Stones of Life*, reveals the simplicity and perfection involved with this concept, while dispelling the many misconceptions and distortions associated with the belief in reincarnation.

Substantial evidence exists to indicate that most ancient people believed in the reincarnation of the soul. Authors W. Raymond Drake and James Churchward both disclosed that the earliest recognized religious belief on Earth was that of reincarnation.[1] Numerous other researchers also make that same claim. The reincarnation process allowed a soul to choose the time and place of its rebirth, during a conjunction when cosmic influences and unfolding events would provide explicit lessons for the evolution of that specific soul. This understanding is also an integral part of Hinduism, which continues to thrive into modern times, albeit with untold modifications and alterations from its original format over the millennia. The reincarnation belief is also apparent within the earliest spiritual teachings of the Egyptians, a concept that did not survive into later times after the emergence of a pantheon of gods around 3150 BC that then controlled humanity. Religious practices in modern Egypt now focus mainly on Islam, along with a few followers of other ideologies such as the Coptic Christian belief.

The earliest recorded religious concept of the Egyptians is contained in the *Pyramid Texts*, which professes that some spectral form of existence survives physical death. It also states that Earth was inseparably connected with and governed by the cosmos. The heavens were believed to be the true home of humanity's spiritual component, while 'heavenly inhabitants' also exerted a powerful influence upon humankind and Earth. Archaic Egyptians clearly knew that the physical body was expendable, and did not survive into the afterlife.[2] They further acknowledged the spiritual elements of the *Ka* and *Ba*, the invisible components that comprise each individual human essence. Their afterlife 'journey' was then followed with a 'new' or subsequent physical life, which was provided through the reincarnation process.

Additional references to reincarnation were contained in numerous ancient Egyptian records, such as an obscure text that Colonel James Churchward called the *Papyrus of Anana*. Anana reportedly was the Chief Scribe and trusted counselor to Pharaoh Seti II during the XIX Dynasty. According to the *c*.1205 BC Egyptian *Papyrus of Anana*: "Men do not live once only and then depart...they live many times in many places, though not always in this world. That between each life there is a veil of darkness...The doors will open at last, and show us all the chambers through which our feet wandered from the beginning."[3]

The early Egyptian concept clearly stated that the body is mortal, while the *Ka* is immortal. The *Ka* may best be described as the commodity Western religions call the soul. The soul or *Ka* enters the body at birth, and is part of the universal spirit, the composition of the Creator. But the soul is not the total constituent or component of an individual's essence or consciousness. It also includes the *Ba*, the other companion commodity associated with each essence, which remains separate from the unity of the current physical body and its *Ka* while in our material realm.

The release of the soul after physical death allows the *Ka* and *Ba* to once again be reunited in the spiritual realm, 'completing' each consciousness. Each released *Ka* brings the most recent life's events, lessons, corrections, failures, and gained knowledge to the previously accumulated whole of that individual essence. Such combined unity, the reuniting of the *Ka* and *Ba*, then reflects the complete conscious awareness of an individual's essence at that point in time, restoring all the memories of past lives lived by each distinct entity. That unified completeness reflects the then-present progress toward perfection obtained by that individual.

The original Egyptian reincarnation belief can be traced back to their god Osiris and subsequent teachers such as the god Thoth. That fact was corroborated by Quintus Tertullian (160-230 AD), the Christian theologian and ecclesiastic writer who noted that the teachings of Thoth were believed to be those associated with the religion of Osiris, the reincarnation doctrine that was taught to the human civilization that existed before the Great Flood.[4] Knowledge of Thoth's teachings is mostly known from the scant fragments of Manetho's writings, which were later preserved by the monk, Georgios Syncellus, around 800 AD. Those teachings consisted of numerous facts about reincarnation that pertained to an individual's soul, with those truths further recognized through self-realization.

Reincarnation was the stated mechanism of immortality, revealing the imperishability of the soul and its dual nature.

Thoth stated that only one fragment of our spirit or soul, its *Ka*, actually enters the physical body, while the other part, the *Ba*, remains in the 'timeless' spiritual or ethereal realm.[5] Thoth further professed that each spirit may select a body of either sex, according to its evolutionary need. Animals were apparently thought to be on a separate evolutionary stream of enlightenment from that of humans, with certain branches of animals such as dolphins and lions thought to be at a higher evolutionary level than other animals.[6]

Olden Egyptian religious belief declared that only the soul ascended into heaven to live with the gods. They knew with certainty that the decayable physical body could not survive death.[7] The later ancient Greek concept of immortality further embraced that notion. They also knew that only the spiritual component, the soul, survived physical death, never the body. The Greeks also believed that the soul was not physical, but merely a single dimension point without spatial size or properties. Plato believed that the universe was divinely created, with all physical creations, including 'nonhuman intelligences among the stars,' possessing an immortal soul.[8]

Only later did ancient cultures start to believe that it was absolutely necessary to preserve the physical body as best possible, such as the mummification practice adopted by Dynastic Egypt. Egyptologist Sir Wallis Budge believed mummification was a form of 'insurance policy,' which allowed the deceased and their families a double assurance of the soul's entrance into heaven. Since such an entrance was thought to be achieved only through a very complex process that involved a series of ceremonies, if any portion or phase of that process might accidentally be overlooked or neglected, then the ceremony could be performed again at a later date over the preserved body.[9] The priests that recited the Ritual of Embalmment included the chief officiating priest known as the *Kher-heb*, and his supporting *Sem* priests.[10] At least ten sets or levels of ceremonial people participated in those elaborate Egyptian after-life ceremonies.

As times changed, so did the influences over the Egyptian culture and its religious beliefs. There was an apparent discontinuity between the much earlier predynastic beliefs and those of the later dynastic periods. Such change is immediately apparent at the very start of the Pharaonic Dynasties in *c*.3150 BC. That date also represented the start of the Ancient Ones' period of exile from Earth. That allowed the BOPH gods to impose new beliefs upon the people of Earth, ones designed to inspire both reverence and fear of such seemingly powerful and superior beings.

Colonel James Churchward revealed that Egyptologist Donald A. Mackenzie detected two different religious beliefs in archaic Egypt. One belief followed Osiris and taught the Paradise of the West (thought to be Atlantis), while a rival belief came from the east.[11] Those rival beliefs existed intermittently, each exuding their influences at various times in both Upper and Lower Egypt, until being united around 3150 BC under King Menes. Those back and forth changes in the religious beliefs of ancient Egypt evidently reflected the turmoil between the Ancient Ones and the BOPH colonists. Those disputes abruptly subsided with the temporary exile of the Ancient Ones around 3150 BC, leaving only their Helpers to continue that struggle.

The later religion then followed by ancient Egypt believed that the afterlife journey of the soul was undertaken in a region of the sky known as the *Duat*, a celestial portal. That cosmic domain was located at the midpoint of a region of space bounded by the constellations Leo, Orion, and Taurus.[12] A similar belief was held by the early natives of the Pacific Northwestern United States, who believed that the Milky Way was the 'Pathway of Souls.'[13] Other cultures that also acknowledged such a 'sky region of the dead' included the Tlingits of Alaska, the Arctic Inuit (aka Eskimos), and the Haida natives of British Columbia, Canada.[14]

The later dynastic Egyptians believed that man's destiny or fate was decided before birth, and was unalterable, concluding that destiny was an immutable commodity.[15] But that is a distortion or misconception of free will choice, at least within the context of future-encountered predestined events. While a future event may be predestined to occur sometime within one's currently chosen life, our free will choice in reacting to that learning event will determine its lasting effect.

Professor Cornelius Loew wrote that the Greeks believed human actions were linked to a cause and effect connection.[16] As previously stated, Greeks also believed in a cause and effect reaction to all human transgressions, acknowledging the existence of karma. That concept was based on the intention or objective behind each action, thereby defining the 'right or wrong' nature of each deed. A connection between karma and Christianity is also apparent in Jesus' statement: "For whatsoever a man soweth, that shall he also reap."[17]

Similarities with the basic tenets of reincarnation can also be found in the religious doctrine of the Hopi clan of the Pueblo Indians. Hopi belief stated that beyond (or perhaps before) our present known universe, there existed six more universes or solar systems marking our 'Road of Life.' In each life, man starts out pure (or more correctly 'neutral,' without blemishes or achievements). The world (the present life reality) either corrupts that life with evil, requiring yet another life on that same level of existence (reliving lessons over again) or gains enlightenment, thus moving that life to the next higher level.[18] The Hopi also conceived that the universe, the domain of the Creator, comprises the most minute particle to the largest; encompassing a region starting from its origin (the Big Bang event 'point'), and extending out to the farthest cosmic edges. Hence, the essence of the Creator is within each of Its creations throughout the universe. The Hopi religious creed appears to be the very essence of the reincarnation belief.

Pythagoras was a widely known educator who spread esoteric teachings and religious concepts through his famous Mystery School at the Greek colony in Crotona, Italy, around 530 BC. Pythagoras embraced reincarnation and taught its principals,

272

believing he was the reincarnation of Euphorbus,[19] the son of Panthus, who was a warrior in the Trojan War, killed by a spear from Menelaus. He formulated a theology of his own, which evolved into a religious belief that survived his death. His theology then became known as the Pythagorean Movement, which was carried on by his many followers.

That doctrine professed sobriety, purity, manners, and temperance. This belief avowed doing no harm to any other living creatures, thus Pythagoreans would not kill or injure any animal. It also believed in the transmigration of the soul and a mathematical basis or relationship that was employed throughout the physical world, where all celestial bodies obeyed the same natural laws. The Pythagorean Movement also believed in a fifth element or force, the last of the natural or basic elements of the universe, which remained undiscovered and hidden from all later Pythagorean followers.

Pythagoras considered numbers to be the essence and basic principle underlying all things. The Monad or Unit was considered the source of all numbers. It has long been interpreted that his followers considered the number ten as having embodied all musical and mathematical proportions, denoting the system of the universe.[20] The relationship of numbers to notes of the musical scale were also equated with the harmony that resulted from vibrations in equal times, or in discord from its converse or opposite condition. Pythagoras taught that all heavenly bodies circled a central star, and described their proportional orbits as the previously mentioned 'music of the spheres,' or the harmonies of the universe.[21] The later 17th century astronomer, Johannes Kepler (1571-1630), essentially refined this basic Pythagorean concept in 1619, formulating his third harmonic law of planetary motion. Pythagoras further believed that the moon was once inhabited,[22] while also professing that the gods were indeed real beings that had imparted divine inspiration and specific knowledge to humans.

After the death of Socrates, Plato (*c*.428-*c*.347 BC) reportedly joined the secret Pythagorean Society and learned its many esoteric mysteries.[23]   Followers of the Pythagorean Movement also utilized a secret sacred symbol, in the shape of a pentagram, to identify their comrades.   The pentagram was believed to contain a unique mathematical measurement or reference known as the 'Golden Section.' That measurement, or more correctly a 'proportional relationship,' later became known as the *phi ratio*, named after the Greek sculptor Phidias.

Phi is considered to be the ideal ratio between two lengths, producing the most aesthetic visual effect. This ratio, calculated as 1:1.61803398,[24] has been consistently incorporated in works of art as well as many famous architectural structures. It also exists throughout nature, found in leaf spacing, snail shells, and other forms of organic life. Pythagoreans believed that *phi* reflected the harmonies of nature, a universal constant of aesthetic proportion that was intrinsic to every object. The *phi ratio*, as contained in the pentagram, was used extensively by Leonardo da Vinci in his numerous depictions of human-form proportions.

The Pythagorean Movement was supposedly derived from Orphism, the mystical religious belief based on the writings of the Greek poet and musician Orpheus.[25]   That conclusion is known from certain 6th century BC writings made by later Pythagorean followers, found buried with them in their graves. The physical existence of Orpheus has been disputed, with some claiming he was merely a legendary character, while others believed he was an actual historic person. His mother was reportedly the muse Calliope, and his father was either Oeagrus, the king of Thrace, or the god Apollo.   Evidently DNA paternity tests were unavailable to even the privileged class of ancient Greece and their gods. Disputes also exist as to whether Apollo or Orpheus was the author of the ancient Orphic hymns.   Those hymns transmitted great knowledge, especially concerning astronomy and cosmology. They were also prophetic, including revelations that the moon had 'divine inhabitants.' Those mystic hymns further revealed that a set of universal cosmic laws governed all phenomena everywhere within the physical realm.

Orpheus is reported to have stated that the heavenly gods were innumerable souls that traveled: "...from planet to planet, and in the abyss of space, lament the heaven they have forgotten."[26] Zeus later condemned Orpheus for revealing the secret *Ancient Wisdom* of the gods. Eventually, he presumably departed Earth for the moon, where he remained, although other accounts claim he was slain by Zeus, "for divulging divine secrets."[27] Orpheus was also considered the most accomplished mortal Greek musician, a person that was also able to move physical objects with his music.

The religious mystic cult known as Orphism reportedly emerged from the hymns and teachings of Orpheus. That belief centered on the revelations of the god Dionysus Zagreus, the son of Zeus and Persephone. Such a belief claimed that humans possess a dual nature, both mortal and divine, or earthly and heavenly; one that also comprised or mingled with 'good and evil.' Humanity was to rid itself of evil by correcting their faults and deficiencies, resulting in complete liberation from further physical trials, thereby reuniting with the Creator.

Such a task was intended to be accomplished through a series of numerous reincarnated lives, ultimately allowing each entity to remain within the divine realm upon perfection of its essence. It further asserted that humans possessed an immortal soul that was released or freed from the physical vessel of its body upon death, thus rejoining an ethereal realm where that soul remained until inhabiting its next body. When a soul was purified of all faults and character deficiencies, that soul could then return to its source, for its permanent reunification with the Creator. Orphism, like numerous other early mystic beliefs, incorporated Earth's earliest spiritual teachings of reincarnation, the spiritual concept first revealed during remotely ancient times by the Ancient Ones.

Chapter 24

Ancient Religions

According to most religious beliefs, there is only one truly supreme and universal Godhead, the Creator. Yet that Supreme Entity is known by different names within the many diverse religions practiced by humankind. Therefore, apparently all religions are merely different expressions referring to the same Creator, although defined by different perceptions held by each faith's human followers. The main differences between most of humanity's organized religions emerge within the ceremonies and rituals followed by those various beliefs. Doctrine pertaining to the supreme nature of the Creator, and the belief that one should live an ethical and just life, are integral parts of most modern religions, with a vast array of distinctions only apparent in more insignificant areas.

Believing in something so strongly that one is willing to forfeit their physical life does not alter the factual reality of what actually exists. The deaths of martyrs do not prove the factual reality of their individual convictions. This concept can best be demonstrated by prevailing beliefs professed during the Dark Ages, a period when all the greatest scientific minds, along with the Church Fathers and leaders, 'knew' that our flat Earth was at the center of a relatively small universe. However, such a strong belief did not change the factual reality of a spherical Earth and other planets circling a central star; all occupying a small portion of a 'common' galaxy, located within an unremarkable part of a vastly larger universe.

F. Max Müller, in his *Lectures on the Science of Religion*, stated: "Men fight about religion on Earth; in heaven they shall find out that there is only one true religion...the worship of God's Spirit."[1] Knowledge of the Creator, apparently revealed from the most ancient oral traditions originally imparted to humanity by the Ancient Ones, was often subsequently distorted through false interpretations. The source behind those distortions apparently originated with the BOPH gods, who deliberately altered that original ancient knowledge. Later, humanity apparently continued that practice of revisionism and its resultant deception for political motives.

Author Jean Sendy stated that anthropologists have noted a metaphysical spirit as an integral element underlying many ancient cultures.[2] That metaphysical aspect was linked with the concept of immortality associated with the reincarnation process and the belief in a superior order that existed throughout the universe. From those most basic concepts, Earth's initial religious beliefs emerged. A review of the earliest formal doctrines revealed a pattern of continuous change and distortion from their original concept, since first being imparted to humankind.

The oldest known religious belief is described as that of the Mother Goddess, traced back to the Cro-Magnons. That may not have been a true religious belief, but rather an 'honor' bestowed on the fertility of the female through the process of childbirth. Another possibility might reflect the reverence bestowed upon certain female beings, perhaps a female Ancient One or Helper, who brought the earliest forms of civilization and knowledge to humans. Still other non-human or spiritual concepts were also apparent, such as those that focused on the celestial bodies of the sun, moon and stars. Again, actual worship is not necessarily indicated by such focus.

Evidence of post-flood veneration of that generic Mother Goddess continued into historic times. The Mother Goddess was evident in the oldest known permanent settlement of Tell

Mureybut (modern day Aleppo, Syria), which dated to 8000 BC. A Bull cult followed, believed associated with the Zodiac Age of Taurus the Bull. The bull or its symbol was worshiped intermittently over the millennia, with perhaps its greatest exposure occurring between 1400 and 400 BC. During ancient times, it was generally believed that all living things on Earth emanated from the body and blood of the bull. The bull was further associated with the moon, linked through the description of a crescent moon as being 'horned' like a bull. That notion may provide further verification that the Lunar Pitris were the 'ancestors' of human life on Earth.

Both the Mother Goddess and the Bull cult were worshiped at Catal Hüyük around 7000 BC. Those cults were intermingled contemporaneously with a Water or Fish god first found at Lepenski Vir, Yugoslavia, in c.5450 BC, and later around 4800 BC in the Ubaid culture of Mesopotamia. Such symbolic cults may not reflect a true religious belief, but rather a veneration of superior beings, ones that were apparently represented by such bull, water, or fish icons.

The earliest specific humanlike god was the Sumerian Enki, who dates to at least 3350 BC. A true religious belief in a pantheon of gods, or Godhead, emerged from the Sumer Kingdom around c.3150 BC, when specific physical superhuman beings were venerated or worshiped. Humanlike gods of ancient epics and mythology then dominated religious beliefs during the ensuing millennia. Around 2000 BC, the Hebrew faith emerged with the patriarch Abraham, who claimed a generic lineage with the Biblical pre-Flood Adam to Noah ancestors.

Those much earlier ancestors were associated with a divine being who created a paradise from which gifts were bestowed upon humans, and knowledge was imparted to humanity. A similar 'generic' patriarchal ancestry was common with numerous other ancient cultures, where benevolent beings bestowed favors and gifts upon humans. Perhaps the Egyptian Netteru, the ephemeral divine beings that reportedly taught humans knowledge and civilization, are some of the better-known benefactors. Only later were those beings described as 'gods.'

The advanced culture of ancient India was contemporaneous with Sumer, Akkad, and Egypt. It had a rich established religious belief of its own, and along with predynastic Egypt, perhaps the one that most closely followed the original concepts associated with reincarnation. Their established belief was later called Hinduism, although with certain known changes or distortions from its original version. A brief exposure of the earliest ancient religions is presented for further enlightenment, as contained in the following basic descriptions.[3]

HINDUISM

Hinduism claims no founder for its religious belief, professing its origin as having been 'eternal and ageless.' Followers also claim no time when their religion did not exist. Hinduism is both a religious belief as well as an established pattern for living life. One of its fundamental beliefs describes the universe as being a great enclosed sphere, one that moves through various cycles, such as a Golden Age followed by a 'degenerative period,' with each prior 'world cycle' being destroyed and recycled again. Such recycling also applies to mortal life, where physical death releases an immortal soul. Those departed souls can then be reborn into anything, including animals or minerals, a process known as transmigration. The specific nature of each subsequent life or existence is based on karma, an accumulated 'merit or demerit' ledger system resulting from consequences caused by all of one's past actions. Bad karma can only be overcome through future good works or acts.

There are two basic types of Hinduism, Worldly Hinduism and Renunciatory Hinduism. Worldly Hinduism professes three *Debts*, namely: study of the *Vedas*, producing a male heir, and sacrificing to the Gods; along with three *Goals*, which focus on: the attainment of material success, cultivation of righteous behavior, and the pursuit of sensual pleasures. Renunciatory Hinduism is based on Upanishad philosophy, the metaphysical and speculative texts dealing with knowledge and meditation. That belief requires abandonment of worldly ways, while striving for the unification of the individual soul with the Godhead's Universal World Soul.

The most ancient and sacred literature of Hinduism is the four *Vedas*, collectively known as the *Mantra* or the *Samhita*. The arranged order of the *Vedas* was believed to have been the work of the great sage, Vyasa, sometime around 3000 BC, although it is believed that the *Vedas* were not recorded in written form until *c*.1500 BC. Prior to then, the *Vedas* were either handed down verbally, or written in an unknown language or recorded form yet to be discovered. The *Vedas* teach the belief in only one Supreme Being, the Creator, known as Brahma, along with lesser beings or deities that are at a higher enlightenment than humans. It is believed that everything physical will revert back from which it came, ultimately being absorbed by the Creator. Their Creator God, Brahma, should not be confused with the Brahmans, who are humans that comprise the fourth and highest class of officiating priests within this religion.

While Brahma is the Creator, some believe the Supreme Being, the All-Father, is comprised of three gods; forming a triad or trinity known as the *Trimurti*.[4] This trinity is comprised of Vishnu as the Preserver, Shiva (aka Siva) as the Destroyer, along with Brahma, the Creator. Although there were a few temples erected to Brahma, no personification of this Creator God is known. Brahma was an unseen God that created the other gods and the universe. Vishnu and Shiva had numerous sites of worship, with statues depicting them as physical beings. These personified gods survive eternally through the reincarnation process, as exemplified by Rama, who reportedly was the seventh reincarnation of Vishnu; or Krishna, who is believed to be Vishnu's eighth incarnation.

Two other religious beliefs, Jainism and Buddhism, are variants of Hinduism. They are included within this category of 'ancient religions' due to their specific Hindu relationship, which by definition is more than a religious belief, professing a designated 'way of life.' Hinduism, Jainism, and Buddhism provide the three 'varieties' of religious mythologies in India, according to W. Norman Brown, a professor of ancient Sanskrit.

JAINISM

Jainism was based on the eighth century BC teachings of Parshva (aka Parsva) who lived sometime between 877 and 777 BC. He was a holy teacher or saint of India, and is believed to have originated Jainism doctrine. But it was Vardhamana (*c*.544-*c*.472 BC, although some records reflect an earlier life from 599-*c*.528 BC), a contemporary of Gotama (the Buddha), who is credited as the founder of this belief as a religion. Vardhamana, a young prince turned preacher, grew in prominence as a religious teacher, and later came to be known as Mahavira, meaning Great Man or Hero. The religious beliefs promoted by Mahavira were thought to be the result of personal enlightenment revealed directly from the gods.

Jainism teaches that the universe has gone through a series of similar cycles, each of extremely long duration, from maximum evil to the best of all states. While in the deteriorating periods or cycles, learning becomes necessary. During those times, a series of 24 'saviors' appear to teach wisdom, knowledge, civilization, art, and laws throughout that 'period of deterioration.' The followers of this religion ascribe supernatural powers to those 'savior teachers,' but did not considered them to be gods; remaining in agreement with Mahavira who did not believe in any physical gods. However, certain special saints or prophets from the remote past were known as the *tirthankaras* (aka *tirthamkaras*). Those ancient beings were once bound or constrained, but eventually gained enlightenment, becoming liberated souls through their own efforts. They were considered the 'founders of the path' by later souls. Such descriptive terms suggest that the *tirthankaras* may have been the Ancient Ones.

Mahavira believed that man was his own worst enemy, making it necessary to conquer individual delusions that were the result of incorrect, blind, perverse, or ignorant beliefs. Mankind must also conquer their propensity toward degenerate behavior. Those that attained such self-mastery were deemed a *Jina*, a spiritual conqueror, and thus became known as a Jain. Jainism rejected the claims of the Brahmans and the *Vedic* rituals, preaching a new ethical doctrine, including the non-injury of all living creatures. The most important tenet of the faith was its insistence upon *Ahimsa* (aka *Ahinsa*), their creed requiring 'harmlessness' to all living creatures.[5] Jainism records were written in both the Sanskrit and Prakrit languages.

This theology also includes the belief in a soul, which is an independent conscious entity that is eternal, formless, and spatial. Jainism professes that an infinite number of souls exist, with each soul being an inherently independent and conscious agent; an eternal, formless entity. The process through which a soul obtained a physical vessel, its body, was by reincarnation. When a soul entered, it pervaded that entire vessel, assuming the size and shape of its entire body.

When released from that physical vessel due to bodily death, the soul severs all connection with that body and once again resumes its 'eternal composition' in its spiritual form, which exists in the ethereal realm. The soul then ceases to have physical size, existing only in that ethereal world. Thus, the soul passes through two phases, a 'bound state' and its 'free state.'

The bound state occurs during physical life, or a series of numerous lives, during which the soul attempts to conquer its deficiencies. During those intermediate phases, the soul possesses differing levels or degrees of imperfection. Any retention of faults from one life to the next is due to wrong beliefs, which include one-sided or blind convictions, along with dubious, perverse, and ignorant beliefs. The freed state occurs at the end of the reincarnation cycle (or cycles) when the condition of perfect bliss is obtained, which is every entity's ultimate and ideal goal. The ethereal freed state is the natural form of each consciousness, the one sought as its permanent state. That can only be achieved over a series of numerous lives of learning, while correcting any remaining imperfections and faults, thereby eventually obtaining a perfected state of bliss.

Jainism views the physical world as an intricate assembly of simplistic parts. Those basic parts are merely individual particles occupying a point in space, and thus could only be defined as being one or perhaps two-dimensional. Such an eternal formless particle, or particles, is the source of all form. This concept is easily recognizable as describing the elemental or subatomic particles of quarks and leptons. Such a remarkable example of ancient understanding of quantum theory, especially during those 'primitive' times, suggests imparted knowledge from an unknown but highly enlightened source. Jainism further proposed that all physical matter exists in either of two forms, namely *fundamental* (at the atomic level) or *aggregate* (in which atoms join in various combinations to produce more complex compounds).

BUDDHISM

This religion was founded in 525 BC by the *Buddha*, a mortal man who was Siddartha Gotama (aka Gautama Siddharta, *c.*565-*c.*485 BC), an Indian prince. His enlightenment was the result of instruction from religious teachers and his own self-introspection, not a revelation directly from the gods. Buddhism is a later form of Hinduism, rejecting large portions of that older belief. The original Buddhism did not worship the Vedic gods, or believe in their divinity. Those gods were thought to be merely 'elevated' or superior beings, susceptible to death and rebirth. Buddhism also rejected the claims of the Brahmans and the Vedic rituals, discarding the Sanskrit language, the caste system, and sacrificial

284

practices. Its doctrine appears to be an attempt to regain what was thought to be the earliest teachings of Hinduism, before its later distortions and changes.

Buddhist teachings, as expressed in the *Dhammapada*, stress a moral and ethical doctrine, including non-injury of all living creatures.[6] Buddhism believes in the concept of reincarnation, including transmigration, with the cycle of rebirth based on acquired karma from prior actions. It is through such karma that all past, ongoing, and future lives are connected. While Buddhism believes in karma, it does not recognize an immortal soul. Its practitioner's ultimate goal is to seek and obtain nirvana. Nirvana represents the state of total enlightenment and liberation (or spiritual purity), a state reached by strictly observing a righteous way of life, while purging all undesirable or negative traits. Dharma is the faith's decrees or doctrines governing the eternal laws of nature and the moral laws of humankind.

Buddhism may be considered a sect of Brahminical Hinduism, where Buddha was believed to be an incarnation of the god Vishnu. It is further believed that the Lamas are divine spirits who voluntarily descend to Earth in human form to promote the welfare of humankind, while perpetuating their divine lineage and concepts into contemporary times. The Lama residing in (or presently exiled from) Tibet is recognized as the chief or highest pontiff of the sect. That temporal monarch is called the Dalai Lama, the ultimate authority within this religious belief.

According to Tibetan records, during the early period of Buddhism, the original *Siddhas*, the perfected beings or saints of this belief who were known as 'the sky-traveling beings,' reportedly ascended while in their physical bodies to the realm of the Dakas. Such a belief might suggest a vague recollection of the Ancient Ones leaving Earth in exile, departing into the realm of outer space. Variants of the Buddhism belief, such as Tantrism, also evolved from the same initial doctrine. Tantra Buddhism, also known as Tantrism, exists in Northern Bengal,

Nepal, and Tibet. Tantrism is also found within some cults of Jainism.

Other Eastern Religions

W. Norman Brown, the previously mentioned professor of Sanskrit studies, discerned the period around the 6th century BC as being a time of great religious and philosophical creativity, as well as one of great economic expansion in both India and Asia as a whole. That specific time period produced such enlightened great men as Lao-tzu, Gotama, Mahavira, Pythagoras, Zoroaster, and Confucius, as well as their prominent religious movements. The creation of numerous formal religions then proliferated as a result of this 6th century BC enlightenment, including those of Taoism, Jainism, Buddhism, Confucianism, Shintoism, and Zoroastrianism.

TAOISM

Unlike the Hindu spiritualistic belief, or the Western God-centric and dualistic belief in some supernatural being, the Chinese are Naturalistic, as reflected in their practice known as Taoism. This ancient wisdom was based on an agricultural culture wherein humans realized their dependence upon nature and its ever changing processes. Taoism ignores human relationships and concentrates on understanding the universe, including its numerous supernatural aspects. Taoism's fundamental concept is of a universe that is in a constant state of change, brought about by two opposing forces, the principles of Yin and Yang. Yin and Yang are conceived as basic elements that are normally in a state of balance, but occasionally undergo temporary disruptions. Taoism developed from the ancient worship of nature, which included deities, some of whom were supernatural beings. One ancient deity was a goddess called Hsi Wang Mu, sometimes associated with the Mother Goddess, as well as with the later

Christian Mother Mary.

The origination of Taoism is credited to Lao-tzu (aka Lao-tse or Li Urh), the 6th century BC author recognized for his great philosophical classic, the *Tao Teh King* (aka *Tao Te Ching*), the *Book of Nature and Intelligence*. That profound work has often been described as being mostly unintelligible without its accompanying commentaries, and was reportedly based on the ideas of the legendary ruler Huang-ti (aka the Yellow Emperor) who civilized China sometime between 2697 and 2595 BC. Lao-tzu supposedly derived many of his beliefs from the *Nei Jing* (*Book of the Yellow Emperor*), a record that originated around *c.*2600 BC, although its content or inspiration was derived from a much earlier but unknown source. Lao-tzu reportedly wrote 930 ethical and religious texts, along with another 70 books about magic; producing a total of 1,000 enlightened manuscripts.[7]

CONFUCIANISM

A younger contemporary of Lao-tzu was Confucius (aka K'ung Tzu and Kung Fu-tzu, 551-478 BC), a descendant within the Shang dynasty. He was not a religious man, but rather both a student and teacher of ancient beliefs, claiming no divinity or direct contact with any deity. From the numerous philosophical beliefs he encountered, Confucianism then formed his teachings. It was not a formal religion with a church and priesthood, but rather a system of virtuous thought; with basic principles for personal conduct, interaction with others, and the pursuit of wisdom. Confucius reportedly stated that the celestial beings, the ancient gods, were the source from which all morality and virtue on Earth had emerged, as a direct result of their early teachings. The virtues of righteousness, propriety, piety, and integrity were stressed. Every human who mastered such virtuous traits then became a *chun-tzu*, a 'perfected being.'

Confucius reportedly also formulated the notable Golden Rule philosophy, believing in a natural sympathy or an ethical intent that existed between all people. He demanded ardent desire and commitment from all of his followers, and stressed education for all classes of people. The revered principals of Confucianism are contained within two groups of writings: the *Wu Ching* (*Five Classics*) and the *Shih Shu* (the *Four Books*).

SHINTOISM

The national religion of Japan is Shintoism, which is not technically a religion, but rather a creed of a political-religiosity system that originated in prehistoric times. It has no stated dogma, moral codes, or sacred writings. However, Shintoism does profess that the Imperial Dynasty of Japan is of a divine nature, with its descendants coming from a long line of physical gods, essentially making it a combined form of hero and ancestor worship. Shintoism contains both polytheistic and animistic elements, believing in invisible powers and natural spirits. Its typical worship site contains multiple separate altars honoring numerous beings. Those recipients of Shinto worship included a group of various individuals, consisting of an important local deity; a revered family ancestor; the Sun goddess; and a national hero or deity. Shinto deities are called *kami*, with Amaterasu being their Grand Goddess. She is revered as both the highest divinity, as well as their greatest ancestress.

Buddhism's arrival to Japan in 552 AD greatly influenced the Shinto doctrine in numerous ways, eventually creating different 'splinter' sects within its original belief. The Zen sect of Buddhism eventually gained an ample number of Japanese followers, which then allowed it to coexist with Shintoism throughout Japan. Zen Buddhism is considered a form or branch of the prior Mahayana Buddhism.

Chapter 25

Evolving Beliefs

ZOROASTRIANISM

Another of the devout ancient beliefs that also solidified into a formal religion during the 6th century BC emerged in ancient Persia. The Persian prophet Zoroaster (aka Zarathuštra) started the religious belief known as Zoroastrianism in *c.*625 BC, when he began receiving revelations from the god Ahura Mazda [Lord Wisdom]. The accounts and tales of Ahura Mazda existed for at least a thousand years before Zoroaster, with humanity eventually elevating him to 'supreme god' around 600 BC. Ahura Mazda was prominent as far away as India, where he was known as a Great Father, according to researcher and author Merlin Stone.[1] After the Persian conquest of Babylon in 539 BC, all the olden Babylonian gods were essentially displaced by Ahura Mazda.

Zoroaster was born in the Eastern Persian territory of Airyana Vaejah, in the land of Media, the area now known as Azerbaijan near the Caspian Sea. The date of his birth is in dispute, as either in the year 660 BC, the most probable date, or in 630 BC. He was precocious as a child, confounding the Magi with his wisdom. He became a hermit, living in a cave on Mount Sabalan, where he eventually heard the Revelation of God. Those revelations were compiled in a doctrine that was recorded as psalms [Gathas] that later formed a major portion of the sacred scripture known as the *Avesta* or *Zend-Avesta*. It is the Bible equivalent of this religion, which Alexander the Great reportedly burned, although his followers, along with the Parsees, later restored it.

Zoroaster was one of the first prophets to preach apocalyptic doctrine and monotheism, worshiping only Ahura Mazda who had six assistants, although the religion also recognized a powerful negative force or deity. Zoroastrianism believed the Creator produced these two mighty beings, both endowed with abilities and powers nearly equal to those of the Creator. Ahura Mazda (aka Ohrmazd, Ormuzd, or the Greek Oromasdes), remained faithful to the Creator, and represented all that was good. The other, Ahriman (the Greek Arimanes), rebelled and became the author of all evil. Such discord is reminiscent of the Ancient Ones and the Destroyers.

Zoroastrianism professes that such opposing pairs as truth and lies, or good and evil, permeated everywhere within the universe. Ahura Mazda was believed to be the one who built the Earth (perhaps an early *First Being*) and formed the Seven Amshaspends (aka Amahraspands, perhaps the *Tridasa*) to fight against the evil Ahriman. It is thought that the conflict between these two opposite forces would be resolved in the final days of an apocalyptic end, with 'Good' eventually triumphing. This religious belief obviously recognized distinctions between the Creator and 'God' (or gods); recognizing 'elevated' physical beings or divinities of both Good (perhaps the Ancient Ones) and Evil (perhaps the Destroyers), which came after the Creator.

Beside its dualistic concept of good versus evil, Zoroastrianism also employs extremely ethical laws, with a highly intellectual dispensation of rule, justice, intent, devotion, integrity, and morality. It could be described as a cause and effect religious belief or way of life. Its belief proposes a non-physical spiritual realm with an afterlife reward in a paradise, or a punishment in a hellish existence. It contained some ritual practices, ceremony, and magic; but no mythology, formal priesthood, or divination. Zoroastrianism did not utilize temples, altars, or statues; but rather offered their sacrifices out in the open, usually on mountain tops. Its informal ministers or promoters, referred to as Magi, were schooled in magic formulas, incantations, and astrology.

All deeds were to be done in accordance with a 'Righteous Order.' According to author Robert Charroux, the Zoroastrian religion held a belief called *Pairi*, which designated a way of life that was in harmony with the cosmos.[2] Any deviation from Pairi led to chaos and disruption, in a manner similar to disobeying the Cosmic Order, which also led to disharmony. Any form of burial for the deceased was prohibited, since it was thought to pollute the land. Zoroastrian customs required the dead to be exposed, enabling the deceased body to be devoured by vultures.

There is much evidence that Zoroastrian religious beliefs strongly influenced the Jewish theology. The *Manual of Discipline* found among the *Dead Sea Scrolls* bears many direct similarities with Zoroastrianism, such as its direct influence on generating the belief in demons and angels, which then emerged within the Judeo-Christian doctrine. Many Greeks, including the philosophers Plato and Aristotle, also embraced Zoroastrian beliefs. Persecution by the Arabs in the 7th century AD caused its Persian believers to flee to India, where they became known as the Parsees, since Pars was another name for ancient Persia.

JUDAISM

Judaism formed as a result of a contractual agreement, The Covenant, between the Semitic god Yahweh and the Hebrew Abraham, perhaps sometime around *c.*2004 BC. This covenant was proposed by Yahweh, which provided for Abraham and his people to honor only Yahweh as their ultimate king and legislator, agreeing to obey His laws, and circumcise all males as a sign of this covenant. Yahweh would then acknowledge the Hebrews as His particular people and be considerate of them, implying a certain level of protection. Yahweh apparently often used affliction to test His people. As long as the people remained faithful to Yahweh's Law, He would not allow them to be defeated by their enemies. Over several ensuing centuries after that contractual agreement, up to 400 years by some accounts, Abraham and his subsequent descendants had continued their nomadic wanderings throughout the Near East.

After the Hyksôs conquered Egypt in 1720 BC, many Hebrews eventually migrated to Egypt seeking work as 'free men.' When the Hyksôs reign finally ended in 1555 BC after the Egyptians regained power, some Hebrews returned to Asia Minor and Canaan, while others remained in Egypt. During that time, Yahweh is reported to have made the same covenant with Moses that He made with Abraham. Not much is known about the Hebrews between their arrival in Egypt and their Biblical Exodus under Moses, but their religion was strongly influenced by Egyptian beliefs. After the Exodus, the Hebrews also became known as the Israelites, with Moses receiving several sets of Laws from God. The *Ceremonial Laws*, the ordinances that regulated the killing of animals, are written in II Chronicles 35:1-13, but were later abolished by Christ according to Ephesians 2:15. Another set of Laws, the *Health Laws*, is contained in Leviticus 11 and Deuteronomy 14. The *Moral Laws* are well known as the Ten Commandments.

During the ensuing forty years of wandering in the desert after their Exodus from Egypt, many Jews rebelled against the strict and rigid discipline of Yahweh, and reverted to worshipping their 'olden gods.' At that time, all gods were visible, physical beings that were known by their personal names. After settling in the land of Canaan, the official religion of Northern Israel remained as the worship of Yahweh, but the Ugarit religions of Baal and Astarte were also followed. Such multiple worship continued from *c.*1400 BC until about 600 BC, when strict monotheism became the rule.

It was under the leadership of Joshua when the Hebrews systematically entered the land of Canaan, the modern day area comprised of Lebanon, Israel/Palestine, and parts of Syria.

Yahweh ordered the genocide of all inhabitants in that area, with Jerusalem becoming the first city to fall under Yahweh's assault. Ugarit was the land in the far northern border region of Canaan, the modern day nation of Syria. Ugarit mythology became a strong influence on the Hebrews, with their god Baal often referred to as the enemy of Yahweh. The first Jewish kingdom started with David, who reportedly also created an eternal covenant with Yahweh. His son Solomon, the second Hebrew king, built the Great Temple in 965 BC, the first 'permanent place' for Yahweh worship. After the death of King Solomon in 931 BC, the Jews further split into two separate nations; a southern state of Judah with its capital in Jerusalem, and the northern kingdom of Israel with its capital in Samaria [Bethel], which was later destroyed by the Assyrians in 722 BC.

After the Southern Nation was well established, the Hebrew state changed from a political nation into a church state professing a religious belief, as the result of reforms initiated by Josiah between 638 and 608 BC. That marked the first true formation of Jewish religious doctrine, rather than merely a political arrangement. In 624 BC, King Josiah stopped the idolatry of other gods and also diminished the influence of the Zodiac. The covenant of 621 BC reaffirmed the original contract binding the Hebrew people and their king with Yahweh for all time. After that act, Yahweh was no longer considered to be merely a city-state god, but also became a world God. Beginning in 597 BC, the Southern Kingdom in Jerusalem was attacked by the Chaldean ruled Babylonian Empire, with Jerusalem's final destruction occurring in 586 BC. The Jewish people then became captives, with some remaining in Jerusalem, while others were forcibly relocated to Babylon. The prophet Ezekiel believed that this exile was a punishment Yahweh inflicted on the Hebrews for their sins, an event that marked the end of the Davidic Dynasty.

Exposure to the Chaldean culture of Babylon proved to be a great influence on the Hebrew people. Jewish belief borrowed heavily from Babylonian religious and occult teachings of the god

Marduk (aka Bel), the chief deity over the pantheon during their time of captivity. A large portion of the esoteric wisdom that comprises the Jewish *Cabala* was derived from mystic records preserved in Chaldean temples, which temple priests claimed were allegedly compiled from ancient knowledge collected over a period of more than 200,000 years.

The Empire of Babylonia was later conquered by Persian King Cyrus in 539 BC, supposedly with the help of the god Marduk. Cyrus liberated all Babylonian captives in 538 BC, and also restored the status of their captive gods, recognizing and honoring the God of Israel, Yahweh. Some liberated Jewish exiles then returned to Jerusalem, which had become a part of the Persian Empire. The Persian conquest and its accompanying Zoroastrian religion also greatly influenced Judaism. The concept of the devil emerged when Lucifer, an 'accuser' in the court of Yahweh, was portrayed as God's enemy. The notion of good and evil was also borrowed from Zoroastrian dualism, while Jewish belief in angels accompanied the Persian concept of demons and devils.

Later in 458 BC, Ezra led a second exodus of about 1,800 Jews that had stayed in Babylon. Ezra, who was known as the Scribe of the Law of the God of Heaven, instituted a sweeping religious reform and revival based upon the Torah. As part of those reforms after 445 BC, only the High Priest was to have direct contact with Yahweh, acting as mediator between God and His people. The Jewish religion did not exclusively survive because of its doctrine or its reforms, but also in large measure because of the tenacity and discipline of the Jewish people themselves.

Under Alexander the Great, the Greek conquest of the Persian Empire followed in 332 BC. The creation of the magnificent city of Alexandria in Egypt brought the Greek culture directly to the Near East. That Greek influence on the Jewish faith became evident when the cult of Zeus was introduced to the Jerusalem Temple in December of 168 AD.[3] Another temple for

Zeus was reportedly also built on Mount Gerizim. Still other competing influences also reemerged, when Anatyahu and Ashim-Bethel were worshipped alongside Yahweh, forming an Israelite/Canaanite trinity, one that followed the concept of the Egyptian trinity.

Rome formed in 753 BC, although dominance from its grand expansion did not emerge until between 500 and 338 BC. As the Greek influence began to gradually diminish, Roman influence seemed to fill that void, most notably when Sparta finally fell to Macedonia in 222 BC. True Roman influence then started around 215 BC during the first Macedonian war, which eventually resulted in Macedonia finally becoming a stable Roman province in 148 BC.

It is believed that the earliest primeval faith of the Hebrews was quite different from changes that developed centuries later during their times in Egypt, Canaan, and Babylon. According to *The Secret Doctrine*, the original Hebrew belief did not worship the gods, they only honored them as 'beings superior to humans.'[4] That was evident when Abraham first chose one of the Elohim, perhaps Sin, as their god, not *vice versa*. The Akkadian god Sin was the patron god of Ur, the city-state in which Abraham lived. As revealed in the <u>First Journal of the Ancient Ones</u>, *Elder Gods of Antiquity*, Yahweh was a 'composite god' based on several different beings.

The later esoteric religion of Moses was apparently abandoned several times, with Yahweh worship replacing it. The proper name 'Yahweh' was evidently then used to indicate all the prior Jewish gods, combining them into one deity. A similar alteration can also be recognized in the treatment of Hebrew laws. The Law of Moses was embraced by the high priests of Judaea, while the Books of Moses that comprise the Pentateuch were not. That cycle alternated between Yahweh worship by King David around 1000 BC, followed by Solomon's worship of numerous other gods. However, Yahweh supremacy eventually returned during the times of Hezekiah.

There is a solid mix of esoteric wisdom, as well as some mythical fantasy, contained in the Bible. There is also much contradiction. *The Secret Doctrine* claimed that early Biblical records, those specifically referring to the conflicts that tested Job, associated Lucifer (later known as Satan) with the 'sons of God.'[5] Isaiah referred to Lucifer as the "bright star of the early morning" and the "Luminous Son of the Morning," calling him Lux.[6] Lucifer was reportedly the first Archangel, older and higher than Yahweh. Only later did the Church demonize him as Satan. Yet the notion of the devil did not emerge until the Persian conquest of Babylonia, a concept borrowed from the Zoroastrian belief. The Chaldean occult teachings and the Persian mysticism encountered during Jewish captivity in Babylon altered many of their earlier religious beliefs.

Some Greeks during the early emergence of Christianity began to worship an Unknown God, believed to be the True God. That deity was not Yahweh, the God of Israel, nor any other group's superhuman personification. That profound change started a concept in which the 'reality of God' is external to the reality of the world, a speculative view of the relationship of the divine with the non-divine. That concept further influenced certain Jewish sects toward the formulation of a religious belief that would later emerge and become known as Christianity.

MITHRAISM

The Mithra cult is believed to be an offshoot, or modified form of Zoroastrianism. According to its records, Mithra was the son of the god Ahura Mazda. Ahura Mazda reportedly first appointed Mithra as "a promptly-sacrificing, loud-chanting priest."[7] Many followers believed that Ahura Mazda eventually yielded his reign of power to Mithra and his wife, Anahita. Mithra was a god of contracts, "the punisher of wrong...who rules as an all-knowing potentate...has a thousand ears and ten thousand eyes...and is sleepless, (ever-)waking."[8] Mithra was the living Spirit, the demiurge who maintained law and order, punishing the wrong, and defending the 'contract.'

Mithra became the leader of the Seven Amshaspends, the Heavenly Hosts that were the Immortal or Holy Spirits. They were considered 'creative forces' consisting of wisdom, mind, truth, devotion, power, health, and life. Such attributes of the Seven Amshaspends suggest an association with the Ancient Ones. Mithra is occasionally identified with the earlier Assyrian and Chaldean god of Babylonia, Shamash. Mithra later became an equally important main god of Rome, spread by the legions of Roman soldiers across the Near East and the Mediterranean. Mithraism often competed with the then emerging Christian belief. Numerous theologians consider Mithraism to be the most important Oriental religious influence on later Christianity, and perhaps the forerunner or nucleus of the Christian faith itself.

Mithra worship first started around 390 BC in ancient Persia, and spread through the Roman Empire in the first half of the 3rd century BC. As Mithraism became well established, it emerged as the prominent 'pagan' religion of the Romans by the middle of the 1st century AD, one actively followed by its Roman soldiers. In 307 AD, the Roman Emperor officially declared the god Mithra to be the "Protector of the Empire."[9] Until the 4th century AD, Mithraism continued to greatly influence Christian belief. The numerous similarities between Mithraism and Christianity caused St. Augustine to declare that the priests of Mithra worshiped the same deity as St. Augustine himself.

The Persian god Mithra was the God of Light, associated with the sun disk, and was known as the Persian Sun god. He was the chief intermediary between the Supreme God of the Universe, the Creator, and humankind. Mithraism professed that man was created in God's image, and believed in equality of life, with all life having value. The sacred texts of Mithraism are lost, but some fragments are known. There were seven grades or levels of initiates, with only the last four levels thought to have access to the secret wisdom and sacred mysteries of this cult. By the first century AD, Mithraism was Christianity's strongest competition.

The similarities between Mithraism and Christianity are startling. Both faiths believed in a messiah sacrificed as atonement for sin; resurrection of the dead followed by eternal life after a final judgment, with a resultant reward in heaven or punishment in hell; and worship on Sunday, the Day of the Sun, in honor of the Sun god, rather than the Jewish Sabbath. Both beliefs celebrated with religious suppers; held ethical standards or requirements; and practiced the ritual of baptism, although the followers of Mithraism utilized the blood of a sacrificed bull, not water.

Mithra was a dying-rising savior; had twelve disciples that represented the twelve 'signs' of the Zodiac; performed miracles such as raising the dead, healing the sick, making the blind see, and the lame walk; with both Jesus and Mithra reportedly possessing the ability to cast out devils. The pagan festival *Brumalia* was part of the celebration of Mithra's birthday on December 25. Mithra's birth was reportedly attended by shepherds, along with Magi who brought gifts to his sacred birth place, the Cave of the Rock.

Mithra's Roman cave-Temple, founded in the first century BC on the Vatican Hill northwest of Rome, was seized by the Christians in 376 AD.[10] The Christian Church later erected its basilicas above those Mithraic caves. It was not until the 4th century AD that the Church finally declared Jesus' birthday to be December 25th, the same birthday attributed to Mithra. That date had even older origins with Horus, the son of Isis, who was also thought to have been born on December 25. The Akkadian god Sin, the Moon god, was further believed to have been born late into the night of December 24, or early during the morning of December 25th.

Attis and Cybele Worship

Still other pagan beliefs, generally known as Mystery Cults, flourished along with Mithraism. They also provided a significant influence on the much later Christian belief. Most pagan gods continued to be worshiped during the early centuries of Christianity, thereby maintaining their supremacy due to their supporters, the mortal priests that perpetuated each cult. Often the main question between those cults was the identity of the 'living god' at any present time.[11] One of the older, more prominent cults was that of Cybele and her consort Attis. As far back as 250 BC, the sacred Attis Festival was observed by the Cybele Cult. Several traditions existed of Attis as the young lover of the goddess Cybele. Most claimed that Attis was a shepherd, who was tied to a tree on a Friday, died, was buried, and on the third day rose from the dead on Sunday, bringing salvation to humanity.

Cybele was believed to be the even earlier Sun goddess, Arinna, who allowed the Hittite kings of Anatolia to rule over its people around c.1900 BC. It is believed that about 1000 BC, Arinna became known as Cybele. Cybele was also closely associated with the Greek and Roman goddess, Rhea, who was the mother of the god Zeus. Hence, throughout Rome, Rhea was also commonly known as Ma Rhea (Maria). Such reverence further substantiates the belief that the later Cybele goddess may have also been the likely prototype for Mary, the mother of Jesus.

The rites, customs, and beliefs of the Attis and Cybele Mystery Cult were brought from Anatolia to Rome by Eunuch Priests sometime before 50 BC, and enjoyed uninterrupted worship until 286 AD. Its eunuch connection is thought to be one of the reasons for the later custom of celibacy among the priesthood, as observed in the early Christian belief, and still practiced by the Catholic faith today. Both Emperors Claudius and Augustus were followers of the Cybele Cult doctrines, thereby making it one of the prominent 'pagan' beliefs during their reigns. During those times, all 'pagan cults' or beliefs were considered to be part of the Ancient Religions, and therefore enjoyed 'protected status' throughout the entire Roman Empire.[12]

Chapter 26

Present Era Religions

CHRISTIANITY

The Jews and Christians were originally one group, with Christianity first emerging as a sect of the Jewish belief. Both John the Baptist and Jesus were believed to be members of the Jewish Essene sect. Early Christianity encompassed an extremely fragmented and diverse set of beliefs, with each group at odds with their counterparts, competing with one another to interpret the life of Jesus. Since the early Christian belief was considered to be a part of the Jewish faith, it was deemed to be a 'protected belief' under the Roman policy that tolerated all 'Ancient Religions.'

The Christian movement mostly went dormant after the crucifixion of Jesus, mainly because no major earthly changes occurred as a result. Most of Jesus' followers were expecting terrible consequences, such as cataclysmic disasters and other apocalyptic events. Christianity was not fully 'resurrected' until the efforts of Paul (originally Saul), a converted Jew. Paul started the writings of the New Testament with his 'Letters,' which commenced around *c*.51 AD with the 'First Letter of Paul.' Paul was later executed, along with the Apostle Peter, in *c*.64 AD.

The early Christian sects continued to be a small part of Judaism. The first Jewish revolt, known as The Great Revolt of Judaea, occurred in 66 AD, led by the Zealots against Roman rule. This was the conflict referenced in the *War Scrolls*, one of the texts comprising the *Dead Sea Scrolls*. The war ended with the defeat of Jerusalem in 70 AD, although the last Jewish fortress, that of Masada, did not fall until 73 AD. Afterward, as a result of that war, the Rabbis replaced the Levite priests as the leaders of the Jewish faith.

A second Jewish war with Rome then took place between 132 and 135 AD, but was not supported by the Christian sects, due to the revolt's leader, Simon Bar Kokhba. He was generally considered to be a Jewish 'pseudo' messiah, but Christians already viewed Jesus as their savior. Thus, Christians resented Bar Kokhba, viewing him as a competitor or impostor to Jesus.

At the conclusion of that second war, the Jews and Christians split, with their separate beliefs becoming competing religions. All thirty of the independent Christian sects that existed at that time were then considered merely a 'superstition,' and thus no longer belonged to one of the ancient religious beliefs. That reclassification caused Christians to lose their protected status under the Roman policy tolerating all Ancient Religions, which the Jewish faith had provided for Christianity. That loss of protective status permitted the later persecution of Christians to occur.

Early Church leaders in Rome and Alexandria started working with Roman governmental officials to unite the Christian sects and the earlier followers of Mithraism, adopting the existing Mithra holidays and festivals as 'holy days' that were then observed for Christianity. The Council of Nicaea in 325 AD decreed the pagan Easter Festival as the resurrection day of Jesus. The Catholic Church, during the Council of Laodicea in 364 AD, then officially changed the observance of the Sabbath, the Seventh Day or the Lord's Day, from Saturday to Sunday. But no Biblical account ever referred to Sunday as holy or sacred, or as being the Day of the Lord, the Sabbath. Then in 397 AD, the Church Fathers lead by Augustine convened the Council of Carthage in North Africa, to decide which books were to be deemed the actual Words of God.

Biblical scholars admit that Jesus was not born in December. Church officials in Rome stated that the actual date of Christ's birth was simply unknown. It was believed to have occurred sometime between early spring and October 15, based on certain descriptions and events found in olden records. The Christian Church festival of Christmas first started in the third century AD. Clement of Alexandria believed Jesus was born on May 20, although some 'questionable' records also stated his belief that November 17, 3 BC was the date of Jesus' birth. But Origen strongly opposed assigning birthdays to the gods, citing it as a sinful practice with a pagan origin. Some Oriental based Christians observe Jesus' birth and baptism on January 6th, the feast of Epiphany.

As with the Roman Empire, the Church also underwent a split into two factions, the Church of Rome and the Eastern Church of Byzantium. The Roman Catholics believed only in councils approved by the Vatican, while the Greek Orthodox Catholics believed only in those approved in Constantinople. The Papacy was not established until 538 AD, when Belisarius, the general of Emperor Justinian (483-565), drove the Ostrogoths from Rome. The Papacy ruled until 1798 when the Pope was taken prisoner by Napoleon's general, Berthier, and was moved to France where he later died in captivity. But such denigration never diminished Papal authority. The Pope's official title, which is also inscribed on his official miter, is *Vicarius Filii Dei*, meaning the *Vicar of the Son of God*, assuring his prominence as the Church's leader on Earth.

The doctrine put forth by the Monophysite sect of the young Christian Church attempted to discredit all references to reincarnation contained in the early gospels. The early Christian Church had initially accepted the doctrine of reincarnation, which had been a main tenet that was promoted by Church Fathers such as Clement of Alexandria and Origen in the third century, along with St. Jerome in the fifth century. The early writings of Origen had specifically suffered constant attacks over the centuries. In

553 AD, the Fifth Ecumenical Congress of Constantinople (aka
Council of Constantinople II) condemned the writings of Origen,
an act authorized by Emperor Justinian, effectively removing
most remnants of the belief in reincarnation from Church
teachings, while declaring any promotion of that concept to be
heresy.

The gospels are individual human interpretations of the
Christian movement. Mark wrote his first gospel in *c.*71 AD,
which was essentially the life story of Jesus, albeit more than 30
years after Jesus' death. Mark's writings were based on human
recollections from memories and stories of Jesus known through
oral tradition, which portrayed Jesus as a miracle worker
(although He reportedly had to attempt one miracle twice before
it worked, and on another occasion supposedly failed after
repeated attempts to perform a specific miracle). It is believed
that Mark had access to a hidden Greek source of information
pertaining to Jesus' life. That still undiscovered Greek collection
is called the *Quella* or *Q Gospel*, known only by scholarly
assumption of what must have been included in such an 'unfound
and secret' document. It is believed to be a volume of quotes or
'sayings' that were supposedly made by Jesus.

Matthew and Luke followed with their gospels, which were
written around 85 AD, often using Mark's gospel as a source for
their writings. Matthew was a Jew who incorporated much
Mosaic Law within his documents. Conversely, Luke was a
gentile who largely ignored Mosaic Law. He was considered to
be a 'romantic' writer who also wrote *Acts*, in which Luke used
the term 'Christian' for the first time. John compiled the fourth
gospel of the New Testament, which is a spiritual work written
around *c.*105 AD. In the 2nd century AD, Marcion then 'created'
the *Four Gospel* canon of the Christian Church. From those
works, a 'secret-of-faith' emerged, which is known by many
Biblical scholars as the *Messianic Secret*. It reportedly reveals
the identity of Jesus, while also concealing the real identity of
Jesus.

Such a seemingly contradictory and perplexing secret might have emerged from certain esoteric documents, known to a select few within the Judean branch of the Essene Brotherhood. Isaiah reportedly founded that sect, which was located in the mountain caves above the shoreline of the Dead Sea. Many years later, Jesus supposedly taught his twelve apostles, who were known members of that same Jewish sect, those corresponding esoteric revelations and truths. Those secretive Essene records reportedly claimed that the prophet Jesus, when 30 years old, visited His mother Mary in Canaan, and then went to Gilgal on the Jordan River where John baptized Him.

According to occult author Eklal Kueshana, secret documents from the Judean branch of that Essene Brotherhood revealed that during Jesus' baptismal full-immersion in the River Jordan, He vacated His physical body, temporarily departing the physical plane, and went to the 'astral plane' of the ethereal realm. That allowed the Archangel Melchizedek to then occupy the physical body previously inhabited by Jesus.[1] It is unclear if Archangel Melchizedek is the same entity as the prophet Melchizedek, the person who lived about the same time as Abraham, sometime around *c*.2000 BC, and formed the Melchizedek Priesthood.

Supposedly, it was the Archangel Melchizedek, while occupying the physical body of Jesus, who then became Christ, the one that brought salvation to humankind. Reportedly, only John the Baptist, Mother Mary, Joseph of Arimathea, and certain Masters within the Judean branch of the Essene Brotherhood knew the true identity of the entity occupying the vacated body of Jesus.[2] Three years later, when the body of Jesus was crucified, Melchizedek reportedly departed that body at its moment of physical death.[3] Three days later, that resurrected body was once again returned to and reoccupied by its prior original entity, the man known as Jesus.[4]

Limited appearances by both the spiritual image of Jesus (represented by Melchizedek), and the physical being of Jesus (in corporeal form animated by the entity known as Jesus) reportedly were made after the Resurrection to a few select people. Supposedly it was Melchizedek who eventually returned to the ethereal realm 40 days after the Resurrection, culminating with His Biblical Ascension into heaven. Other reports indicate that the physical entity, Jesus, then lived out the remaining 'natural life' of His material body at various European sites, mainly in France, Ireland, and England, along with Mary Magdalene who supposedly became His wife.

GNOSTICISM

The Gnostic religious belief formed as a combination of the Jewish heritage and doctrine, blended with secret Christian terminology that was often derived from Mystery Cults. It further incorporated certain ideas from Eastern religions, emerging as one of the earliest Christian sects. Parts of this belief were reportedly based on esoteric traditions and secret wisdom received from a divine or higher realm that was supposedly divulged by Jesus to a select few followers who had attained 'maturity of thought.' Such knowledge was imparted to those 'chosen humans' through initiation into a secret doctrine of God, a 'hidden level' above that possessed by the priests and bishops, who were limited to offering only 'common' traditions.

This branch of Christianity dates its origins during the actual lifetime of Jesus, and became a main Christian sect by 50 AD. Gnosticism continued to grow between 80 and 330 AD, until certain orthodox Christians began to denounce it as heresy. It survived that ensuing persecution to a limited degree by meeting secretly in secluded locations, while also hiding their esoteric records and gospels from threatened destruction. Gnosticism's greatest following occurred during its spread by the Greek Marcion and Valentinus during the mid-second century AD. Their direct involvement provided notable credibility to this sect. Around 140 AD, Valentinus claimed to have learned the secret teachings of Gnosticism from Theudas, one of Paul's early disciples. Gnosticism was also spread by the teachings of Theodotus between *c*.140 and 160 AD.

Its connection with Greek philosophers further provided a link between the Divine Logos and the mind of the adept, allowing select initiates access to a higher level of secret wisdom and esoteric teachings. St. Irenaeus (*c*.140-202 AD), a Christian prelate and Father of the Church who later became the Bishop of Lyons, was an active opponent of calling Gnosticism a heretical belief. Although he defended Gnosticism, he is often described as anti-Gnostic since his writings attacked heretical notions that were falsely assigned to Gnosticism, and thus often misinterpreted.

Valentinus divulged an esoteric Gnostic belief in different levels of gods, the highest one being the original and unknowable divinity, the Creator, along with several levels of lesser divinities. The Creator was the 'God beyond God,' with the latter god referring to the Chief God that ruled over Earth. That lesser god of Earth reportedly merely served as the 'instrument of the higher powers.' Those higher powers were below the supreme level of the Creator, but above the lesser god of Earth.[5] This multilevel division of divine beings was also accepted and strongly promoted by Marcion, who noted a sharp contrast between the vengeful God of the Old Testament and the forgiving God of love portrayed within the New Testament.

Valentinus described the Creator God as the: "[Root] of the All, the [Ineffable One who] dwells in the Monad. [He dwells alone] in silence...since, after all, [He was] a Monad, and no one was before Him...."[6] He further clarified the distinction between the two gods, stating that the lesser divine being served as the instrument of the higher powers. Valentinus also stated that the lesser god of Earth: "...who reigns as king and lord, who acts as a military commander, who gives the law and judges those who violate it,"[7] was the God of Israel. Gnostic scholar and author, Dr. Elaine Pagels, quoted the Gnostic teacher, Justinus, who described the Lord's shock, terror, and anxiety: "...when he discovered that he was not the God of the Universe."[8]

The extant written Gnostic record consists of 52 Coptic papyri texts, which included early secret Christian gospels. Those texts were found in 1945, stored in jars and hidden among the cliffs of the mountains near the town of Nag Hammadi, Egypt. Some of the texts were similar to the teachings of the *Followers of Righteousness* discovered with the *Dead Sea Scrolls*, which are usually associated with the Jewish Essene sect. The gospels of the New Testament are dated between *c*.70 and 110 AD, while these Gnostic gospels are dated slightly earlier from *c*.50 to 100 AD. The Gnostic texts also contain some gospels that are completely unknown within the New Testament. Those include the Gospel of Thomas, Gospel of Philip, Gospel to the Egyptians (aka The Sacred Book of the Great Invisible Spirit), Gospel of Mary [Magdalene], Gospel of Truth, the Secret Book of James, the Apocalypse of Paul, the Apocalypse of Peter, and the Letter of Peter to Philip. Some Gnostic gospels, especially the Gospel of Philip, contradict or differ with certain accounts of Jesus that are contained within the 'accepted' New Testament gospels.

Much of the scholarly knowledge of the Gnostics and their belief system is derived from the writings and descriptions of anti-Gnostic texts written by competing Christian sects of the 2nd and 3rd centuries AD. Much of their true tenets and doctrine can only be inferred from ritual descriptions and comments in those anti-Gnostic texts. Nearly all surviving Gnostic records were written in the Coptic language. That resulted when Gnosticism spread to Egypt during the late 2nd century AD. The Nag Hammadi documents found in 1945 reflect those known Coptic translations, and represent the bulk of extant records and knowledge of Gnosticism, although they represent only a small portion of the original Gnostic record, texts, and beliefs.

Gnostic beliefs contained fantastic elements of mythology, and a cosmology consisting of multiple levels of heavens, each assigned to a divine being or god. It further involved many mystical conclusions and practices, with numerous elements different than the present Christian teachings. According to the prominent Gnostic researcher Professor G.R.S. Mead, author of the early 20th century book, *Fragments of a Faith Forgotten*, the Gnostics believed that the gods were civilizers and teachers of infant races; equating those Divine Instructors with the serpent.

Gnostic belief further revealed that the origins of humankind emerged from what was called a 'divine spark.' That divine spark was derived from the lesser divinities that 'fell to our world,' or were sent here by either higher divine beings or the Creator, and were then combined with a degenerate mortal lifeform of Earth, resulting in our human species. Humans were thus believed capable of reuniting with their higher divine elements, perhaps even attaining the level on which the Creator exists, by eliminating or overcoming the evil characteristics or faults retained by humanity. Such purging of all human 'character deficiencies' would produce a 'perfected being,' thus allowing such a 'corrected entity' to then return to its 'proper home' within the ethereal realm.

Some Gnostic sects even believed that the souls of humankind were completely alien to Earth, belonging to a different celestial realm. Perhaps the essence of Gnosticism was its view that the spiritual element possessed by humanity must be liberated from a physical world that is basically deceptive, evil, and oppressive.

One of Gnosticism's main 'lesser divinities' was Sophia, meaning 'Wisdom,' who reportedly was 'not of Earth origin.' An evil god, the demiurge, later emerged from her family, taking credit for all past accomplishments; becoming known as and often called 'the creator.' Obviously, a late arrival could not have created all that came before, and hence could not be the True Creator, the Supreme Force that initiated the Big Bang genesis of our universe. The Gnostics identified that later god as Yahweh, the demiurge or 'living spirit,' the one declared by many to be the God of the Old Testament. It was also thought that such a 'false god' made every effort to keep humanity in a state of ignorance, by concentrating only on material desires and goods, thereby keeping the celestial truth hidden from humans. That false god reportedly punished any attempt by humanity to acquire knowledge and truth. For that reason, the Gnostics did not associate God the Father of the New Testament, the Father of Jesus, with the God of the Old Testament; thus discounting the Old Testament texts and excluding those writings from their faith.

Gnosticism also did not accept that the Godhead had ever taken human form; hence neither Yahweh nor Jesus could be the true supreme Creator. The Gnostics knew that Yahweh was only one deity among many. He was often referred to as 'the God of Gods' and 'the Lord of Lords,' clearly signifying other gods and lords beside Himself. Originally, Yahweh was merely one of the Elohim, who were also called the Nefilim and the 'Genii of the Seven Planets.' The Gnostics identified Yahweh with evil, calling him Ialdabaoth (aka Ildabaoth), the Son of Darkness.

Ialdabaoth was also called the child of the egg, sometimes associating him with Manu of India. He was the son of Sophia Achamoth (aka Sophia Faith), who was the daughter of Sophia (aka Sophia Wisdom or the Divine Wisdom), who was both the Mother Goddess and the Holy Ghost of early Christianity. Ialdabaoth is quoted as saying: "I am Father, and God, and above me there is no one."[9] His mother (Sophia) replied: "Do not lie, Ialdabaoth; for the father of all, the primal Anthropos (the first man) is above thee, and so is *Anthropos*, the Son of *Anthropos*."[10]

Origen (*c*.185-*c*.254 AD), one of the foremost proponents of Gnosticism, was born in Alexandria, Egypt, and was a student of Clement of Alexandria. He was a Christian layperson, writer, teacher, and theologian who spent 28 years instructing both pagans and Christians. He is generally considered to be the most accomplished Biblical scholar of the early Church, who specialized in Old Testament writings. Origen developed the concept of Christ as the Logos, or Incarnate Word, the Father of Eternity. He believed that the Son is subordinate to the Father in power and dignity, and strongly believed in reincarnation. He was denied priesthood in the Church due to an ongoing political conflict with his regional Bishop.

The olden initiated Fathers of the Church, such as Clement of Alexandria (aka Clemens Alexandrinus) and Origen (aka Origenes), made specific references to what can be identified as the Ancient Ones. Origen, commenting on the Books of Celsus (which were destroyed by the Church Fathers) spoke of a ladder of creation with seven gates, or Seven Heavens. Clement of Alexandria also wrote: "...these Heavenly Architects, emanate from the Great Supreme Infinite One, and evolved the material universe from chaos."[11] These statements appear to be references to the Ancient Ones, as the builders and purveyors of civilization throughout the universe.

Further, the dragon was the symbol for the Logos of the Gnostics, yet another icon of the Ancient Ones. Both Church Fathers believed that the moon was Yahweh's living symbol, with Yahweh originally considered to be a lunar god.[12] This tends to reinforce the theory that the God of Abraham was the Akkadian god Sin, the Moon god. Iao, the Gnostic mystery god, was also known as the Regent of the Moon, according to Origen. Iao was also reported to have once been the leader of the gods. According to Diodorus, "The Jews claim that Moses received their [religious Laws] from Iao."[13] Iao is often associated or equated with Yahweh and Ialdabaoth.

Gnosticism observed that the leader of the lesser gods who ruled over Earth would randomly change or be replaced periodically. The new rulers were sometimes female, a fact known from references made to the 'Ruling One.' In Hebrew, the word 'One' is *Achath* in its feminine form, and *Achod* in the masculine form. The acknowledged use of both forms within their olden sacred records would suggest a gender change at the head of the divine leadership from time to time.

One text found with the Nag Hammadi documents, *Thunder, Perfect Mind*, contains a poem spoken in the voice of a feminine divine being. Additional references to a female deity are also found in the text, *On the Origin of the World*, wherein the God of Earth was chastised for His boast made to the angels when He stated, "I am God, and no other one exists except me."[14] According to that narrative, when God made such a statement He sinned against all of the 'Immortal Ones.' When [Sophia] Faith saw the impiety of that chief ruler, she was angry, saying: "You err, [blind god]. An enlightened, immortal humanity exists before you!"[15] The *Hypostasis of the Archons*, another text found with the Nag Hammadi documents, describes the creation of the first man, Adam, by 'Mother'; linking such a birth or 'creation' with the oldest recognized religious reverence on Earth, the veneration of the Mother Goddess.

Still other Gnostic texts speak of God as a *dyad*, a creation embracing both masculine and feminine elements. Other references also refer to a feminine element, thereby celebrating God as both Father and Mother. Additional texts describe such a Divine Mother as part of an original couple, the 'Mother of the All' and the 'Primal Father,' reminiscent of the Sumerian primordial couple, Tiamat and Apsu. That Divine Mother was also called [Sophia] Wisdom, the one that brought about the God of Israel (Yahweh) as her agent.

A few 'pagan' Gnostic sects were alleged to have also existed. Such a belief may have been merely conjecture or misunderstanding, since Gnostic doctrine was partially influenced by Persian Zoroastrianism and Mithraism, along with certain Jewish occult teachings that originated in ancient Syria and Palestine. Portions of the Gnostic esoteric beliefs were actually incorporated much later into the Jewish mystical philosophy of *Cabala*. Gnostic beliefs also became a strong influence on Manichaeism, a Persian religion that likewise was in competition with Christianity. Moreover, Gnosticism contributed greatly to the much later concepts and teachings of Theosophy and existentialism, as well as to the writings of Carl Jung, the noted Swiss psychologist.

312

Roman Emperor Constantine persecuted the Christian sects that did not include the Old Testament teachings within their beliefs, in an effort to consolidate all the fragmented sects into a cohesive universal Christian belief. Gnosticism was especially affected by that relentless persecution, with its teachings later labeled as heresy by the Church. It survived after 330 AD, but only to a limited degree, by hiding its esoteric documents and meeting in secret locations.

Catharism, a religious belief followed by the Cathari in western Europe and the Albigenses in Southern France during the 11th and 12th century AD, derived much of its beliefs from both Gnosticism and Manichaeism. Manichaeism was an outgrowth from Mitharism during the 3rd century AD, a doctrine that was also greatly influenced by certain Gnostic beliefs. Catharism was eventually deemed to be a form of heresy, and suffered severe persecution from the Church.

NAZARENES

The Nazarenes were another early Christian sect comprised of Hebrew believers who observed a combination of Jewish rituals, Christian tenets, and mystery cult customs. Followers of this sect including the 'Initiates of Christos,' with Christos being the Jewish 'savior king.' It also claimed John the Baptist as a member, although most records indicate he remained a 'maverick' within the Jewish Essene sect. Later, the Nazarenes were politically persecuted and ultimately disbanded, with some of its remnants absorbed into the 'accepted' Church after the fourth century AD.

Their record was the *Codex Nazareus*, the scriptures of the Nazarenes, which contained beliefs very similar to those of the Gnostics. They believed the creative phases of Earth were brought about by acts of a female spirit, the *Spiritus*, the Holy Spirit or perhaps the Mother Goddess, who was portrayed as an evil power or influence over Earth. They were aware of the various stages or different versions of humankind, and believed that the newest or latest man created by (or from) the Lunar Pitris was inferior, since it did not possess a 'divine soul.'

Such a statement is believed to acknowledge that humans were not 'heavenly beings,' even though the humanlike Lunar Pitris were considered divine. The Nazarenes referred to the *principes*, the Genii, as the Sons of Light that fought against the dark ones, the Ancient Ones. This reflected their belief in the dual and equal levels of good and evil powers, similar to the Zoroastrians. It further reflected the success of the BOPH gods to demonize the Ancient Ones.

MORMONS

One modern religion, The Church of Latter Day Saints, claims its origins during the era of ancient religions. Followers of this belief are also known as Mormons. Joseph Smith founded the Mormon Church in 1830, after having been called to the ministry by a visitation from God in 1820, and from later encounters with an angel called Moroni, who first appeared to Mr. Smith in 1823. Angel Moroni identified himself as the incarnation of an ancient human that lived many centuries ago. In 1827, the prophet Joseph Smith was reportedly guided to ancient buried annals, which had been hidden by an earlier 'chosen people.' Certain sections of those records were written on brass plates, with other portions engraved on sheets of gold. Also hidden with those annals were two special stones, referred to as the *Urim* and *Thummin*, which were attached to an ancient breastplate. The Urim and Thummin were known as the 'Interpreters,' since those stones allowed the translation and understanding of their archaic records. Those ancient metal plates reportedly disappeared after they were translated, supposedly taken by an angel of the Lord.

During repeated visitations over several years, God and the angel Moroni further informed Mr. Smith that the universe contained many inhabited planets. Mormon doctrine also states that there are *Governing Stars*, which reign over other planets belonging to their *Order*.[16] It was further divulged that God inhabits a physical body of flesh and blood, the same form of being from which man was fashioned, and lives on a planet in the star system of Kolob.[17] The Kolob star system is also one of those Governing Stars, believed to be the main star in the Order that reigns over all the other planets in the universe. Certain Egyptian depictions contained in the *Book of Mormon* have been interpreted as identifying Kolob with the Egyptian name 'Oliblish.' Although the earliest humanlike God referenced in the *Book of Mormon* was interpreted to be Jesus, as discerned by later Mormon commentators, such a conclusion would have required Jesus to have lived almost 2500 years before His own birth.

A summary of the Mormon Doctrine states that humans are immortal spiritual beings occupying physical bodies. The spiritual component is believed to be the source of intelligence and personality of its core entity, rather than specific to its body. The goal of physical life is to improve spiritually, eventually obtaining the devout state that mirrors the Supreme Being. All beings are given free will choice in all their actions, but consequences are attached with each of their choices. Ethics are considered an important commodity in achieving that desired state of perfection. Mormon creed also asserts a certain kinship between the white race and the divine.

According to Mormon belief, the colonization of North America occurred soon after the 'confusion of tongues' that ensued from the Tower of Babel event, which some have dated around *c*.2400 BC. God then first instructed Jared, a righteous Jewish man living in Canaan at that time, to collect pairs of animals along with plant seeds; a mandate similar to His earlier instructions to Noah. God's chosen group included Jared, his brother, their families, and some friends; totaling 22 people. Those chosen people then traveled through the wilderness to ultimately arrive along the seacoast at a place called Moriancumer.

At Moriancumer, God instructed the group to build eight windowless barges to His exact specifications. Those special vessels were described as submersible craft, evidently of a 'dish shape,' with each vessel internally lighted by two 'strange stones' that glowed. Those special stones were provided by God, and were described as "clear and white…as transparent glass."[18] After the four years of construction that was required to complete those vessels, God unleashed savage winds, rains, and floods on all the lands. The eight vessels were launched into the 'great waters' (presumed to be the Atlantic Ocean via the Mediterranean Sea), and were propelled to the Promised Land by the fierce storm winds. After a voyage lasting 344 days, God's chosen group reached the American shore, due to divine guidance and help.[19]

Those people were then called the Jaredites, named after their leader. An advanced state of civilization was quickly established, but its culture later became extinct around the 6th century BC. They were then reportedly followed by a second group of Jewish colonists from Jerusalem during the reign of King Zedekiah in 598 BC. That date coincides with the historical emergence of certain 'new' ancient Central American and Mexican civilizations. It also occurred during that prominent period within the previously highlighted 6th century BC 'spiritual movement,' which led to the expansion of human enlightenment. That second group, reportedly led by the prophet Lehi, traveled down the Red Sea, then headed east to the Indian Ocean, and later crossed the Pacific, landing on the western shores of South America. There, they separated into two tribes called Nephites and Laminites, with each group named after their leader.

Reportedly, those two tribes formed great settlements in South America and also colonized certain portions of North America. Near the end of the 4th century AD, a war ensued between those two civilizations, resulting in the extermination of the Nephite people. The only Nephites that escaped were Mormon and his son, Moroni, apparently as a result of divine intervention. They were then commanded by God to conceal the ancient annals of their ancestors, by burying them within the hill of Cumorah, in Ontario County, New York. That was the location where the last battle between the Nephites and Laminites reportedly took place.

Those annals were written on thin metal tablets of either gold or brass that were then bound by rings in 'book form'; the collection that is now known as the *Book of Mormon*. Those annals became a part of the Mormon Bible, and contain the complete religious history and knowledge of the people that supposedly colonized the Americas. The *Book of Mormon* discusses the same gods and angels that were worshipped in the Near East. It also stated that God eventually brought massive punishment and destruction in the form of a nuclear holocaust on the Laminite people in 34 AD, about the time of the crucifixion of Jesus. The great Mormon cities of Zarahemla and Moroni were reportedly destroyed during that holocaust.

ISLAM (Muslims)

The Islamic faith was founded in Arabia around 630 AD by the prophet Muhammad (569-632 AD). It formed as a culmination of instructions and visions that Muhammad had received from Archangel Gabriel since 609 AD. It prospered as a powerful reaction against existing Arabian pagan cults. Islam, which means 'surrender to God,' sanctioned an aggressive desire to obtain converts, including the use of 'forceful means.' Islamic practitioners are known as Muslims, with unfaithful people called Infidels. This faith conceives God only in spirit form, and never depicts God in any physical personification. Islam also drew in part on Jewish sources during its start, whereupon God manifested Himself unto Muhammad through the Archangel Gabriel. It was Gabriel that reportedly instructed Muhammad to be God's messenger on Earth, in order to reveal God's will. Angel Gabriel divulged revelations contained on divine tablets that Muhammad later recorded, with his subsequent document

317

becoming known as the *Koran* (aka *Qur'an).*

Such divulged knowledge is also referred to as the Hidden Book or the Preserved Tablets. Another record, the *Sunna*, is considered a secondary source of Islamic tradition, one based on the teachings and actions (the examples) of Muhammad, as transmitted by the *Hadith*, an oral tradition not written down until the 9th century AD. Since the *Hadith* is based on the opinions and commentary of early Muslim clerics, it is not considered to be infallible, unlike the *Koran*.

Islamic belief is monotheistic, with Allah being the frequent name of the supreme God of Islam, although a total of "Ninety-nine Names of God" have been counted.[20] Islamic belief states that God provided a proper nature to all of creation, resulting in a harmonious order to the cosmos. Allah is believed to be the same God or Supreme Being as the one of the Jewish faith, who was called Yahweh. Yahweh was also reported to be 'God the Father' (of Jesus) within the Christian faith. Adam, the first man, is considered to be the first prophet of Islam, thereby claiming the same ancestral lineage as the Hebrews. Although Allah was not considered to be a Moon god, the Islamic faith is associated with the crescent moon as its universal symbol.

That lunar connection is thought to be due to the Feast of Fast Breaking, the Eid al-Fitr, which is one of two obligatory festivals established by Muhammad. This feast marks the end of Ramadan, the holy month of fasting and faith renewal. The *Hadith* establishes the Eid Festival as the morning after the observance of the new crescent moon. The crescent moon was also the symbol of the Sumerian BOPH god Enki, who was known as the Horned One, a reference to the 'horn points' of the moon during its crescent phase.

Muslim warriors from Greater Arabia spread Islam during the 7th century AD. They conquered surrounding lands as far west as Spain and as far east as central Asia. An ensuing Muslim empire then formed, which dominated the world's trade routes, while excelling in the arts and sciences. Similar to other Eastern

318

religions, Islam is a 'way of life.' It prescribes a society governed by *Sharia*, or Islamic Law, which applies to every aspect of Muslim life. This religion has five basic requirements, known as the Pillars of Islam. They include a belief in only one God, with Muhammad as His final messenger; prayer five times each day; tithing to the needy, known as Zakat; fasting during Ramadan; and completing the Hajj, a pilgrimage to Mecca at least once during each follower's lifetime.

Islam eventually split into different followings, with as many as 72 separate sects known to exist, differentiated by cultural distinctions within each practicing country. The Sunni branch is considered to be its main sect, emphasizing personal devotion, blended with local practices. It is the one followed by most Asian Muslims, including those living on the Indian subcontinent where its belief is often favored by the lower castes. The Sufis, the Sunni mystics, had originally spread Islam into Asia, where it also became known as Sufism. The Sunnis believe that the first four Caliphs, their olden supreme religious Arab rulers, were the rightful successors to the Prophet Muhammad. A 7th century AD rivalry then split the faith, based on who should be Muhammad's rightful heir as caliph. The momentous schism that followed created two main Islamic factions, with one following the descendants of Abu Sufyan, those known as the Umayyads or Sunni sect; and a rival group, the followers of Aga Khan, who formed the Shia sect (aka Shiism, or the Shiite sect of Islam).

Shiism, the second largest branch of Islam, then formed as a dissident faction from Sunnism. It has its own distinct rituals and a highly organized clerical hierarchy. It is the predominate faith in Iran and Iraq, and is also followed by some in Afghanistan, Pakistan, and Tajikistan. The Shia sect or Shiites insist that their leaders be descendants of Ali, the fourth caliph of Arabia who was a son-in-law of Muhammad. Islam's third major sect, Wahhabism, was founded in Saudi Arabia. It is based on literal translations of the *Koran*, while rejecting any mysticism or veneration of saints. Still other smaller sects developed, such as the Ismailis. That faction developed from the Shia sect, and shares many beliefs that were derived directly from Gnosticism. The majority of Muslims that represent the Ismailis sect predominately live in India and Pakistan.

Ancient Religions and the Ancient Ones

One can not escape the many remaining 'veiled references' to the Ancient Ones and the *Elder Gods* theory, which can be detected throughout the numerous original religious beliefs previously reviewed.[21] Although these testimonials are distorted, usurped, and hidden in numerous different ways, collectively they reveal the legacy these 'divine beings' bestowed upon Earth. The many common references and universal accounts seem to suggest, if not confirm, the essential premise of two distinct and divine (enlightened) groups of beings that were often at odds with one another. Those two groups from the 'heavens' intervened within the natural development of Earth and its inhabitants, imparting civilization to humanity during our formative archaic times. Additionally, the degree of intellect demonstrated by such highly evolved abstract spiritual concepts suggests those beliefs were legacies revealed by 'divine beings,' not self-conceived thoughts and ideas originated by humans.

Chapter 27

Fortuitous Legacy

After the temporary departure of the Ancient Ones around $c.3150$ BC, the gifts that had been bestowed upon Earth ceased. The legacy left by those teachers and purveyors of true civilization were then confiscated by the BOPH gods and utilized exclusively for their own use. The few devices not in the possession of the BOPH gods or their human followers eventually fell into disrepair, or were otherwise possessed by humans incapable of understanding the underlying nature of the technology employed in their use. Over time, all such gifts eventually deteriorated, although primitive copies of certain devices were eventually reproduced, utilizing the limited capabilities of the BOPH gods. Still other implements were essentially lost to subsequent Earth cultures, perhaps until the eventual return of the Ancient Ones.

Since the Ancient Ones' exile, the BOPH gods had overseen the welfare and fate of humans, while remaining purposely separated from humanity. Over time, their seclusion increased, with the BOPH gods becoming approachable only by their high priests on ceremonial occasions or other specified dates. Due to their smaller population numbers compared to humans, the gods had to increasingly depend upon their human priests, kings, and armies to carry out their dictates and achieve their intended goals. Ancient texts state that it was the gods (the BOPH gods) that spread the tradition of kingship, first installing their offspring from unions with human 'mortals.'

Later, the gods designated certain loyal humans to be 'puppet rulers,' to reign over the ever increasing human population. The

BOPH gods viewed humans merely as slaves, using them mostly as servants. As competition between individual city-state gods increased, infighting resulted over land, power, and prestige. Due to those political conflicts, the BOPH gods divided regions of the Earth into separate domains assigned to each prominent god.

The BOPH gods realized they were no match for the many human inhabitants of Earth that greatly outnumbered them. Thus, absolute control over humans became their ultimate objective. That was partially accomplished through the gods' occasional display of their awesome weapons, along with use of advanced technology that would have been perceived as 'magical' to a primitive culture. Such demonstrations helped to create the tight control over large groups of humans by a small number of select overseers, who enforced the restrictive laws decreed by the BOPH gods.

Such notable control 'by the few over the many' is referenced in numerous ancient texts. Per Deuteronomy 32:8, "When the Most High...separated the sons of Adam, He set the bounds of the people according to the number of the children of Israel." Such a statement seems to indicate a deliberate redistricting, separating certain bands of humans from other groups, to diminish the potential sum of their combined power. Such tight control was intended to divide the populace into separate tribes, diminishing any potential impact and capability that might result from their combined greater numbers. That was most evident in the city-state divisions of Sumer and Akkad, where a separate patron god reigned over each city's inhabitants. Strict restraint over human actions resulted, which was the very practice the BOPH gods had previously criticized and later demonized the Ancient Ones for having imparted and enforced under the auspices of the Cosmic Order.

The BOPH gods succeeded in creating a mystique around their true vulnerability and mortal composition, which was maintained through their limited appearances among humans, as well as their generally secluded lifestyle on Earth. That was achieved by living in relative isolation on remote, inaccessible mountainous locations. Legends state that during the early history of Earth, after the gods became established over the various human lands, the 'Greater Gods' (those Chief Gods that reigned over each city-state) established residency high within various mountain retreats. Such sites made it difficult for humans to learn about the BOPH gods' many limitations and frailties, or their true source of power, their utilization of high technology devices.

Those remote mountainous sites were generally difficult to access, except by aerial means. Such inaccessible abodes are confirmed throughout the mythological and religious texts of many ancient cultures. Records consistently reference their deities as 'gods of the mountains,' mostly invisible and rarely seen, except by select 'human messengers' chosen to carry out specific tasks as directed. Such high altitudes, with its corresponding lower atmospheric pressure and oxygen content, provided a more pleasant environment for the BOPH gods in which to live, one more closely reflecting their prior homebase on Mars.

It should be noted that those mountainous locations would have also provided the best communication advantage with Mars, Earth's closest neighbor. While there was never an 'invasion' of Earth by the relocated BOPH beings from their Martian base, they were apparently limited to only periodic communications between the two planets, according to certain archaic texts. An Akkadian copy of an earlier Sumerian text, referred to as *Prophecy Text B*, stated: "If [Mars] is very red, bright...Enlil will speak to the great Anu."[1] Such mention of a distinct color and brightness may refer to ideal or enhanced conditions during which communication would have been increased or expanded between the two worlds. That could have been the result of the close opposition between Mars and Earth, a condition that occurs on a predictable cyclic basis due to each planet's orbital attributes. This close proximity of Mars to Earth varies between 764 and 810 days, or roughly every 26 months based on a 787 day average; with each 'opposition' lasting about 2.5 months. A unique 'close opposition' condition 'recently' occurred in August of 2003 when Mars was at its closest position to Earth in over 700 years.

There was a fascination with Mars throughout primordial times, spawning numerous myths about the planet. Both the Sumerians and Akkadians called Mars *Nergal*, the Death Star, perhaps referring to its dying environmental status. Egyptians called Mars *Hor Dshr*, meaning Horus the Red, and also called it the Eastern Star. Later, the 19th and 20th Dynasties of Egypt called Mars *Heru-khuti* (*Harmachis* in Greek), and depicted it in the form of a hawk's head wearing a triple crown. Hindu myth called Mars *Nr-Simha*, meaning the man-lion. The Chinese called Mars *Huoxing*, the Fire Star. Mars was called *Madim* in Hebrew astrology, according to Rabbi Joel C. Dobin.[2] It was called *Al-Qahira* (aka *El Khira*) in Arabic, while in Latin, Mars originally was *Mavors* or *Mamers*. Author Brinsley le Poer Trench noted that the supernatural Helpers of the Hopi, the kachinas, were said to have originated from the skies, and were sometimes linked with Mars. Mr. Trench also reported that the earliest belief associated with Mars was its original role as a Guardian of the Solar System, not its association with war. He further stated that the Hebrew God, Yahweh, was originally a Lord of Mars, according to arcane literature.[3]

In non-mountainous regions of Earth, the gods were said to inhabit subterranean tunnels and secret caverns. Such dank, cool, and dark living environments would have also reflected the underground accommodations at their previous Martian base. The BOPH gods preferred not to leave those agreeable environments unless absolutely necessary. On this point, a misconception exists. The BOPH gods did not attempt to completely conceal their existence or arrival on Earth, only their mortal frailties and the true source of their 'supernatural' powers. The opposite may be more accurate, realizing that the greater the number of humans that knew of the BOPH gods, the more converts, followers, and worshipers they would gain.

With the exception of sexual intimacy, the BOPH gods did not consider humans to be their equal. Early documents reveal even the best supporters and friends of humankind, such as Ea, Enki, and Ra, were still intimidating figures to humans. It was clear that most BOPH gods considered humans to be lower lifeforms, to be used as they chose. Inter-family marriage between brother and sister nobility was the common tradition during ancient times. That was an attempt to preserve an untainted royal bloodline, perhaps one directly linked with the BOPH gods. The continuation of such bloodlines was to assure that the transfer of power made to subsequent generations remained firmly with the BOPH beings.

Their sexual promiscuity may have undermined that desire. The BOPH gods classified their offspring that resulted from unions with humans as demigods, a level above humans but below gods. The biological and genetic compatibility between humans and the BOPH beings had been established during much earlier times, since they both shared the same basic ancestral origins from universal spores that had evolved on an outer planet within our solar system. Although later descendants were differentiated and altered through both manipulation and environment over time, both human and outer planet humanlike beings shared essentially the same genetic composition from a common source.

As subsequently fewer 'pure' descendants were produced, those resulting from unions between two BOPH beings, demigods became the next 'level' to inherit rule over Earth. Select and arranged bloodline marriages, which prevailed into later times, helped assure a continuation of rulers whose genetic composition reflected those of the 'superior' BOPH beings, at least on some level. Over an extended period of time, the dilution of the BOPH gods' bloodline through interbreeding with various levels of demigod/human offspring reached a steady-state of 'mix,' resulting in a single strain on Earth. It would appear that present humans are hybrids, having evolved from a combination of sources. Those sources included an indigenous Earth species, mixed with genetically modified extraterrestrial humanlike beings, along with a later admix from the BOPH gods and Helpers, those slightly less altered descendants of the 'original seed.'

Essentially, that same otherworldly bloodline flowed through the humanlike Helpers of the Ancient Ones, the ones that chose to remain on Earth to continue the spread of civilization and knowledge to humans. Accounts indicate that their group had initially stayed to themselves once their daily duties were completed, remaining separate from the primitive humans they were educating. They undoubtedly initially raised families within the confines of their own species or bloodlines. Later, as their isolation from the departed Ancient Ones increased, they eventually joined the cultures they were educating, becoming an integral part of those tribes. Those humanlike Helpers, the teachers of those clans, often became the rulers and leaders over their human followers. Over the centuries, as their numbers dwindled due to persecution by the BOPH gods and the lack of any replacement Helpers from the exiled Ancient Ones, the Helpers eventually married human spouses, thus further perpetuating hybrid offspring on Earth.

With an eye toward the day when the Ancient Ones' temporary exile from Earth would end, the BOPH gods wished to tightly control the planet's inhabitants so as to shape the desired human reaction upon their return. As a result of those efforts, the previously mentioned suppression of knowledge became an essential objective of the BOPH gods, making any subsequent human enlightenment extremely difficult to achieve. Only the few humanlike Helpers of the Ancient Ones, who chose to stay on Earth after the exile, were left to spread truth and enlightenment. The quick rate of growth, as well as the advanced societies promised by the BOPH gods, existed for only a very select few. Those recipients were the loyal human pawns that did the bidding of the BOPH gods, while reigning over their fellow humans as dictators.

Growth, advancement, and knowledge ended up being more restricted and controlled under the BOPH gods than the prior regulated but open-ended progress offered by the Ancient Ones. Recognizing the technological achievements that existed more than 5,000 years ago, humanity's expected obtainment should be well beyond its current level, had progress not been restrained by the BOPH gods' freeing Earth from the 'terrible constraints' imposed under the Cosmic Order of the Ancient Ones.

The suppression of any knowledge that might reveal the mission and nature of the Ancient Ones, along with their many contributions to Earth, became the easiest way for the BOPH gods to affirm their own base of power and control over humanity during the early years. Later, they demonized the Ancient Ones, but took full credit for all their prior accomplishments, which had been made during their contact with Earth over millions of years. A similar degradation of the Ancient Ones' Helpers that remained on Earth after the 'temporary exile' also ensued, accounting for various narratives describing devils, demons, and 'fallen angels.'

The indoctrination of the human populace to the political views of the BOPH gods was a necessary step to assure the 'brainwashed' support of Earth's inhabitants. The conversion of humans to the side of the BOPH gods was to assure humanity's allegiance upon the eventual return of the Ancient Ones from temporary exile. That future return will necessitate a vote by humans to either join with the Ancient Ones and align with the Cosmic Order, or reject that association and remain an 'independent' world under the control of the BOPH gods.

For whatever reason, a further transition also ensued, one involving the BOPH gods themselves. Some time after 300 AD, religious organizations and their human leaders first started to hide the very existence and true nature of the BOPH gods, thus altering their actual physical composition, converting them into 'spiritual beings.' Such deception further combined the deeds of various BOPH gods into the acts of a single invisible deity, a god that only those religious leaders apparently had access to, thus becoming that deity's main 'representatives.'

Such actions were implemented to further control the masses, while promoting their own agendas. That early transitional period might also reflect the dwindling number of 'pure bred' BOPH beings, those untainted with earthly human DNA. That predicament might have provided those trusted human 'insiders,' the kings and high priests appointed by the BOPH gods, to create their own inroads into the real power structure on Earth.

That transition toward human leaders, especially religious ones after 300 AD, assured that the origins, accomplishments, and nature of the Ancient Ones also remained hidden. But such action also distorted the true nature of the BOPH gods, perhaps much the same way that world governments apparently now try to hide the truth concerning UFOs during modern times. Such a cover-up would not only protect the dwindling number of BOPH gods, but also elevate those human 'insiders' or leaders into greater positions of power. That subsequent transition required the BOPH gods to be described as merely spiritual beings, ones 'invisible' to mortal humans.

Such a manufactured mystique, which was created for the remaining BOPH gods, along with the blossoming of human 'insider' influence and power, can first be detected during the early Roman Empire. The pagan gods of the numerous Ancient Religions of Rome were kept supreme because of their mortal priests that perpetuated those cults. Power shifts from one cult to another often resulted from claims professing their deity as the true 'living god' at any one time. An earlier but more limited transition was evident between 1800 and 1500 BC, when certain BOPH gods started to make only 'miraculous' appearances to reveal their 'will' to select humans, assuring their continued compliance. Still other early indications of such 'behind-the-scenes' hidden powers were evident to Josephus, the first century AD historian. He was referenced in Robert Graves' 1958 book,

The White Goddess, which stated: "The Essene initiates, according to Josephus, were sworn to keep secret the names of the Powers who ruled their universe under God...."[4] But conversion from physical gods into a single, invisible, supreme deity was not a quick transition, having occurred over a period of time encompassing nearly two millennia.

However, that slow transformation also allowed the few 'pure-blood' BOPH gods to remain completely hidden. Over many centuries, their 'supernatural' powers and advanced devices were likewise hidden, perhaps permitting their later 'invention' during specific future times to assure acquisition of additional wealth and power when needed. Further, the prior common occurrence of seeing 'gods' traveling in air craft was eventually lost to human memory by 1500 BC. Hence, an occasional unexplained supernatural event or enigmatic appearance of 'spiritual beings' was subsequently declared a miracle or revelation from God, with flying objects becoming a rarity.

Those infrequent sightings would have included craft of either the BOPH gods, the Helpers, or even a 'scout' vessel of the Ancient Ones checking on Earth during their exile. To later humans, those sightings became mysterious and unexplained events, which continued throughout history. Only in more recent times have such occurrences become known as UFO sightings, with the idea of extraterrestrial beings then permeating the thoughts of humanity. Such an unconventional premise has now been promoted and expanded by authors of futuristic fiction, motion picture productions, and television dramas depicting possible otherworldly life.

Yet the phenomenon of extraterrestrial beings and UFOs is not exclusive to our modern age, since those anomalous incidents have been continuously reported since ancient times. Records referring to times before 3000 BC, such as epic Sanskrit accounts, clearly described advanced aerial craft as common occurrences. That situation changed over ensuing centuries, with perhaps the next or earliest subsequent reference to aerial craft resurfacing around 1500 BC. Royal annals recorded during the Egyptian XVIIIth Dynasty described a number of 'fire circles' within the sky that were more brilliant than the sun.[5]

Later Greek accounts described 'blazing wheels' or 'fiery wheels' with flashing spokes that were flying high in the heavens.[6] The Roman historian, Pliny the Elder, recorded second century BC accounts of 'nocturnal suns' seen moving across the night sky. He also described a c.100 BC account of a 'burning shield' that darted across the sky at sunset, traveling from west to east, which emitted a trail of sparks.[7] Pliny recorded another account from c.76 BC of a spark falling from a star that became as large as the moon as it approached Earth, becoming a 'burning lamp' that then returned to the night heavens where it vanished.[8]

Similar sightings continued to be recorded over ensuing centuries, but were often described by the Church as religious portents or an 'ominous sign.' Authors Chuck Missler and Mark Eastman discussed documented UFO occurrences that started during ancient times and continued into 1993 AD, as disclosed in *Project Delta*, a 1994 book written by former NASA research scientist Richard F. Haines.[9] Those reputable accounts of aerial craft since c.1500 BC further attest to the effectiveness of the suppression, distortion, and elimination of references to the Ancient Ones made by the BOPH gods, starting shortly after their c.3150 BC temporary exile.

Both the Ancient Ones and the BOPH gods, as well as perhaps even a few 'independent' extraterrestrial explorers, each with their own different agendas, likely piloted those ancient craft. While the Ancient Ones undoubtedly continued their civilizing and nurturing efforts with other distant infant races, they also continued their monitoring and 'restricted contact' with Earth, even into modern times. That would have involved maintaining a base on our moon and perhaps on Mars, if the last of the Martian based BOPH beings had either died or been relocated to Earth.

Some extraterrestrial visitors have been described as having vastly different appearances. That conceivably indicates involvement by a number of different species or races. Such descriptions include a humanlike 'Nordic-type' of large, white, handsome humanoid beings; an amphibious or reptilian creature; a type of feline race; and certain small 'childlike' beings that possess large heads, slanted almond-shaped eyes, and spindly arms and legs of humanoid shape that are commonly called *Grays*.

The Vonjinda (aka Vondjina), the creator gods of the central Kimberly district of Australia, are depicted as resembling the Grays. An insect species is also noted, often described as similar in appearance to a large praying mantis. Others include a batlike creature with webbed-finger hands, known from Ancient Peruvian legends as Oryana, a goddess that arrived in a glimmering celestial craft from the heavens. Accounts of other completely alien appearing creatures are also described, ones often described as possessing a 'horrifying' appearance.

Some researchers believe that UFO occupants are benevolent beings that wish to share their advanced knowledge, or warn of impending disasters, or perhaps even create a new hybrid species from human DNA to populate a 'new' Earth or maybe an entirely different world. Others believe in more sinister motives behind the UFO phenomenon, ones concealed within a massive deception. Still others assert that more than one type of being, either of extraterrestrial or interdimensional origin, may be associated with UFOs, each with different objectives.

Some even consider the enigmatic beings associated with UFOs to be divine saviors, replacing the Godhead and ushering in the prophesied 'end-times' of salvation for humankind. Such a belief rejects more conventional religious teachings, focusing attacks primarily toward the Christian faith. Those attacks typically portray Christianity as a 'great deception.' Such a belief, one professing the 'deception' of humanity, is apparently being advanced through a political agenda intended to exploit the masses. Sources warning of such deceptions are numerous, and include Revelations 12:9, which claims: "And the great dragon was cast out, that old serpent, called the devil, and Satan, which deceiveth the whole world: he was cast out into the earth, and his angels were cast out with him." Followers are admonished to be ever watchful for false prophets, and remain vigilant against any deception they might encounter.

Yet another aspect that is often associated with this 'deception' plan is an ever present or persistent desire to establish a one-world government, replacing the sovereignty of nations with a global multiculturalism that would be entirely under a single unified central control. Such an institution would make it much easier to usurp absolute power over our planet, since only one governing body would be involved, rather than a number of independent ones.

The absence of an extraterrestrial attack, or their creation of peaceful diplomatic relations, or even public contact with Earth seemingly reflects some 'interim period' that awaits the end of the Ancient Ones' temporary exile. Perhaps that banishment period also afforded Earth a certain 'protected status' from potential invasion, until a final 'affiliation decision' is made by humanity. Perhaps a new phase of human indoctrination might have already begun, with humanity being slowly directed toward considering the reality of otherworldly beings. The next step might be to acknowledge the existence of extraterrestrial life, while planting doubts as to their motives and purpose, thereby instilling fear and mistrust. Such actions might reflect preparations by the descendants of the BOPH gods for the return of the Ancient Ones and humanity's ultimate choice between measured progress, knowledge, and protection with the Ancient Ones; or independence, but with no restrictions, help, or security.

Chapter 28

The UFO Phenomenon

Extraterrestrials involved with Earth are generally believed to be visitors from another galaxy, or at least from beyond our own solar system. The main difficulty with such otherworldly lifeforms visiting and observing Earth's development is found in humanity's perceived limitations involved with distant space travel. The vast expanses involved, even to Earth's closest star systems, represent distances that would require travel at impossible speeds, over time durations that would be adverse to humans, and thus apparently also to the physiology of other alien beings.

Perhaps means and methods yet beyond human comprehension are involved in these excursions. A one-way journey from our closest star system, Alpha Centari, would require light speed travel in excess of four years duration, utilizing an inconceivable power source requiring an enormous quantity of some unknown fuel. However, light speed is considered to be a physical impossibility, based on accepted astrophysical assumptions.

Accepting that roughly nine billion years had transpired within the early universe prior to the formation of Earth; numerous planets similar to the conditions and environments of our world certainly could have existed during that time. Conceivably, some type of life could have formed on some similar world, leading to the later evolution of intelligent beings. Those beings could have also created advanced societies capable of producing notable inventions and discoveries.

Within a civilization's capacity to reach fantastic levels of scientific achievement, such a culture would likely acquire the ability to avoid or cure most disease while extending physical life. Due to such an expansive level of advanced medical practices, that planet would eventually experience overpopulation of their homeworld, which would prompt development of space travel methods allowing that planet's inhabitants to seek out 'expansion places' to colonize. Thus, it could be deduced that space travel would be one of the naturally occurring evolutionary products or consequences that would eventually emerge from most advanced civilizations.

Such galactic travel might involve conveyance procedures or techniques beyond our present comprehension. Those methods and movements might even utilize naturally occurring celestial structures or commodities. Albert Einstein first predicted the bizarre object known as a stellar black hole, a 'gravity well' that forms when a star at least three times the mass of our sun expends its nuclear fuel and then collapses. That condition would result in an immensely dense central core, producing a gravitational force so powerful that nothing can escape, not even light.

Data from the Chandra X-ray telescope have indicated the possible existence of a massive black hole near the center of our Milky Way Galaxy. Further studies led by Frederick Baganoff at Massachusetts Institute of Technology concluded that a supermassive black hole 24,000 light years from Earth was indeed located at the center of our galaxy.[1] Scientists generally believe that most spiral galaxies were formed around a similar black hole. Black holes are estimated to number in the billions, situated at various locations throughout the universe.

Charles Berlitz reported in his 1989 book, *The Dragon's Triangle*, that theoreticians such as Cambridge mathematician Roger Penrose have formulated the possibility of utilizing black holes for galactic travel. Their theory speculates that a vessel could enter a large, rotating black hole below its event horizon, the point at which matter and energy are drawn into the black hole and disappears. That craft might then utilize some other dimensional realm to perhaps emerge at a vast distance within our own universe by exiting through a 'white hole,' which is thought to expel energy and matter beyond its own event horizon.[2]

Great misunderstanding seems to exist concerning black holes, as well as any potential passage they might contain that could possibly link remote locations throughout the cosmos. It is now fully accepted that travel through black holes is an impossibility. They apparently have no exit, only incredible forces of gravity that would retain and crush any matter that entered it. That is the conclusion of physicist Kip Thorne, a recognized authority on both black holes and wormholes at the California Institute of Technology. However, Dr. Thorne does accept the theoretical premise that some type of travel through wormholes might be a possibility.

Wormholes are essentially 'tunnels' within the fabric of space-time. Such conduits represent a 'folding of space-time,' linking remote locations of space through 'hyperspace' as a 'short-cut' route. Dr. Thorne further believes that hyperspace wormhole passages exist only on the quantum level, and are much too small for conventional space travel utilization. But at the quantum level, it is believed that particles may routinely traverse those incredibly small wormholes.

For humans to effectively utilize those infinitesimal passageways, wormholes would have to be enlarged and held open by some external means. That might be accomplished by accessing minuscule quantum level wormholes and modifying them through some yet unknown process. That modification might be accomplished using huge amounts of exotic matter known as 'negative energy' to accomplish the feat. That energy could theoretically enlarge and maintain such a conduit, allowing 'conventional passage' through them over the duration of any travel.

In his controversial book *Abduction*, Dr. John Mack divulged that a beam of light was the mechanism utilized by some UFOs to facilitate certain abductions. First hand experiences with such a 'transport beam' reportedly described a vibratory tingling sensation within the body of the abductee, when exposed to that light beam. The reported resultant consequence was a seeming dissolution or diffusion of the abducted physical body, creating a temporary 'transparent state.' In that transparent state, the molecular structure of the affected body is then reportedly transported in layers within that beam of light. Such a light beam evidently transforms one state of physical matter into another state, although the original object retains its residual general shape, one comparable to a 'ghost image.'[3]

Still other researchers believe that extraterrestrials and their UFO craft may be visitors from another dimension, or perhaps even time travelers from our own future space-time continuum. Such speculation proposes that the method of arrival to our reality may not be conventional, as one might usually think of space travel. Rather, it may involve transversable wormholes, time travel, dimensional portals, or some vastly advanced mastery over the natural laws of physics.

Increasingly, eyewitness reports of such unidentified metallic appearing craft describe them as changing shape or separating into multiple objects, while other accounts claim that numerous individual pieces had merged into a single vessel. Still others describe craft that appear and disappear within an instant, or display maneuvers including right-angle turns and 180-degree directional changes, all accompanied by acceleration rates beyond known physical limits. Many visual accounts describe apparent abilities of UFOs as doing the 'impossible,' although such mysterious events can only be corroborated with minimal empirical evidence. Yet UFOs appear on radar, allow limited aerial pursuits by military aircraft, and sometimes even leave certain slight but tangible trace evidence of their status as physical objects at their reported landing sites.

Indications that such unidentified craft are tangible or physical vessels can also be found in the cliff drawings, rock paintings, and cave art made by ancient cultures. Such pictorial evidence depicts craft of various shapes and designs, which are also similar to reports describing modern UFOs. Such allegedly observed craft tend to indicate they are not only physical objects, but may also involve the transport of numerous different species from diverse homeworld origins, due to the dissimilar ship configurations and different designs associated with their distinct vessels.

Yet the apparent physical composition of those craft are precisely the reason UFO reports are often discounted. Numerous reports of modern UFOs describe objects behaving as massless aircraft while in flight, often displaying right-angle turns at over 15,000 miles per hour. Their incredible rates of acceleration and sudden stops are impossibilities for any physical object, based on our known laws of physics. Such apparently improbable maneuvers would create inertial forces that should crush both the craft and its occupants.

Seemingly, only a virtually massless craft could perform such feats of maneuverability that defy known physical laws. However, a contrary conclusion may be more likely, one recognizing that our understanding of the laws of physics is at best fragmentary, with insufficient knowledge to explain all phenomena. Perhaps the best proof that such craft could be of extraterrestrial origin is derived from the simple fact that no earthly government has attempted to register, license, ticket, or tax such vehicles...as yet.

These sightings tend to support the possibility that the inhabitants of those craft might be from another dimension, perhaps a parallel universe or even from some bizarre multi-universe. Such speculation requires that some vague hyperdimensional domain exists outside our known space-time continuum, one beyond our physical senses and present perspective. By definition, spaces occupying more than three spatial dimensions are referred to as *hyperspaces*. Euclid's many discoveries, along with Albert Einstein's theories of relativity, provide a basis from which such domains could be possible. The concept of hyperspaces may also provide the missing element that might allow unification of the four basic physical forces, an endeavor that eluded the genius of such advanced intellects as Albert Einstein and James Maxwell.

Research and experimentation conducted by Theodr Kaluza at the University of Konigsberg, Germany, has identified a five-dimensional domain, integrating the realms of both light and gravity with our known three-dimensional reality.[4] Elsewhere, some have integrated the affirmed commodity of 'time' with an additional enigmatic 'hidden' domain, thereby creating a 'new' five dimensional reality. Theoretical physicists, in their attempt to explain the totality of our universe through String Theory, generally support these 'unseen dimensions.' The complex equations associated with String Theory actually requires or predicts six additional 'curled-up' dimensions in addition to the presently recognized four dimensions that conventional physics can directly measure; which include the three spatial dimensions, along with the commodity called 'time.'

String physicists have extended the construct of our universe into a potential ten dimensional domain, consisting of our four measurable dimensions, plus those six bizarre dimensions that are intertwined or 'curled' into infinitesimally small spaces the size of the Planck Length, making them discernible only through indirect means. Calculations by physicist Oskar Klein determined the size of the Planck Length to be 10^{-33} centimeters,[5] a value supported by theoretical physicist Michio Kaku,[6] although Stephen Hawking approximates the Planck Length at 10^{-35} centimeters;[7] with either size being 100 billion times smaller than the proton.[8] Such proposed conceptual spaces define a domain too small to be directly probed, or even detected experimentally.

Still other theoretical physicists add an additional '11th dimension,' one described as a membrane (aka Brane),[9] which then allows each eleven-dimensional reality or 'individual universe' to be separated by that 'membrane' from all other multidimensional universes, if such other 'parallel realities' might actually exist outside our domain. Nevertheless, be advised that Superstring Theory should not be confused with 'cosmic strings,' those theoretically dense but thin tubular structures that formed the original massive nucleating sites that allowed the eventual formation of stars, solar systems, and galaxies sometime after the start of the Big Bang event.

Particle physicist Yoshiro Nambu of the University of Chicago first proposed the basics for Superstring Theory in 1970. But the theory of superstrings did not become more widely accepted until around 1984, when physicists John Schwarz from the California Institute of Technology and Michael Green, then with the University of London, proposed the conceivable solutions for the mathematical difficulties associated with its concept. String Theory hypothesizes that all matter is composed of nothing but the harmonies created by vibrating strings, with those vibrating strands of energy underlying all subatomic particles, and thus comprise anything larger that those particles might also eventually form.

The different vibrational patterns and/or frequencies of those energy strands are what allow each assembly or collection of those strings to eventually become unique commodities and form different elements or molecular combinations. Such a commodity perhaps even blurs the distinction between the two forms of existence, which can be classified as being either energy or matter. Such a hypothesis is eerily reminiscent of the ancient Pythagorean belief in the *harmony of the spheres*, with their different vibrational rates. Such one-dimensional string elements are thought to resonate in multiple spatial dimensions, with their smallest vibration or movement perhaps forming the quantum or underlying unit of gravity,[10] which some define as a 'graviton.'

Superstring Theory provides explanations for the arbitrary properties of elementary particles. According to the current standard model, elementary particles such as quarks are described as dimensionless points. But as defined by Superstring Theory, such particles or strands exist as unimaginably short, one-dimensional 'strings,' extending to about 10^{-33} centimeters in one spatial dimension. Such energy particles exist as either 'closed loops,' the resultant configuration from a single string forming a circle after its ends join together; or as 'open strings,' a condition where its ends remain non-joined, or two different strings join at one end only to form an even longer 'open string.' The lowest energy state for any string is a near-non-vibrating state, which is thought to occur mainly within the free-state of a single 'straight' or 'open' string that has yet to bond. Such strings can collide with other single or joined strings, either momentarily or permanently, thus creating an infinite number of various configurations and/or energy levels.

Some vexing problems emerge from this theory, where quarks and leptons require a domain possessing nine spatial dimensions and one temporal dimension, which is perhaps also separated from other similar or 'parallel' realms by a membrane. Bosons, or gauge bosons, the family of 'carrier' or 'exchange' particles that includes light photon particles, then theoretically require the existence of 25 spatial dimensions, plus one temporal dimension.[11] Such 'extra' and undetected spatial dimensions, which are beyond the known three-dimensional ones we perceive within our physical world, are thought to be 'compacted' ones. Such undetectable dimensions may exist as 'curled-up' ones, in a manner similar to a roll of paper wound tightly as in a scroll. Such rolled-up two dimensional surfaces would therefore appear as a 'line' within such a realm, or as a 'string.' Even if correct, this theory still offers no explanation as to why nature would possess such strange and permanently compacted spatial 'multidimensions.'

One appealing feature of this theory is its natural ability to unify all four fundamental forces of nature, including gravity. In fact, gravitational involvement is actually required by this theory, which emerges from the motions of particle interaction. Without the implication or application of such a theory, unification efforts have eluded all past attempts by our most brilliant minds.

Rather than a parallel universe that remains separate from our known one (or some alternate imperceptible reality or even an analogous series of layered orthogonal universes), perhaps UFOs merely utilize such a domain (or numerous such domains) as corridors in which to traverse great distances. One might consider such realms or dimensions as 'alternate routes.' A simplification would be the comparison of traversing from one point on Earth to another, either over land, or by a separate but different route through air. Prior to our 18th century 'lighter-than-air' balloon technology, great distances could only be displaced through arduous land or sea travel, or a combination of both. But later technology allowed air travel through an entirely different medium of gasses. Such hyperdimensional domains may provide a similar travel realm, as did the gasses comprising Earth's atmosphere for air transport. Both might simply allow an alternate mode of conveyance, one distinctly different from more conventional displacement methods.

Entering such hyperdimensional domains might disengage a traveler from their conventional space-time reference, while also prohibiting the laws of physics from affecting its traveling mass. It is hypothesized that such a domain might not be linear, implying an absence of any passage of 'time' as conventionally understood. Additionally, such travel might then allow an ability to simply 'reenter' the physical world at any specifically designated time or spatial location desired.

Upon entering such an exotic domain, any travel would seemingly require some form of 'alteration' to the mass being transported; perhaps utilizing some sort of atomic transformation or 'conditioning' involving 'molecular control.' Such a 'modified' mass, with dispensation from all known physical laws, might somehow choose to exit that hyperdimensional domain at some predetermined portal. Upon exiting, the traveler would then reenter the normal physical domain of space-time at some distant location, with little or no time having expired since first leaving their departure point within our perceived physical realm.

Some researchers and spiritualists believe that such an unseen realm may be the natural home of the disembodied soul, the basic essence of each individual. Such a domain might be the spiritual realm referenced by many religious beliefs. Certain scientists also refer to this unknown and unconfirmed realm as 'subspace.' Such a spiritual dimension or reality is thought to be a sea of conscious energy devoid of all matter; one incapable of containing any physical substance or creatures, only their spiritual essence or ethereal counterpart. Speculative thought imagines such a realm to be an actively functioning society, one existing concurrently with our physical world.

The term 'space,' or outer space, represents the vast physical volume of the universe, but not the realm outside that boundary, which may contain the spiritual or non-corporeal domain. The Sanskrit term *akasha* includes both the spiritual and the physical realms. A link is believed to remain between physical life and its counterpart (or aspect) in the spiritual realm. It is generally accepted that humans are composite beings, possessing both a physical and spiritual component. Physical beings generally have difficulty in accepting or perceiving such a nonphysical realm.

The Urantia Book reveals non-corporeal intelligent life that does not assume physical density, but still interacts with physical life within our material universe. Such 'spiritual entities' are believed to represent a highly evolved consciousness, one no longer required or deemed necessary to take physical form for interaction with our physical world. Such entities may be compatible within both the spiritual and material domains. Those dual realm entities are often described as primarily existing in subspace, the non-physical arena of 'nothingness' outside of our universe. Yet such beings are purportedly also able to interact within our physical universe.[12]

Remote viewers have reportedly made contact with such a subspace realm, and the spiritual beings that inhabit it. Remote viewers allegedly are capable of visiting 'targets' during a type of out-of-body or paranormal experience. Some remote viewers, including Courtney Brown, the remote viewer mentioned in the earlier chapter on the Cosmic Order, believe that the evolution of both subspace and the physical realm are interlinked or dependent upon one another.

Therefore, some believe the evolution of physical life is necessary to enact a corresponding evolution in subspace. Dr. Brown thinks that a group of subspace beings are attempting to assist physical beings within our material universe toward a mutual evolution. He further believes that a subspace revolt called the Lucifer Rebellion took place in the distant past, which involved this subspace group.[13] A similar premise is also expressed in *The Urantia Book*.[14]

Notable scientists including Eric Laithwaite, Edward Delvers, and Bruce DePalma have also postulated the existence of another dimension, one referred to as a 'mechanical dimension.'[15] They have concluded that differences can be detected between identical masses as they relate to gravity, depending on whether the mass is in a rotating or stationary state. That conclusion was deduced from a number of experiments concerning the interrelationship between rotationally imparted inertia and its effect on gravity. Such a concept suggests that mechanical properties of a mass can be altered by rotation, with rapidly rotating masses gaining inertia while storing that energy as an 'inertial field.' That field is physically detectable by its effect on electrical circuits within the vicinity of those rotating masses, wherein their frequency of oscillations is reduced.

Such a conferred 'inertial property' might be an additional 'mechanical dimension' from which energy could be extracted from its surrounding gravitational field, thereby also weakening its ability to attract matter.[16] Additionally, sufficient energy might also be extracted from that same 'mechanical dimension' to further overcome the remaining attractive force of gravity, while imparting that same potential to other 'companion' objects, such as a spacecraft and its occupants, which are acted upon within that affected surrounding gravitational field. The conversion of inertial forces potentially produced by rotational motion might eventually be harnessed to negate the attraction of gravity, creating a form of 'antigravity' that could then be used to alter or control some of the known physical laws governing our universe.

The inconceivably rapid acceleration rates exhibited by suspected extraterrestrial craft would be damaging to both living tissue and the structural integrity of the craft, unless an essentially massless condition existed. However, a force that would accelerate every affected structural or living molecule individually would eliminate any associated damaging stress. Thus, if all accelerated components were acted upon individually by some unknown process, such a craft would be able to negate gravity by producing a reactance directly with any gravitational field.

Our present concept and understanding of matter and energy is incomplete. An advanced species might have evolved to a level where physical or quasi-physical control over particle or quantum physics became a reality. It is known that solid objects are merely an illusion, their actual composition consisting of a very porous underlying structure. Solidity is perceived due to the 'shell' created by electrons orbiting its nucleus, in a manner similar to the way a fan blade appears as a 'circular solid' during high-speed rotation. Bonds of attraction on an atomic level maintain that shell. A level of enlightenment might eventually be achieved that would allow molecular bonds to perhaps be altered by 'thought-power' or some other yet-unknown conversion process, thus mastering the ability to change matter into pure energy, then back to matter again.

Such mastery over physical matter, either through evolutionary advancements in thought-control or utilization of scientific devices, might eventually allow a quasi-physical or semi-corporeal state of existence. Perhaps creatures capable of altering, suspending, or weakening their molecular bonds can approximate the realm of fundamental particles, or become compatible with that domain; a realm believed to be exempt from the conventional laws of physics. In such an altered quasi-physical state, the instantaneous force of gravity might be able to be harnessed or utilized. Gravity is the force that keeps the planets in their orbits, while binding the solar system together. It further organizes the galactic composition of the universe, while regulating each galaxy in its internal motion and relationships with other surrounding celestial formations.

Speculation was presented earlier that subspace transport might be possible if physical beings underwent some form of alteration or transformation, thereby creating a temporary condition permitting such travel. That conditioning may involve molecular control or require a further spiritual evolution of our species, which might create a new mind/body connection for controlling and utilizing such subspace corridors for travel. Scientist and author Adrian Clark postulated the possibility of eventually obtaining such molecular control over our physical body through the use of brain activity,[17] perhaps with the use of advanced devices to produce such an altered physical state.

In any case, time would be another commodity that would have to be considered for such extended travel. However, the speed-of-light 'velocity limit' is believed to apply only within the physical world, not in subspace where displacement is thought to be instantaneous. If so, linear time would not exist in subspace, or have any effect on occupants within that realm. Time is sequential only in the physical world and comprises merely one aspect of our tangible realm. Hence, all events are thought to occur simultaneously in subspace, perhaps in layers or phases.

Conceivably, once such travel is completed, a reuniting or reconvergence of an 'altered' object's molecular bonds could once again be achieved, returning that object to the ordinary or normal space-time continuum and its applicable universal laws of physics. Similar manipulation of bonds, matter, and energy may even allow access to multiple different realms. Perhaps the spiritual realm is the elementary or quantum dimension, one ultimately accessible by enlightened beings at will. If so, then the essence of those enlightened beings might temporarily 'exit' their physical body, enter the spiritual domain, and reenter the physical realm instantaneously at a far distant location, inhabiting or temporarily 'taking over' another physical body or mass at that new location. Rather than physical beings altering their state of existence, perhaps it is 'space' or the surrounding environment that undergoes modification or change through some still unknown process, thereby producing the same 'conduit effect,' along with its massive displacement result.

Even with humanity's progress in unlocking the fundamental characteristics of quantum physics, along with numerous theoretical models attempting to explain the nature of our universe and physical existence, it becomes evident that a great deal yet remains unknown. Whatever the mechanism utilized by intelligent otherworldly beings to make contact with Earth, most extant evidence suggests such contact has been made with our world since its most remote epoch, and continues to be made well into modern times. The mere absence of a 'provable' explanation for an occurrence does not discount or negate the reality that such an event actually occurred.

Chapter 29

Speculative Thought

Superstring Theory defines the temporal dimension of 'time.' Time is misconstrued as being linear and absolute, but is actually a relative commodity, as demonstrated by Albert Einstein. We base chronology, the concept of 'time lines,' on one event within a moment of time occurring after a prior event, building a linear sequence that is relative to all other events. That concept breaks down when this belief is applied to the definition of 'eternity,' which starts at infinity and continues throughout infinity. But cosmology calculates a finite point for the creation of our universe, an event that occurred some 13.7 billion years ago. From the study of cosmology, an understanding can be deduced that space, time, and matter all had a simultaneous origin that emanated from the Big Bang event. Physicists refer to that event as a singularity, which had a finite point of existence within the history of our universe. Based on the acceptance of a fixed starting point, the probability of an implied 'end point' to the universe is also suggested. Sanskrit texts allude to the existence of prior universes, indicating a series of finite starting-and-stopping points for those prior realities. But such a conclusion contradicts the concept of infinity.

Time may not even be contiguous, a concept that often surfaces in regressive hypnosis sessions during attempts to recover 'past lives.' Such contradictions emerge from accounts of out-of-sequence 'prior' lives, ones that took place in non-chronological order, wherein a past life had occurred during some time in the future, relative to other past lives that followed, or even to one's present life. Such conundrums make sense when we realize that it is only the learning events that are the important part of those subsequently chosen lives, rather than the progression of linear time. Hence, a specific time period that occurred prior to one's last contemporary existence may offer the best lesson from which corrections of character deficiencies might occur. Therefore, linear time is a misconception, as explained by Dr. Einstein when he stated that: "...the distinction between past, present, and the future is only a stubbornly persistent illusion."[1]

Time itself is conceived as our fourth physical dimension, a concept inherent to Euclid's discoveries; the premises upon which Albert Einstein based his theories of relativity. Therefore, time is a physical reality that varies with acceleration, mass, and gravity. A time measurement device, such as a clock, will operate faster in a weaker gravitational field than will an identical timepiece placed within a stronger field. Any mass able to escape from our known physical realm would thus also be free of the constraints of time, at least as we understand them.

According to Einstein's Theory of Relativity, nothing can travel faster than the speed of light at 186,282 miles per second, the generally accepted universal 'speed limit.' But with exposure to a combination of atomic and electromagnetic-effect conditions, laboratory-produced light beams have apparently traveled much faster than normal light speed. Dr. Lijun Wang of the NEC Research Institute in Princeton, New Jersey, has claimed speeds of 300 times that of normal light through a specially prepared chamber of cesium gas.[2] Such speeds produce an effect that allows light to exit a chamber before it even enters it, verging on the definition of time travel. Claims of other superluminal speeds resulting from use of different mediums and environments also exist.

Such greater than light speed transport is now considered possible, due to the strange phenomenon called 'quantum tunneling.' Such a 'tunneling effect' has been demonstrated through utilization of special media, guides, or barriers. The concept behind such superluminal speed is based on the quantum theory of 'chance and probability,' which is associated with matter in the quantum realm, where all possibilities, including the 'impossible,' can happen in equal likelihood.

New calculations based on Einstein's General Theory of Relativity suggest that faster than light speed travel through wormholes might be possible. According to Sergei Krasnikov, a Russian theorist and relativity expert at the Pulkovo Observatory in St. Petersburg, a new type of large, stable wormhole that is compatible with the known laws of physics is possible. Such a theory suggests that an 'exotic matter' can be created literally out of nothing, when space and time are curved in the right way. Such an altered wormhole is theorized to then be capable of creating its own supply of exotic matter to continue its enlargement and also maintain its 'opening.'[3]

A propulsion device utilizing such a theoretical system might be capable of generating some form of artificial gravimetric force that could be projected through a tube or waveguide to create a 'wave front' ahead of the craft in the intended travel direction. That might be accomplished by using a portable, low-energy accelerator focusing particles on an exotic material such as Element 115, resulting in a series of high energy waves that somehow work against or repel the force of gravity. Such a resultant force would then attract or 'drag' the craft toward the site or point where the wave front was projected. Upon reaching that projected focal point, the wave front would dissipate, allowing another new artificial gravimetric force to again be generated and projected ahead of the ship. The process could be repeated in a continuous cycle of projections to displace vast distances. Speed control might be accomplished by lengthening or shortening the duration of each artificially created 'gravity well' projection, while directional maneuverability of the craft might be facilitated through the precise or 'directed' placement of each generated wave front.

Reportedly, modern UFOs use a similar type of propulsion, based on alleged secret 'reverse engineering' performed on 'downed' UFO craft. Those vessels supposedly contained one or more generators capable of producing 'gravity waves'; an amplifier to enhance that force; and a 'horn' to direct or focus such artificially produced wave forces. That 'horn' was described as a device similar to those found in microwave ovens that are used to emit electromagnetic radiation.[4]

Such a process evidently involved the creation of a 'jump range,' the 'desired distance' to be traversed or displaced with each created effect. Its range would depend on the magnitude of the gravimetric distortion capable of being produced by each craft's specific generator. A 'gravity wave' would be directed in front of the craft toward its desired destination at a determined point (based on the range capacity of the generator within each craft) within the fabric of space-time, producing a 'gravity well.' Each gravity projection would then distort that space-time location, warping that point in space into a gigantic narrow loop, creating a 'near-fold' condition.

Such a loop would bring two distant points from opposite edges of each distorted loop much closer to each other. The massive 'gravity well' associated with such a distortion would also drastically slow the passage of time. With a craft traveling at only 'minimal' velocity, it would be able to traverse that temporarily 'folded' or 'shortened' distance, all during a dilated time period (of slowly moving chronological time). The desired 'jump range' distance could then effectively be displaced by the craft within a minimal period of time, at a relatively slow rate of speed.

Upon reaching its desired 'targeted' distance, the gravemetric projection is released, with space-time returned to normal. The process is then repeated for the next 'jump,' allowing vast distances to be cumulatively accomplished even by a small craft, utilizing relatively modest equipment. A larger mothership, with much greater gravemetric projection equipment, would be able to displace vastly larger 'jump ranges,' allowing for more extensive galactic travel abilities. Material objects involved with such a process would likely undergo some form of phase change or alteration upon entering such 'distorted' space. That likelihood may account for the reported 'changeable' appearances of certain UFOs before they 'vanish,' due to the extreme distortion of surrounding light waves (thereby distorting the image of that object while in 'conditioned space').

Another common observation associated with modern UFO sightings involves reported 'light flashes' seen just before the craft speeds away or disappears. It is known that electrons do not emit radiation while they normally orbit within one of their energy levels. But when an electron drops (transitions) from a higher energy level to a lower level, its atom emits (radiates) a photon of electromagnetic energy. Such emission transfer involves an energy loss that is then balanced by absorbing a photon of energy at random from its surrounding environment, raising that other electron to a higher energy level. This photon emission phenomenon, which results from such a balanced energy exchange, might account for the glow, flashes, or other visual light evidence often associated with UFO craft. This same light emission phenomenon may somehow also be connected with or utilized by the Ancient Ones, perhaps as a 'protective shield' or during the use of some type of transport device, thus prompting their epithet as the Shining Ones.

In 1917, Einstein postulated that empty space is not totally empty, but rather contained a kind of 'invisible energy.' Such 'dark energy' was theorized to act in a reverse manner to gravity, causing galaxies to repel one another, rather than attract. Einstein dismissed this theory because he felt it was too bizarre. But an April 2001 news release reported that new celestial evidence suggests just such a repulsive force actually exists, and that same repulsive force has surpassed or overwhelmed the known force of gravity during the last several billion years.[5] Perhaps some mechanism to harness this 'dark energy' has been perfected by certain advanced extraterrestrials sometime during the last few billion years. Such 'mechanical' utilization of naturally occurring anti-gravity forces might also provide the source of propulsion that would allow craft to perform the amazing feats described by those who have reportedly observed modern UFOs in flight.

Still other enigmatic phenomena, ones contrary to orthodox beliefs concerning the laws of physics, have been created in laboratory settings. Research done at the University of California, San Diego, created an extraordinary environment using a palm-sized array of small copper rings suspended between a grid of copper rods. Microwaves in that environment behave in reverse, without breaking other known physical laws.[6] Perhaps other electromagnetic wavelengths might also act in a reverse manner, although it is unknown if such a supposition has yet been evaluated. However, such experimentation indicates that phenomenon beyond our present comprehension can and does exist, regardless if they can be fully explained or not.

Equally mystifying commodities and phenomena may take place all around our physical world without ever being perceived by our human senses. It is only logical to reject or doubt situations that defy understanding, realizing that humans think in purely physical terms. Yet a multitude of processes occur outside our perception, which we accept without question. Electromagnetic radiation, such as in the form of radio broadcasts, remains unknown to us until an extraneous device, a radio receiver, is used to access that 'invisible' commodity.

The underlying reality of our universe, as well as the void that may extend outside its limits, might be equally imperceptible. The universe is composed of energy and matter, with matter being the condensed form of energy. The essence of our being, our soul, may be pure energy, since it is believed to extend beyond the physical realm and possess a non-material composition. By mastering some still unknown thought process or power, the condensation of pure energy into a quasi-physical state of being might produce an illusion of a somewhat visible form within the physical world. Conversely, thought projection by an enlightened entity of their 'pure energy essence' might allow that entity (in its form as an 'energy essence') to travel in an unknown realm or dimension. Such travel capabilities might include an ability to instantaneously transport to distant locations or realms. Perhaps a similar mechanism is associated with the alleged process involved with 'thought-travel' or 'remote viewing.'

Evolution may be more a function of our spiritual component rather than our physical part. The elemental nature of our existence, that commodity referenced as our essence, soul, or consciousness is what animates and bonds with the physical vessel used to experience material life. That bond is broken at death, releasing that consciousness back to the spiritual realm for further introspection, prior to rebonding with a new vessel later in the physical world. Perhaps the spiritual realm is the elementary or quantum dimension, one ultimately accessible by such enlightened beings at will. It may also be the realm utilized for 'travel' associated with remote viewing. If so, then enlightened beings might temporarily 'exit' their physical body, enter the spiritual domain, and reenter the physical realm instantaneously at some far distant location.

The universal laws of physics presumably apply only to physical objects of a size larger than fundamental particles. Elementary particles interact within their domain under a different set of rules or parameters, as defined by the laws of quantum mechanics. The composition of physical objects is merely the combination of lesser collections of ever simpler and smaller admixtures, down to the subatomic level. A level of thought-power might eventually be attained allowing an entity to control molecular bonds, perhaps even to change matter into pure energy, and later back to matter. It is believed that pure energy, or self-energy, need not be in any particular shape, but may attain form as desired. Hence, some method of molecular control over organic matter could eventually lead to a quasi-physical state, or semi-corporeal form of 'energy being.' In such an altered state, physical laws may not apply, allowing light speed and beyond.

It may be possible to alter inanimate matter in a similar fashion, thereby also exempting it from the laws of physics. Such alteration of matter might first require its conversion into pure energy, or undergo elimination or 'weakening' of its molecular bonds to produce an even more porous structural amalgamation. It was previously stated that solid objects are merely illusions, containing proportionally vast porous spaces between its orbiting electrons and its nucleus. Bonds that are altered or 'controlled' could allow for expanded 'open spaces' through which other 'conditioned' or modified objects might pass. Such an altered state could possibly allow those conditioned solid objects to pass through other solid matter, with minimal molecular disturbance or displacement. Such a quasi-physical or 'loosely unbound aggregate' of atomic particles might presumably be capable of light speed velocities, while being compatible with its negative effects.

If such 'molecular controlled' matter is exempt from the constraints of physical laws, solid objects might 'disappear' when 'altered,' or allow the division of an object into multiple articles of different shapes and forms. Reported witnesses of UFO sightings have often described just such phenomena. Speed limits and physical laws would likely no longer apply to such quasi-objects, allowing fantastic phenomena to ensue. Similar to a liquid or gas assuming the shape of its containment vessel, solid objects might be altered through control of bonds at the atomic level, allowing entry of their cohesive essence into an unknown realm. Such abilities might someday be obtainable by higher evolved beings, thereby allowing mastery over the laws of physics.

Perhaps a highly technical device or mechanism is used for such molecular control. Or possibly some form of advanced thought control might be involved, one using electromagnetic radiation produced by, or correlated with brain activity. But even such altered matter would still require a propulsion device. The brutish, massive rockets used by present era space missions are generally limited, merely utilized as a single-use engine to attain escape velocity from Earth's gravity to exit its atmosphere. Hence, their future usage as a multi-mission exploration vehicle for travel from one planet to another becomes very restrictive or impossible, due to the inherent limitations associated with its huge fuel storage needs. Other more efficient methods have been proposed, including simple ion engines or yet-to-be-developed 'antimatter drives.' The simplest atom of antimatter consists of an oppositely charged nucleus (comprised of a neutron and an anti-proton) orbited by a 'positron,' a positive-charged electron.

It has been concluded that equal amounts of matter and antimatter were created as a result of the Big Bang event. When those two opposite forms of matter collide, they annihilate each other, releasing vast quantities of energy. Since nearly all the antimatter is apparently now absent from our present universe, scientists have questioned why any 'regular' matter would still remain. One would surmise that an equal amount of antimatter would have eliminated a like amount of ordinary matter. One answer might be found from work done by a team of physicists at Stanford University. They discovered differences in the rate of degeneration between the quicker decaying antimatter and its ordinary counterpart, a condition referred to as a 'charged-parity violation.'[7]

However, such rare antimatter still exists, with small quantities of antihelium 3 having been produced in the laboratory, along with a few atoms of antimatter reportedly detected in outer space. The controlled introduction of opposing matter and antimatter particles always results in annihilation of the combined masses in the form of an immense energy release, one exponentially enhanced by a factor equivalent to the speed of light squared, from Einstein's $E=MC^2$ equation. Essentially, the oppositely charged sub-atomic particles orbit and spin in reverse, canceling-out each other, providing a totally complete conversion of physical matter into pure energy.

That is the theoretical principle behind the antimatter 'warp core drive' of *Star Trek* fame, where antimatter is stored in a magnetic field, isolating it from its 'normal matter' counterpart. When a stream of antimatter particles is focused (using the fictitious dilithium crystals) with a stream of its corresponding 'common matter,' all while harnessed within a containment chamber, a tremendous energy release results. Such a reaction requires only a small quantity of mass, in contrast with its ensuing huge energy production release, thereby necessitating only minimal fuel storage for this extremely efficient theoretical form of propulsion.

Author Eric Norman speculated that the source of fuel for UFOs might be derived by 'breaking down' water into its elementary atoms of hydrogen and helium, utilizing those gasses to produce energy. Consistent reports describe UFOs hovering around large bodies of water, or even drawing water from lakes and oceans. Mr. Norman also hypothesized that UFO propulsion devices use the force of gravity in an attraction-repulsion manner in outer space, and as an electromagnetic force while within a planet's atmosphere, based on reported UFO contacts.[8] Mastery over gravity appears to be the key element in achieving such 'unlimited' space travel.

Mass of any size attracts every other particle with a gravitational force proportional to the product of their masses, divided by the square of the distance separating them. Gravitational fields act instantaneously, while extending to infinity, although the gravitational effect of any body of matter diminishes with its increased distance from any other affected mass. The force of gravity keeps the planets in their orbits and binds together all solar systems. It further organizes the galactic composition or distribution within the physical universe, while guiding each galaxy within its internal motion. It defines the relationships between all cosmic formations and their collective interaction with each other.

Yet gravity can be counteracted. A body in space becomes 'weightless' when it 'balances' the force of gravity through the creation of an equal and opposite force acting against its effect. That results when downward or gravitational forces nearly equal the upward or inertial forces. Such gravity 'counteraction' renders any spacecraft and its contents 'weightless,' as if in a free-fall state. That same steady-state condition occurs when an object achieves 'orbit' around another mass, the result of the inertial force (the radial or centrifugal force in the case of an orbit) acting away from the mass-center of attraction, or center-of-gravity, of the body being orbited.

Beyond the speculative nature of the method, mode, or state of composition of UFO craft or the creatures piloting them, evidence suggests that extraterrestrial beings have been contacting Earth since primordial times. Those initial or earlier alien beings, or perhaps another different species of otherworldly lifeforms, evidently continued to visit and perhaps even inhabited Earth during various times. Such interspecies contact has apparently continued into modern times. If true, their intent and purpose remain the subject of diverse speculation.

Humans tend to think of space travel in terms of a 'mission,' with those missions focused on specific activities. Upon completion, the crew returns to their homeworld and reunites with their families. For that reason, many intelligent people dismiss the possibility of extraterrestrial life visiting Earth, since the vast distances involved from the closest star system, even traveling at light speed, would entail decades away from families. Further, the increase in frequency and number of UFO sightings would indicate that various diverse species are visiting Earth from numerous different worlds, requiring even more distant and lengthy round trip travels.

Such beliefs discount the more likely scenario that those 'visits' are not round trips, but rather dedicated life-long duties involving many subsequent generations of descendants, born into the same service as their parents, fulfilling an ongoing mission that never ends. 'Home' might be a huge mothership or numerous temporary 'bases' on nearby uninhabited worlds close to each 'targeted' planet. Local bases, such as those on Mars or the moon of Earth, would not require vast distances or lengthy travel times to periodically visit Earth on a routine basis. Such bases would likely also be utilized by the Ancient Ones during their extended exile period, permitting their monitoring of human development prior to their eventual return to Earth.

Those lunar bases might even be evidenced from the numerous enigmatic domed structures that occasionally appear on its surface, or perhaps from the apparent underground caverns that have been detected. The dark side of the moon would allow mostly undisturbed privacy for such bases and their affiliated activities. Governments with satellite and probe reconnaissance would be aware of such bases, even if denying their existence to people within their own nation. That might be especially true of the United States, as the only modern nation to have visited the moon.

Some might argue that the manned Apollo missions to the moon would have detected some evidence of those occupied bases, but those landings involved only very limited areas. Further, not all findings were released by NASA to the public. Moon bases may continue to exist, demonstrated by the sudden appearance of structures, such as the huge 12 mile long bridgelike creation over the Sea of Crisis first observed in 1954.[9] Other objects were described as dome-like structures as large as 700 feet in diameter,[10] which started to suddenly appear around 1865.[11] Such structures usually appeared near or in craters, such as those within the depressions of Plato, Plinius, and Hyginus. The last confirmed dome sighting by the noted English astronomer, Dr. H. P. Wilkins, was in 1953,[12] at the first apex of the early phase of the modern UFO phenomenon.

NASA compiled an extensive study of unexplained lunar lights and objects, both stationary and moving, which were reported to have occurred over several centuries. Four distinguished scientists, including Dr. Patrick Moore, compiled that 1968 study, titled the *Chronological Catalogue of Reported Lunar Events*.[13] That study documented hundreds of mysterious lunar observations. Other independent scientific groups also conducted similar studies, with one report claiming over 800 sightings, while another group compiled more than a thousand.[14] Astronomer Morris Jessup, when he was with the University of Michigan, believed the lights and dome-like structures were large UFOs on the moon's surface.[15]

The area of the first manned moon landing, the Sea of Tranquility, was photographed initially by the 1966 NASA Orbiter 2. Anomalies were detected, including several strange spires or obelisks that ranged in height from 40 to 75 feet, with one as tall as 150 feet, along with a large rectangular pit located just west of that tallest spire. However, NASA never revealed their on-site evaluation conducted by Apollo 11 of those anomalies. According to Dr. Farouk El Baz, a former NASA geologist who later became a research director at the Smithsonian Institution, NASA did conduct secret investigations of those anomalies.[16] Dr. El Baz stated that NASA was specifically "looking for something," and added, "not every discovery has been announced."[17]

Still other former NASA employees, such as engineer Fred Steckling, have claimed that numerous apparently artificial structures were detected on the moon. Many of those structures were photographed by various moon probes, including the five Lunar Orbiters and certain Apollo missions, as well as observations/photos while utilizing Earth-based telescopes. Such anomalies included the large five-miles long by one-mile wide 'platform' south of the Archimedes Crater in the Mare Imbrium region and what appeared to be an enormous 'glasslike structure' over Mare Crisium.[18]

With hundreds of credible 'moving light' reports on the surface of the moon, plus the sudden appearance of apparently artificial structures or abrupt landscape changes viewed by reputable astronomers, along with the UFO encounters NASA astronauts had during their moon missions, perhaps the moon is not so lifeless. Earth's moon might still be utilized by the Ancient Ones as a base of operation during their temporary exile. In fact, numerous researchers outside NASA have speculated that such past or present habitation may have been the reason for the accelerated 'crash' program undertaken to first reach the moon. Such 'habitation' was strongly suspected, based on data retrieved by probes from both the United States and the Soviet Union, prompting their 'race to the moon.' Perhaps the desire for first contact with our nearest neighbor was an effort to claim any abandoned advanced technology that might be found there.

As rapidly as the manned lunar missions were enacted, they were just as suddenly stopped. The original Apollo Program included a total of ten trips to the moon, comprised of one 'fly-over' (Apollo 10) and nine 'manned landings.' But only a total of six manned landings were completed (Apollo 13 was the 'troubled' flight that returned without landing), with Apollo 17 ending the program; even though the remaining two missions, Apollo 18 and 19, were already funded, with their hardware purchased. Some NASA scientists speculated that the agency was fearful of a potential UFO encounter with our astronauts, one that they would not be able to keep secret.[19]

Another speculation was that NASA had sufficient proof that the moon had been or was a base for otherworldly beings and 'chose not to pursue or press the issue.' Others believe that any further manned missions were unnecessary, since all that could be learned from the 'dead' world had been discovered. Yet numerous scientists at NASA contend that the Apollo Missions had created more questions, contradictions, and confusion about the moon than existed before the program. Seemingly, more research and evaluation should therefore be in order, not less.

Chapter 30

The Return

A general change in attitude toward the possibility of extraterrestrial life can be perceived during more recent times, with a majority of our population now believing that otherworldly life likely exists elsewhere within our universe. This current position may reflect the years of 'conditioning' of our human population by the descendants of the BOPH gods and their human 'insiders.' Those efforts have evidently been preparing Earth for the inevitable return of the Ancient Ones, if the *Elder Gods* theory is correct.

However, any verification of UFO encounters and alien life would be a serious challenge to present religious, scientific, and governmental paradigms. Therefore, a precise plan undoubtedly was devised long ago to implement such preparatory conditioning. Perhaps numerous different plans have been enacted over the ages, by each of the various affected and informed institutions, in order to deal with the inevitable return of the Ancient Ones from exile. Religious leaders have long warned that the 'Fallen Ones' may return to Earth and once again subject it to their rule.

In the New Testament, Chapter 13 of Mark divulges the signs and calamities preceding the Second Coming, and warns of false Christs and false prophets. One would expect our Savior's return to the physical realm to be a very joyous event, rather than an ominous and threatening one. Equally surprising is the anticipated end of the world often associated with such a return, which has also been characterized by others as a 'great non-event.'

Similar dire warnings emerge from other religious records and numerous modern prophets. Those declarations attempt to alert humanity of impending ecological or natural disasters, while imploring restraint regarding weapons of mass destruction. They also urge curtailment of experimentation into areas that humanity does not yet fully understand, such as the processes of cloning and genetic manipulation. Surprisingly, such dreadful warnings also herald a New Age for a few 'chosen people,' one emerging from the forewarned chaos.

Since the 1947 Roswell crash, a fascination with aliens and UFOs can be detected in the news media, the entertainment industry, various new 'religious movements,' and numerous other cultural venues within human society. That focus has led to a sizable majority of Americans now accepting the probable existence of otherworldly beings. How those beings are portrayed to the masses will certainly help shape human reaction toward our 'first contact' with them.

This purposeful orchestration, which may slowly reveal the likelihood of extraterrestrial beings, would seemingly be the intended result of a carefully planned conditioning of humanity. That intent would be the eventual shaping of our predetermined reaction and opinion regarding such contact, with that effort directed toward the results desired by the descendants of the ancient BOPH beings.

In 1960, NASA released a Brookings Institution study evaluating effects on our society from a potential disclosure that would reveal the existence of extraterrestrial life. The study concluded that the exposure of otherworldly beings could lead to: "...sweeping changes or even the downfall of civilization," adding: "societies... have disintegrated when confronted by a superior society."[1] It is believed that the very foundations of government, religion, science, and civilization would be undermined by such disclosure if those beings were a superior species. Without doubt, 'public' extraterrestrial contact would stagger psychological and social aspects of humanity. President

Ronald Reagan's September 21, 1987 address to the United Nations contained a reference to a possible alien threat from beyond this world.[2] Many have since speculated that he may have had specific classified information concerning the actual potential for such an otherworldly threat.

Two dilemmas seem to be at the forefront of modern UFO concern. The first one questions why extraterrestrial beings appear to be so secretive, or otherwise appear to accept governmental concealment and suppression of their actual existence. The answer may emerge from the evolving and continuing story of the Ancient Ones, which may ostensibly be associated with the modern UFO phenomenon. If true, the coy refusal by UFO occupants to make 'open' contact with humanity may be their continuing adherence with the arrangement made thousands of years ago, which prevented such contact or intervention with the affairs of humankind until their exile ended. Their occasional covert interaction with a few select humans apparently does not breach terms of that ancient exile agreement.

The second dilemma focuses on governments around the world that possibly suppress the knowledge of extraterrestrial life and their surveillance of Earth. An organized cover-up is the usual explanation for such suspected continuing suppression. The 1947 Roswell crash may be the defining moment that formulated the modern approach for dealing with this conundrum. Recall that newspapers and lower level personnel within the military, along with numerous civilian observers from a wide array of the population, all readily acknowledged the factual nature of those initial crash reports regarding an extraterrestrial craft.

Apparently, some unseen power quickly instructed the military at its highest level to suppress that account. Those high level military advisors subsequently advised various heads of government that 'nothing had really happened, it was simply a weather balloon.' The government then instructed the press to 'down play' the crash story. The event was transformed into a charade perpetrated on the general populace, evidently in an effort to suppress the real truth.

According to certain UFO researchers, including Vance Davis and Jim Marrs, Presidents Truman and Eisenhower supposedly had knowledge of alien beings and their visitations to Earth; although they decided to keep such facts hidden, due to the belief that the general public would panic.[3] Other leaders feared such knowledge would undermine the very foundations of our centuries old nation and its benchmark enterprises; including our financial institutions, civic organizations, universities, and industrial giants and defense contractors, as well as the very essence of the cultural structure of humanity itself. It was also believed that proof of alien beings would ultimately destroy religious institutions, while further revealing the military's inability to ultimately protect the public.

It is the further contention of Messrs. Davis and Marrs that the remote viewing records of the military confirm that UFOs are alien spacecraft. Pilots of such craft are alleged to be aliens from several different worlds, who supposedly represent different alien species, some of which are at war with one another.[4] Those aliens are not necessarily aligned with each other, nor have they evidently finalized any specific contract or agreement with any governmental agency of Earth.

Public suppression of knowledge concerning otherworldly visitors would require the cooperation of numerous agencies. Such infusion may be evidenced by the placement of military personnel in certain powerful positions within influential agencies. Collectively, their hidden agenda might be to shape public opinion toward a desired specific outcome. Evidently, that would be the continuation of the demonization of the Ancient Ones, although there are some indications that certain insiders might be resisting that directive.

Author Graham Hancock reported that governmental lobbyist and researcher Dan Ecker had noted that many civilian workers within NASA were replaced with people from the Department of

Defense during the tenure of Daniel Goldin, who was the chief administrator of NASA during the time of those appointments. Mr. Ecker also believed that NASA appeared to become more covert in their actions and informational releases during Dr. Goldin's administration.[5] Others have also detected that same trend, believing that NASA may have had a hidden agenda, one influenced by something beyond the pure pursuit of scientific knowledge. Such an agenda is often believed to be the cover up of significant evidence that would reveal the true nature of the anomalous structures photographed on Mars, as well as NASA's knowledge pertaining to the existence of UFOs and extraterrestrial life.[6]

On August 6, 1996, Daniel Goldin approved a press release stating: "NASA Scientists Find Evidence of Life on Mars."[7] But that was the apparent discovery of merely bacterial life found within a meteorite that had drifted to Earth from Mars. Some believe that this was the start of an orchestrated global strategy by governmental and scientific agencies, which was undertaken to openly acknowledge the reality of extraterrestrials while still withholding other more specific knowledge, such as information concerning the Cydonia region of Mars.

The Space Act of July 29, 1958, the Act from which NASA was originally formed, required NASA to make public all information they possessed. But that Act also exempted certain data, actually requiring it to be withheld under federal statute, along with any information deemed essential to protect our national security. Hence, NASA actually has a duty to withhold some information.[8] NASA, as a United States agency, has always been closely associated with national defense and security. Still, author Don Wilson reported that Robert D. Barry of the 20th Century UFO Bureau claimed that a classified NASA document, namely KMI-8610.4, orders astronauts to report any UFO encounters or sightings as pieces of regular NASA spacecraft.[9]

The aforementioned 1960 released Brookings Institution report further urged NASA to control information pertaining to evidence of any extraterrestrial life if ever found, for reasons of public security. A CIA report from a scientific advisory panel on UFOs, which was held from January 14th through the 18th, 1953, asserted that continued reporting of UFO encounters would create a threat to the orderly functioning of the protective organizations within our government.[10] It also advised that even NASA's scientists should be excluded, when possible, from knowledge or proof of extraterrestrial life, if it should eventually be found.

However, some merit may exist for such a secretive policy. Any adverse public opinion that might lead to potential civil disruption and mob violence would certainly influence governmental disclosures concerning sensitive matters, including UFOs and alien life. It is generally believed that numerous governments from around the world have direct knowledge of extraterrestrials, but withhold it from their people. Since governments apparently can do little or nothing to either stop or alter UFO activity, any acknowledgment of those extraterrestrial visitations would merely declare openly their powerless position in such matters.

Nations may merely be postponing their public confirmation until they have an opportunity to adequately deal with this dilemma, perhaps by negotiating with these otherworldly visitors. Until then, their policy of denial apparently continues. Such 'information management' may also reflect a campaign designed to slowly acclimate humans to the reality of advanced extraterrestrial life. This slow release of information, presented at various perceived 'proper times,' could subjectively influence and prepare Earth's populace for the inevitable First Contact. Such conditioning could help negate any civil chaos and mob violence. But manipulation of facts withheld until a more appropriate time would merely delay the inevitable. Perhaps Daniel Goldin's unexpected departure from NASA at the end of 2001 might eventually alter that agency's persistent prior policy of withholding certain 'sensitive' information.

Withheld data, such as national security information, may be a legitimate application of non-disclosure. The speculation that certain knowledge is occasionally being suppressed by some governmental agencies may have its origins rooted throughout history. A consistent belief over the centuries suggests that a secret society of 'masters,' or a group of 'wise men,' has directed human events through their sporadic exposure of advanced knowledge and complex technology of a 'metaphysical nature.' This secret group is believed to have either direct or indirect control over the governments of many nations, and hence the world collectively. This frightening concept of an unseen group directing human events has apparently existed continuously throughout our history. If such a conspiracy against humanity is true, it renders our culture to be merely a puppet society, one directed by an unknown agency for some still unknown purpose.

Candidates for these secret societies have occasionally been identified. They include: The Knights of the Temple, Sons of Liberty, the Knights Templar, the Sovereign & Military Order of Malta (SMOM), the I Am Society, Teutonic Knights, The Assassins, The Illuminati, the Thule Society, the Vril Society, the Rosicrucians, the Edelweiss Society, Freemasonry, the League of the Just, the Theosophical Society, the Pythagoreans, and even the Gnostics; to name just a few of the many possibilities over the years. The Bilderbergs (Builderberg Group/Conference), the Bohemian Club (Bohemian Grove), along with certain financial institutions such as the House of Rothschild are other similar 'globalist' candidates. The occasional sinister forces behind certain Christian Orders, such as the Dominicans who ran the Inquisition, may also fit into this category. Such secret societies have spawned numerous conspiracy theories wherein a few 'Dark Leaders' supposedly exercise global rule from behind the scenes as a *de facto* one-world governmental influence or New World Order.

Modern researchers such as Vance Davis and Jim Marrs further contend that a secret war is being waged behind the scenes for control of Earth. They contend that much of their belief theories have been confirmed or exposed from governmental records acquired through remote viewing, a program that was originally overseen and conducted by the military. Messrs. Davis and Marrs think that the country is being run by a handful of 'global elitists' operating from their influential positions or posts within secret societies, such as the Council on Foreign Relations or the Trilateral Commission. Such organizations are reportedly utilized to pass along directives and orders, while executing their own secret agenda.[11] Conspiracy theorists believe that such a sinister force is operating behind the scenes; dictating policy and wielding the true power over Earth, or at least strongly influencing the power behind governments and military agencies. They further contend that the media is controlled, dominated, or owned by this select group of policy makers, with centralized control being wielded from three major media groups or consortiums.

If such groups of Dark Leaders do exist, they would likely be the descendants of the BOPH gods. Their agenda, which was handed down from their ancient ancestors, would be simple. It would involve humanity's preparation for the eventual return of the Ancient Ones after expiration of their exile period. The desired outcome would be to produce a dubious populace that would greatly distrust the returning Ancient Ones, viewing their return as an ominous and threatening event. Their ultimate goal would be humanity's rejection of any unification or allegiance with the Cosmic Order, as well as with the regulated rate of growth and help offered by the Ancient Ones.

If the hypothesis presented in this writing is correct, Earth might be nearing the end of that agreed upon separation from the Cosmic Order and the Ancient Ones. The Mayans, one of the most meticulous and concise cultures known for their record keeping, dated our planet's current period as starting on August 13, 3113 BC, and predicted its end on December 21, 2012 AD. Although purely speculative, that period might reflect the duration of Earth's separation from the Ancient Ones. The increased sightings of UFOs since 1947 might signify a heightened early reconnaissance of Earth by the Ancient Ones, in preparation for reestablishing direct contact. Such contact would also initiate humanity's possible reinstatement with the Cosmic Order, if the people of Earth, through their informed choice, should so decide.

During the Ancient Ones' suspected 5,125 years of exile, the plan adopted by the BOPH beings to assure future control over Earth and its population was to keep humanity in a constant state of warfare and turmoil, while demonizing the Ancient Ones as an evil entity. This is evident throughout most ancient texts and many religious beliefs. Their plan continues into modern times, with the steadily diminishing governmental denials of UFOs and extraterrestrial life, evidently accompanied by a policy intended to portray otherworldly beings as potentially evil entities awaiting their moment to attack and take over Earth, ultimately enslaving its people. If that was really the case, what defense could Earth offer against such a superior power?

Our recent period of rapid advancement in scientific inventions and discoveries might reflect a deliberate and artificially accelerated growth of Earth's technological progress. The later descendants of the BOPH beings could have planned such an accelerated period of progress to occur just prior to the return of the Ancient Ones, in an attempt to negate any need or desire for their advanced technological assistance. Any such offer of help and guidance could then be characterized by the BOPH descendants as simply being unnecessary, especially considering the required surrender of certain human 'freedoms' as mandated by the Cosmic Order.

With implementation of the apparent political strategy intended to negate any need for a partnership with the Ancient Ones, the BOPH descendants' ultimate argument would then be that such an alliance comes with too high a price to be worthwhile. Upon rejection of the Ancient Ones and their

Cosmic Order, the BOPH descendants could then continue to control and restrain humanity, just as they have throughout the past.

It would appear that the descendants of the BOPH gods have attempted to keep humans ignorant and in a continuous state of war since the temporary exile of the Ancient Ones. Such a condition would negate normal cultural progress and help control population numbers. Such prior control may have been accomplished over the ages through various wars, religious domination and persecutions, and global plagues. It may have also been accompanied with restraint of growth and knowledge over extended periods of time, as evidenced throughout the Dark Ages. While many past cultures believed they were living during the 'End Times' of humanity, perhaps we really are, depending on the impending choice made by humankind.

Meanwhile, the benefactors that bestowed the numerous legacies to humanity during ancient times have been continuing their never-ending mission to civilize emerging species elsewhere. Those same benefactors, who were perhaps directed by the Creator to guide, domesticate, and educate infant races throughout the universe, have continued those duties on other developing worlds. It is also conceivable that during the exile period of the Ancient Ones, they have continued to monitor Earth from a distance, and may have even maintained bases on our moon and perhaps on Mars. Their observations of human progress and our development as a species will supply the criteria from which those benefactors will formulate their future plans for Earth and their final evaluation of humanity. Might anyone believe that the Ancient Ones would be completely pleased with what they have observed on Earth over the past 5,000 years?

References

Chapter 1

1 Matthew Fordahl, "Scientists Take Photo Of Early Universe," Associated Press article in The Ledger, Lakeland, Fla., 4-27-2000.

2 Ibid.

3 Marcia Dunn, "Probe to Study Remnants of Creation," Associated Press article in The Ledger, Lakeland, Fla., 7-1-2001.

4 Murry Hope, *The Sirius Connection: Unlocking the Secrets of Ancient Egypt* (hereafter called *The Sirius Connection*), Element Books, Rockport, Mass., 1996, p. 154.

5 Ibid.

6 Matthew Fordahl, "Scientists Take Photo Of Early Universe," op. cit.

7 James Glanz, "Cosmic Clue May Give Answer to Big Bang," New York Times article in The Ledger, Lakeland, Fla., 11-26-1999.

8 Sharon Begley, "Scientists Go on Hunt For the 'Dark Energy' Filling In the Universe," Science Journal article in the Wall Street Journal, 10-18-2002.

9 Richard Golob and Eric Brus, *The Almanac of Science and Technology*, Harcourt, Brace, & Jovanovich Inc., Florida, 1990, pp. 470-472. See also James Glanz, "Claims About 'Dark Matter' Particles Raise Skepticism," New York Times article in The Ledger, Lakeland, Fla., 2-20-2000.

10 Richard Golob & Eric Brus, *The Almanac of Science and Technology*, op. cit., p. 470. See also "Scientists ID Half of Missing Universe Mass," New York Times & Associated Press, 1997; & James Glanz, "Claims About 'Dark Matter' Particles Raise Skepticism," op. cit.

11 John Johnson, Jr., "Scientists Discover Dark Matter Proof," Los Angeles Times article printed in the Tampa Tribune, 5-16-07.

12 Radio interview with Richard C. Hoagland on the *Coast to Coast AM* program with Art Bell. See also Enterprise Mission Web site @ www.enterprisemission.com.

13 Ibid.

14 John Biemer, "New Evidence Found of Milky Way Black Hole," Associated Press article in The Ledger, Lakeland, Fla., 9-6-2001. See also Washington Press release, "Study: Black Holes Dominated Universe," article in The Ledger, Lakeland, Fla., 3-14-2001.

15 Holy Bible, Genesis 1:6; and Psalm 19:1. See also *Rig Veda* 1.154.3, p.226 & 1.185.2, p. 204, trans. and ed. by Wendy Doniger O'Flaherty, Penguin Books, New York, 1981.

Chapter 2

1   *The Book of Enoch* (*2 Enoch* or *The Book of the Secrets of Enoch*), Chapter V; reproduced in *The Forgotten Books of Eden*, Ed. Rutherford H. Platt, Jr., Bell Pub., New York, 1980, p. 83.

2   *I. P. Cory, Ancient Fragments,* Second Ed., William Pickering, Pub., London, 1832, p. 286. See also Sir John Gardner Wilkinson, *The Manners and Customs of the Ancient Egyptians,* Vol. II, Ed. by Samuel Birch, John Murray Pub., London, 1878; from Ch. XII, Cosmogony of Iamblichus, p. 505.

3   W. Norman Brown, *Mythology of India* section in *Mythologies of the Ancient World,* ed. by Samuel Noah Kramer, Anchor Books, New York, 1961, pp. 287-288. See also *Rig Veda, Creation Hymn* 10.129, op. cit., p. 25.

4   Alexander G. Higgins, "Experiment Yields Evidence Supporting 'Big Bang' Theory," Associated Press article in The Ledger, Lakeland, Fla., 2-11-2000.

5   Ibid.

6   Washington, D.C. press release, "Organic Molecules Found in Space," 1-13-2000.

7   H. P. Blavatsky, *The Secret Doctrine,* Theosophical University Press, Pasadena, Calif., 1988 printing of the original 1888 edition, p. 366.

8   *The Urantia Book,* The Urantia Foundation, Chicago, 1955, pp. 152, 154, & 236.

9   Ibid., pp. 136, 258-260, & 262.

10 Sharon Begley, "Scientists Revisit Data on Mars With Minds More Open to Life," Wall Street Journal, 10-27-06.

11 Erich von Däniken, *The Gold of the Gods,* Bantam Books, New York, 1974, pp. 64-65.

Chapter 3

1   William McCall, "Study: Extinction Recovery Takes a Long Time," Associated Press article in The Ledger, Lakeland, Fla., 3-9-2000.

2   Ibid.

3   Graham Hancock, *Fingerprints of the Gods*, Crown Pub., New York, 1995, p. 477.

4   Radio interview with Gregg S. Braden on the *Coast to Coast AM* program with Art Bell.

5   Paul Recer, "Fossil Find Suggests Arctic Once as Balmy as Today's Florida," Associated Press article in The Ledger, Lakeland, Fla., 12-18-1998. See also W. Raymond Drake, *Gods and Spacemen of the Ancient Past*, Signet Books, New York, 1974, p. 106; & Eric Norman, *Gods, Demons and Space Chariots*, Lancer Books, New York, 1970, p. 115.

6   Funk & Wagnall's New Encyclopedia, 1983 ed., vol. 13, p. 271. See also M. Don Schorn, *Elder Gods of Antiquity*, Ozark Mountain Publishing, Huntsville, AK., 2007, pp. 141 & 149.

7   Andrew Tomas, *We Are Not The First*, Bantam Books, New York, 1973, p. 24. See also Herbie Brennan, *Martian*

Genesis, Dell Pub., New York, 1998, p. 36; & M. Don Schorn, *Elder Gods of Antiquity*, op. cit., p. 140.

8   Andrew Tomas, *We Are Not The First*, op. cit., p. 24. See also Craig and Eric Umland, *Mysteries of the Ancients: Early Spacemen and the Mayas* (hereafter referred to as *Mysteries of the Ancients*), Walker and Co., New York, 1974, p. 159.

9   Peter Kolosimo, *Not of this World*, Bantam Books, New York, 1973, p. 8. See also M. Don Schorn, *Elder Gods of Antiquity*, op. cit., p. 140.

10 Carl Sagan, *Cosmos*, Ballantine Books, New York, 1985, p. 285.

11 Craig and Eric Umland, *Mysteries of the Ancients*, op. cit., p. 94. Affected area included Oregon, Idaho, Nevada, and Northern California. Additional geological evidence indicates that New Mexico and parts of Arizona also experienced volcanic eruptions and lava cover.

Chapter 4

1   *Parade Magazine*, Parade Publications, New York, January 21, 2001 issue.

2   Paul Recer, "Photos: Jupiter Moon Racked by Volcanoes," Associated Press article in The Ledger, Lakeland, Fla., 5-19-2000. See also Candice Hughes, "Quest for Life Centers on Jupiter Moon," Associated Press article in The Ledger, Lakeland, Fla., 10-14-1999.

3   Robert S. Boyd, "Europa May Have Life-Supporting Ocean," Knight-Ridder Newspapers, 1998. See also Thomas H. Maugh II, "Europa's Ice: What Lies Beneath?" Los Angeles Times article in The Tampa Tribune, Tampa, Fla., 9-11-2000.

4   Washington, D.C. press release, "6 New Planets Found Orbiting Other Stars," 11-30-1999. See also William Schiffmann, "Scientists Point to Other Solar Systems," Associated Press, 1999.

5 By-line El Paso, Texas, "Scientists Discover Jupiter-size Planet," wire service article in The Tampa Tribune, Tampa, Fla., 8-5-2000.
6 Paul Recer, "Team Finds 2 Smaller Planets," Associated Press article in The Ledger, Lakeland, Fla., 3-30-2000. See also William Schiffmann, "Scientists Point to Other Solar Systems," Associated Press, 1999.
7 Ibid.
8 Ibid.
9 Ibid. See also Paul Recer, "Planet Systems Discovered," Associated Press article in The Ledger, Lakeland, Fla., 1-10-2001; & David H. Levy, "The Search For Other Worlds," *Parade Magazine,* op. cit., 9-30-2001, pp. 4-6.
10 Alicia Chang, "Scientists Say Planet Sighting Confirmed," Associated Press article in The Ledger, Lakeland, Fla., 4-30-05. See also Associated Press article, "Light From Distant Planets Is Captured," The Ledger, Lakeland, Fla., 3-23-05.
11 By-line Washington, "5th Planet Orbiting Nearby Star Found," Washington Post article in The Tampa Tribune, 11-7-07.
12 William J. Broad, "Maybe We are Alone in the Universe," New York Times article in The Ledger, Lakeland, Fla., 2-9-2000.
13 Ibid.
14 Robert S. Boyd, "Scientists Call, But E.T. Doesn't Answer," Knight-Ridder Newspapers article in The Ledger, Lakeland, Fla., 4-13-2000.
15 Ibid.
16 Matthew Fordahl, "NASA's Future Mars Missions Unaffected by Orbiter's Loss," Associated Press article in The Ledger, Lakeland, Fla., 9-26-1999. See also Paul Recer, "Mathematical Error Led to Loss of Mars Climate Orbiter," Associated Press article in The Ledger, Lakeland, Fla., 11-11-1999; "Polar Lander," The Ledger, Lakeland, Fla., 12-4-1999;

& Marc Kaufman, "Mars Photos Most Dramatic of Rover's 900-Day Mission," Washington Post article printed in the Tampa Tribune, 10-7-2006.

17 Paul Recer, "Experts Confident Of Life Beyond Earth," Associated Press article in The Ledger, Lakeland, Fla., 10-15-1998.

18 Joseph B. Verrangia, "Scientists Find Unique Microbes," Associated Press, January 2002.

19 Chuck Missler and Mark Eastman, *Alien Encounters,* Koinonia House, Coeur d'Alene, Idaho, 1997, p. 127. See also Michael Denton, *Evolution: A Theory in Crisis,* Adler and Adler, 1986, p. 250.

20 Chuck Missler and Mark Eastman, *Alien Encounters,* op. cit., p. 130.

21 *Nature,* vol. 294:105, Nature Pub. Group, New York, November 12, 1981. See also Chuck Missler and Mark Eastman, *Alien Encounters,* op. cit., p. 129.

Chapter 5

1   Michael Pollak, "Neanderthal Isn't Extinct Online," New York Times article in The Ledger, Lakeland, Florida, 5-9-1999.

2   Paul Recer, "Experts Confident Of Life Beyond Earth," Associated Press article in The Ledger, Lakeland, Fla., 10-15-1998.

3   Eric Chaisson, *Cosmic Dawn,* Berkley Books, New York, 1984, p. 169.

4   Cal Tech press release dated 7-24-1997, referenced by Graham Hancock, *The Mars Mystery,* Three Rivers Press, New York, 1998, p. 181.

5   Sharon Begley, "Forget That Ape-Man," Wall Street Journal, 7-11-2002.

6   Ibid.

7   John Noble Wilford, "Fossil Discovery Fuels Missing-Link Debate," New York Times article in The Ledger, Lakeland,

Fla., 4-25-1999. See also Peter Svensson, "Early Man Shown to be Smarter," Associated Press article in The Ledger, Lakeland, Fla., May 1999.

8 Paris, France press release, "Fossil Suggests Nice Neanderthals," 10-13-2001.

9 Washington, D.C. press release, "Neanderthal Bones Date to Human Era," 10-26-1999.

Chapter 7

1 Such a 300 million year 'headstart' is based on dating of meteorite rocks determined to be from the asteroid belt that later impacted Earth, which have been dated at 5.0 billion years old; yet Earth did not form until only 4.7 billion years ago, a difference of 300 million years.

2 Washington Press release, "Crystal May Prove Life on Mars," 1998. See also Paul Recer, "NASA Defends Theory of Life on Mars," Associated Press article in The Ledger, Lakeland, Fla., 8-5-1998.

3 Ibid.

4 *Icarus*, vol. 36, 1978, as ref. by Graham Hancock, *The Mars Mystery*, op. cit., p. 40.

5 Donald W. Patten and Samuel L. Windsor, *The Scars of Mars*, Pacific Meridien Pub., Seattle, 1996, p. 69. See also Graham Hancock, *The Mars Mystery*, op. cit., p. 47.

6 Paul Recer, "Meteorite May Offer Clues to Life," Associated Press article in The Ledger, Lakeland, Fla., 10-13-2000.

7 Ibid.

8 Ibid.

9 George Hunt Williamson, *Other Tongues – Other Flesh*, Amherst Press, Amherst, Wisc., 1953, p. 172.

10 Robert S. Boyd, "Saltwater Found in Meteorite," Knight-Ridder Newspapers article in The Ledger, Lakeland, Fla., 8-27-1999.

11 Some stray chunks that broke from orbit in the asteroid belt and later impacted our planet display a composition striking

similar to Earth. Analysis of these specimens reveals no 'foreign' substances or elements that are not also found on Earth. The age of such specimens are dated at 5.0 billion years, making the extraterrestrial parent at least 300 million years older than Earth.

12 M. Don Schorn, *Elder Gods of Antiquity*, op. cit., pp. 116-119.

13 The Roche Limit calculates that gravitational stresses and electromagnetic forces would destroy an invasive body of similar density if it approached closer than 2.44 times the radius of the parent body. See also Walter Sullivan, *We Are Not Alone*, Signet Books, New York, 1966, p. 47; & Graham Hancock, *The Mars Mystery*, op. cit., p. 39.

14 Warren E. Leary, "3-D Map Shows Texture of Mars," New York Times article in The Ledger, Lakeland, Fla., 5-28-1999.

15 George Hunt Williamson, *Other Tongues – Other Flesh*, op. cit., p. 181.

16 Ibid., pp. 178-179.

Chapter 8

1 Graham Hancock, *The Mars Mystery*, op. cit., p. 30.

2 Donald W. Patten and Samuel L. Windsor, *The Scars of Mars*, op. cit., p. 69. See also Graham Hancock, *The Mars Mystery*, op. cit., p. 47.

3 Graham Hancock, *The Mars Mystery*, op. cit., pp. 156-157.

Chapter 9

1 Nicholas Wade, "DNA Study Traces First Family Tree," New York Times, 2000.

2 William J. Broad, "Findings Boost Case For Martian Ocean," New York Times article in The Ledger, Lakeland, Fla., 12-10-1999. See also Warren E. Leary, "3-D Map Shows Texture of Mars," New York Times article in The Ledger, Lakeland, Fla., 5-28-1999; & Science News article,

"Discovery Sheds Light on Mars' Past," Tampa Tribune, 1999.

3 Michael Pauls & Dana Facaros, *The Travelers' Guide to Mars*, Cadogan Books, London, 1997.

4 Paul Recer, "Mars Dust Storm May Alter Odyssey Flight Plan," Associated Press article in The Ledger, Lakeland, Fla., 10-12-2001.

5 NASA's 1976 Viking 1 orbiter photograph, Frame No. 70A13 & 35A72.

6 Ibid.

7 Ibid.

8 Richard C. Hoagland, *The Monuments of Mars*, North Atlantic Books, Berkeley, Calif., 1987, p. 26. See also Graham Hancock, *The Mars Mystery*, op. cit., p. 10.

9 Radio interview with Richard C. Hoagland on *Coast to Coast Am* radio program. See also Web site @ www.enterprisemission.com.

10 Ibid.

11 NASA's Mariner 9 orbiter, infrared image, Frame No. 4209-75 (ref. NASA created photograph, number 75-H-604).

Chapter 10

1 *Velikovsky Reconsidered,* the eds. of Pensee, Warner Books, New York, 1976, p. 266.

2 Immanuel Velikovsky's contributing article included in the New York Times article, *"Man Walks on Moon,"* referenced in *Velikovsky Reconsidered,* eds. of Pensee, op. cit., pp. 265-267. Article based on thermoluminescence studies conducted at Washington University, St. Louis, Mo., headed by R. Walker. Studies concluded that disturbances responsible for the anomalies possibly occurred around 8000 BC, but the limited data base for extracted material at any lunar site would create a wide swing in such subjective dating.

3 Based on statements contained in *The Kumarbi Myth* (sometimes known as *The Story of Alalu, Anu, and Kumarbi,*

and also as *The Struggle for Kingship Among the Gods),* as referenced in *The Hittites,* O. R. Gurney, Penguin Books, Maryland, 1954, p. 190.

4 Ibid.

5 Ibid.

6 See First Journal of the Ancient Ones, *Elder Gods of Antiquity,* op. cit., pp. 159, 161, & 169 for supportive indications of Alalu's association with Lepenski Vir.

7 *The Epic of Gilgamesh,* English trans. by N. K. Sandars, Penguin Books, Baltimore, 1968, pp. 38 & 120. Dilmun is referenced as the Land of the Living (the Land of the Immortals), where the gods took the Sumerian hero, Ziusudra (the Akkadian Utnapishtim) after the Great Flood, granting him immortality, and allowing him to live among the gods.

8 Geological and archaeological evidence establishes that the area that later became Eridu was submerged until c.4900 BC. At that time, the waters had sufficiently evaporated, forming marshlands, which only became livable through the use of canals, which later served as irrigation for farming the rich delta land that had been 'reclaimed.'

9 *Enuma elish,* Akkadian version, Tablet IV, line 42; reproduced in *The Ancient Near East,* ed. by James B. Pritchard, Princeton University Press, New Jersey, 1958, p. 37.

10 Geoffrey Bibby, *Looking for Dilmun,* Penguin Books, New York, 1980. The book presents substantial suggestive evidence that the Dilmun culture migrated to Sumer from Bahrain; and also states that Enki was the first god of Dilmun, presumably before becoming a god at Eridu and throughout Mesopotamia.

11 As known from the 300 Igigi stationed in the heavens, per the *Enuma elish,* Akkadian version, Tablet IV, line 42; reproduced in *The Ancient Near East,* ed. by James B. Pritchard, op. cit., p. 37.

12 That date for Enlil's emergence on Earth is known from the Jemdet Nasr period, which occurred between c.3250 and 2850 BC; the period in which Enlil ruled over the gods.

13 Descriptions of apparent nuclear weapons and nuclear blasts are numerous in ancient Sanskrit texts, such as the *Mahabharata,* Book I, trans. & ed. by J.A.B. van Buitenen, University of Chicago Press, Chicago, 1980, and the *Rig Veda,* trans. by Wendy D. O'Flaherty, Penguin Books, New York, 1981; as well as Mesopotamian texts such as the *Lament for the Destruction of Ur,* trans. Thorkild Jacobsen, reproduced by Cornelius Loew, *Myth, Sacred History, and Philosophy,* Harcourt, Brace & World, New York, 1967, pp. 29-30.

14 The Olmec and Mayan Long Count, as based on the Goodman-Martinez, Hernandez-Thompson calculation, started in 3113 BC; a date of some significance to numerous cultures.

Chapter 11

1 *Rig Veda,* trans. by Wendy D. O'Flaherty, Penguin Books, New York, 1981, Hymn 1.32: *The Killing of Vrtra,* 1.32.2, 8 & 11, pp. 149-150.

2 Graham Hancock and Robert Bauval, *The Message of the Sphinx,* Three Rivers Press, New York, 1996, p. 225.

3 Murry Hope, *The Sirius Connection,* op. cit., pp. 213-214.

4 Ibid., p. 214. See also G.R.S. Mead, *Thrice Greatest Hermes,* Theosophical Pub. Soc., London, 1906, Vol. III, pp. 136, 143, & 147-148.

5 *Virgin of the World,* fragment reportedly written by Thoth, reproduced by G.R.S. Mead, *Thrice Greatest Hermes,* op. cit., Vol. III, p. 122. The term 'Architect' was also a common epithet used in Sanskrit texts as an apparent reference to the Ancient Ones. Such epithets will be further examined in Chapter 14 of this text.

6 *Virgin of the World,* reproduced by G.R.S. Mead, *Thrice Greatest Hermes,* op. cit., Vol. III, p. 122. See also Murry Hope, *The Sirius Connection,* op. cit., p. 69.

7 *Virgin of the World,* reproduced by G.R.S. Mead, *Thrice Greatest Hermes,* op. cit., Vol. III, p. 122.

8 Ibid. p. 123.

9 Ibid., p. 124.

10 Dr. Elaine Pagels, *The Gnostic Gospels,* Vintage Books, New York, 1981, p. 44.

11 Frank Waters, *Book of the Hopi,* Ballantine Books, New York, 1976, pp. 202 & 222.

12 Ibid., pp. 202, 222, 231-235.

13 Ibid., p. 203.

14 Ibid., pp. 82-83, & 202.

15 Ibid., pp. 203-204.

16 Ibid., pp. 171 & 221.

17 Ibid., p. 171.

18 Murry Hope, *The Sirius Connection,* op. cit., pp. 84-85.

19 Ibid., p. 85.

20 Letter written in the name of The Great House of her grace, Sekhmet Montu, to author Murry Hope. Letter contained a scribal translation of a reportedly olden Ammonite esoteric history account, portions reproduced by Murry Hope, *The Sirius Connection,* op. cit., pp. 65-67.

21 Ibid., pp. 65-66.

22 Ibid., p. 66.

23 Ibid.

24 Ibid.

Chapter 12

1 *Enuma elish,* Akkadian version, Tablet IV, lines 105 & 137; reproduced in *The Ancient Near East,* ed. James B. Pritchard, Princeton University Press, New Jersey, 1958, pp. 34 & 35.

2 *Mahabharata,* Book I, trans. & ed. by J.A.B. van Buitenen, op. cit., 1.58.46, p. 138.

3   Ibid., 1.71.5, pp. 175-176.
4   *Rig Veda,* trans. by Wendy D. O'Flaherty, op. cit., Footnote 23, p. 156. See also Hymn 1.32.8 &11, p. 150; & Hymn 3.31, pp. 151-154.
5   Ibid., pp. 23 & 225. See also Hymn 1.154, p. 226-227; Hymn 3.31.12 & 13, p. 150; Hymn 5.85.5, p. 211; Hymn 10.81.2, p. 35; & Hymn 10.82, p. 36.
6   Ibid., Hymn 3.31.12, p. 153.
7   Ibid., Hymn 2.12.1, p. 160; & Hymn 7.86.1, p. 213.
8   Ibid., p. 225. See also Hymn 1.154.3, p. 226.
9   H. P. Blavatsky, *The Secret Doctrine,* op. cit., p. 32.
10 Zecharia Sitchin, *When Time Began,* Avon Books, New York, 1993, p. 7.
11 Derk Bodde, *Myths of Ancient China,* Sect. 2, contained in *Mythologies of the Ancient World,* ed. Samuel Noah Kramer, op. cit., p. 386.
12 Charles Berlitz, *Mysteries From Forgotten Worlds,* Dell Pub., New York, 1972, p. 199.
13 *The Urantia Book,* op. cit., pp. 602-604.
14 Ibid., p. 198.
15 Ibid., pp. 611-615, 619-620, & 808.
16 Timothy Wyllie, *Dolphins*Extraterrestials*Angels,* Bozon Enterprises, 1984.
17 Mircea Eliade, *The Myth of the Eternal Return,* English trans. by Willard R. Trask, Bollingen Ser., New York, 1954, p. 91. See also Derk Bodde, *Myths of Ancient China,* Sect. 3, contained in *Mythologies of the Ancient World,* ed. Samuel Noah Kramer, op. cit., p. 392.
18 Ibid.
19 Derk Bodde, *Myths of Ancient China,* Sect. 3, contained in *Mythologies of the Ancient World,* ed. Samuel Noah Kramer, op. cit., p. 393.
20 Ibid.
21 Ibid., p. 390.

22 Ibid.
23 Zecharia Sitchin, *The 12th Planet,* Avon Books, New York, 1978, pp. 96-97.
24 *The Kumarbi Myth* sometimes known as *The Story of Alalu, Anu, and Kumarbi,* and also as *The Struggle for Kingship Among the Gods,* referenced in *The Hittites,* O. R. Gurney, Penguin Books, Maryland, 1954, p. 190.
25 *The Vishnu Purana,* trans. by H. H. Wilson, John Murray Pub., London, 1840, Book V, Ch. XXXVII, p. 608.
26 Murry Hope, *The Sirius Connection,* op. cit., p. 68.

Chapter 13

1 William L. Langer, ed., *Western Civilization*, American Heritage Pub., N.Y., 1968, p. 31.
2 *Rig Veda*, trans. by Wendy D. O'Flaherty, op. cit., pp. 37, 70 & 223. See also H. P. Blavatsky, *The Secret Doctrine*, op. cit., p. 202.
3 W. Raymond Drake, *Gods and Spacemen In The Ancient East*, Signet Books, New York, 1973, p. 225.
4 *Papyrus of Ani*, Chapter 17, Sect. 112, (part of the Egyptian *The Book of the Dead*), translated by Sir E. A. Wallis Budge, British Museum, London, 1895. See also W. Raymond Drake, *Gods and Spacemen In The Ancient East*, op. cit., p. 136-137 & 139.
5 Ibid.
6 Ignatius Donnelly, *Atlantis: The Antediluvian World*, rev. by Egerton Sykes, Grammercy Pub., New York, 1949, p. 156.
7 Robert Graves, *The White Goddess*, Faber & Faber, London, 1958. See also Brinsley Le Poer Trench, *The Sky People*, Award Books, New York, 1970, p. 23.
8 Elaine Pagels, *The Gnostic Gospels*, op. cit., pp. 44, 65 & 148. See also H. P. Blavatsky, *The Secret Doctrine*, op. cit., pp. 197 & 449.

9   *Enuma elish*, Akkadian version, all of Tablet V & most of Tablet VI; reproduced in *The Ancient Near East*, ed. James B. Pritchard, op. cit., pp. 35-37.

10 *3 Enoch* (aka *Hebrew Book of Enoch*), trans. by Hugo Odeberg, Cambridge University Press, Cambridge, England, 1928. See also George C. Andrews, *Extra-Terrestrials Among Us*, Llewellyn Pub., St. Paul, MN., 1995, p. 56.

11 *The Mahabharata*, Book I, trans. & ed. by J.A.B. van Buitenen, op. cit., introduction, p. xxi & p. 6.

12 Rudolf Anthes, *Mythology in Ancient Egypt*, Sect. 4, contained in *Mythologies of the Ancient World*, ed. Samuel Noah Kramer, op. cit., p. 36.

13 Murry Hope, *The Sirius Connection*, op. cit., p. 103.

14 Samuel Noah Kramer, *Mythology of Sumer and Akkad*, Sect. on Sumer, contained in *Mythologies of the Ancient World*, ed. Samuel Noah Kramer, op. cit., p. 95.

Chapter 14

1   *Book of Dzyan*, Stanza III.7., reproduced in H. P. Blavatsky, *The Secret Doctrine*, op. cit., p. 29.

2   H. P. Blavatsky, *The Secret Doctrine,* op. cit., p. 355.

3   *Book of Dzyan,* Stanza III.7: "Behold Him (the Creator) lifting the veil...for the Shining Ones," (p.29); Stanza IV.2: "...the Primordial Seven...have learnt from our Fathers (the Creator and the prior universes)...." (p.30); & Stanza V.3: "He (the Creator) is their (the Ancient Ones) guiding spirit and leader." (p.31); reproduced in H. P. Blavatsky, *The Secret Doctrine,* op. cit., ref. pages.

4   H. P. Blavatsky, *The Secret Doctrine,* op. cit., pp. 88 & 573.

5   I. P. Cory, *Ancient Fragments,* Ed. by E. Richmond Hodges, Reeves & Turner, London, 1876, pp. 10 & 12.

6   Ibid.

7   H. P. Blavatsky, *The Secret Doctrine,* op. cit., p. 167.

8   W. Raymond Drake, *Gods and Spacemen In The Ancient East,* op. cit., p. 42. See also Eric Norman, *Gods and Devils From Outer Space,* Lancer Books, New York, 1973, p. 35.

9   Eric Norman, *Gods and Devils From Outer Space,* op. cit., pp. 36, 156-157.

10 H. P. Blavatsky, *The Secret Doctrine,* op. cit., pp. 480 & 601.

11 *Book of Dzyan,* Stanzas II.5. (p. 28), IV.2. (p. 30), & V.1. (p. 31); reproduced in H. P. Blavatsky, *The Secret Doctrine,* op. cit., ref. pages.

12 H. P. Blavatsky, *The Secret Doctrine,* op. cit., p. 344.

13 Ibid., p. 446.

14 Ibid., p. 290.

15 Frank Waters, *Book of the Hopi,* op. cit., p. 183.

16 W. B. Henning, "A Sogdian Fragment of the Manichaean Cosmogony," in *Bulletin of the School of Oriental and African Studies* XII, 1948, p. 313; as reproduced by M. J. Dresden, *Mythology of Ancient Iran,* Sect. 1c., contained in *Mythologies of the Ancient World,* ed. Samuel Noah Kramer, op. cit., pp. 341-342.

17 Brinsley le Poer Trench, *Temple of the Stars,* Ballantine Books, N.Y., 1974, pp. 46 & 49.

18 Ibid., p. 50.

19 Ibid.

20 *The Mahabharata,* Book I, trans. & ed. by J.A.B. van Buitenen, op. cit., pp. 436 & 443.

21 Graham Hancock and Robert Bauval, *The Message of the Sphinx,* op. cit., pp. 200 & 201.

22 Ibid., p. 201.

23 H. P. Blavatsky, *The Secret Doctrine,* op. cit., pp. 579 & 613. See also James Churchward, *The Lost Continent of Mu,* Paperback Library, New York, 1968, p. 125.

24 H. P. Blavatsky, *The Secret Doctrine,* op. cit., p. 344.

25 James Churchward, *The Lost Continent of Mu,* op. cit., p. 142.

26 Ibid., pp. 19 & 151.

27 H. P. Blavatsky, *The Secret Doctrine,* op. cit., p. 436.

28 H. P. Blavatsky, *The Secret Doctrine,* op. cit., Vol. II. The Puranas reference a 4,320,000 year cycle called Mahayuga, see *The Secret Doctrine,* p. 655.

29 Ibid., p. 434.

30 Thor Heyerdahl, *Early Man and the Ocean,* Doubleday & Co., New York, 1979, p. 108.

31 James Churchward, *The Sacred Symbols of Mu,* Paperback Library, New York, 1968, p. 56.

32 H. P. Blavatsky, *The Secret Doctrine,* op. cit., p. 446.

33 Ibid., p. 127.

34 Ibid., p. 128.

35 Murry Hope, *The Sirius Connection,* op. cit., pp. 213-214.

36 Ibid., p. 208.

37 Ibid.

38 Zecharia Sitchin, *When Time Began,* op. cit., pp. 298-299.

39 Ibid., p. 304.

40 Brinsley le Poer Trench, *Temple of the Stars,* op. cit., p. 57.

41 Ibid., p. 67.

42 Graham Hancock and Robert Bauval, *The Message of the Sphinx,* op. cit., p. 268.

43 W. Raymond Drake, *Gods and Spacemen In The Ancient East,* op. cit., p. 43.

44 Ibid., p. 87.

45 George C. Andrews, *Extra-Terrestrials Among Us,* op. cit., p. 47.

46 W. Raymond Drake, *Gods and Spacemen In The Ancient East,* op. cit., p. 88.

47 H. P. Blavatsky, *The Secret Doctrine,* op. cit., p. 312.

48 W. Raymond Drake, *Gods and Spacemen In The Ancient East,* op. cit., p. 135.

49 *Papyrus of Ani,* trans. by E. A. Wallis Budge, Chapter 18, lines 86-99. See also W. Raymond Drake, *Gods and Spacemen In The Ancient East,* op. cit., pp. 134-135.

50 E.A.E. Reymond, *The Mythical Origin of the Egyptian Temple,* Manchester University Press- Barnes & Noble, New York, 1969, p. 77.

51 H. P. Blavatsky, *The Secret Doctrine,* op. cit., p. 70. See also Ellen Gunderson Traylor, *Noah,* Living Books, Wheaton, Ill., 1988.

52 W. Raymond Drake, *Gods and Spacemen In The Ancient East,* op. cit., p. 225.

53 Ibid., p. 224.

54 Rupert Furneaux, *Ancient Mysteries,* Ballantine Books, New York, 1993, pp. 37-38.

55 Ibid., p. 39.

56 Ibid., p. 38.

57 Letter written in the name of The Great House of her grace, Sekhmet Montu, to author Murry Hope. Letter contained a scribal translation of a reportedly olden Ammonite esoteric history account, portions reproduced by Murry Hope, *The Sirius Connection,* op. cit., pp. 65-67.

58 Jacques Bergier, *Extraterrestrial Visitations from Prehistoric Times to the Present* (hereafter called *Extraterrestrial Visitations*), Henry Regnery Co., Chicago, Ill., 1973, p. 108.

59 Ibid., p. 106.

60 Ibid., p. 104.

61 Ibid., pp. 108-109.

62 Ibid., p. 99.

63 Ibid.

Chapter 15

1 Brinsley le Poer Trench, *Temple of the Stars*, op. cit., pp. 130-131.

2 *The Mahabharata*, Book I, trans. & ed. by J.A.B. van Buitenen, op. cit., p. 3.

3 James Bailey, *The God-Kings & The Titans*, St. Martin's Press, New York, 1973, p. 186.

4 *The Mahabharata*, Book I, trans. & ed. by J.A.B. van Buitenen, op. cit., p. 439.

5 W. Raymond Drake, *Gods and Spacemen In The Ancient East*, op. cit., p. 55.

6 H. P. Blavatsky, *The Secret Doctrine*, op. cit., p. 407.

7 Cyrus H. Gordon, *Canaanite Mythology*, contained in *Mythologies of the Ancient World*, ed. Samuel Noah Kramer, op. cit., p. 201 & footnote #10, p. 217.

8 E. A. Wallis Budge, *Egyptian Magic*, Citadel Press/Carol Pub., New York, 1991, p. 79.

9 H. P. Blavatsky, *The Secret Doctrine*, op. cit., p. 674.

10 Peter Kolosimo, *Not of this World*, op. cit., p. 35.

11 H. P. Blavatsky, *The Secret Doctrine*, op. cit., p. 446.

12 *Valentinian Exposition*, 22.19-23, based on the Nag Hammadi Documents; as contained in Elaine Pagels, *The Gnostic Gospels*, op. cit., p. 37. See also H. P. Blavatsky, *The Secret Doctrine*, op. cit., p. 446.

13 H. P. Blavatsky, *The Secret Doctrine*, op. cit., p. 480.

14 Ibid., p. 650.

15 Ibid., p. 198.

16 From the writings of Basilides, contained in Charles W. King, *The Gnostics and Their Remains*, 2nd edition, David Nutt Pub., London, 1887, p. 76.

17 Ibid., p. 77.

18 Ibid.

19 *Poemanders*, Sect. 9, 14, & 16, trans. by G.R.S. Mead, in *Thrice-Greatest Hermes*, Vol. II, op. cit., pp. 7, 9, 10-11.

20 From *Apocryphon of John*, contained in *The Nag Hammadi Library in English*, Ed. by James MacConkey Robinson, the Coptic Gnostic Library Project, Brill Pub., Boston, 1988, p. 111.

21 H. P. Blavatsky, *The Secret Doctrine*, op. cit., p. 196.

22 Ibid., pp. 432-433.

23 Ibid., pp. 647 & footnote on p. 648.

24 G.R.S. Mead, *Thrice Greatest Hermes*, Vol. III, op. cit., p. 300.

25 W. Raymond Drake, *Gods and Spacemen of the Ancient Past*, op. cit., p. 133.

26 Erich von Däniken, *In Search of Ancient Gods*, G. P. Putnam's Sons, N.Y., 1974, pp. 88-89.

27 Various guest interviews, including aerospace engineer, Robert Lazar, on the *Coast to Coast AM* radio program.

28 Walter Sullivan, *We Are Not Alone*, op. cit., p. 202.

29 Ibid., pp. 203-205.

30 W. Raymond Drake, *Gods and Spacemen In The Ancient East*, op. cit., p. 17.

31 *The Mahabharata*, Book V, (*The Book of the Effort*), as ref. by Andrew Tomas, *We Are Not The First*, op. cit., p. 117.

Chapter 16

1 Jean Sendy, *Those Gods Who Made Heaven & Earth*, Berkley Medallion Books, New York, 1972, p. 35.

2 H. P. Blavatsky, *The Secret Doctrine*, op. cit., p. 577.

3 James Churchward, *The Lost Continent of Mu*, Paperback Library, New York, 1968, p. 114.

4 H. P. Blavatsky, *The Secret Doctrine*, op. cit., p. 208.

5 Moshe Hallamish, *An Introduction to the Kabbalah*, trans. by Ruth Bar-Ilan and Ora Wiskind-Elper, State University of New York Press, Albany, NY, 1999, pp. 152-155.

6 Naacal Tablet No. 1231, ref. by James Churchward, *The Lost Continent of Mu*, op. cit., p. 24.

7 H. P. Blavatsky, *The Secret Doctrine*, op. cit., p. 446.

8 Warren Smith, *Lost Cities of the Ancients-Unearthed!*, Zebra Books/Kensington Pub., New York, 1976, p. 214.

9 Rudolf Anthes, *Mythology in Ancient Egypt*, Sect. 4, contained in *Mythologies of the Ancient World*, ed. Samuel Noah Kramer, op. cit., p. 38.

10 Ibid., Sect. 8, p. 77.

Chapter 17

1 Joseph Campbell Video Lecture Series on Mythology (first segment): *The Hero's Journey*, produced by Mythology Ltd., in association with Pantechnicon Productions, Inc., 1987.

2 *Valentinian Exposition* 22.19-23, from the Nag Hammadi texts; reproduced by Elaine Pagels, *The Gnostic Gospels*, op. cit., p. 37. See also H. P. Blavatsky, *The Secret Doctrine*, op. cit., p. 446.

3 Elaine Pagels, *The Gnostic Gospels*, op. cit., p. 44.

4 Ibid., pp. 44 & 65.

5 *The Book of the Dead* (Egyptian), including *The Papyrus of Ani*, Chapter 108, Sect. 4, translated by Sir E. A. Wallis Budge, op. cit. See also H. P. Blavatsky, *The Secret Doctrine*, op. cit., p. 674.

6 Elaine Pagels, *The Gnostic Gospels*, op. cit., pp. 65-66.

7 H. P. Blavatsky, *The Secret Doctrine*, op. cit., pp. 657-658.

8 W. Norman Brown, *Mythology of India*, Sect. 6, contained in *Mythologies of the Ancient World*, ed. Samuel Noah Kramer, op. cit., p. 310.

9 Robert Graves, *The Greek Myths: Volume 1*, Penguin Books, Maryland, 1955, p. 35.

10 H. P. Blavatsky, *The Secret Doctrine*, op. cit., p. 394.

11 Robert Graves, *The Greek Myths: Volume 1*, op. cit., p. 27.

12 Frank Waters, *Book of the Hopi*, op. cit., p. 166.

13 Cyrus H. Gordon, *Canaanite Mythology*, contained in *Mythologies of the Ancient World*, ed. Samuel Noah Kramer, op. cit., p. 214.

14 M. J. Dresden, *Mythology of Ancient Iran*, Sect. 3b., contained in *Mythologies of the Ancient World*, ed. Samuel Noah Kramer, op. cit., pp. 352-353.

Chapter 18

1 Cornelius Loew, *Myth, Sacred History, and Philosophy*, op. cit., pp. 33, 42 & 69.

2   H. P. Blavatsky, *The Secret Doctrine*, op. cit., pp. 273 & 634.

3   Samuel Noah Kramer, *Mythology of Sumer and Akkad*, contained in *Mythologies of the Ancient World*, ed. Samuel Noah Kramer, op. cit., p. 99 & 115.

4   Rig Veda, Hymn 10.190.1, trans. and ed. by Wendy Doniger O'Flaherty, op. cit., p. 34. See also W. Norman Brown, *Mythology of India*, Sect. 2, contained in *Mythologies of the Ancient World*, ed. by Samuel Noah Kramer, op. cit., pp. 284-285.

5   Rudolf Anthes, *Mythology in Ancient Egypt*, Sections 7, 8 & 9, contained in *Mythologies of the Ancient World*, ed. Samuel Noah Kramer, op. cit., pp. 59, 79 & 88. See also Graham Hancock and Robert Bauval, *The Message of the Sphinx*, op. cit., p. 278.

6   Rudolf Anthes, *Mythology in Ancient Egypt*, Sections 7 & 9, contained in *Mythologies of the Ancient World*, ed. Samuel Noah Kramer, op. cit., pp. 59-60 & 90.

7   Graham Hancock and Robert Bauval, *The Message of the Sphinx*, op. cit., pp. 278–279.

8   Ibid., pp. 276 & 278.

9   Frank Waters, *Book of the Hopi*, op. cit., p. 1.

10 Ibid., pp. 171 & 221.

11 *The Book of Abraham*, Ch. 3:3, contained in *The Pearl of Great Price*, Pub. by The Church of Jesus Christ of Latter-Day Saints, Salt Lake City, Utah, 1989, p. 34.

12 *The Book of Abraham*, Ch. 3:3&16, contained in *The Pearl of Great Price*, op. cit., pp. 34-35.

13 *The Urantia Book*, op. cit., pp. 258-260 & 262.

14 Ibid.

15 Courtney Brown, *Cosmic Voyage*, Onyx Books, New York, 1996.

16 Ibid.

17 Ibid.

18 James Churchward, *The Lost Continent of Mu*, op. cit., p. 23.

19 Ibid., p. 24.
20 Ibid., p. 27.
21 Ibid., p. 23.
22 Ibid., p. 27.

Chapter 19

1   H. P. Blavatsky, *The Secret Doctrine*, op. cit., p. 263.
2   *Poemanders*, Sect. 16, translated by G.R.S. Mead, contained in his *Thrice Greatest Hermes*, Vol. II, op. cit., p. 11.
3   Ibid, Sect. 26, p. 16.
4   I. P. Cory, *Ancient Fragments*, ed. by E. Richmond Hodges, op. cit., p. 19.
5   H. P. Blavatsky, *The Secret Doctrine*, op. cit., pp. 249-250 & 415.
6   Rudolf Anthes, *Mythology in Ancient Egypt*, Sect. 6, contained in *Mythologies of the Ancient World*, ed. Samuel Noah Kramer, op. cit., p. 57.
7   *The Egyptian Book of the Dead* (aka *The Book of Going Forth by Day*), Plate 11, Inscription 146, trans. by Dr. Raymond O. Faulkner, Chronicle Books, San Francisco, 1998.
8   Sir E. A. Wallis Budge, *Egyptian Magic*, op. cit., p. 171.
9   *The Rig Veda*, trans. by Wendy D. O'Flaherty, op. cit., footnote 3, p. 199.
10 H. P. Blavatsky, *The Secret Doctrine*, op. cit., p. 415.
11 Ibid., p. 312. See also *The Book of the Dead*, (Egyptian), including *The Papyrus of Ani*, Plate X, Lines 45-46, translated by Sir E. A. Wallis Budge, op. cit., pp. 283-284.
12 Graham Hancock, *The Mars Mystery*, op. cit., p. 273.
13 Rudolf Anthes, *Mythology in Ancient Egypt*, Sect. 7, contained in *Mythologies of the Ancient World*, ed. Samuel Noah Kramer, op. cit., p. 67.
14 Ibid., pp. 65-67.
15 Fragments from the writings of Panodorus, as reproduced by W. Raymond Drake, *Gods and Spacemen of the Ancient Past*,

op. cit., pp. 123-124. Also ref. fragments contained in W. Williams, *Primitive History, From the Creation to Cadmus*, J. Seagrave, Chichester, England, 1789, p. 508.

16 W. Raymond Drake, *Gods and Spacemen of the Ancient Past*, op. cit., p. 55.

17 H. P. Blavatsky, *The Secret Doctrine*, op. cit., p. 132.

18 Ibid., p. 104.

19 Egyptologist Professor Walter Emery stated that the type of graves and any evidence of the Shemsu-Hor disappeared after c.3150 BC, according to his *Archaic Egypt*, Penguin Books, Baltimore, Maryland, 1963.

20 Frank Waters, *Book of the Hopi*, op. cit., p. 202.

21 Ibid., pp. 82, 83 & 84-87.

22 Ibid., p. 87.

23 Robert Charroux, *Masters of the World*, Berkley Medallion Books, New York, 1974, p. 79. See also Robert Charroux, *Legacy of the Gods*, Berkley Medallion Books, New York, 1973, Chapt. 6, 7, & 10.

24 *1 Enoch* (aka *The Book of Enoch*), Chapter 15, lines 8-9, trans. by R. H. Charles, Clarendon Press, Oxford, 1912. See also Chuck Missler and Mark Eastman, *Alien Encounters*, Koinonia House, Coeur d'Alene, ID, 1997, p. 241.

25 Chuck Missler and Mark Eastman, *Alien Encounters*, op. cit., p. 241.

26 *Virgin of the World*, fragment reportedly written by Thoth, reproduced by G.R.S. Mead, *Thrice Greatest Hermes*, Vol. III, op. cit., p. 121-123. See also Murry Hope, *The Sirius Connection*, op. cit., p. 69.

27 Murry Hope, *The Sirius Connection*, op. cit., p. 69.

28 James H. Breasted, *A History of Egypt*, Charles Scribner's Sons, New York, 1912 & 1937, p. 378. See also Immanuel Velikovsky, *Oedipus and Akhnaton*, Pocket Books, New York, 1980, pp. 60, 62 & 92.

29 Ignatius Donnelly, *Atlantis: The Antediluvian World*, rev. by Egerton Sykes, op. cit., pp. 281-282 & 286-288.

30 F. H. Brookbank, *Egyptian Gods and Heroes*, Harrap & Co., London, 1914. See also Eric Norman, *Gods and Devils From Outer Space*, op. cit., p. 83.

31 Murry Hope, *The Sirius Connection*, op. cit., p. 39.

32 Ibid., pp. 39-40. See also *Quest for the Past*, Reader's Digest Eds., Pleasantville, New York, 1984; & Martin Merzer, "Site May Be Linked To 1st Floridians," Miami Herald article in The Ledger, 6-4-2000.

33 Thomas Bulfinch, *Mythology of Greece and Rome*, Collier Books, New York, 1962, p. 327.

34 Ibid., p. 328.

Chapter 20

1 William Howells, *Back of History*, Natural History Library, U.S.A., 1963, pp. 33-34.

2 Moshe Hallamish, *An Introduction to the Kabbalah*, trans. by Ruth Bar-Ilan & Ora Wiskind-Elper, op. cit., p. 109.

3 Warren Smith, *Lost Cities of the Ancients-Unearthed!*, op. cit., pp. 314-315.

4 H. P. Blavatsky, *The Secret Doctrine*, op. cit., pp. 131 & 167.

5 Murry Hope, *The Sirius Connection*, op. cit., p. 63.

6 *Book of Dzyan*, Stanza IV, Verse 5, line 3, as contained in H. P. Blavatsky, *The Secret Doctrine*, op. cit., p. 31.

7 Ibid., Stanza V, Verse 5, p.32.

8 Brinsley le Poer Trench, *Temple of the Stars*, op. cit., p. 51.

9 *Book of Enoch* (*2 Enoch* or *The Book of the Secrets of Enoch*), Chapter XX; reproduced in *The Forgotten Books of Eden*, ed. Rutherford H. Platt, Jr., op. cit., p. 88.

10 H. P. Blavatsky, *The Secret Doctrine*, op. cit., various commentaries.

Chapter 21

1 H. P. Blavatsky, *The Secret Doctrine*, op. cit., Vol. 2, p. 366.

2 George F. Creuzer, as referenced from p. 441 of *Egypte*, and quoted by H. P. Blavatsky, *The Secret Doctrine*, op. cit., Vol. 2, p. 367.

3 Per fragments from the writings of Panodorus, ref. by H. P. Blavatsky, *The Secret Doctrine*, op. cit., Vol. 2, pp. 368-369.

4 Zecharia Sitchin, *When Time Began*, op. cit., p. 299.

5 *Book of Enoch* (*2 Enoch* or *The Book of the Secrets of Enoch*), Chapter XXIII, verses 2 & 3; reproduced in *The Forgotten Books of Eden*, ed. Rutherford H. Platt, Jr., op. cit., p. 89.

6 Zecharia Sitchin, *When Time Began*, op. cit., p. 304.

7 H. P. Blavatsky, *The Secret Doctrine*, op. cit., p. 657.

8 Ibid., Vol. 2, pp. 371-372. See also Brinsley le Poer Trench, *Temple of the Stars*, op. cit., pp. 130-131.

9 W. Raymond Drake, *Gods and Spacemen of the Ancient Past*, op. cit., p. 82.

10 W. Raymond Drake, *Gods and Spacemen In The Ancient East*, op. cit., p. 55. See also Brinsley Le Poer Trench, *The Sky People*, op. cit., pp. 46 & 155-156.

11 W. Raymond Drake, *Gods and Spacemen In The Ancient East*, op. cit., p. 85.

12 H. P. Blavatsky, *The Secret Doctrine*, op. cit., Vol. 2, p. 210.

13 Ibid., p. 379.

14 Graham Hancock & Robert Bauval, *The Message of the Sphinx*, op. cit., pp. 236, 242, & 270.

15 Ibid., footnote #1, p. 321.

16 Murry Hope, *The Sirius Connection*, op. cit., p. 10.

17 Graham Hancock and Robert Bauval, *The Message of the Sphinx*, op. cit., footnote #5, p. 322.

18 Ibid., p. 264.

19 Ibid. See also footnote #5, p. 322.

20 Al-Masudi, *Akhbar al Zaman*, manuscript excerpt reproduced in Ignatius Donnelly, *Atlantis: The Antediluvian World*, rev. by Egerton Sykes, op. cit., p. 274.

21 Brinsley le Poer Trench, *Temple of the Stars*, op. cit., p. 115.

22 Ibid.

23 Graham Hancock and Robert Bauval, *The Message of the Sphinx*, op. cit., pp. 18 & 52.

24 Alan and Sally Landsburg, *In Search of Ancient Mysteries*, op. cit., p. 21.

25 Charles Berlitz, *Atlantis: The Eighth Continent*, op. cit., pp. 134-135. See also Charles Fort, *The Book of the Damned*, op. cit., p. 132.

26 Erich von Däniken, *In Search of Ancient Gods*, op. cit., p.173.

27 Eric Norman, *Gods and Devils From Outer Space*, op. cit., p. 91.

28 Andrew Tomas, *We Are Not The First*, op. cit., p. 54.

29 Ibid, p. 48.

30 Ibid.

31 Alan and Sally Landsburg, *The Outer Space Connection*, op. cit., p.14.

32 Ibid., p. 52.

33 Warren Smith, *Lost Cities of the Ancients-Unearthed!*, op. cit., p. 311.

34 Known as the Konig Batteries, named after Dr. Wilhelm Konig who discovered the artifacts and recognized their use. See Erich von Däniken, *The Eyes of the Sphinx*, Berkley Books, New York, 1996, p. 170; Alan and Sally Landsburg, *The Outer Space Connection*, op. cit., p.132; and Charles Berlitz, *Atlantis: The Eighth Continent*, op. cit., p. 139.

35 Andrew Tomas, *We Are Not The First*, op. cit., p. 95, quote taken from the *Agastya Samhita*.

36 David Hatcher Childress, *Lost Cities of Atlantis, Ancient Europe & The Mediterranean*, op. cit., p. 19.

37 Erich von Däniken, *The Eyes of the Sphinx*, op. cit., pp. 172-173. See also Charles Berlitz, *Atlantis: The Eighth Continent*, op. cit., p. 140.

38 Erich von Däniken, *The Eyes of the Sphinx*, op. cit., pp. 172-173. See also E. A. Wallis Budge, *Egyptian Magic*, op. cit., p. 47; and James Churchward, *The Sacred Symbols of Mu*, op. cit., p. 110.

39 E. A. Wallis Budge, *Egyptian Magic*, op. cit., p. 47.

40 Such as Item #6347 in the Cairo Museum. See Erich von Däniken, *In Search of Ancient Gods*, op. cit., p. 171.

41 Ibid. See also Charles Berlitz, *Atlantis: The Eighth Continent*, op. cit., p. 143.

42 Erich von Däniken, *In Search of Ancient Gods*, op. cit., p. 172. See also Charles Berlitz, *Atlantis: The Eighth Continent*, op. cit., p. 142.

43 Erich von Däniken, *In Search of Ancient Gods*, op. cit., pp. 178-179.

44 Cartography data derived from various sources, including but not limited to: Charles H. Hapgood, *Maps of the Ancient Sea Kings*, Chilton Books, N.Y., 1966; M.H.J. Th. Van Der Veer and P. Moerman, *Hidden Worlds*, Bantam Books, N.Y., 1975; David Hatcher Childress, *Lost Cities of Atlantis, Ancient Europe & The Mediterranean*, op. cit.; J. V. Luce, *The End of Atlantis*, Bantam Books, New York, 1978; Jacques Bergier, *Extraterrestrial Visitations*, op. cit.; Charles Berlitz, *Atlantis: The Eighth Continent*, Ballantine Books, New York, 1985.

45 Ibid.

46 Ibid.

47 Ibid.

Chapter 22

1 Murry Hope, *The Sirius Connection*, op. cit., p. 204.

2 Graham Hancock and Robert Bauval, *The Message of the Sphinx*, op. cit., p. 236.

3   *Kore Kosmu*, Excerpt XXIII, sect. 29, as translated in *Hermetica* (Sir Walter Scott trans.) and reproduced by Graham Hancock and Robert Bauval, *The Message of the Sphinx*, op. cit., p. 132.

4   *The Sacred Sermon*, translated by G.R.S. Mead and contained in his *Thrice Greatest Hermes*, op. cit., Vol. II, p. 83. See also Graham Hancock and Robert Bauval, *The Message of the Sphinx*, op. cit., p. 34.

5   Graham Hancock and Robert Bauval, *The Message of the Sphinx*, op. cit., p. 214.

6   Murry Hope, *The Sirius Connection*, op. cit., p. 208.

7   G.R.S. Mead, *Thrice Greatest Hermes*, Vol. I, op. cit., p. 124. See also Murry Hope, *The Sirius Connection*, op. cit., p. 208.

8   G.R.S. Mead, *Fragments of a Faith Forgotten*, Theosophical Pub. Soc., London, 1900.   See also George C. Andrews, *Extra-Terrestrials Among Us*, op. cit., p. 62.

9   Murry Hope, *The Sirius Connection*, op. cit., p. 201.

10 Ibid., pp. 3 & 201.

11 Ibid., p. 205.

12 Zecharia Sitchin, *When Time Began*, op. cit., pp. 159-160.

13 Ibid., pp. 148 & 160.

14 H. P. Blavatsky, *The Secret Doctrine*, op. cit., p. 650.

15 Ibid. See also *Encarta 98 Encyclopedia*, 1998 Ed., Microsoft Corp., Redmond, WA., 1997, Topic: "Seven Liberal Arts."

16 W. Raymond Drake, *Gods and Spacemen In The Ancient East*, op. cit., p. 119.

17 Immanuel Velikovsky, *Oedipus and Akhnaton*, op. cit., pp. 86 & 88.

18 Eric Norman, *Gods and Devils From Outer Space*, op. cit., pp. 95 & 98.

19 James Churchward, *The Sacred Symbols of Mu*, op. cit., p. 17.

20 Ibid., p. 23.

21 H. P. Blavatsky, *The Secret Doctrine*, op. cit., p. 432.

22 Lewis Spence, *The History of Atlantis*, Bell Pub., New York, 1968, pp. 189-190.

23 Frank Waters, *Book of the Hopi*, op. cit., p. 254.

24 Ibid.

25 Ibid., p. 367.

26 Ibid., p. 264.

27 Theodore Vrettos, *Alexandria: City of the Western Mind*, The Free Press (Div. Simon & Schuster), New York, 2001, p. 170. See also *Encarta 98 Encyclopedia*, op. cit., Topics: "Neoplatonism" & "Eusebius of Caesarea."

28 Jacques Bergier, *Extraterrestrial Visitations*, op. cit., p. 132.

29 Ibid.

30 Ibid., p. 126.

31 Ibid., p. 127.

Chapter 23

1 W. Raymond Drake, *Gods and Spacemen In The Ancient East*, op. cit., p. 1 & James Churchward, *The Lost Continent of Mu*, op. cit., p. 93.

2 E. A. Wallis Budge, *Egyptian Magic*, op. cit., p. 182.

3 James Churchward, *The Sacred Symbols of Mu*, op. cit., p. 87.

4 Murry Hope, *The Sirius Connection*, op. cit., p. 215.

5 Ibid., pp. 106 & 213. See also Erich von Däniken, *The Eyes of the Sphinx*, op. cit., p. 25.

6 Ibid.

7 E. A. Wallis Budge, *Egyptian Magic*, op. cit., p. 182.

8 Cornelius Loew, *Myth, Sacred History, and Philosophy*, op. cit., pp. 230, 267, & 272-273.

9 E. A. Wallis Budge, *Egyptian Magic*, op. cit., pp. 183-184.

10 Ibid., p. 192.

11 James Churchward, *The Lost Continent of Mu*, op. cit., pp. 93-94.

12 Graham Hancock, *The Mars Mystery*, op. cit., p. 163.

13 Sybil Leek, *Reincarnation: The Second Chance*, Bantam Books, New York, 1975, p. 93.

14 Ibid.

15 E. A. Wallis Budge, *Egyptian Magic*, op. cit., p. 222.

16 Cornelius Loew, *Myth, Sacred History, and Philosophy*, op. cit., p. 208.

17 Galatians 6:7, *The Holy Bible*, New Testament, King James Version, Cambridge University Press, Great Britain, 1994.

18 Frank Waters, *Book of the Hopi*, op. cit., pp. 33 & 202-203.

19 Thomas Bulfinch, *Mythology of Greece and Rome*, op. cit., p. 276.

20 Perhaps the olden interpretation of the number 10 is incomplete. It may be merely a distortion of the integers 1 & 0, the basics for binary code used in computer operations.

21 Thomas Bulfinch, *Mythology of Greece and Rome*, op. cit., pp. 276-277.

22 From *Discovery of a New World*, by the English Bishop, John Wilkins, 1644, as referenced by Don Wilson, *Secrets Of Our Spaceship Moon*, Dell Pub., New York, 1979, p. 247.

23 Don Wilson, *Secrets Of Our Spaceship Moon*, op. cit., p. 247.

24 Graham Hancock, *The Mars Mystery*, op. cit., p. 108.

25 Cornelius Loew, *Myth, Sacred History, and Philosophy*, op. cit., p. 231.

26 Don Wilson, *Secrets Of Our Spaceship Moon*, op. cit., p. 245.

27 Ibid., p. 246.

Chapter 24

1 F. Max Muller, *Lectures on the Science of Religion*, p. 257; as referenced by H. P. Blavatsky, *The Secret Doctrine*, op. cit., "Introductory," p. xli.

2 Jean Sendy, *Those Gods Who Made Heaven & Earth*, op. cit., p. 35.

3 Descriptions of ensuing religions were verified using numerous sources, including but not limited to: Archie J. Bahm, *The World's Living Religions*, Dell Pub., New York, 1964; Gerald L. Berry, *Religions of the World*, Barnes & Noble, New York, 1956; Funk & Wagnall's New

Encyclopedia, 1983 ed., op. cit.; *I Ching*, Raymond Van Over, Ed., Trans. by James Legge, Mentor Books, New York, 1971; *Mahabharata*, Book I, trans. & ed. by J.A.B. van Buitenen, op. cit.; *Rig Veda*, trans. by Wendy D. O'Flaherty, op. cit.; Cornelius Loew, *Myth, Sacred History, and Philosophy*, op. cit.; Merlin Stone, *When God was a Woman*, Barnes & Noble, New York, 1993; Ralph Linton, *The Tree of Culture*, Vintage Books, New York, 1959; Sybil Leek, *Reincarnation: The Second Chance*, op. cit.; *Mythologies of the Ancient World*, ed. Samuel Noah Kramer, op. cit.; Stuart Piggott, *Prehistoric India*, Penguin Books, Baltimore, Maryland, 1952; & H. P. Blavatsky, *The Secret Doctrine*, op. cit.

4   H. P. Blavatsky, *The Secret Doctrine*, op. cit., p. 355.

5   Archie J. Bahm, *The World's Living Religions*, op. cit., p. 92. See also Ralph Linton, *The Tree of Culture*, op. cit., p. 196.

6   Sybil Leek, *Reincarnation: The Second Chance*, op. cit., p. 130.

7   H. P. Blavatsky, *The Secret Doctrine*, op. cit., "Introductory," p. xxv.

Chapter 25

1   Merlin Stone, *When God was a Woman*, op. cit., p. 74.

2   Robert Charroux, *Masters of the World*, op. cit., footnote p. 249.

3   Leonhard Rost, *Judaism Outside the Hebrew Canon*, Abingdon, Nashville, TN., 1976, p. 38.

4   H. P. Blavatsky, *The Secret Doctrine*, op. cit., footnote p. 492.

5   Ibid., p. 70. See also Job 2:1.

6   Ibid.

7   M. J. Dresden, *Mythology of Ancient Iran*, Sect. 3b.ii., contained in *Mythologies of the Ancient World*, ed. Samuel Noah Kramer, op. cit., p. 350.

8   Ibid., Sect. 3b.i., p. 347.

9 David Adams Leeming, *The World of Myth*, Oxford University Press, N.Y., 1990, p. 197.

10 Ibid., p. 199.

11 Leonhard Rost, *Judaism Outside the Hebrew Canon*, op. cit., p. 94.

12 Preceding descriptions of religions and beliefs were verified using numerous sources, including but not limited to: Archie J. Bahm, *The World's Living Religions*, op. cit.; Gerald L. Berry, *Religions of the World*, op. cit.; Funk & Wagnall's New Encyclopedia, 1983 ed., op. cit.; *I Ching*, Raymond Van Over, Ed., Trans. by James Legge, op. cit.; *Mahabharata*, Book I, trans. & ed. by J.A.B. van Buitenen, op. cit.; *Rig Veda*, trans. by Wendy D. O'Flaherty, op. cit.; Cornelius Loew, *Myth, Sacred History, and Philosophy*, op. cit.; Merlin Stone, *When God was a Woman*, op. cit.; *Mythologies of the Ancient World*, ed. Samuel Noah Kramer, op. cit.; Stuart Piggott, *Prehistoric India*, op. cit.; Robert Charroux, *Masters of the World*, op. cit.; Leonhard Rost, *Judaism Outside the Hebrew Canon*, op. cit.; Vance Ferrell, *Christmas, Easter, and Halloween: Where Did They Come From?*, Pilgrims Books, Beersheba Springs, Tenn., 1997; & H. P. Blavatsky, *The Secret Doctrine*, op. cit.

Chapter 26

1 Eklal Kueshana, *The Ultimate Frontier*, The Stelle Group, Chicago, Ill., 1963, p. 166.

2 Ibid.

3 Ibid., pp. 167-168.

4 Ibid., p. 168.

5 Elaine Pagels, *The Gnostic Gospels*, op. cit., p. 44.

6 Ibid., p. 37.

7 Ibid., p. 44.

8 Ibid., p. 70.

9 From the writings of *Irenaeus*,1.30.6., reproduced in Elaine Pagels, *The Gnostic Gospels*, op. cit., p. 148.

10 Ibid.

11 James Churchward, *The Sacred Symbols of Mu*, op. cit., p. 56.

12 H. P. Blavatsky, *The Secret Doctrine*, op. cit., p. 387.

13 James Churchward, *The Sacred Symbols of Mu*, op. cit., p. 85.

14 *On the Origin of the World*, 103.9-20; reproduced in Elaine Pagels, *The Gnostic Gospels*, op. cit., p. 34.

15 Ibid.

16 The Book of Abraham, 3:2-3, & 9, contained in *The Pearl of Great Price*, Pub. by The Church of Jesus Christ of Latter-day Saints, Salt Lake City, Utah, 1989, p. 34.

17 Ibid., Abraham 3:9, 11-12, & 16. See also The Book of Mosiah, 7:27, p. 162.

18 The Book of Ether, 3:1, contained in *The Book of Mormon*, Pub. by The Church of Jesus Christ of Latter-day Saints, Salt Lake City, Utah, 1989, p. 492.

19 Ibid., Ether 6:11, p. 497.

20 Betty Kelen, *Muhammad: The Messenger of God*, Pocket Books, New York, 1977, p. 67.

21 Preceding descriptions of religions and beliefs were verified using numerous sources, including but not limited to: Archie J. Bahm, *The World's Living Religions*, op. cit.; Gerald L. Berry, *Religions of the World*, op. cit.; Funk & Wagnall's New Encyclopedia, 1983 ed., op. cit.; Cornelius Loew, *Myth, Sacred History, and Philosophy*, op. cit.; Merlin Stone, *When God was a Woman*, op. cit.; *Mythologies of the Ancient World*, ed. Samuel Noah Kramer, op. cit.; Eklal Kueshana, *The Ultimate Frontier*, op. cit.; Elaine Pagels, *The Gnostic Gospels*, op. cit.; James Churchward, *The Sacred Symbols of Mu*, op. cit.; Vance Ferrell, *Christmas, Easter, and Halloween: Where Did They Come From?*, op. cit.; H. P. Blavatsky, *The Secret Doctrine*, op. cit., *The Book of Mormon*, op. cit.; *The Pearl of Great Price*, op. cit.; & Betty Kelen, *Muhammad: The Messenger of God*, op. cit.

Chapter 27

1 Zecharia Sitchin, *When Time Began*, op. cit., p. 333.
2 Michael Pauls and Dana Facaros, *The Travelers' Guide to Mars*, Cadogan Books, London, 1997.
3 Brinsley Le Poer Trench, *The Sky People*, op. cit., p. 29.
4 Robert Graves, *The White Goddess*, op. cit. See also Brinsley Le Poer Trench, *The Sky People*, op. cit., p. 23.
5 George Hunt Williamson, *Other Tongues – Other Flesh,* op. Cit., pp. 284-285.
6 George William Cox, *Tales of Ancient Greece,* Jansen McClurg & Co., Chicago, 1879, p. 52
7 Pliny [the Elder], *The Natural History of Pliny,* trans. By John Bostock & H. T. Riley, Geo. Bell & Sons, London, 1893, p. 63.
8 Ibid.
9 Richard F. Haines, *Project Delta: A Study of Multiple UFO,* L.D.A. Press, Los Altos, Calif., 1994, as referenced by Chuck Missler and Mark Eastman, *Alien Encounters,* Koinonia House, Coeur d'Alene, ID, 1997, pp 66-67.

Chapter 28

1 John Biemer, "New Evidence Found of Milky Way Black Hole," Associated Press article in The Ledger, Lakeland, Fla., 9-6-2001. See also Washington Press release, "Study: Black Holes Dominated Universe," article in The Ledger, Lakeland, Fla., 3-14-2001.
2 Charles Berlitz, *The Dragon's Triangle*, Fawcett Books, New York, 1989, p. 199.
3 John E. Mack, *Abduction*, Macmillan Pub., New York, 1994, p. 354.
4 Chuck Missler and Mark Eastman, *Alien Encounters*, op. cit., p. 94.
5 Ibid. See also Richard Golob and Eric Brus, *The Almanac of Science and Technology*, op. cit., p. 457.

6   Michio Kaku, *Hyperspace: A Scientific Odyssey Through Parallel Universes, Time Warps, and the Tenth Dimension*, Anchor Books/Doubleday, N.Y., 1994, p. 16 & footnote #4, p. 335.

7   Stephen Hawking, *The Universe In A Nutshell*, Bantam Books, N.Y., 2001, Glossary, p. 206.

8   Michio Kaku, *Hyperspace: A Scientific Odyssey Through Parallel Universes, Time Warps, and the Tenth Dimension*, op. cit., p. 16.

9   Stephen Hawking, *The Universe In A Nutshell*, op. cit., margin note, p. 54.

10 Chuck Missler and Mark Eastman, *Alien Encounters*, op. cit., pp. 94-95.

11 Richard Golob and Eric Brus, *The Almanac of Science and Technology*, op. cit., p. 458.

12 *The Urantia Book*, op. cit., pp. 149-150, 161, & 184-190.

13 Courtney Brown, *Cosmic Voyage*, op. cit.

14 *The Urantia Book*, op. cit., p. 601.

15 Robert L. Dione, *Is God Supernatural?*, Bantam Books, New York, 1976, pp. 143 & 144.

16 Ibid., pp. 148-149.

17 Adrian V. Clark, *Cosmic Mysteries of the Universe*, Parker Pub., N.Y., 1968, pp. 170-171.

Chapter 29

1   Chuck Missler and Mark Eastman, *Alien Encounters*, op. cit., p. 223.

2   James Glanz, "Speed of Light May Not be the Limit," New York Times article in The Ledger, Lakeland, Fla., 5-30-2000.

3   Robert Matthews, "Wormholes for Space Travel Might Exist," New Scientist article in The Ledger, Lakeland, Fla., 4-15-2000.

4   As described by certain 'insiders' such as aerospace engineer Robert Lazar, a civilian scientist who once worked at the

secret government facility known as Area 51, located in the Groom Lake region of the Nevada desert. See also Web site @ www.coasttocoastam.com.

5 Wire service report, "The Idea That Einstein Hated," article in The Ledger, Lakeland, Fla., 4-8-2001. See also Sharon Begley, "Scientists Go on Hunt For the 'Dark Energy' Filling In the Universe," Science Journal article in the Wall Street Journal, 10-18-2002.

6 Alexandra Witze, "Physicists Discover New Material That Runs in Reverse," Dallas Morning News article in The Ledger, Lakeland, Fla., 3-23-2000.

7 Matthew Fordahl, "Team of Physicists Hopes to Unlock Mystery of Universe's Matter," Associated Press article in The Ledger, Lakeland, Fla., 7-7-2001.

8 Eric Norman, *Gods and Devils From Outer Space*, op. cit., p. 119.

9 Don Wilson, *Secrets Of Our Spaceship Moon*, op. cit., pp. 13 & 228.

10 Ibid., p. 206.

11 Ibid., p. 208.

12 Ibid., p. 206.

13 *Chronological Catalog of Reported Lunar Events*, NASA Technical Report number R-277, Washington, D.C., July 1968.

14 Don Wilson, *Secrets Of Our Spaceship Moon*, op. cit., p. 25.

15 Ibid., p. 35.

16 Ibid., p. 25.

17 Ibid.

18 Platform south of Archimedes Crater per NASA photo 109H3 from Lunar Orbiter IV, as printed by National Geographic, Nov. 1972, pp. 250-251; 'Glasslike' structure over Mare Crisium per NASA photos 177H3, 191H3, 192H3, & 54H2 from Lunar Orbiter IV, early vintage - 1968 microfilm archive; with both sites and photos reported by Fred

Steckling, *We Discovered Alien Bases On The Moon*, GAF Publishing, Los Angeles, 1981.

19 Don Wilson, *Secrets Of Our Spaceship Moon*, op. cit., p. 261.

Chapter 30

1   1960 Brookings Institution Report to the 87th Congress, Calendar 79, Report 242, re. NASA, as ref. by Chuck Missler and Mark Eastman, *Alien Encounters*, op. cit., p. 193.

2   Chuck Missler and Mark Eastman, *Alien Encounters*, op. cit., p. 293.

3   Combined interview with Vance Davis and Jim Marrs on *Coast to Coast AM* radio program. See also Web site @ www.coasttocoastam.com.

4   Ibid.

5   Graham Hancock, *The Mars Mystery*, op. cit., p. 19.

6   Ibid., pp. 19-20.

7   Chuck Missler and Mark Eastman, *Alien Encounters*, op. cit., p. 9.

8   Graham Hancock, *The Mars Mystery*, op. cit., pp. 122-123.

9   Don Wilson, *Secrets Of Our Spaceship Moon*, op. cit., p. 56.

10 Graham Hancock, *The Mars Mystery*, op. cit., p. 124.

11 Combined interview with Vance Davis and Jim Marrs on *Coast to Coast AM* radio program. See also Web site @ www.coasttocoastam.com.

SELECTED BIBLIOGRAPHY

I. Manuscripts, Books, and Texts:

Alonzo, Gualberto Zapata, *An Overview of the Mayan World*, Litoarte Printing, Mexico, 1987.

Andrews, George C., *Extra-Terrestrials Among Us*, Llewellyn Pub., St. Paul, Minn., 1995.

Ardrey, Robert, *African Genesis*, Dell Publishing, New York, 1961.

Asimov, Isaac, *Please Explain*, Dell Publishing, New York, 1973.

Bahm, Archie J., *The World's Living Religions*, Dell Publishing, New York, 1964.

Bailey, James, *The God-Kings & The Titans*, St. Martin's Press, New York, 1973.

Bergier, Jacques, *Extra-Terrestrial Visitations From Prehistoric Times to the Present*, Henry Regnery Co., Chicago, 1973.

Berlitz, Charles, *The Mystery of Atlantis*, Avon Books, New York,1969.

-----*Mysteries From Forgotten Worlds*, Dell Publishing, New York, 1972.

-----*Atlantis The Eighth Continent*, Ballantine Books, New York, 1985.

-----*The Dragon's Triangle*, Fawcett Books, New York, 1989.

Berry, Gerald L., *Religions of the World*, Barnes & Noble, New York, 1956.

Bibby, Geoffrey, *Looking for Dilmun*, Penguin Books, New York, 1972.

Blavatsky, Helena P., *The Secret Doctrine*, Theosophical Publishing, New York, 1988, (reprint of original 1888 Theosophical University Press edition).

Blum, Ralph, *Beyond Earth: Man's Contact with UFO's*, Bantam Books, New York, 1974.

Blumrich, Josef F., *The Spaceships of Ezekiel*, Bantam Books, New York, 1974.

Book of Mormon, The Church of Jesus Christ of Latter-day Saints, Salt Lake City, Utah, 1989.

Bramley, William, *The Gods of Eden*, Avon Books, New York, 1993.

Breasted, James H., *A History of Egypt*, Charles Scribner's Sons, New York, 1937.

Brown, Courtney, *Cosmic Voyage*, Onyx Books, New York, 1996.

Budge, (Sir) E. A. Wallis, *Egyptian Magic*, Citadel Press/Carol Publishing, New York, 1991.

Bulfinch, Thomas, *Mythology of Greece and Rome*, Collier Books, New York, 1962.

Campbell, Joseph, *The Masks of God: Primitive Mythology*, Viking Press, New York, 1959.

Carlotto, Mark, *The Martian Enigmas: A Closer Look*, North Atlantic Books, Berkeley, Calif., 1991.

Cayce, Edgar Evans, *Edgar Cayce On Atlantis*, Warner Books, New York, 1968.

Ceram, C. W., *Gods, Graves, and Scholars*, Bantam Books, New York, 1972.

Cerminara, Gina, *The World Within*, Signet Books, New York, 1957.

Chaisson, Eric, *Cosmic Dawn*, Berkley Books, New York, 1984.

Charroux, Robert, *Legacy of the Gods*, Berkley Medallion Books, New York, 1973.

-----*Masters of the World*, Berkley Medallion Books, New York, 1974.

Chatelain, Maurice, *Our Ancestors Came From Outer Space*, Dell Publishing, New York, 1978.

Childress, David Hatcher, *Extraterrestrial Archaeology*, Adventures Unlimited Press, Stelle, Illinois, 1995.

-----*Lost Cities of Atlantis, Ancient Europe & The Mediterranean*, Adventures Unlimited Press, Stelle, Illinois, 1996.

Churchward, James, *The Lost Continent of Mu*, Paperback Library, New York, 1968.

-----*The Children of Mu*, Paperback Library, New York, 1968.

-----*The Sacred Symbols of Mu*, Paperback Library, New York, 1968.

-----*The Cosmic Forces of Mu*, Paperback Books, 1970.

Clark, Adrian V., *Cosmic Mysteries of the Universe*, Parker Publishing, New York, 1968.

Corliss, William R., *Mysteries of the Universe*, Thomas Y. Crowell Co., New York, 1967.

-----*Ancient Man: A Handbook of Puzzling Artifacts*, The Sourcebook Project, Glen Arm, Md., 1978.

Cory, I. P., *Ancient Fragments*, Second Ed., William Pickering, Pub., London, 1832.

-----*Ancient Fragments*, Ed. by E. Richmond Hodges, Reeves & Turner, London, 1876.

Cox, George William, *Tales of Ancient Greece,* Jansen McClurg & Co., Chicago, 1879.

Cross, Jr., Frank Moore, *The Ancient Library of Qumran*, Anchor Books, New York, 1961.

Darling, David, *Deep Time*, Delacorte Press, New York, 1989.

Darwin, Charles, *The Origin of Species*, Mentor Books edition of the 1859 original, N.Y., 1958.

Day, Michael H., *Fossil Man*, Bantam Books, New York, 1971.

De Camp, L. Sprague, *Lost Continents*, Ballantine Books, New York, 1975.

-----*The Ancient Engineers*, Ballantine Books, New York, 1984.

Dempewolff, Richard F., Ed., *Lost Cities and Forgotten Tribes*, Pocket Books, New York, 1974.

Diaz de Arce, G. H., *Of Gods and Men*, Dorrance & Co., Philadelphia, 1975.

Dimont, Max I., *Jews, God, and History*, Signet Books, New York, 1962.

Dineley, David, *Earth's Voyage Through Time*, Knopf Books, New York, 1974.

Dione, Robert L., *God Drives A Flying Saucer*, Bantam Books, New York, 1969.

-----*Is God Supernatural?*, Bantam Books, New York, 1976.

Donnelly, Ignatius, *Atlantis, The Antediluvian World*, revised by Egerton Sykes, Gramercy Publishing, New York, 1949.

Downing, Barry H., *The Bible and Flying Saucers*, Berkley Books, New York, 1989.

Drake, W. Raymond, *Gods and Spacemen In The Ancient East*, Signet Books, New York, 1973.

-----*Gods and Spacemen of the Ancient Past*, Signet Books, New York, 1974.

Dudley, Donald R., *The Civilization of Rome*, Mentor Books, New York, 1962.

Ebon, Martin, *Atlantis: The New Evidence*, Signet, New York, 1977.

Edwards, Frank, *Strange World*, Bantam Books, New York, 1969.

Edwards, I.E.S., *The Pyramids of Egypt*, Viking Press, New York, 1972.

Egyptian Book of the Dead, The (aka *The Book of Going Forth by Day*), trans. Dr. Raymond O. Faulkner, Chronicle Books, San Francisco, 1998.

Eliade, Mircea, *The Myth of the Eternal Return*, Eng. Trans. by Willard R. Trask, Bollingen Serv., New York, 1954.

-----*Essential Sacred Writings From Around The World*, HarperCollins Pub., New York, 1977.

412

Emery, Walter, *Archaic Egypt*, Penguin Books, Baltimore, Maryland, 1963.

Encarta 98 Encyclopedia, Microsoft Corp., Redmond, WA., 1997.

Epic of Gilgamesh, Penguin Books, Baltimore, Maryland, 1964.

Evslin, Bernard, *Gods, Demigods, & Demons: An Encyclopedia of Greek Mythology*, Scholastic Inc., New York, 1975.

Ferrell, Vance, *Christmas, Easter, and Halloween: Where Did They Come From?*, Pilgrims Books, Beersheba Springs, Tenn., 1997.

Finley, M. I., *The Ancient Greeks*, Penguin Books, New York, 1982.

Frankiel, Tamar, *The Gift of Kabbalah*, Jewish Lights Publications, Woodstock, VT., 2001.

Funk & Wagnalls New Encyclopedia, ed. Phillips, Robert S., Lippincott & Crowell Pub., U.S.A., 1983.

Furneaux, Rupert, *Ancient Mysteries*, Ballantine Books, New York, 1978.

Golob, Richard, and Brus, Eric, Eds., *The Almanac of Science and Technology*, Harcourt Brace Jovanovich, Orlando, Florida, 1990.

Gordon, Cyrus H., *The Ancient Near East*, Norton & Co., New York, 1965.

Graves, Robert, *The Greek Myths* (vol. 1), Penguin Books, Baltimore, Maryland, 1955.

-----*The White Goddess*, Faber & Faber, London, 1958.

Gribbin, John, *Companion to the Cosmos*, Little, Brown & Co., New York, 1996.

Gribbin, John and Mary, *Fire on Earth: In Search of the Doomsday Asteroid*, Simon and Schuster, N.Y., 1996.

Gurney, O. R., *The Hittites*, Penguin Books, Baltimore, Maryland, 1954.

Hallamish, Moshe, *An Introduction to the Kabbalah*, trans. by Ruth Bar-Ilan and Ora Wiskind-Elper, State University of New York Press, Albany, N.Y., 1999.

Hamilton, Edith, *Mythology*, Mentor Books, New York, 1953.

Hamlyn, Paul, *Egyptian Mythology*, Westbook House, London, 1965.

Hancock, Graham, *Fingerprints of the Gods*, Crown Publishers, New York, 1995.

-----*The Mars Mystery*, Three Rivers Press, New York, 1998.

Hancock, Graham, and Bauval, Robert, *The Message of the Sphinx*, Three Rivers Press, New York, 1996.

Hapgood, Charles H., *Maps of the Ancient Sea Kings*, Chilton Books, New York, 1966.

Harrison, R. K., *The Archaeology of the Old Testament*, Harper & Row, New York, 1966.

-----*Old Testament Times*, Eerdmans Publishing, Grand Rapids, Mich., 1970.

Hawkes, Jacquetta, *History of Mankind* (vol. 1, pt. 1: *Prehistory*), Mentor Books, N.Y., 1965.

Hawking, Stephen, *A Brief History Of Time*, Bantam Books, New York, 1990.

-----*The Universe In A Nutshell*, Bantam Books, New York, 2001.

Herodotus, *History of Herodotus*, trans. by George Rawlinson, ed. by Manuel Komroff, Tudor Publishing, New York, 1941.

Heyerdahl, Thor, *Early Man and the Ocean*, Doubleday & Co., New York, 1979.

Hoagland, Richard C., *The Monuments of Mars*, North Atlantic Books, Berkeley, Calif., 1987.

Holy Bible, King James Version, Cambridge University Press, Great Britain, 1994.

Hope, Murry, *The Sirius Connection: Unlocking the Secrets of Ancient Egypt*, Element Books, Rockport, Mass., 1996.

Howell, F. Clark, *Early Man*, Time-Life Books, New York, 1968.

Howells, Willaim, *Back of History*, Natural History Library, U.S.A., 1963.

I Ching, Van Over, Raymond, Ed., (Trans. James Legge), Mentor Books, New York, 1971.

Jeffrey, Grant R., *The Signature of God*, Frontier Research Publications, Toronto, 1996.

Jessup, Morris K., *The Case For The UFO*, Bantam Books, New York, 1955.

Johnson, George, and Tanner, Don, *The Bible and the Bermuda Triangle*, Logos Intl., New Jersey, 1976.

Jordon, Michael, *Encyclopedia of Gods: Over 2,500 Deities of the World*, Pub. by Facts On File, Inc., New York, 1993.

Josephus, *Josephus [Complete Works]*, trans. by William Whiston, Kregel Publishing, Grand Rapids, Mich., 1972.

Kaku, Michio, *Hyperspace: A Scientific Odyssey Through Parallel Universes, Time Warps, and the Tenth Dimension*, Anchor Books/Doubleday, New York, 1994.

Kelen, Betty, *Muhammad: The Messenger of God*, Pocket Books, New York, 1977.

Keyhoe, Donald E., *Aliens From Space*, Signet Books, New York, 1974.

King, Charles W., *The Gnostics and Their Remains*, David Nutt Pub., London, 1887.

Kitto, H. D. F., *The Greeks*, Penguin Books, Baltimore, Maryland, 1957.

Kolosimo, Peter, *Not of this World*, Bantam Books, New York, 1973.

Kramer, Samuel Noah, Ed., *Mythologies of the Ancient World*, Anchor Books, New York, 1961.

Kueshana, Eklal, *The Ultimate Frontier*, The Stelle Group, Chicago, Ill., 1963.

Landsburg, Alan and Sally, *In Search of Ancient Mysteries*, Bantam Books, New York, 1974.

-----*The Outer Space Connection*, Bantam Books, New York, 1975.

Langer, William L., Ed., *Western Civilization*, American Heritage Publishing, New York, 1968.

Langley, Noel, & Cayce, Hugh Lynn, Ed., *Edgar Cayce On Reincarnation*, Paperback Books, New York, 1967.

Leach, Marjorie, *Guide to the Gods*, ABC-CLIO, Inc., Calif., 1992.

Leek, Sybil, *Reincarnation: The Second Chance*, Bantam Books, New York, 1975.

Leeming, David Adams, *The World of Myth*, Oxford University Press, New York, 1990.

Leonard, George, *Somebody Else Is On The Moon*, Pocket Books, New York, 1976.

Leonard, R. Cedric, *Quest For Atlantis*, Manor Books, New York, 1979.

Lewis, L. M., *Footprints on the Sands of Time*, Signet Books, New York, 1975.

Linton, Ralph, *The Tree of Culture*, Vintage Books, New York, 1959.

Loew, Cornelius, *Myth, Sacred History, and Philosophy*, Harcourt, Brace & World, N.Y., 1967.

Luce, J. V., *The End of Atlantis*, Bantam Books, New York, 1978.

McDaniel, Stanley V., *The McDaniel Report*, North Atlantic Books, Berkeley, Calif., 1993.

Macgowan, Kenneth, and Hester Jr., Joseph A., *Early Man in the New World*, Natural History Library/Anchor Books, New York, 1962.

Mack, John E., *Abduction*, Macmillan Publishing, New York, 1994.

Mahabharata, trans. & ed. by J.A.B. van Buitenen, University of Chicago Press, Chicago, 1980.

McGaa, Ed, *Native Wisdom*, Four Directions Pub., Minn., 1995.

Mead, G.R.S., *Fragments of a Faith Forgotten*, Theosophical Pub. Society, London, 1900.

-----*Thrice Greatest Hermes*, Vol. I, II, & III, Theosophical Pub. Society, London, 1906.

Missler, Chuck, and Eastman, Mark, *Alien Encounters*, Koinonia House, Coeur d'Alene, ID., 1997.

Mitchell, Edgar D., and Williams, Dwight A., *The Way of the Explorer*, G. P. Putnam's Sons, New York, 1996.

Montgomery, Ruth, *Threshold to Tomorrow*, Putnam's Sons, New York, 1982.

-----*Aliens Among Us*, Ballantine Books, New York, 1985.

Moore, Patrick, *New Guide to the Moon*, Norton & Co., New York, 1976.

New York Public Library Desk Reference, Simon & Schuster, New York, 1989.

Norman, Eric, *Gods, Demons and Space Chariots*, Lancer Books, New York, 1970.

-----*Gods and Devils From Outer Space*, Lancer Books, New York, 1973.

Osborne, Harold, *South American Mythology*, The Hamlyn Publishing Group, New York, 1968.

Pagels, Elaine, *The Gnostic Gospels*, Vantage Books, New York, 1981.

Patten, Donald W., and Windsor, Samuel L., *The Scars of Mars*, Pacific Meridien Publishing, Seattle, 1996.

Pauls, Michael, & Facaros, Dana, *The Travelers' Guide to Mars*, Cadogan Books, London, 1997.

Pauwels, Louis, and Bergier, Jacques, *Morning of the Magicians*, Avon Books, New York, 1963.

Pensee editors, *Velikovsky Reconsidered*, Warner Books, New York, 1976.

Pfeiffer, John E., *The Emergence Of Man*, Harper & Row, New York, 1969.

Piggott, Stuart, *Prehistoric India*, Penguin Books, Baltimore, Maryland, 1952.

Pliny, *Natural History,* trans. by John Bostock & H. T. Riley, Geo. Bell & Sons, London, 1893.

Popul Vuh, trans. by Dennis Tedlock, Simon and Schuster, New York, 1985.

Pritchard, James B., Ed., *The Ancient Near East*, Princeton University Press, New Jersey, 1958.

Quest for the Past, Reader's Digest Eds., Pleasantville, New York, 1984.

Ramayana, trans. and ed. by Aubrey Menen, Greenwood Press, Westport, Conn., 1972.

Rappoport, Angelo S., Ph.D., *Ancient Israel Myths & Legends*, Volumes 1, 2, & 3, Bonanza Books, New York, 1987.

Reymond, E.A.E., *The Mythical Origin of the Egyptian Temple*, Manchester University Press/Barnes & Noble, New York, 1969.

Rig Veda, (translation and selections by Wendy D. O'Flaherty), Penguin Books, N.Y., 1981.

Rost, Leonhard, *Judaism Outside the Hebrew Canon*, Abingdon, Nashville, Tennessee, 1976.

Roux, Georges, *Ancient Iraq*, Penguin Books, New York, 1983.

Sagan, Carl, *Cosmos*, Ballantine Books, New York, 1985.

Schorn, M. Don, *Elder Gods of Antiquity*, Ozark Mountain Publishing, Huntsville, AK., 2008.

-----*Reincarnation...Stepping Stones of Life*, Ozark Mountain Publishing, Huntsville, AK., 2009.

Scott-Elliot, W., *The Story of Atlantis and the Lost Lemuria*, Theosophical Publishing, London, 1968.

Sendy, Jean, *Those Gods Who Made Heaven & Earth*, Berkley Medallion Books, N.Y., 1972.

Sitchin, Zecharia, *The 12th Planet*, Avon Books, New York, 1978.

-----*The Stairway to Heaven*, Avon Books, New York, 1983.

-----*The Wars of Gods and Men*, Avon Books, New York, 1985.

-----*The Lost Realms*, Avon Books, New York, 1990.

-----*When Time Began*, Avon Books, New York, 1993.

-----*Genesis Revisited*, Avon Books, New York, 1990.

-----*Divine Encounters*, Avon Books, New York, 1996.

Smith, John Maynard, *The Theory of Evolution*, Penguin Books, Baltimore, Maryland, 1958.

Smith, Warren, *The Secret Forces of the Pyramids*, Zebra Books, New York, 1975.

-----*Lost Cities of the Ancients-Unearthed!*, Zebra Books/Kensington Pub., New York, 1976

Spence, Lewis, *The History of Atlantis*, Bell Publishing, New York, 1968.

Spencer, John Wallace, *No Earthly Explanation*, Bantam Books, New York, 1975.

-----*Limbo of the Lost*, Bantam Books, New York, 1973.

Steckling, Fred, *We Discovered Alien Bases On The Moon*, GAF Publishing, Los Angeles, 1981.

Stone, Merlin, *When God was a Woman*, Barnes & Noble, New York, 1993.

Sullivan, Walter, *We Are Not Alone*, Signet Books, New York, 1966.

Temple, Robert, *The Sirius Mystery*, Destiny Books, Rochester, Vermont, 1987.

The Book of Mormon, Pub. by The Church of Jesus Christ of Latter-day Saints, Salt Lake City, Utah, 1989.

The Book of the Dead (Egyptian), including *The Papyrus of Ani*, translated by Sir E. A. Wallis Budge, British Museum, London, 1895.

The Forgotten Books of Eden, ed. Rutherford H. Platt, Jr., Bell Pub., New York, 1980.

The Four Gospels and the Revelation, trans. by Lattimore, Richard, Farrar-Straus-Giroux, New York, 1979.

The Nag Hammadi Library in English, Ed. by James MacConkey Robinson, the Coptic Gnostic Library Project, Brill Pub., Boston, 1988.

The World's Last Mysteries, Reader's Digest, Pleasantville, New York, 1980.

Tomas, Andrew, *We Are Not The First*, Bantam Books, New York, 1973.

Traylor, Ellen Gunderson, *Noah*, Living Books, Wheaton, Ill., 1988.

Trefil, James, *The Edge of the Unknown*, Houghton Mifflin, New York, 1996.

Trench, Brinsley le Poer, *The Sky People*, Award Books, New York, 1970.

-----*Temple of the Stars*, Ballantine Books, New York, 1974.

Umland, Craig and Eric, *Mystery of the Ancients: Early Spacemen and the Mayas*, Walker and Co., New York, 1974.

Urantia Book, The Urantia Foundation, Chicago, 1955.

Vallee, Jacques, *UFO's in Space: Anatomy of a Phenomenon*, Ballentine Books, N.Y., 1974.

Van Der Veer, M.H.J. Th., and Moerman, P., *Hidden Worlds*, Bantam Books, New York, 1975.

Van Doren, Charles, *A History of Knowledge*, Ballantine Books, New York, 1992.

Velikovsky, Immanuel, *Worlds in Collision*, Pocket Books, New York, 1977.

-----*Earth In Upheaval*, Pocket Books, New York, 1977.

-----*Oedipus and Akhnaton*, Pocket Books, New York, 1980.

Vishnu Purana, trans. by H. H. Wilson, John Murray Pub., London, 1840.

Von Däniken, Erich, *Chariots of the Gods?*, Bantam Books, New York, 1971.

-----*Gods From Outer Space*, Bantam Books, New York, 1972.

-----*In Search of Ancient Gods*, G. P. Putnam's Sons, New York, 1974.

-----*The Gold of the Gods*, Bantam Books, New York, 1974.

-----*The Eyes of the Sphinx*, Berkley Books, New York, 1996.

Vrettos, Theodore, *Alexandria: City of the Western Mind*, The Free Press, New York, 2001.

Warner, Rex, *The Greek Philosophers*, Mentor Books, New York, 1958.

Waters, Frank, *Book of the Hopi*, Ballantine Books, New York, 1969.

Wigoder, Geoffrey, Ed., *The Encyclopedia of Judaism*, The Jerusalem Publishing House, Ltd., Jerusalem, Israel, 1989.

Wilkinson, Sir John Gardner, *The Manners and Customs of the Ancient Egyptians*, Vol. II, Ed. by Samuel Birch, John Murray Pub., London, 1878.

Williams, W., *Primitive History, From the Creation to Cadmus*, J. Seagrave, Chichester, England, 1789.

Williamson, George Hunt, *Other Tongues – Other Flesh*, Amherst Press, Amherst, Wisc., 1953.

Wilson, Don, *Secrets Of Our Spaceship Moon*, Dell Publishing, New York, 1979.

Wyllie, Timothy, *Dolphins * Extraterrestrials * Angels*, Bozon Enterprises, 1984.

II. Articles and Reports

Antczak, John, Spacecraft Faces Fierce Radiation in Flyby of Jupiter Moon, Assoc. Press, 1999.

Associated Press Report, New-star Nursery Found in Heavens, 1993.

-----Stardust Contains Earthly Compounds, 1997.

-----Wooden Spear Discovery Shows Man Hunted Earlier Than Thought, 1998.

-----Ancient Site Found, 1998.

-----Light From Distant Planets Is Captured, 2005.

Begley, Sharon, Scientists Go on Hunt For the 'Dark Energy' Filling In the Universe, Wall Street Journal, 2002.

-----Forget That Ape-Man, Wall Street Journal, 2002.

-----Scientists Revisit Data on Mars With Minds More Open to 'Life,' Wall Street Journal, 2006.

Biemer, John, New Evidence Found of Milky Way Black Hole, Associated Press, 2001.

Boyd, Robert S., New Planets Thrill Astronomers, Knight-Ridder Newspapers, 1996.

-----Europa May Have Life-Supporting Ocean, Knight-Ridder Newspapers, 1998.

-----Saltwater found in Meteorite, Knight-Ridder Newspapers, 1999.

-----Scientists Call, But E.T. Doesn't Answer, Knight-Ridder Newspapers, 2000.

Broad, William J., Findings Boost Case for Martian Ocean, New York Times, 1999.

-----Think You're From Mars?, New York Times, 1999.

-----Maybe We Are Alone in the Universe, New York Times, 2000.

Callahan, Rick, Comet May Be Made Of Early Material, Associated Press, 1999.

Chang, Alicia, Scientists Say Planet Sighting Confirmed, Associated Press, 2005.

Cooke, Robert, Scientists Discover New Evidence That Universe Began With Big Bang, Newsday, 1995.

Crenson, Matt, Cosmologists Bringing Universe Into Focus With Math, Associated Press, 1996.

-----Unexpected Particle Observation May Advance Physics, Associated Press, 2001.

Davis, Bob, A Universal Mystery Is Said to be Solved, Wall Street Journal, 1991.

Dunn, Marcia, Probe to Study Remnants of Creation, Associated Press, 2001.

Egan, Timothy, Study of Prehistoric Human Inconclusive, New York Times, 1999.

Fordahl, Matthew, Team Finds Evidence of Early Oxygen-Producing Organisms, Associated Press, 1999.

-----NASA's Future Mars Missions Unaffected by Orbiter's Loss, Associated Press, 1999.

-----Scientists Take Photo of Early Universe, Associated Press, 2000.

-----Team of Physicists Hopes to Unlock Mystery of Universe's Matter, Associated Press, 2001.

Glanz, James, <u>Cosmic Clue May Give Answer to Big Bang</u>, New York Times, 1999.

-----<u>Claims about Dark Matter Particles Raise Skepticism</u>, New York Times, 2000.

-----<u>Speed of Light May Not be the Limit</u>, New York Times, 2000.

-----<u>Light Taken From 186,000 miles per Second to Zero and Back</u>, New York Times, 2001.

Hatton, Barry, <u>Skeleton May Help Clarify Genesis Of Man</u>, Associated Press, 1999.

Higgins, Alexander G., <u>Experiment Yields Evidence Supporting "Big Bang" Theory</u>, Associated Press, 2000.

Hotz, Robert Lee, <u>Universe is 12 or 13 Billion Years Old</u>, Los Angeles Times, 1999.

Hughes, Candice, <u>Quest for Life Centers on Jupiter Moon</u>, Associated Press, 1999.

Johnson, John Jr., <u>Scientists Discover Dark Matter Proof</u>, Los Angeles Times article printed in the Tampa Tribune, 5-16-07.

Kaufman, Marc, <u>Mars Photos Most Dramatic of Rover's 900-Day Mission</u>, Washington Post, 2006.

Leary, Warren E., <u>3-D Map Shows Texture of Mars</u>, New York Times, 1999.

Levy, David H., <u>What Rocks Say</u>, Parade Magazine, Parade Pub., New York, August 2, 1999.

-----<u>Why We Have A Moon</u>, Parade Magazine, Parade Publications, N.Y., November 5, 2000.

-----<u>When It Storms on the Sun</u>, Parade Magazine, 2001.

-----<u>The Search for Other Worlds</u>, Parade Magazine, 2001.

Loft, Kurt, <u>Ion Engines</u>, Tampa Tribune, 1997.

Matthews, Robert, Wormholes for Space Travel Might Exist, New Scientist, 2000.

Maugh, II, Thomas H., Europa's Ice: What Lies Beneath?, Los Angeles Times, 2000.

McCall, William, Study: Extinction Recovery Takes a Long Time, Associated Press, 2000.

Merzer, Martin, Site May Be Linked to 1st Floridians, Miami Herald, 2000.

New York Times report, Study Maps `Seat of Intelligence', 2000.

-----(with Associated Press), Scientists ID Half of Missing Universe Matter, 1997.

Paris (France) press release, Fossil Suggests Nice Neanderthals, 2001.

Pasternak, Judy, New Light on Black Holes, Los Angeles Times, 1992.

Pollak, Michael, Neanderthal Isn't Extinct Online, New York Times, 1999.

Recer, Paul, Satellite Finds Possible Presence of Dark Matter, Associated Press, 1993.

-----Evidence of Huge Asteroid Uncovered, Associated Press, 1997.

-----NASA Defends Theory of Life on Mars, Associated Press, 1998.

-----Experts Confident of Life Beyond Earth, Associated Press, 1998.

-----Astronomers Find 2 New Planets, Associated Press, 1998.

-----Fossil Find Suggests Arctic Once as Balmy as Today's Florida, Associated Press, 1998.

-----Mathematical Error Led to Loss of Mars Climate Orbiter, Associated Press, 1999.

-----Study: Rapid Climate Change Possible, Associated Press, 1999.

-----Team Finds 2 Smaller Planets, Associated Press, 2000.

-----Scientists Say Photos Depict Signs of Lakes on Ancient Mars, Associated Press, 2000.

-----Photos: Jupiter Moon Racked by Volcanoes, Associated Press, 2000.

-----Meteorite May Offer Clues to Life, Associated Press, 2000.

-----Mars Dust Storm May Alter Odyssey Flight Plan, Associated Press, 2001.

-----Astronomers Open Way to New Planets, Associated Press, 2001.

-----Astronomers Find Evidence For Black Hole Phenomenon, Associated Press, 2001.

-----Planet Systems Discovered, Associated Press, 2001.

Schiffmann, William, Scientists Point To Other Solar System, Associated Press, 1999.

Schmid, Randolph E., Oldest Fossil Life Sign Found, Associated Press, 1999.

Siegel, Lee, Discovery Backs Big Bang Theory, Associated Press, 1992.

Siegfried, Tom, Conferees Agree to Disagree About God, Dallas Morning News, 1999.

Svensson, Peter, Early Man Shown to be Smarter, Associated Press, 1999.

Tampa Tribune Science News article, Discovery Sheds Light on Mars' Past, Tampa, Fla., 1999.

-----(By-line: El Paso, Texas) Scientists Discover Jupiter-size Planet, 2000.

Todt, Ron, Human Site May Be Earliest in Hemisphere, Associated Press, 2000.

Urry, Meg, The Secrets of Dark Energy, Parade Magazine, Parade Pub., N.Y., May 27, 2007.

Verrangia, Joseph B., Scientists Find Unique Microbes, Associated Press, 2002.

Wade, Nicholas, Scientists Extend Human Cells' Life Span, New York Times, 1998.
-----DNA Study Traces First Family Tree, New York Times, 2000.

Warren, Jere and Baker, David, The Missing Link, Knight-Ridder, 1995.
Washington Post Report, Antimatter Cloud Detected, 1998.
-----5th Planet Orbiting Nearby Star Found, 2007.
Washington Press release, Crystal May Prove Life on Mars, 1998.
-----6 New Planets Found Orbiting Other Stars, 1999.
-----Neanderthal Bones Date to Human Era, 1999.
-----Organic Molecules found in Space, 2000.
-----Study: Black Holes Dominated Universe, 2001.
Wilford, John Noble, Fossil Discovery Fuels Missing-Link Debate, New York Times, 1999.
-----Human Family Gets Larger, New York Times, 2001.
-----Cosmic 'Building Block' Detected, New York Times, 2001.
Wire Service report, Polar Lander, 1999.
-----Earth May Have Rolled Long Ago, 1999.
-----Fossils of Ancient Migrants Found, 2000.
-----The Idea That Einstein Hated, 2001.
-----Scientists Discover Jupiter-size Planet, By-line El Paso, Texas, 2002.
Witze, Alexandra, Jets From Black Hole May Answer Puzzle, Dallas Morning News, 1997.
-----Physicists Discover New Material that Runs in Reverse, Dallas Morning News, 2000.

Zaloudek, Mark, <u>Paleontologists Dig Up Florida's Past Millennia</u>, Lakeland Ledger, 1999.

M. Don Schorn

About the Author:

M. Don Schorn started his professional career in 1968 with a thermoplastics molding company. As a graduate mechanical engineer, he combined his interests in plastics and cars working for several manufacturers supplying component parts to the automotive industry. Mr. Schorn continued his postgraduate education with a curriculum in Plastics Technology and individual course study in various technical and managerial programs. His extensive manufacturing and design experience led to the development of a number of new processing techniques and numerous patentable innovations.

Utilizing his extensive plastics and manufacturing background, Mr. Schorn later joined a Detroit manufacturers' representative firm as a product development specialist. Working with various OEM automotive divisions, he assisted in finalizing product specifications and part designs, ISO quality criterion and certifications, along with direct marketing and sales efforts. After a successful professional career spanning more than 27 years, he retired early at the beginning of 1995 to pursue a second career in writing.

Since then, M. Don Schorn has studied cosmology, paleoanthropology, geology, and archaeology, along with extensive analysis of ancient records and sacred texts. Those studies provided both comprehension and factual data necessary to complete five manuscripts as of this date. Four of those books are non-fiction works, including the trilogy collectively known as the *Journals of the Ancient Ones*, which introduces the *Elder Gods* theory that reveals Earth's primordial development and the emergence of humankind. The author's other non-fiction work, *Reincarnation...Stepping Stones of Life*, is an enlightening examination of the reincarnation concept and its implementation as a way-of-life. Mr. Schorn's first fictional work is his *Emerging Dawn* novel, which details a near-future global search for ancient artifacts that are connected with the Mayan *End-Time* prophecy anticipated to occur on December 21, 2012.

Other Books Published
by
Ozark Mountain Publishing, Inc.

For more information about any of the above titles, soon to be released titles, or
other items in our catalog, write or visit our website:

OZARK
MOUNTAIN
PUBLISHING

PO Box 754
Huntsville, AR 72740
www.ozarkmt.com
1-800-935-0045/479-738-2348 Wholesale Inquiries Welcome